Also by Keri Arthur

The Dark Angels Series

DARKNESS UNBOUND
DARKNESS RISING
DARKNESS DEVOURS
DARKNESS HUNTS
DARKNESS UNMASKED
DARKNESS SPLINTERED
DARKNESS FALLS

The Souls of Fire Series

FIREBORN
WICKED EMBERS

CITY OF LIGHT

AN OUTCAST NOVEL

KERI ARTHUR

A SIGNET SELECT BOOK

SIGNET SELECT
Published by New American Library,
an imprint of Penguin Random House LLC
375 Hudson Street, New York, New York 10014

This book is an original publication of New American Library.

First Printing, January 2016

Copyright © Keri Arthur, 2016
Penguin Random House supports copyright. Copyright fuels creativity,
encourages diverse voices, promotes free speech, and creates a vibrant culture.
Thank you for buying an authorized edition of this book and for complying
with copyright laws by not reproducing, scanning, or distributing any part of
it in any form without permission. You are supporting writers and allowing
Penguin Random House to continue to publish books for every reader.

Signet Select and the Signet Select colophon are trademarks of
Penguin Random House LLC.

For more information about Penguin Random House, visit penguin.com.

ISBN 978-0-451-47350-9

Printed in the United States of America
10 9 8 7 6 5 4 3 2 1

This book is dedicated to Miriam and Kaz.
Without their help, Tiger would not be complete.

CHAPTER 1

It was the whispering of the ghosts that woke me.

I stretched the kinks out of my bones, then glanced at the old metal clock on the far wall to confirm what I instinctively knew. It was barely six p.m., so night hadn't fallen yet. The ghosts were well used to my seminocturnal patterns, so something had to be wrong for them to wake me early.

I swung my legs off the bed and sat up. The tiled floor chilled my feet and the air was cool, though slightly stale. Which probably meant one of the three remaining purifiers had gone offline again. It was a frustrating problem that had started happening more often of late, thanks to the fact that parts for the decades-old machines just weren't made anymore. And while there *was* one place where I probably could scavenge the bits I needed to repair them, it was also something of a last resort. Chaos was not a place you entered willingly. Not if you valued life and limb.

But if one of the purifiers *had* gone down again, then I

either had to risk going there or close off yet another level. I might be able to survive short-term on foul air, but I still needed to breathe.

Gentle tendrils of energy trailed across my skin, a caress filled with the need to follow. But it was a touch that held no fear. Whatever disturbed the ghosts was not aimed at our bunker deep underground.

I slipped on my old combat clothes and boots, then grabbed my jacket and rose, shoving my arms into the sleeves as I walked across to the door at the far end of the bunk room. A red warning light flashed as I neared it.

"Name, rank," a gruff metallic voice said. Over the years I'd named it Hank, simply because it reminded me somewhat of the cranky custodian who'd run the base exchange. He still haunted the lower floors, although he tended to avoid both me and the children.

"Tiger C5, déchet, lure rank."

I pressed my thumb against the blood-work slot. A small needle shot out and took the required sample, but the door remained securely closed. Even though I'd adjusted the power ratios and cut several levels out of the security net, it still took an interminably long time for the system down here to react. But then, with only one hydrogen-fueled generator and the banks of solar batteries powering the system during the day, *everything* was slow. And I couldn't risk firing up a second generator when I needed at least two running at night to cope with the main defense systems. I had only three generators in total and—with parts so scarce in the world above—I had to be careful. That meant conserving the system where I could and doing continual maintenance.

The scanner finally kicked into gear. After checking my irises, the door beeped and swung open. The corridor beyond was cold and dark, the metal walls dripping with condensation. Ghosts swirled, their little bodies wisps of fog that drifted along in blackness.

The sounds of my footfalls echoed across the stillness, hinting at the vastness of this underground military bunker. And yet this was the smallest of the three bases humans had used during the race war—a war that might have lasted only five years but had forever altered the very fabric of our world.

The shifters—with their greater strength, speed, and the capacity to heal almost any wound—should have wiped the stain of humanity from Earth. But humans had not wasted the many years leading up to the war, and the bioengineering labs, which had initially produced nothing more than body part replacements for the sick and dying, had gone into full—and secret—production. These labs had created not only an enzyme that gave humans the same capacity to heal as the shifters, but also the designed humanoid. Or déchet, as we'd become known.

It said a lot about humanity's opinion of us that we were given a nickname that meant "waste product."

Most of us hadn't come from human stock, but were rather a mix of shifter and vampire, which gave us most of their strengths and few of their weaknesses. We'd been humanity's supersoldiers—designed to fight and to die without thought or feeling—and we'd almost turned the tide of the war.

Almost.

But not all of us had been trained strictly as soldiers, just as not all of us were unfeeling. There were a few who'd been created with more specific skills in mind—chameleons able to alter their flesh at will, and who'd been tasked with either seduction and intelligence gathering or assassination.

I was one such creation.

Of course, while humans might have designed us to be frontline soldiers in their battle with the shifters, they'd never entirely trusted us not to turn against them—even if they'd made that all but impossible through a mix of chemical and medical interventions. Which meant there'd been areas in this base that, as a déchet, I'd been banned from entering.

But as the sole survivor of the destruction that had hit this base at the war's end 103 years ago, I'd made it my business to fully explore every available inch. The shifters had, in an effort to ensure the base could never be used again, blocked off all known access points into the base by pouring tons of concrete into them. While this had taken out sublevels one to three, it still left me with six others— and those six were huge. Which was hardly surprising since this had once been the home to not only a thousand-strong complement of déchet, but to all those who had been responsible for our creation and training.

I passed through several more security points—points that, like the one at the bunkhouse, were fixed and unalterable— and eventually made my way into the tight, circular stairwell that led to the surface level. These stairs had been one of two routes designed as emergency escapes for the humans in charge of the various sections of the Humanoid Development Project, so its presence had been unknown to all but a few and it had been designed to withstand anything the shifters could throw at the base. As it turned out, it had also withstood the concrete.

It had taken me close to a year to find this tunnel, and a couple more to find the second one, but they gave me much-needed access points to the outside world. It might be a world I ventured into only once or twice a month—generally when food or equipment supplies were low or when the need for company that was flesh-and-blood rather than ghostly became too strong to ignore—but that didn't assuage the need to know what was going on above me on a regular basis. Being able to venture out, to watch from shadows and distance, was all that had kept me sane in the long century since the war. That and the ghosts.

I reached the surface level and pried open the hidden escape panel. Sunlight poured in through the dome over the building's remains, shielding it from the elements and further decay. This level had once contained the day-to-day operational center of the HDP, and the battered remnants had become part of a museum dedicated to the history of a war no one wanted to see repeated. Of course, it was also a museum created by the shifters, so it emphasized both the foolishness and waste of war and also the evils of gene manipulation and bioengineering. The body-part industry and all the benefits it had once provided were now little more than bylines in history.

And though fewer and fewer were visiting the museum these days, one of the most popular exhibits still seemed to be the old tower that held all the remaining solar panels. They might be an antiquated and curiously inadequate technology to those alive today, yet the panels continued to power not only the systems that had been preserved on this floor for demonstration purposes, but all of mine.

The ghosts surrounded me as I walked across the foyer, their ethereal bodies seeming to glow in the fading streams of sunlight bathing the vast open area. As ever, it was little Cat who kept closest, while Bear surged forward, leading the way.

Both he and Cat had always considered me something

of a big sister, even though we déchet shouldn't have even understood the concept. Our closeness was primarily due to the amount of time I'd spent in the nursery unit in the years leading up to the war. Even during the war, those lures not out on assignment or in a recovery period were put to use in the nurseries; our task had been to teach and to protect the next generation of fighters.

Because despite what the shifters had believed, there'd been only a finite supply of us. Our creators had discovered early on that while the use of accelerant increased the speed of *physical* growth, it did not enhance mental growth. Déchet might have been designed to be nothing more than superhuman soldiers able to match the strength and speed of shifters, but sending your rifle fodder out with the body of an adult and the mind of a child really defeated the purpose of their creation. So while they'd halved our development time, they hadn't been able to erase it completely.

I came to the tower and unlocked the thick metal doors that led to the rooftop stairwell, then unlatched the silver mesh behind them. There was enough shifter in my blood that my skin tingled as I touched it, but it wasn't as deadly to me as it would have been to a full-blood. I slipped through the mesh and ran up the old concrete stairs, breathing air that was thick with disuse and age. Visitors wanting to see the ancient solar technology did so from the special observation platform that had been built to one side of the tower rather than accessing the panels through the tower itself, simply because the old tower was considered too dangerous. For the last couple of years there'd been talk of tearing it down before it actually fell, but, so far, nothing had actually happened. I hoped it never did. I wasn't entirely sure what I would do if it was knocked down and I was left with only the decaying generators to power my underground systems.

We reached the metal exit plate at the top of the stairs. It was also silver, but it was so scarred with heat and blast damage that it no longer looked it. I drew back the bolts and pushed the plate open.

The children flung themselves into the glorious sunset, and that alone told me there was nothing dangerous nearby. But there was no shaking the years of training, even though the need for such measures had long since passed. I drew in a deep breath and sorted through the various scents, looking for anything unusual or out of place. There was nothing. As I climbed out of the stairwell, a slight breeze tugged at my short hair, and I looked up to see the dome's panels had fissured yet again. It was an odd fact that this section of dome failed regularly. It was almost as if the old tower wanted to feel the wind and the rain on its fading bones. It just might get that wish tonight, because the heaviness of the clouds so tinted by the sun's last dance of the day suggested it wasn't going to be a good night to be out on the streets.

Not that there was *ever* a good night to be out on them.

I zipped up my jacket and walked through the banks of solar panels to the old metal railing that lined the rooftop. The walls of Central City rose before me, and, beyond them, a sea of glass and metal that shone brightly under the strengthening glow of the UV light towers perched on top of the massive metal D-shaped curtain wall. There were also floodlights on the rooftops of the many high-rises, all of them aimed at the streets in an effort to erase any shadows created by either the buildings or the wall itself.

Lying between Central and the bunker's dome was the main rail line, which transported workers in glowing, caterpillar-like pods to the various production zones that provided the city with the necessities of life. But with dusk coming on, there was little movement in the yards, and the city's drawbridge had already risen, securing Central against the coming of night.

The inhabitants of Chaos—which was the long-accepted name given to the ramshackle collection of buildings that clung to the curved sides of Central's curtain wall—had no such protection. It was an interconnected mess of metal storage units, old wood, and plastic that was ten stories high and barely five wide. The upper reaches bristled with antennas and wind turbines that glimmered in the wash of light from Central's UV towers, but the lower reaches of Chaos already lay encased in darkness. Lights gleamed in various spots, but they did little to lift the gathering shadows.

And it was in these shadows that the vampires reigned supreme.

The shifters might have claimed victory in the war, but in truth, the only real winners had been the vampires. While they'd never been a part of the war—or of society in general—their numbers had certainly grown on the back of the war's high death toll. They were creatures untouched by the basic needs of the living. Water, power, sanitation—the very things humanity considered so vital—had no impact on the way vampires lived their lives, because their lives consisted of nothing more than hunting their next meal. And though they preferred to dine on the living, they were not averse to digging up the dead.

Before the war, most cities had relied solely on the UV towers to stop the vampires. But the cities of old had been built on a network of underground service tunnels, which gave the vampires access and protection. With most of these cities lying in ash and ruin after the war, the shifters had taken the chance to rebuild "vampire-proof" cities for both victor and vanquished to live in. So not only were there massive curtain walls and UV towers around every major city, but services now ran aboveground, in special conduits that had been "beautified" to disguise what they were.

Chaos, unprotected by either lights or walls, and still sitting on many of the old service tunnels, was regularly hit by the vampires—but neither the inhabitants of Chaos nor those in charge of Central seemed to care.

Of course, vampires were no longer the only evil to roam the night or the shadows. When the shifters had unleashed the bombs that had finally ended the war, they'd torn apart the very fabric of the world, creating drifting doorways between this world and the next. These rifts were filled with a magic that not only twisted the essence of the landscape, but also killed anyone unfortunate enough to be caught in their path. That in itself would not have been so bad if the Others had not gained access into our world through many of these rifts. These hellish creatures— creatures the humans and shifters had named demons, monsters, and death spirits, although in truth no one really knew if they were from hell or merely another time or dimension—had all found a new and easy hunting ground in the shadows of our world.

But at least one good thing had come from their arrival— it had finally forced shifters and humans to set aside all differences and act as one against a greater foe.

And yet humanity's fear of vampires had not been usurped by this newer evil. Even *I* feared the vampires, and I had their blood running through my veins. It didn't make me safe from them. Nothing would.

Ghostly fingers ran down my arm and tugged at my fingertips. I followed Cat as she drifted toward the left edge of the building, my gaze scanning the old park opposite. The shadows growing beneath the trees were vacant of life, and nothing moved. Nothing more than the wind-stirred leaves, anyway. I frowned, moving my gaze further afield, studying the street and the battered remnants of what once had been government offices, trying to uncover what was causing the little ones so much consternation.

Then I heard it.

The faint crying of a child.

A *young* child, not an older one, if the tone of her voice was anything to go by.

She was in the trees. At dusk, with the vampires about to come out. An easy meal if I wasn't very quick.

I spun and ran for the stairs. The ghosts gathered around me, their energy skittering across my skin, fueling the need to hurry. I paused long enough to slam down the hatch and shove the bolts home, then scrambled down the steps three at a time, my pace threatening to send me tumbling at any moment.

At the bottom I again stopped long enough to lock up behind me. I might have an instinctive need to save that child—a need no doubt born of my inability to save the 105 déchet children who'd been in my care the day the shifters had gassed this base and killed everyone within it—but I wouldn't risk either discovery or the security of our home to do so.

The ghosts swirled around me, urging me to hurry, to run. I did, but down to the weapons stash I'd created in the escape tunnel rather than to the front door. I fastened several automatics to the thigh clips on my pants, then strapped two of the slender machine rifles—which I'd adapted to fire small sharpened stakes rather than bullets—across my back. Once I'd grabbed a bag of flares and threw several ammo loops over my shoulders, I was ready to go. But I knew even as I headed for the main doors that no amount of weaponry would be enough if the vampires caught the sound of either the child's heartbeat or mine.

The dome's security system reacted far faster than mine, the doors swishing open almost instantly. The passcodes might change daily, but I'd been around a long time and I knew the system inside out. Not only had the motion and heat sensors installed throughout the museum been programmed to ignore my lower body temperature, but I'd installed an override code for the outer defenses that didn't register on the daily activity log. I might be flesh and blood most of the time, but as far as the systems that protected this place were concerned, I was as much a ghost as the children who surrounded me.

Once the laser curtain protecting the front of the dome had withdrawn, I headed for the trees. Cat and Bear came with me, their ethereal forms lost to the gathering darkness. The others remained behind to guard the door. It would take a brave—and determined—soul to get past them. The dead might not be the threat that the vampires were, but the astute didn't mess with them, either. They might be energy rather than flesh, but they *could* both interact with and manipulate the world around them if they so desired.

Of course, the smaller the ghost, the less strength they had. My little ones might be able to repel invaders, but they could not hold back a determined attack for very long. I just had to hope that it didn't come to that tonight.

City Road was empty of any form of life and the air fresh and cool, untainted by the scent of humanity, vampire, or death. No one—living or dead—was near.

So where was the child? And why in hell was she alone in a park?

I ran into the trees, breathing deeply as I did so, trying

to find the scent of the child I'd heard but gaining little in the way of direction.

Thankfully, Cat seemed to have no such trouble. Her energy pulled me deeper into the park as the stamp of night grew stronger. Tension wound through my limbs. The vampires would be rising. We had to hurry.

Bear spun around me, his whisperings full of alarm. Like most of us created in the long lead-up to the war, there was no human DNA within his body. In fact, despite his name, he was more vampire than bear shifter and, in death, had become very attuned to them.

They were rising.

Sound cracked the silence. A whimper, nothing more.

I switched direction, leapt over a bed of old roses, then ran up a sharp incline. Like the crying I'd heard earlier, the whimper died on the breeze and wasn't repeated. If it hadn't been for Cat leading the way so surely, I might have been left running around this huge park aimlessly. While my tiger-shifter blood at least ensured I had some basic tracking skills, basic wouldn't cut it right now. Cat, while not trained to track, was almost pure tabby. Her hunting skills were both instinctive and sharp.

The urgency in her energy got stronger, as did Bear's whisperings of trouble.

The vampires had the scent. They were coming.

I reached for more speed. My feet were flying over the yellowed grass, and the gnarled, twisted tree trunks were little more than a blur. I crested the hill and ran down the other side, not checking my speed, my balance tiger sure on the steep and slippery slope.

I still couldn't see anything or anyone in the shadows, but the desperation in little Cat's energy assured me we were getting close.

But so, too, were the vampires.

Their scent began to stain the breeze, a mix of decay and unwashed flesh that made me wish my olfactory senses weren't so keen.

Where was the damn child?

I reached for a rifle, unlocked the safety, and held it loose by my side as I ran. Bear whisked around me again, whispering reassurances, his energy filled with excitement as he raced off into the trees. Seconds later I heard his whimper, strong at first but fading as he ran away from us. If the vampires took the bait, it would give us time to find our quarry. If not, I would be neck deep in them and fighting for life.

I broke through the trees and into a small clearing. Cat's energy slapped across my skin, a warning that we were near our target. I leapt high over the remnants of another garden bed, and saw her. Or rather, saw the bright strands of gold hair dancing to the tune of the breeze. She was hiding in the shattered remains of a fallen tree. Beside that tree lay a man. I couldn't immediately tell if he lived. The scent of death didn't ride his flesh, but he didn't seem to be breathing, either. Though I could see no wounds, the rich tang of blood permeated the air—and if I could smell it, the vampires surely would. Bear's diversion probably wouldn't last much longer.

I dropped beside the stranger and rolled him over. Thick, ugly gashes tore up his chest and stomach, and his left arm was bent back unnaturally. I pressed two fingers against his neck. His pulse was there—light, erratic, but there.

Yet it was the three uniform scars that ran from his right temple to just behind his ear that caught my attention. They were the markings of a ranger—a formidable class of shifter soldier who'd once been used to hunt down and destroy the déchet divisions, and who now formed the backbone of the fight against the Others. While it was unlikely this ranger would know what I was by sight or scent—especially given that lures had been genetically designed *not* to have any of the telltale déchet signatures—he still wasn't the sort of man I wanted anywhere near either me or my sanctuary.

Especially *not* when there were nearly three platoons—or, to be more precise, ninety-three—of fully trained adult déchet haunting the lower levels. The children might have few memories of the hideous way the shifters had killed everyone at the base, but the same could not be said of the adults.

I shifted my focus to the log and the strands of golden hair blowing on the breeze.

"Child, you need to come with me." I said it as gently as I could, but the only response was a tightening of fear in the air. But it was fear of *me* rather than the situation or even the night.

Cat spun around me, her energy flowing through my body, briefly heightening my sense of the night. The vampires would be here soon.

The urgent need to be gone rose, but I pushed it down. Dragging the child from the log would only make her scream, and that in turn would make the situation a whole lot worse. Noise was our enemy right now. The vampires weren't the only dangers night brought on—many of the Others tended to hunt by sight and sound.

"The vampires are coming, little one," I continued, even though I was talking to scarcely more than a strand of hair. "Neither of us are safe here."

"Jonas will protect me. He promised." Though her words were stilted, there was nothing in the way of fear or uncertainty in them. Which was odd.

"Jonas is injured and can't help anyone right now." *Not even himself.* I hesitated, then added, "We need to get out of here before the vampires arrive."

She didn't respond for a moment. Then a dirt-covered cherub face popped up from the hollow of the tree. She scanned me, then stated flatly, "I won't leave without Jonas. I *won't.*"

"Jonas is unconscious, but I'm sure he'd want me to get you to safety rather than worrying about him."

She continued to study me, her blue eyes wide and oddly luminous. I had a strange feeling that the child understood all too clearly just what I was saying—and her next words confirmed that. "I won't leave him here to die. I won't let you leave him for the vampires. You have to save him."

"Child—"

"No," she said, her lip trembling. "He saved me. And he'll save you. You can't leave him here to die."

I frowned. He'd save me? A ranger? Even if he didn't realize what I was, it was an unlikely scenario, given rangers had been notorious for forsaking the wounded. And if he *did* realize . . . I thrust the thought away with a shudder and simply said, "His wounds are fairly serious—"

"Promise me you'll help him!"

Cat spun around me, her whisperings filled with urgency. If we didn't get moving soon, we'd be dead. Given I had no wish to die, I had to either snatch the child and race her—screaming—to our sanctuary, or do as she wished. The first would attract all manner of trouble other than the vampires, but to help a ranger . . .

I took a deep breath and released it slowly. I might have been trained to seduce rather than destroy, but that didn't alter the fact that shifters had eradicated everything and everyone I knew or cared about. It went against every instinct I had to save this one.

And yet the instinct—need—to save this child was stronger still.

"Okay, I'll help him."

She eyed me for a moment, a little girl whose gaze seemed far too knowing. "You promise?"

"Yes."

Cat whisked through me. The image of the vampires flowing through the trees rose like a deadly black wave. We had five minutes, if that.

"Who's that?"

The child's blue gaze wasn't on me, but rather on the energy that was Cat as she hovered near my shoulder. I raised an eyebrow. "You can see Cat?"

"Cat? What sort of name is that?"

"It's short for Catherine," I said. Which it wasn't, but I had no idea where this child was from or how much she might have been taught about the war and déchet. Those who'd created us hadn't afforded us real names—couldn't humanize the military fodder in any way, after all. So they used the breed of shifter we'd been designed from, and whatever number we were of that breed. Cat was number 247 in production terms. And while it was unlikely our names would be a giveaway, I wasn't about to take a chance. Not when there were still shifters alive today who'd survived the war. "Mine's Tig."

She didn't ask me what it was short for. Her gaze went from Cat to me, then back to Cat. "She's not real. You are."

"She might not have flesh, but she's as real as you and me."

The little girl frowned and stood. She was wearing a smock that was grimy and blood-splattered, and there were half-healed slashes all over her arms and legs. Anger rose within me, then swirled away. I needed to make sure we were safe before I could allow any reaction to those cuts.

Because those cuts were too sharp, too straight, to have been caused by anything other than a blade.

"How can she have no body and be real?"

There was still no fear in her voice, and no apparent realization just how close to disaster we truly were. I wondered briefly if she was human. She didn't smell like it, but then, she didn't exactly smell like a shifter, either.

"Because not everything that is real has human flesh."

I clipped the rifle onto a loop on my belt and squatted beside the ranger as Cat's energy hit again. Images slashed through my mind—dark beings running through the trees, their hunger surging across the night. We needed to go. *Now.*

I gripped the man under his shoulder and heaved him over mine. "Do you have a name?"

She hesitated, and then said, almost shyly, "Penny."

"We need to go, Penny." I thrust upward, my legs shaking under the stranger's sudden weight. Holding him steady with one hand, I unclipped the rifle and rested my finger against the trigger. "Run with Cat. She'll take you into a safe place. Wait for me there."

The little girl's lips trembled a little. "And Jonas?"

"Jonas and I will be right behind you."

She nodded, then scrambled over the tree trunk and ran after the energy that was Cat as she retreated through the trees. I followed, Jonas's body a dead weight that allowed no real speed or mobility.

Bear reappeared, his whisperings full of warning. I ran up the hill as the night around me began to move, to flow, with evil.

They were close.

So close.

But there was something else out there in the night. It was a power—an energy—that felt dark. Watchful. At one with the vampires and yet separate from them.

And instinct suggested I needed to fear that darkness far more than the vampires who swept toward us.

I cursed softly and pushed the thought away. One threat at a time. I needed to survive the vampires before I worried about some other, nebulous threat. "Bear, I need your help here."

His energy immediately flowed across mine, allowing me to see everything he saw, everything he felt. While this level of connection wasn't as deep as some we could achieve, *any* bond between the living and the dead could be deadly. All magic had a cost, an old witch had once warned me. While my ability to link with the ghosts wasn't so much magic as a mix of psychic abilities and my own close call with death, it still taxed both my strength *and* theirs. And it could certainly drain me to the point of death if I kept the connection too long.

But for certain situations it was worth the risk—and this was certainly one of those situations.

There was at *least* a score of vampires out there, which meant this wasn't the usual hunting party. If I'd been alone, if I hadn't promised to keep Jonas safe, I would have shadowed and run. The vampires might sense me in *this* form, but if I became one with the night—became little more than dark matter, as they could—then it was harder for them to pick me out from their own. I knew *that* from my time in the war, when the vamps had overrun a village I'd been assigned to.

But I *had* promised, and that left me with little choice. Using the images Bear fed me as a guide, I raised the rifle and fired over my shoulder, keeping the bursts short to conserve ammunition. The needle-sharp projectiles bit through the night and burrowed into flesh. Three vampires went down and were quickly smothered by darkness as other vampires fell on them and fed. The scent of blood flooded the night, mingling with the screams of the dying.

I crashed through yet another garden bed, my feet sinking into the soft soil. A deeper patch of darkness leapt for my throat, and the pungent aroma of the dead hit. I flipped the rifle and battered him out of the way with the butt, then switched it into my other hand and fired to the right, then the left. Two more vamps down.

I leapt over a fallen branch. Jonas's weight shifted, making the landing awkward and losing us precious speed. Sweat broke out across my brow but I ignored it, grabbing the ranger's leg to steady him as I ran on.

"Bear," I said, my voice little more than a pant of air. "Light."

Ethereal fingers tugged at the bag of flares by my side and lifted one. Energy surged across the night and light exploded, a white ball of fire surrounded by a halo of red.

It was bright enough to force them back, but they didn't go far. They knew, as I did, that the flare would give me only a minute, at most.

And they knew, like I did, that a little ghost probably wouldn't have the energy to light a second flare so soon after the first.

I ran on as hard as I could. The dome's lights beckoned through the trees, forlorn stars of brightness that still seemed too far away.

The flare guarding our back began to sputter, and the black mass surged closer. I fired left and right. The nearest vampires swarmed their fallen comrades, while those at the back flowed over the top of them, hoping to be the ones to taste fresher, sweeter flesh.

Thirteen vampires left, if I was lucky. It might as well have been a hundred for all the hope I'd have if they dragged me down.

Sweat stung my eyes and dribbled down my spine, and my leg muscles were burning. But the end of the park was now in sight. The old tower's searchlights suddenly came on, hanging free from both the tower and the dome, supported by ghostly forms. Their sunshinelike light swept City Road and provided a haven of safety if I could get to it.

Fifty yards to go.

Just fifty yards.

Then the flare went out and the vampires hit us.

Chapter 2

I fell into a tangle of tearing claws and raking teeth. My rifle went flying and, for a moment, the sheer weight of their numbers overwhelmed me, as did their desperation to taste my flesh. It stung the air, filling my lungs with its stench and bludgeoning my mind with the certain knowledge that death would be my fate if I didn't damn well *move*.

I released my hold on Jonas and surged to my feet, shaking the vampires from my back as I freed the weapons clipped to my thighs. Claws slashed at my shoulders, teeth tore into my flesh, and all I could see was a wall of stinking death on legs.

I fired the weapons around in a circle, first killing the ones ripping at my flesh, then aiming at the black mass surrounding me. Several vampires went down, each one torn apart by the ravenous creatures around them, but I shot for speed, not accuracy, and I missed as many as I got.

The chambers on the automatics clicked over to empty,

and I didn't have time to reload. I reached for the remaining machine rifle and fired in one smooth motion. The vampires shadowed and the stakes went through their vapor, thudding harmlessly into the trees beyond them.

Vampires might be insatiable monsters, but they aren't stupid.

Energy surged across the night—my little ghosts, coming to help. Ethereal fingers tore at the pack and pulled out the flares while others reached for the stinking creatures closest to us, tossing them back into the night and forming a small but important clear way.

Then the energy riding the night sharpened and the flares came to life, lining the clear way and leading us to safety.

I grabbed Jonas by one leg, pulled him out from underneath the pile of putrid flesh, and then dragged him along behind me as I ran for the dome.

Fifty yards had never seemed so far.

The half dozen remaining vampires surged forward with us, their desperation thick and heavy in the air. One foolishly attempted to cross the line of flares, but his flesh was instantly set alight the moment the sputtering brightness touched his skin. He went up in a whoosh of flame, providing even more light, more protection.

Then the flares began to die. I hit the ring of safety provided by the searchlights, but didn't slow. I dragged the unconscious ranger across the road, no doubt doing more damage to his back than had been already done to his front. It didn't matter. Nothing mattered, except getting inside the dome and switching the security system to full.

Because the vampires were now tossing rocks at the hovering searchlights.

One light went down and the shadows crowded closer. I reached the security panel and punched in the code. As I did, the second searchlight went out and the vampires surged.

The ghosts screamed a warning.

The doors began to slide open. I dove inside, saw that Penny was safe, then pulled the ranger in and punched the panic button beside the door. It slammed shut just as the black tide hit it, and the force of their weight caused the heavy metal to ring like a death knell.

It would be *our* death knell if the system wasn't kicked into full gear. I leapt over the ranger and ran for the main control panel, my fingers flying over the keys as I fired the system to full life.

Glass shattered and Penny screamed.

I swung around and raised the rifle. The vampires were breaking into the dome via the fissured panels. I scanned the upper panels, wondering where the laser curtain was, then said, "Cat, get her down the stairs."

Cat's energy whipped away from me, spun around the little girl, and then leapt away toward the stairs. Penny followed unbidden, her fear tainting the air, as sharp as the smell of death now squeezing through the shattered panels.

I pressed the trigger and fired continually at the area that had been breached. It briefly forced a retreat, but I knew they were probably only waiting for my ammunition to run out. As a light atop the rifle chamber began to flash a warning that it was nearing empty, I glanced at the control panel. What in hell was taking so long?

The rifle clicked over to empty and the vampires surged again. I threw the weapon aside and drew my knives, the sheer blades glowing an unnatural green in the shadowed darkness. The vampires screamed, a harsh sound filled with anticipation and hunger. But as they fought one another to get through the breach first, the mesh of lasers finally unfurled down the walls, ringing the room with their deadly light and slicing any and all flesh in their way.

We were safe.

And it was all I could do not to collapse in sheer and utter exhaustion. I sheathed the knives, then bent over, my palms pressed against my bloody knees to keep them locked in position as I sucked in breath and battled the tide of relief and fear that suddenly threatened to overwhelm me.

Death had been close this time. So, *so* close.

The little ones crowded around me, their tingly lips kissing my cheeks and their whisperings a mix of excitement and reassurance. Amusement ran through me. At least *they'd* enjoyed themselves.

I took a deep, shuddering breath, then straightened. Blood dribbled from my wounds and splattered across the floor, but I ignored it. The wounds weren't deep, and I'd heal quickly enough. Our makers had ensured that when they'd made us—couldn't have either the rifle or bedroom fodder out of action for too long, after all.

The ranger lay where I left him, sprawled on his back near the door. Blood seeped from underneath his shoulders— testament to the damage I'd done when I dragged him—but neither guilt nor remorse plucked at my conscience. Had the situation been reversed, I had no doubt he would have left me for the vampires while he made his escape.

And if I hadn't made that promise to Penny, I'd have done exactly the same.

"Bear," I said softly. He whisked around to the front of me, his little form humming with expectation. He liked helping; he always had. "Could you ask Cat to take Penny to the labs via tunnel D? Tell her we'll meet them there."

Tunnel D was the first of the main tunnels not filled with concrete. Tunnels A to C were as impassable today as they had been when they'd first pumped concrete into this place.

Bear made a happy little noise and sped off to complete his mission. I walked across to the ranger and knelt beside him. His pulse was still erratic, but it seemed stronger. Maybe his natural healing abilities were kicking in.

Which meant I'd better get him downstairs and re-strained. I'd been in more than a dozen shifter camps during my time in the war, and I'd witnessed the fate of captured déchet. I had no desire to have such destruction wreaked on me.

I dragged him up onto my shoulders again and headed for the stairs. A half dozen little forms drifted ahead of me, but most of them stayed behind to keep watch over both the security systems and the few remaining vampires who still prowled outside.

Which was odd. The vampires were smart enough to realize when their prey was beyond reach, and they'd attempted to breach this building often enough in the past to know that once the complete system was running, there was no getting through it.

So what was it about this ranger and the child that made them desperate enough to keep battering the walls and flinging themselves at the lasers?

Or did they, I wondered, remembering that odd darkness I'd sensed behind the vampires, have little other choice? Were they being controlled by something—or someone—else?

That was a terrifying prospect if true. But how could it be? It wasn't as if anyone—human or shifter—could actually communicate with them. I'm sure vampires did have some form of language, but it certainly wasn't one the rest of us could understand.

Maybe Penny would know what was going on—although to be honest, it didn't matter if she didn't. My task now was to fulfill my promise to her, then get them both out of here—and as fast as possible. Whatever they were involved in, whatever trouble dogged their heels, *we* didn't need it. The world had buried and forgotten us, and I very much wanted to keep it that way.

I made my way down the stairs and into the rarely used darkness that was D tunnel. My footsteps echoed against the metal floor, a sharp tattoo of sound that my little flotilla of ghosts happily danced to. As we neared the end of the tunnel, the metal flooring gave way to undulating concrete, evidence of how close this tunnel had come to being filled. I ducked through the half-collapsed doorway into the foyer of level four, the area that had housed the main medical facilities for the bunker's combatant déchet divisions. Several of the rooms closest to the tunnel that led up to level three had been flooded by concrete, but the rest of this level had survived intact. The medical equipment—although undoubtedly out-of-date by today's standards—still worked. Why the shifters hadn't destroyed these machines along with all the equipment in both the creation labs and the nurseries, I had no idea, but I'd thanked the goddess Rhea many a time over the years for that one piece of luck. I might be able to heal myself as well as any shifter, but there were still times that using a machine was infinitely better. Like when I'd fallen from the damn museum roof and broken my leg. The machines had turned a week of recovery into a day.

Penny swung around as I entered the room, and her relief was palpable.

"You're here."

I raised an eyebrow as I lowered the ranger onto one of

the mediscan beds. I stripped off the remnants of his torn and bloodied shirt and tossed it in the nearby garbage chute, then laid him down. The soft foam enveloped his body, and the bed instantly began to emit a soft beeping sound—his heartbeat, amplified by the light panel above.

"You were told I would be. Why would you expect otherwise?"

"Because people lie."

Yes, they did, but it was unusual for someone so young to say that with such surety. "And who has been lying to you? Jonas?"

The light panel shimmered as I pressed several buttons. Jonas's biorhythms came up—his brain activity was high. Either he was close to waking, or he was having some pretty vivid dreams. I glanced down at his face. His eyes weren't moving under their closed lids, but that didn't mean anything. I pressed another button. Metal clamps slid over his ankles and right arm. I might have been bred to be as strong and as fast as most shifters, but he was a ranger, lean and muscular. It was better to be safe than sorry.

I set the scanner in motion, then glanced at Penny. She was studying me with solemn eyes. "Who lied to you, Penny?"

"The man."

"What man?" I said patiently.

"The man who killed my family."

I glanced at the crisscrossed mass of scars that decorated her arms, and again anger washed through me. "Why did he kill your family?"

She half shrugged. "He just did."

"Did Jonas or the police catch him?"

"No." She hugged her arms across her chest, as if she was trying to comfort herself. Yet there were few tears in her eyes and no emotion in her voice as she asked, "Is Jonas going to be okay?"

I glanced at the scan results. No major internal damage, and aside from the broken arm, no major limb damage. "I think so."

"He was poisoned, you know."

I blinked and looked at her again. "Poisoned?"

She nodded. "He told me. He said we had to get back to Chaos quickly, because only Nuri could heal him."

Chaos. The one place on Earth I really *didn't* want to go. And it wasn't a reluctance that stemmed from the fact that its inhabitants were a broken mix of thieves, murderers, whores, and drug gangs, as well as Central's unwanted or forgotten, all of them trying to scrape by the best way they could. No, it was the sheer and utter *closeness* of it all. Everything and everyone literally lived on top of one another; there was no space, no air, hardly any light, and certainly little room to move. I'd been there only once, but I'd wanted to run screaming from it after only a few minutes.

And that was where Penny was expecting me to take her—my own private version of hell. I took a slow, steadying breath, then said, "Is that where you live?"

"Nuri does. I live in Central."

So what in hell were she and the ranger doing in the park, at night? It made no sense. "Did Jonas say what he was poisoned with? Or how?"

"He was scratched."

Poison had often been administered that way during the war, but I wouldn't have thought it to be practical these days. Not when the mediscan beds could detect—and treat—all known ailments and poisons. "By whom?"

"The man."

Suspecting I'd only get a repeat of her previous answer if I asked the next logical question, I simply said, "Let's see what the machine says before we start worrying."

"He'll die," she said, in that same solemn little tone. "You promised you'd look after him."

"I am, trust me."

She didn't say anything, but it was evident she didn't exactly trust me, either. But I guess that was to be expected, given everything she'd obviously gone through.

Nothing in the results suggested the ranger had been poisoned, so either Penny was misinformed or whatever had been used on Jonas had been created *after* the war and therefore was not in the system's databanks. I set the machine to HEAL. Mechanical arms reached down from the ceiling, carefully realigning the ranger's arm before the lasers kicked in to set it.

I turned to fully face Penny. "Why don't we go get something to eat while Jonas is patched up?"

Her nose screwed up. "I'm not hungry."

"Well, I am." I gently touched a hand to her back and pushed her reluctant figure toward the door. Despite her cherub face, her skin was cool and her body skeletal. She might not want food right now, but she desperately needed it. I guided her down the hall and into the small dispensing kitchen that had once served as a break area for the staff on this level. There was only one machine working these days, and the coffee it produced was pretty vile, but it was still better than nothing. I hit the button for a strong black, then glanced down at her. "I know you're really not hungry, but surely you could manage a small protein meal?"

She shook her head, studying me solemnly, the steadiness of her gaze oddly disturbing.

"What about something to drink? A soda? Milk?"

"You have milk? Real milk?" Her voice was surprised more than interested.

I smiled wryly. "No, not real. It's powder-based but drinkable."

Her nose screwed up again, and I can't honestly say I blamed her. The powdered stuff was little more than a chemical stew, and it certainly tasted like it. But real milk was rarer than gold, and it definitely wasn't in the price range of the average Joe in Central—even if he *had* a decent job and wage. And it was damnably hard to steal something that wasn't available in the sort of establishments I could risk theft in.

I silently handed her some water, then heated a protein meal for myself, collected my coffee, and walked across to one of the small, padded benches lining the far wall. She didn't follow, just watched me, the cup in one hand and the torn fingers on the other clenching and unclenching.

"I'm not going to hurt you, Penny," I said softly.

"I know."

I studied her for a moment, wondering if her unnatural calmness was merely shock or something more serious. "Why don't you tell me how your parents died?"

"I told you, they were attacked—"

"By the man who lied to you," I finished for her. "Do you know his name?"

She shook her head, then raised the cup and took a sip. A shudder ran through her thin frame. "That's awful."

"It's recycled and does taste a little tart, but it won't kill you."

"I can't drink it." She placed the cup on the floor beside her feet, then clasped her hands in front of her stomach. "I really need to see if Jonas is okay."

"That screen up there"—I pointed to the light screen flickering above the main door—"will let us know when the healing cycle has finished. Tell me how you know Jonas."

"He's my uncle."

"You're a shifter?"

I couldn't help the edge of surprise in my voice. She really *didn't* smell like a shifter. Jonas did—at a guess I'd say he was panther, not only because most rangers tended to be cats of some kind, but because of the mottled, night-dark color of his hair. It was the usual indicator of species. Mine was a mix of white and black, and my eyes were blue, because my genes had come from the rarer white tiger.

Penny nodded solemnly. "He's my mom's older brother."

"Was it just you and Jonas who survived the attack?"

She shook her head. "Jonas wasn't there when Mum and Dad were killed. He found me later and rescued me."

"From where?"

"From where I was hiding from the man."

Something flashed in her eyes. Something dark and angry and very unchildlike. I frowned, once again oddly uneasy. There was something amiss here, with her, but I just couldn't put my finger on it.

Yet the ghosts were watching her with fascination and absolutely no sense of disquiet. They surely wouldn't be so relaxed if they'd sensed anything untoward, especially given that their sense of these things was usually more finely tuned than mine.

"Can you describe the man for me?"

She studied me for a minute, then pointed at me and said, "He wore combat pants like yours, but though he walked through the shadows he wasn't comfortable in them. Not like you."

Something twisted inside me. My combat pants had been

made with a special gray material that took on the colors of its surroundings and made us near invisible from a distance. Like the shirt—also gray, but patterned with darker swirls—they were déchet *specific*, designed not only to withstand the rigors of war, but to carry the many weapons warrior-trained déchet were proficient with. There was a ton of both still in the base exchange and, with the war long over, I'd taken to wearing them. The only people who'd look twice were shifters who'd survived the war, and most of those generally weren't found in the areas of Central I visited.

"So this man was a soldier?"

She shrugged. "I suppose so. He fought Jonas, and almost won."

The twisting ramped up a notch. Only a highly trained fighter could ever hope to beat a ranger, even in this day and age. I touched my cheek. "Did he have an inked bar code here?"

Her gaze followed my fingers. "Bar code?"

I hesitated. "It would be black, and look like lots of little lines squashed together."

She shook her head. "No. He was almost see-through, and he didn't really have a face. Just big eyes and a squashed nose."

So not a déchet, but something far, *far* worse. She'd described—almost to the letter—the creatures commonly called wraiths. They were one of the Others, but, unlike most, they seemed to have a distinct plan and purpose beyond murder and mayhem. The only trouble was, no one—as far as I was aware—had yet discovered that purpose.

But why would a wraith kill Penny's parents and only slash her up? That wasn't their usual mode of operation. Generally, if a wraith crossed your path, you were dead. No ifs, buts, or second chances.

The light screen above the door flickered to life, indicating the mediscan bed had finished the healing process. I tossed my half-eaten meal in the nearby recycle bin and rose.

"Is Jonas better now?" Penny said, her expression solemn as she studied the screen.

"Let's go see." I waved a hand for her to precede me, and sipped my coffee as I followed. The ghosts trailed alongside us, a flotilla of humming happiness. Which again made me question the drifting sense of unease within me.

An amber light flashed on the control monitor above Jonas's bed. I frowned and pressed a couple of buttons. Though the ranger's wounds had been healed, his vital signs were becoming unstable and there was no indication as to why.

"He's been poisoned," Penny repeated softly. "We have to get him to Nuri, otherwise he'll die. I don't want him to die. He's all I have left."

"He won't die." I flicked the screen across to view the blood work. There was nothing there—certainly no sign of any abnormality in his tox results. And yet he wasn't waking up, and his condition was worsening.

I looked at Penny. "Are you sure he didn't say what he was poisoned with?"

She shook her head, and I bit back a growl of frustration.

"Please," she said. "We have to get him to Nuri. He said it was his only chance."

I blew out a breath, glanced at the screen, then closed my eyes and said, "Okay, but we can't go now. We have to wait until the morning."

"But—"

"Penny," I said, gently but firmly. "The night belongs to the vampires, and we'll all die if we go out there now. We'll just have to hope he hangs on until tomorrow."

Besides, there was no way I was going into Chaos at night. In that place, vampires certainly *weren't* the biggest threat to life.

Her bottom lip quivered, but no tears filled her eyes. Maybe she couldn't cry. Maybe she was all out of tears.

"Can I stay here with him?"

"Yes." I picked her up and sat her on the next bed. "Snuggle down, little one. The bed will keep you warm, and the ghosts will keep you company."

"Where are you going?"

"Just to check how the system is holding up against the vampires. I'll be back soon."

She nodded and lay down. Her eyes drifted closed and, within minutes, she was asleep. I glanced up at the light screen. Her core temperature was low, but everything else seemed to be okay. I pressed a button, setting the machine to do a full scan, then turned and headed out. Bear and Cat came with me; the others stayed behind, happily gossiping with one another. After so many years of just having me to talk to and about, I thought wryly, this had to be the most exciting thing that had ever happened to them.

I didn't immediately go check the system, however. I headed instead down to the ninth level—the level where, in the long years immediately after this place had been cleansed, I'd taken what little remained of everyone who'd died here. The ghosts of the adult déchet had followed their bones, but the humans who'd died here had not, and I had no idea where they'd gone. I knew humans believed that while most souls moved on after death, a person who'd been taken before their time could *not*. Did that mean everyone other than Hank—who was the only human ghost I'd seen over the years—had moved on? I didn't know— and, to be honest, had no real desire to find out. I might owe humanity for my existence, but I certainly owed them nothing else.

The farther down I went, the closer I got to them, the more their anger grew. They were well aware of just who I'd brought into our home.

I took a deep breath and said, "I apologize for bringing our foe into your midst, but he will not be here long. He saved the young child's life, and you cannot harm him in any way."

The only response was a sharpening of the anger. It crawled across my skin like fire, burning where it touched. And while I could—through physical contact with their energy—see and talk to these déchet as I might the living, I wasn't about to tempt fate that way. Of course, they might not give me an option.

"I know you're unhappy, but I had no choice. And the war is long ended."

Energy surged across my skin, creating a fleeting connection that was intense and filled with hate.

It will never be over for us, a deep voice said. *We were soldiers, created to kill, and death has not ended that directive.*

"But you cannot kill without orders." And even as I said it, I crossed mental fingers, because I really had no idea if that was true one hundred years down the track.

And that, came the harsh reply, *is the only reason the ranger still lives.*

Relief spun through me. At least that meant they were one less problem I had to worry about.

I would not, however, the voice added, *bring him down here. Directives and conditioning have been known to fail.*

And with that warning ringing in my ears, the connection died and the ghosts left. I retreated.

A check upstairs revealed the remaining vampires still

prowled around the building, looking for a way in. While that was not unusual, there was an intensity to their movements that was troubling. It was almost as if they were being ordered to do so—and yet, I'd never heard or seen any evidence that vampire society had any sort of hierarchy.

I cleaned up the mess I'd made in the museum area, then patrolled the rest of the complex out of habit. Once I was sure everything was secure and the system was working fine, I headed down to the bunk room, where I gave myself a booster shot against whatever viruses and infections the vamps' claws and teeth might have held. It was something I really didn't need, but taking it at least took the stress off my body's self-healing properties. By the time I'd had a shower and changed my clothes, a couple of hours had slipped past. Penny was still asleep, but the ranger stirred, his lean, muscular body bathed in sweat as he unconsciously fought the restraints holding him in place. A glance at the light screen confirmed his core temperature was rising.

I downgraded the bed's temp setting, then introduced a strong sedative. He calmed almost instantly, but his brain activity remained high, and his core temp wasn't going down. That wasn't good, especially when the machine wasn't picking up a reason. But then, these machines *were* old. Who knew what sort of poisons the world had developed since their creation?

Frowning, I turned around and studied Penny's results. Even after the full scan, there didn't appear to be anything unusual other than a lower than normal core temp. So why did I still have a gut feeling that all was not well?

Maybe it was just the guilt. Maybe I would never be able to look at a child in trouble and not be certain there had to be something more I could do to help.

Cat drifted into my vision. Ghostly palms gently cupped

my face as her energy ran through me, full of reassurance. I smiled and kissed her fingertips, feeling the warmth in them and half wishing they could once again hold flesh. But that, too, was something that was never going to be.

I blew out a breath, half-annoyed at the sudden wash of melancholy, and walked across to the chairs near the door. Here I perched, keeping an eye on both of the monitors as the long night rolled slowly by.

Penny eventually woke and almost instantly said, "It's dawn."

I raised an eyebrow. *I* knew it was nearly dawn because my DNA was sensitive to the coming and going of the sun, but it was rare to find a shifter similarly attuned. Not when they were this deep underground, anyway.

"Yes, it is." I rose from my chair. "Would you like some breakfast?"

She shook her head. "We need to take Jonas to Nuri."

My gaze flicked to the readouts. He'd definitely gone downhill over the last couple of hours, but he wasn't at death's door just yet. "Penny," I said, as gently as I could. "You need to eat. You won't be any help to Jonas if you make yourself sick."

"No!" Her voice was strident, angry, and again that darkness flashed briefly in her eyes.

I frowned, my gaze flicking to the ghosts. They didn't seem alarmed. "Okay, we'll go. But I need to get some supplies first, just to make sure we're safe."

She nodded and almost instantly calmed down. I spun on my heel, leaving her in the company of the ghosts as I made my way to a secondary gun cache two levels down. I grabbed several automatics and a couple of clips, and hid them all under a long, hooded trench that I'd stolen from Central last winter. I thought briefly about altering my appearance, but decided against it. It took a lot of energy to initiate a shift, though once achieved it was easy enough to maintain as long as I ate sensibly and slept properly. But right now, it was probably more prudent to save my strength for whatever might await in Chaos. Besides, if what I'd seen on the surface a month ago was any indication, my black-and-white-striped hair would be deemed rather mild.

I headed to medical supplies to collect an airchair. Though there was no way known I could take it into Chaos—doing so would be nothing short of issuing an invitation to be attacked—I could at least use it until we reached the bunker's South Siding exit. The less distance I had to carry the shifter, the better.

Penny hadn't moved when I got back. She simply sat on the bed staring at Jonas. Maybe she was willing him to live or something.

I detached him from the bed's sensors, then carefully lifted him up and placed him on the chair. Once I'd strapped him in, I glanced at Penny. "Ready to go?"

She nodded, her little face solemn as she jumped off the bed. The ghosts swirled around, excited and happy that we were once again moving. It wouldn't last—not when they realized we were not only heading back up to the surface, but going out.

"Bear, lead the way."

He hummed contentedly and did as bidden, guiding us through the myriad tunnels. As we neared the exit, the tunnel became strewn with the rubble and debris that had drifted in over the years thanks to the overflow from the nearby drains. The air was a putrid mix of humanity, rotting rubbish, and the muddy scent of the trickle of water that was still known as the Barra River. Like many things in this world of ours, its course had been forever altered when the bombs had been unleashed.

The thick steel grate covering the exit came into sight, and the green light flashing to one side indicated the outer system was still in full security mode. Thankfully, the laser net protected only the dome itself, and, with any luck, the museum staff would blame the system going briefly offline on a computer glitch, as they had in the past.

I powered down the airchair, then walked around to the control box and quickly typed in the twelve-digit code. This tunnel had been designed as a means of escape and, as such, didn't have scanner facilities. I'd never bothered upgrading the old gateway simply because few people ventured down this part of the Barra—it was too close to one of the rifts.

The grate slid noisily open. Penny lunged forward, but I grabbed her, holding her back.

"Hush," I said, as she opened her mouth to protest. "Wait until we know it's safe."

She pouted. I ignored her and listened to the sounds of a city stirring to life, sorting through the layers, trying to find anything that might indicate someone was close. There was nothing.

"Okay," I said and released her.

She ran out but stopped several feet away from the entrance, sucking in the air as if desperate to fill her lungs. I snorted softly. It didn't smell *that* bad underground.

I glanced back at the ghosts. "Keep this entrance safe for me. I'll be back by sunset."

Hands patted me good-bye—although both Cat and Bear were already outside, waiting. They'd always been more adventurous than the younger ones, preferring to be with me whenever possible rather than stay in the home that was also their tomb. I wasn't entirely sure whether it was due to our deeper connection, or whether it was simply a matter of their being older than the rest. Either way, I was always happy to have their company.

I dragged Jonas off the chair, then walked out of our sanctuary. Once the grate had closed, I turned and looked around.

Sunrise tinted the sky with rose and lavender, and the scent of rain was still in the air. It would be brilliant if it *did* rain again, because the inhabitants of Central and Chaos would be too busy scurrying for cover to worry about the three of us. It also meant there would be less chance of our being seen returning.

Central's metal drawbridge was still raised against the night, and the nearby rail siding was filled with pods that were shadowed and silent. No one would be close to them until the sun had fully risen. Humanity had become very fearful of darkness—and with good reason.

My gaze went to Chaos, and a shudder went through me. Even in full sunlight it was a place of shadows; in the half-light of a dawn barely risen, it rose forbiddingly above me, a grimy, gritty mass that blighted the metal to which it clung.

I glanced down at Penny. "Where does this Nuri live?"

"In Chaos," she answered.

"Where in Chaos? It's a big place." And not someplace I wanted to wander about aimlessly. Humans and shifters might now live together in relative peace, even in habitats like Chaos, but that didn't mean it wasn't a dangerous place for strangers to venture.

She hesitated. "Chang Puk district."

Which wasn't overly helpful given how little I knew about Chaos and its districts. "What level is that?"

"Five."

So midlevel. Which meant it was more than likely this Nuri had some standing. In Chaos, the higher the level you lived on, the more power or wealth you had. It was the same in Central, except that it was the city's heart—and the safety that came with being as far away from the walls as was possible—that drew the wealthy. "Where on five?"

Rather unhelpfully, she shrugged.

Irritation surged, but I forced it aside. She was only a child, even if she did sometimes seem far older. "We can't just wander around, Penny. That would be dangerous."

And make us a target. If you didn't move with purpose through the various levels, you were inviting trouble from the gangs and thugs who ran a good portion of the place.

Her gaze drifted to Jonas and her expression became distant yet oddly intent. After a moment, she said, "Nuri lives in Run Turk Alley."

Which was the mercenary district, as far as I knew. In some ways that was better than the upper levels, where the whores, gang leaders, and drug kingpins lived. At least I had a chance of blending in with the mercenaries. Even though I'd been bred to infiltrate and seduce, I would never have passed as a whore. There was a coarseness—a rapacity—in the ladies who traded their wares within Chaos that I doubted I could achieve or fake.

I shifted Jonas's weight to a more comfortable position, then resignedly moved forward. There were only two entrances into Chaos—this south one, and the other at the far north end. A single roadway that followed the sweep of the curtain wall connected the two, but there were a myriad of lanes and footpaths branching off this main artery, as well as a slew of stairs and ladders that connected the various levels.

Penny trailed behind me, as did the two ghosts. Their

thoughts were a mix of excitement and dread, and I had no doubt there would be lots of stories shared and embellished with those who'd remained behind. Penny's expression gave away little, which again struck me as odd. Given she'd never been to this place before, I would have expected at least a little fear. Chaos was not exactly the most welcoming of places to look at.

As we neared the little footbridge that crossed the two-feet-wide remnant of what once had been the main water source for Central's founders, the air began to shimmer and spark. The energy that caressed my skin was dark and unhealthy in feel, and unease crawled through me. Though this rift hadn't moved in years, that didn't mean it couldn't or wouldn't explode into action.

Didn't mean something couldn't or wouldn't come through it, despite the growing strength of daylight.

I'd seen some of those things. I had no desire to fight them.

I increased my pace, and Penny trotted along after me, seemingly oblivious to the danger that waited not very far away. But then, few humans or shifters could actually see them. It seemed to be something only those who were either psychically or magically gifted could do.

The day was growing brighter, casting splashes of red and gold across the silver curtain wall. Or, at least, along the flat front of it. There was little enough silver visible across the rest of it for dawn to paint, covered as it was by Chaos.

We strode up the hill toward the six-feet-wide gap that was the south entrance. On either side were the garishly decorated metal containers that made up much of Chaos's ground level, and which supported the weight of everything above it. There were no windows or ventilation slots cut into any of these; they were basically little more than metal boxes that were used as shops, factories, and trading posts, and they found life only once the sun was up. The inhabitants of Chaos might show little concern about the vampires, but they didn't invite trouble, either. When dusk came, those who worked here retreated to at least the next level, and all ladders and stairs were either drawn up or locked down. It didn't often help, but the illusion of safety was better than nothing, I suppose.

My pace slowed as I neared the entrance. "Are you sure Nuri's in Run Turk Alley on the fifth level?"

"Yes."

Her gaze was on the ranger rather than me, and with good reason. Given the way I was carrying him, I couldn't actually see his features, but I could feel the heat in his skin, the sweat that stained his clothes, and the tremors that raked his body. Whatever he'd been given, it continued to take a toll on his body, despite his natural healing abilities.

I resolutely strode into Chaos. The shadows closed in immediately, and the fear of being caged—of having no room and no air—swiftly followed. It was a fear that had been born in the stinking, bug-filled cesspit I'd once been thrown into after the shifter general I'd been assigned to had begun to suspect I might be a traitor. That pit would have been my tomb had it not been for Sal—a déchet assassin, and one of the few friends I'd had apart from the children. How he'd found me I have no idea, but he'd undoubtedly saved my life.

Of course, it was a debt I'd never get the chance to repay. As far as I knew, no other déchet had survived the shifters' determined destruction of everyone and every-thing related to the HDP.

I swallowed heavily and forced my feet on, my gaze on the grimy, wet, and littered ground rather than the too-close graffiti-strewn metal walls and doors that lined the roadway.

No cars or motorbikes ever came into Chaos—there simply wasn't the room, especially when the traders all opened their doors and their operations spilled into the street itself.

Our footsteps echoed in the thick silence, and above us, life stirred. I glanced up, even though there was nothing to see except the crusted metal ceiling that seemed far too close. But I knew what was up there—layer upon layer of crammed apartments that weren't much larger than the shipping containers they all rested on. I also knew that those who controlled this place would now be aware of our presence. Who those people actually were, I had no idea. Nor did I wish to ever find out.

We pressed on, splashing through water that was thick and oily while trying to avoid the muck that dripped steadily from the ceiling. Rubbish lay in gathering drifts, emitting a stench that was a putrid mix of rotting fish and human waste. While Central grudgingly provided some necessities—basic water and sanitation facilities (though not garbage pickup, as evidenced by the waste), some medical facilities, and irregular postal services—black-market trading was common, and what wasn't stolen was either hunted for in the park near my bunker, or fished from the rerouted Barra, a good kilometer away from here.

We found an unlocked staircase and moved up. The entrance to the next level was sealed, so I drew one of the guns and shot the lock off. The sharp sound echoed. If the powers that be actually *hadn't* been aware of our presence, then they certainly were now. But it wasn't like I had much other choice. Jonas seemed to be getting heavier, and I wasn't entirely sure how much longer I could keep carrying him.

We moved swiftly through the next two levels, but by the time we'd reach the fourth, we were no longer alone.

No one approached us, but they watched, and they followed, and the air was thick with hostility.

"We're almost there." I was trying to reassure Penny as much as myself, but if her expression was anything to go by, she was once again oblivious to the danger surrounding us.

We reached the fifth level. I paused at the top of the stairs, looking left and right, and—after mentally flipping a coin—headed left. If this Nuri was a healer of some distinction—and I suspected she might be—then she was likely housed toward the middle of the complex, which would provide more protection from vampire attacks than the outer reaches.

I scanned the haphazard signage as we passed each off shoot lane or walkway, and eventually found the one we wanted. It was little more than a three-feet-wide path that wove through a mess of houses—each one little more than a ten-feet-wide collection of scavenged wood, steel, and plastic—and whose owners lounged against the outer wall, smoking and drinking. Every one of them was armed. Run Turk Alley was, as I'd heard, mercenary central.

I shifted my grip on Jonas, freeing a hand without making it too obvious I was ready to reach for a weapon. We headed down, weaving our way through a sea of rubbish, stares, and outstretched feet. No one stopped us or said anything, but they didn't move out of our way, either. I stumbled more than once, wrenching my already screaming back and leg muscles as I struggled to remain upright.

Eventually, I saw a small sign that simply read NURI'S. While it was just another wood-and-metal building coated with years of grime, graffiti, and advertising posters, it was three times the size of the others in this street. It also had several windows, all of which were barred—a necessity in this area, no doubt.

Penny squeezed past me and ran ahead to open the door. I followed her into the brightly lit confines and was almost immediately hit by the stink of alcohol. But a more surprising—and dangerous—scent closely followed. There were shifters in this place.

While it was highly unlikely any of them realized what I was, I couldn't help the instinctive need to retreat. I could fight—all déchet could, even those of us who had been trained in the art of seduction. But the war had been a long time ago, and fighting had never been my main skill set. There were far too many shifters in this bar for me to have a chance of survival should they decide to attack.

I stopped several feet in from the door and transferred Jonas to a sturdy-looking table. Then I scanned the room. The woman standing behind the bar was human, and the shifters were all seated at one of the tables crowding the far end of the small room. There were a half dozen of them— four men and two women—and all looked to be in fighting condition. It was an impression amplified by the many weapons strapped to their bodies.

Relax, I told myself silently. *Breathe.*

But my heart still raced, and my fingers itched with the need to reach for a weapon. I resisted the urge and remained where I was, emoting a calm I certainly didn't feel. Cat and Bear crowded close, their energy stinging my skin, making it twitch.

"Jesus H. Christ!" the woman at the bar said, her abrupt comment cutting through the thick silence and making me jump. "What the hell happened to Jonas?"

She strode out of the gloom, a tea towel that had seen better days slung over one shoulder. She was short and fat, with rosy cheeks and wiry, steel gray hair that ballooned around her head like a sea of slender, twisting snakes.

She didn't look the least bit menacing and, for that reason alone, I very much suspected she was the most dangerous person in the room. In fact, the force of her energy electrified the air, so that she appeared surrounded by a halo of flickering, fiery blue.

"According to Penny, Jonas has been poisoned," I said, when it became obvious Penny wasn't going to answer. "I was advised to bring him here."

Her gaze pinned mine and, in the brown depths, I saw sharp intellect and great power. This was Nuri; of that I had no doubt.

"And who the hell are you?" While her voice was still brusque, her touch was gentle as she gripped Jonas's cheeks and studied him intently.

"No one important."

"Well, no one important," she said, her gaze still on the ranger though I had no doubt she was very aware of my every move. "Would you like to tell us how you came to be in a position to help these two? I suspect there's a bit of a story behind it."

I shrugged, my gaze flicking to the watching shifters. Their attention hadn't wavered, and their hands were resting a little closer to their guns. My tension ramped another notch, as did the caress of power from my two ghostly guards.

We needed to get out of here before this situation became nasty. These people were too alert, too ready for action. It was almost as if they'd been expecting us.

"She rescued us," Penny piped up. "From the vampires."

The woman looked up at that. Her gaze swept down my length, then came up to rest on my face again. It felt like she was clawing away the layers of skin and seeing exactly what I was.

"And just how many vampires are we talking about?"

"Not many," I said, at the same time that Penny said, "At least a score."

"It might have seemed that way, but honestly, it wasn't." I forced a smile. "And now that these two are safe, I *really* have to go."

The ghosts flung themselves around me, urging me to hurry, needing, wanting to leave as much as I did. I took a step back. No one moved to stop me. The old woman continued to study me, seeing too much, suspecting too much.

"At least tell us your name," she said, "so that we may say a prayer for you over dinner tonight."

"Her name is Tiger," Penny said, and, with all the innocence of a child, added, "She's a déchet."

My gaze snapped to her. *How the hell . . . ?* But the rest of the thought was snatched away as energy exploded around me. It came from the woman, from the shifters, and, more dangerously, from my little guards.

"No," I said, and flung out a hand, snatching back the power Cat had already begun to discharge. Then something pricked the side of my neck and the world went dark.

CHAPTER 3

Waking was painful.

My head felt like it was full of roaches trying to claw their way out, and my body was on fire. Sweat poured from my forehead and down my spine, and the T-shirt I wore under my jacket was soaked.

But none of that mattered. Understanding the situation *did*. And that meant concentrating every bit of awareness on my surroundings and what was going on.

I guess the most obvious fact was that I still lived, which surprised me. Given everyone's reactions, I'd expected the opposite.

I lay sprawled against cold metal, and the air was not only heated and still, but also ripe with the scent of urine and rubbish. There was no one close—no one I could smell or hear, anyway. I was fully clothed, and—despite the ache in my head and the fire in my body—unhurt. But the weight of my weapons was gone; no surprise there, especially if they'd believed Penny—and the question of how she'd known my true name let alone even *suspect* I was déchet was a point I could worry about once I'd escaped. *If* I escaped.

I opened my eyes, only to be greeted by a light so harsh I blinked back tears. Vampire lights. They were using *vampire* lights on me. I would have laughed had I not felt so shitty.

While I couldn't actually become light—as I could become shadow—I could certainly make it *appear* as if I had. It was a skill that had allowed me to get out of situations like this in the past. If a cell appeared empty—if it appeared the prisoner had already escaped—there was little reason to lock said cell back up.

Of course, it *wasn't* a skill that all déchet had, just those of us designed to be lures and assassins—and we'd been few enough in number.

Little fingers patted my face. It was a reassuring touch, but both Cat and Bear were confused and angry, and their emotions stung the air. I opened my hand and briefly wrapped my fingers around the energy of theirs.

"It'll be okay," I said softly. "We'll be okay."

They hummed, happy that I was awake but not really reassured. I pushed upright, but far too fast. Pain hit like a sledgehammer, so sharp it felt like my head was about to split apart. I hissed and hugged my knees to my chest, breathing slowly and deeply until the sensation faded. Once it did, I studied my surroundings. The room was little more than a ten-feet-square metal box—which was huge in a place where space was at a premium—and had obviously been, at one point in its life, a storage container, as there were no windows and the walls were pockmarked with welded-over drill holes that must have once held shelving in place. Silver mesh covered all four walls and the ceiling.

This was a room designed to hold shifters and vampires, meaning Nuri's place was more than just a bar. And though this prison *should* have set off my fear of enclosed spaces, it didn't. Maybe it was the light. Or maybe the fear of not knowing what these people wanted or intended was drowning out everything else.

I glanced at the door. It, too, was silver-coated and made of thickened steel, with only a minute space between the bottom of the door and the floor. Even so, I might be able to get out that way, but not until the weakness that assailed my body eased. Shadowing in light was extremely hard and not always successful; to have *any* hope of escaping that way, I needed full strength.

I studied the ceiling again, squinting against the harshness of the lights. I couldn't see anything to indicate I was being monitored, but that didn't mean I wasn't.

Bear, I thought. *Explore.*

He hummed with pleasure and whipped through me, connecting us on a level far deeper than what we'd achieved in the park, because *this* time, the connection lingered once he pulled free.

I closed my eyes and saw through his.

There was a dark lane little more than a foot and a half wide just beyond my cell, and the air stirred sluggishly, suggesting there was a vent of some sort nearby. Bear spun around, but there were no other buildings behind my cell—nothing but a glimpse of stained silver that was Central's curtain wall. Unbidden, he turned again and moved down the little lane, checking the small rooms to the left and right, finding nothing but wet, musty darkness. But as he drifted toward a short flight of stairs, voices began to edge across the silence—thick, angry voices. Bear followed the sound into a room slightly larger than mine. A half dozen chairs that had seen better days encircled a small electric stove on which several blackened pots sat. One held little more than water, and the other some sort of meat and vegetable mix.

The voices were coming from the next room. Bear whisked through the wooden door, then stopped. We were back in the bar. One of the shifters—a female—leaned against the bar while Nuri stood in the middle of the room, her hands on her hips as she glared at the second of the shifters. He was a thickset man with a mass of golden hair and yellow eyes. *Lion,* I thought, as Bear drifted closer.

"Fuck it to hell, Branna," Nuri all but exploded. "Did you have to use the Iruakandji on her?"

Iruakandji. No wonder it felt like I was knocking on death's door. That particular drug had been developed in the latter part of war by the HDP, but rarely used. While it *did* kill shifters with great alacrity, it had proven unviable as a weapon not only because it was extremely costly to make, but because it was just as deadly to déchet, no matter how little shifter blood they had in them.

What was even more interesting, though, was the fact this lot not only had access to it, but kept it close enough to use.

"If there's even the *slightest* possibility she's a fucking déchet," Branna said, flinging his arms out wide to emphasize his point, "then what does it matter? They're supposed to be dead, and now she is."

"Most of us are supposed to be dead, Branna. Does that mean you're going to use the poison on Jonas? Or Ela?"

"He'd better not try," the brown-haired woman said without looking up, "or he'll find his balls shoved in the back of his fucking throat."

Branna grimaced. "Look, that's totally different, and you know it."

"What I *know*," Nuri said, "is that the déchet were designed to kill *all* shifters on sight. And yet this woman—if she *was* a déchet, and we have no real proof that she was—saved not only Penny, but a *ranger*. I wanted to know why."

"Well, it's one of life's little questions that's going to have to remain a mystery, isn't it, because I can't fucking undo what I did."

And he didn't want to, if his expression was anything to go by. Although if they were expecting me to be dead, then they were going to be pretty disappointed. When the HDP made those who were destined to become lures, they'd ensured we were immune to all known toxins and poisons. They had to, because that's generally how lures killed when tasked to do so. Which didn't mean we suffered no ill effects—we did. We just didn't die from them—though I'd certainly prayed to Rhea to swiftly take both the little ones *and* me when they'd filled our bunker with Draccid.

But then, Draccid was a particularly insidious gas that entered the body through breath or via exposed flesh, and melted you from the inside out. It was a hideous way to die—something I knew because I'd come very close to death myself. In fact, the strong psychic connection I had with Cat and Bear was undoubtedly due to the fact that they'd not only died in my arms, but that some of our DNA had mingled on that dreadful day.

But being immune didn't make me immortal. Far from it. Any regular weapon that would kill a vampire could kill me, with the exception of light.

"I just wish you'd fucking *think* before you react for a change!" Nuri swung around and headed for the door. "I dreamed of her coming for a reason, Branna, and—"

She stopped abruptly and stared at the empty space where Bear hovered. And given the slight narrowing of her gaze, I had no doubt she was aware not only of *him*, but of my link with him.

"Well, well, well," she added. "Maybe all is not as lost as we thought. Branna, go see if Jonas is awake and aware, and get him to meet me down in the cell if he is."

He muttered something under his breath, but turned on his heel and disappeared through another doorway.

Nuri took a step in our direction. "So, little ghost—"

Bear turned and fled before she could finish, and I can't say I blamed him. He wasn't used to confronting someone like her—hell, *I* wasn't used to confronting someone like her, but obviously, I soon would be.

Bear whisked into the cell, and I held out my hand. He came to rest on my palm, and I flooded our connection with soothing energy. After a while, he calmed down enough to sever the link, then drift upward, hovering near the ceiling. Cat remained near my left shoulder, her energy dancing across my skin like tiny fireflies.

I took a deep breath and released it slowly, but it didn't do much to ease the tension that ripped through my burning limbs. Damn it, I *needed* to get out of here! I might often hunger for company that was solid rather than ghostly, but I'd rather spend another hundred years alone with my ghosts than endure five minutes in the company of people like these.

The big question was, though, would I even last long enough to escape?

Nuri might want to question me, but she'd made no mention of actually keeping me alive *after* that.

I flexed my fingers. I had to stop worrying over things I could do nothing about. It was time to focus on the things I *could*—like the storm of poison ripping through my body.

I crossed my legs and closed my eyes, focusing on my

breathing, on every intake of air as it washed through my nostrils and down into my lungs, until a sense of calm began to descend. It was in this state that my body had been designed to fast-track healing, and, after a few heartbeats, the fire in my flesh began to ease, as did the ache in my head.

The cell door retracted. I didn't open my eyes, concentrating on the repair, desperate to get as close to full working order as was possible. Even so, I knew the first person to step into the room was Nuri. Interestingly, she didn't have any particular scent, although the smell of ale, soap, and water clung to her clothes. It wasn't *her*, though.

She didn't say anything, didn't do anything. She just stood there, studying me. After several moments, I realized she was waiting for Jonas. He eventually arrived and filled the air with the scent of cat, wind, and evening rain—an odd but interesting combination. But there was also a darkness to his scent that had the hairs along the back of my neck rising. There was anger and barely controlled violence in that darkness, and it reminded me forcibly that whatever else this man was, he belonged to a breed of soldier that had single-mindedly mutilated and killed my kind.

Nuri finally walked around me, her steps light despite her large frame. My skin twitched at her closeness, crawled with the sense of her power.

The ghosts crowded closer, their little bodies pressed against mine, their fear and anger clawing at my inside. *Calm, just stay calm,* I whispered internally, not entirely certain who I was trying to reassure—them or me.

As Nuri's fiery presence retreated toward the doorway, I finally opened my eyes.

Only to meet Jonas's gaze.

Something within me tightened; it wasn't fear, but something far more base. I'd been specifically designed to be like honey to a bee when it came to shifters, but a side effect was that I was inordinately attracted to them. And even though there was far more to me than the task for which I'd been bred, I couldn't entirely deny my nature. Not even now, in a situation as uncertain as this.

If he felt even an inkling of attraction, it certainly wasn't showing—not in his scent, and not in his expression or body language. In fact, not even the darkness I sensed within him showed in those vivid, cat-green depths. Indeed, given the casual way he leaned a shoulder against the door frame, it would have been easy to believe he wasn't particularly interested in either me or whatever was about to happen.

At least he appeared to be over whatever it was that had assailed him—even if his sun-browned skin still seemed pale and his cheeks held a slight gauntness that made his sharp nose look even more aristocratic. Even with that nose—or maybe *because* of it—he could definitely be called handsome. But not classically so—there was a roughness to his features that made them far more interesting than beautiful.

"Why did you attack me?" My words came out stronger than I expected, and for that I was grateful. If I was to have any hope of convincing them I wasn't déchet, then I couldn't give any indication that the drug they'd administered had had any effect.

"Penny said you were déchet." The back of Nuri's skirts swished like some gigantic black curtain as she stopped near the doorway. "And she's not a child inclined to untruths."

"Penny also said that she'd never met you," I replied evenly. "And that is patently untrue."

"No, it isn't, simply because we haven't met in person. I know of her only through the dreams."

"Meaning what? That you're some kind of witch?"

"Some kind." She crossed her arms and leaned against the wall. Obviously I'd been right in guessing she was full human, because the silver curtain had no effect on the unprotected areas of her skin.

"So you take the word of a child you've never actually met, and attack the stranger responsible for saving both her and one of your own? Nice. Real nice."

"Perhaps not, but our reaction is understandable if you are what Penny says you are."

"I'm not. You should be able to see that just by looking at me."

"Unlikely," Jonas growled. His voice was deep, rich, and oddly melodious, despite the anger within it. I doubted he'd originated from anywhere around here, as those from both Central and Chaos seemed to have a more guttural edge. "There were many rumors during the war about déchet who bore neither the marks nor the scent of their kind."

I raised an eyebrow. "And there were just as many rumors stating they could fly and walk through walls. Neither of those were true, from what I've read. Besides, didn't your lot ensure all remaining déchet were obliterated after the war?"

"And yet you apparently live in the remains of one of their major bases," Nuri noted. "And wear the military uniform of the déchet."

"I live in a couple of rooms, one of which is a storeroom containing—among other things—tons of uniforms," I corrected. "Last I heard, that wasn't a crime."

"It is when you're carrying weapons not seen since the war," Jonas growled. "And you're using tunnels that were supposed to be blocked."

"The main entrances *are* blocked," I replied, with a calm I certainly wasn't feeling. Despite his nonchalance, it was obvious he wanted to fight—wanted to attack—and the strength of that desire was so strong it rolled across my skin like a heated caress. And there was a tiny, insane part of me that wished—longed—for that caress to be real rather than mere emotion. "As I said, there are only a couple of usable areas."

"Not according to Penny," he said.

"Penny's a child. I wouldn't take everything she says as gospel."

"Penny's not what—"

"Jonas, enough," Nuri cut in softly, making me wonder just what the shifter had been about to reveal.

I shifted my gaze to her. "I'm not a déchet, but whether you choose to believe that is entirely up to you."

"Perhaps," she said. "Wipe your cheek."

I raised an eyebrow. "You could have checked my cheek when I was unconscious."

"We tried." Levity briefly touched her voice. "But I'm afraid your ghosts were rather reluctant to let us close to you."

Then how in hell had they gotten me into the cell? Magic? I eyed Nuri for a moment, suspecting that might well be possible.

Thank you for trying, little ones, I said, then scraped the end of my sleeve across my cheek as ordered. There was no identifying bar code hidden by face paint, nothing inked into my skin or under it. Our creators had been well aware that their seducers and assassins needed to be totally unidentifiable by normal déchet means.

Nuri frowned. "Nothing. And yet—"

"Nothing obvious," the shifter cut in, "but that doesn't prove anything. Penny isn't often wrong."

He uncrossed his arms and revealed a small silver

cylinder. I couldn't help a mental snort. It seemed I wasn't the only one who had access to wartime technology. That cylinder produced a spectrum of light similar to ultraviolet, and it was the only light that could reveal the tattoo inked into the cheekbones of soldier déchet.

He flicked it on. The light hit my cheek, caressing my skin with its cold heat. Had I possessed any more vampire than I did, it would have burned.

Something flickered in the shifter's eyes—disappointment mixed with frustration, perhaps.

"So," Nuri said, snapping my attention away from Jonas. "It would seem you *aren't* a déchet."

"As I believe I've already said," I replied. "But I'm guessing the revelation of that fact doesn't mean you'll actually let me go."

Amusement briefly crinkled the corners of her eyes. "Well, not yet, but only because I believe you might be able to help us."

"I've helped you already, and look where it's gotten me." My gaze flicked back to Jonas. "I should have let the vampires tear you apart, shifter."

His expression hardened, and I hadn't thought that was possible. "So why didn't you?"

"Because I promised Penny I wouldn't."

"As you so aptly pointed out not so long ago, Penny's a child. You could have easily taken her and left me to die."

"No, I couldn't—"

"Because of that promise," Nuri said softly, "and because you could not bear to see another child die."

A chill went through me. I glanced sharply at her, but her gaze was unfocused, distant. *Mind reader,* I thought. *Or, perhaps, a mind seeker.* Unlike telepaths, seekers couldn't directly read thoughts. Instead, they picked up a mix of emotion and mental images, and made judgments from those. In some ways, I was a seeker myself. Catching the emotive output of our targets was part of the reason why lures had been such successful spies. Either way, it meant I'd have to watch what I thought and imagined around her.

"My reasons for rescuing them are really not important." I said it louder than necessary in an effort to snap the other woman from her dream. "So why don't we get back to discussing whatever it is you actually want from me?"

Nuri blinked and her gaze refocused. But something decidedly dangerous glimmered briefly in her eyes. It oddly reminded me of the darkness I'd seen stirring in Penny's, and it made me uneasy. Something was going on with these people. Something more than just kidnapping a stranger who'd rescued two of their own.

The ghosts stirred, and their energy stung the air, a gentle reminder of the hell they could release if I gave the word.

But I couldn't do that yet. The simple fact was, even if I could get past these two, there were still the woman and the lion shifter. And if I managed to overpower *them*, the rest of Chaos stood between us and the safety of our bunker.

If it became clear they intended to kill me, however, then I'd unleash hell and take my chances. I wouldn't go down without a fight. Not ever again.

Nuri said, "As I said, all we really want is your help."

I laughed, and it was a bitter sound. "So instead of merely asking, you attempt to poison me and then you lock me up. Great way to gain my trust, I must say."

"Why in hell would you expect trust, given Penny's declaration?" Jonas retorted. "You're a trained killer—"

"*If* I were a déchet, then yeah, your reaction *might* have been understandable," I snapped back. "But I'm not. The mere fact I'm sitting here talking to you after being injected with Iruakandji proves that."

"The Iruakandji also proves you are not full shifter, or else you would be far sicker," Nuri commented, with another warning look at Jonas. "So what are you, precisely?"

"I'm the result of a shifter-and-human pairing." The lie was automatic, and the only real way I could explain the fact I'd basically escaped the major effects of the drug. Humans were—for reasons I didn't understand—immune to it. My gaze flicked to Jonas's as I added, "And we all know what shifters feel about half-human bastards, even in this day and age, don't we?"

He snorted. "There's no human in you. I would smell it if there were."

I raised an eyebrow. "So you're saying my mother—may Rhea be gentle with her soul—was lying?"

"Either she was, or you are."

"Jonas, enough." Nuri's gaze was again intense, and her expression somewhat distracted. I kept still, both in body and thought. After a moment, she grunted and added, "What we need from you is simply your anonymity."

My eyebrows rose. "Meaning what?"

"Meaning, we've done a quick record search, and there's no one in Central's system who matches your description. That will be a bonus when it comes to investigating what has happened to Penny."

"I never said I was from Central." And if they could access Central's records, they were far more than mere mercenaries. So what were they doing here in Chaos?

"No, you did not." Nuri hesitated. "According to Penny, you had no trouble seeing at night, and that might also be of benefit."

My confusion deepened. "Why?"

"Because even before the war, all of us who live in the cities—both human *and* shifter—had grown too used to the lights. As a result, we are all but night blind." Nuri studied me for a moment, then added, "As you would know if you grew up in this place. Or any other major city, in fact."

I ignored the intent behind that statement, my gaze roaming from her to Jonas and back again. "You live in Chaos, not Central. This place is nothing *but* shadows."

"Shadows are not night. There is a difference, trust me."

I contemplated them. It certainly explained the light both in the bar and here. It also explained why the upper reaches of Chaos had a greater percentage of light per dwelling than the lower. More money meant more access, and more access meant greater safety.

And it meant that if I *did* get out of this room, I could very easily get free. I was at home in the darkness; they were not.

If they were telling the truth, that is.

"So every child born today suffers this problem?"

"Not all, certainly. There are always a few genetic throwbacks born in every generation. But Jonas is the only one in our unit who isn't night blind."

A chill went through me. Unit was an altogether too military-sounding word for my liking. And yet there was nothing about Nuri herself that spoke of military experience.

Her expression wasn't giving anything away, and I couldn't feel anything along the emotive lines. "Why are you investigating what happened to Penny and her parents? Why isn't the corps doing so?" My gaze flickered to the ranger. "Or is this where you come into the story?"

"I'm not corps." It was bluntly said, but there was an edge to his voice that hinted at anger. I briefly wondered if there was ever a time when he actually felt something *other* than anger.

"But you were." My gaze went to the three slashes stretching down from his right temple. "Otherwise you would not bear their markings."

"I *was*," he agreed. "But I now work with Nuri."

"As a mercenary?" It was, I believed, what they wanted everyone to think, but something about this whole situation—and them—didn't sit right.

She nodded. "We are all mercenaries, of one sort or another."

I raised an eyebrow. "Meaning you sell your seeker skills to those who can afford you?"

"Interesting that you noticed my ability in that area," she drawled. "There are few enough these days who have even heard of seekers, let alone are able to tell if they're being read."

"There are few about these days who can see ghosts," I replied evenly. "But you and I can."

"Suggesting you are also something of a reader."

"Something," I agreed, in much the same manner as she had earlier.

She smiled and tilted her head a little. "I like you."

I raised my eyebrows again. "Which doesn't mean you won't set your dogs on me if it suits your purpose."

She laughed, a startling, huge sound in the confined space of the cell. "It doesn't indeed. Although they're mostly cats rather than dogs." She shifted her weight from one foot to the other. "But to answer your question, yes, I do sell my skills, and there are plenty willing to pay. Central might hold itself up as a great and worthy city, but for many it has lost its shine."

Meaning what, exactly? I had no idea, but I guessed that was no surprise given the only contact I had with Central was either raids for supplies or quests to ease more basic needs.

"So why aren't the corps investigating the attack?" My gaze flicked to Jonas again. "And why were you two in the old park if Penny was attacked in Central?"

"Because Penny wasn't in Central when I rescued her," Jonas replied.

"And Central's councillors *are* investigating the attack," Nuri added. "But they can't use the corps. They can't afford to."

I frowned. "Why not?"

"Because this attack is not the first, and they do not want the general population becoming aware that incursions by the wraiths are increasing in frequency."

"How many are we talking about?"

"Fourteen over the past two years."

Fourteen. By Rhea . . . "All from Central?"

"Ten from Central, four from Chaos. Ours were blamed on vampires, but the remainder were not."

"Then what is the council doing to stop them? And how are they even getting into the city?"

"No one knows." Nuri's voice held a grim edge. "No rifts have appeared within Central, and the lights should have killed any wraith that breached the walls."

Then how in the hell could the wraiths be snatching these children? They couldn't. Someone—or some*thing*—else had to be at the heart of all this.

"So you two got involved when Penny's family was attacked?" I paused, remembering Nuri's comment. "Or are you the nonofficial investigators?"

If they were, I could *not* get mixed up in the situation.

Not even if there were other children involved. I might be able to fool Nuri and Jonas, but the government had access to records and equipment these two would never have.

"We were not involved until Penny went missing."

Which didn't mean they weren't on the government payroll now. "How long ago did the attack happen?"

"Four months ago. She was the fourteenth child taken."

Fourteenth *child*. I closed my eyes again, fighting back the fury. I couldn't get involved. I really *couldn't*. But that didn't stop my asking, "Why would wraiths kill the parents and snatch the children? That's not the way they usually operate."

"If we knew what they were up to," Jonas said, his voice dark, "we might actually have some chance of stopping them."

"Meaning the other missing children weren't with Penny?"

"No. She somehow escaped wherever she was being held," Nuri said heavily. "And contacted me via dreams only two days ago."

If Penny was also a seeker—and the fact she'd contacted Nuri via dreams suggested that was very much the case— then it certainly explained how she'd known my name and what I was. She'd simply plucked the information from the emotive swirl of my thoughts. Or maybe even from the ghosts—after all, as a seeker she could both see and communicate with them, and the younger children might not have been aware of the dangers in telling her.

"And she can't tell you anything about where she was kept or what they were doing?"

"Nothing. She has no memory of that time, beyond what she has already told you."

"So what is it, exactly, you want me to do?"

Nuri contemplated me for a moment, and unease swept through me. I didn't like that look. Didn't like the sharpening of anger radiating from the shifter.

"There's one thing Penny probably didn't tell you," she said eventually. "Her parents weren't killed at night, but rather the middle of the day."

"Impossible," I said immediately. If there were two truths in this world, it was that neither vampire nor Other could stand the touch of the sun.

"So we'd all thought," she agreed. "But the truth cannot be denied. We are dealing with a new breed of wraith. One that has gained full immunity to the sun."

CHAPTER 4

"Impossible," I repeated. "If the Others have somehow gained such immunity, they would have swarmed the surface by now."

"True," Nuri said. "Which suggests this immunity is not widespread. And we also think it is not a natural development."

"Why would you think that?"

"Because Penny is not what she once was."

Meaning that uneasy sense of wrongness I'd been getting every time I'd studied her hadn't been so far off the mark. But if that were the case, why hadn't the ghosts reacted to her? If there *had* been something deeply wrong with her, they should have, because ghosts were innately sensitive to the energy output of others.

"Again, I have to ask why you'd think that."

"There is a darkness in her spirit that was not there two years ago. And because Penny's family, like many others who now lie dead, signed up for a lucrative drug-testing program at that time."

My frowned deepened. "Why would any family risk their lives testing unknown drugs?"

"Because it generally isn't much of a risk. The drugs have usually undergone years of exhaustive testing, and these types of rollouts are usually the last step before release."

"And because it pays a lot of money," Jonas added. "Many of the families involved were living on the edge of poverty."

"If they were living on the edge of poverty, they wouldn't have been in Central." They would have been in Chaos. From what I'd seen over the years, those in charge had little time or patience for those who did not pay their way.

"A statement that shows how little you know of life in Central," Nuri murmured. "And Chaos is certainly *not* filled with her refugees or outcasts. It is filled with the free."

I blinked. "You mean, people willingly live here? They choose this place over the safety of cities like Central?"

"There are worse things in this world than the vampires and Others, and many of them hide under the veil of civility and lights." She waved a hand. "But that is neither here nor there, and does not alter the facts of what has happened."

"So if these drug trials are the one connection," I said, "why hasn't the company involved been investigated?"

"Because governments will always actively protect their assets and their asses, no matter what they might say otherwise," Jonas commented, his expression not altering but sarcasm rich in his voice.

Nuri pushed away from the wall, her skirts swishing as she walked around me. The power rolling from her took away my breath, and the ghosts stirred uneasily. That they didn't like her wasn't surprising given the situation, but while I hated the fact that she'd contained me, for some strange reason I could hold no real dislike for her on a personal level. In fact, I had a suspicion she was probably the fairest—or, at least, the most nonjudgmental—human I was ever likely to meet.

"The company has been investigated—inconspicuously, of course," she said. "And it has been cleared of any connection."

"So you're at a dead end, so to speak?"

"Yes."

"Then how is my anonymity going to help you?" Though I tried to keep my voice even, I couldn't help the edge in my tone. "I'm not an investigator, or even a mercenary. And why in hell would my night sight be considered a bonus in a city that is nothing but light?"

She paused behind me and my neck crawled. I very much suspected she could kill me without even touching me.

"What, exactly, you might be is a question still to be resolved."

The chill running through me grew stronger. I resisted the urge to rub my arms and remained still.

"However," she continued, "we would not need your help if it were merely a matter of hunting a sunlight-enabled killer." She moved again, reappearing to the side of me. "What we appear to be dealing with is far more problematic than that."

She might be one of the fairest humans I was ever likely to meet, but she was also one of the wordiest. And getting to the point quickly and precisely was apparently one power she *didn't* have.

She stopped in front of me again and added, "Because despite Winter Halo being cleared, I still feel there is some connection between either the company or the government itself, and the wraith attack on Penny's family and her subsequently being taken by them."

Meaning, I gathered, that she'd seen it in her dreams. And no government in their right mind would act against a company in which they were invested based on the dreams of a witch. "Surely no one in the government would want the wraiths to gain sunlight immunity. That makes no sense."

"Agreed," Nuri said. "But I still believe there is some sort of connection between that company and the wraiths. We need you simply because we cannot infiltrate Winter Halo. We all have histories, and any security check done would flag those histories."

Another chill went through me. A full security check might well flag more than mere history for me. "And did it not occur to you that I'm living where I am simply because I have no other choice?"

"Yes. But when I dreamed of your arrival, I foresaw that you have no history in this place—and that, as I said, is a bonus."

"It's also a problem." My voice remained even despite the chill and the ever-increasing churning in my stomach. "I have no papers, I'm not chipped, and I don't even have a credit account. Getting *any* sort of job is next to impossible."

Nuri waved a hand. "We can set up a radio frequency ID easily enough."

Perhaps, but it might take only a blood sample or a deep iris scan to reveal the truth about me. The destruction of everything related to the déchet program might have been complete in my bunker, but there'd been two others involved in our production, and who knew what files might have survived in them. Even if nothing *had*, it simply wasn't worth the risk of exposure. No matter how deep the urge was to rescue those children.

"If you can set up a new identity for me, what's stopping either of you from doing the same for yourselves?"

"The fact that our faces are known. We may be able to move around Central without problem, but presenting with a different ID *will* raise alarms in the wrong quarters."

And what were the wrong quarters? Military or government? "Why would this company even employ someone like me? It's not like I have many skills."

"From what Penny said, you can fight," Nuri commented. "And that is all they require. That, and the fact you're—at least in part—a cat shifter. Winter Halo is currently hiring security guards."

I frowned. "And they're specifically looking for cat shifters? Why?"

"We don't know."

There were entirely too many things they didn't know, in my opinion. I switched my gaze to Jonas. "You didn't answer my question before—why were you and Penny in the park? Where did you actually find her?"

He contemplated me for a moment, and then his gaze flicked to Nuri's. I had an odd feeling the two were conversing, even though I could catch no hint of it in the emotive output coming from either of them. Did that mean they were both readers, or was this communication ability confined to the two of them? There'd been some evidence during the war that shifters could communicate with select members of their pack, although it wasn't something I'd ever witnessed.

After a moment, Jonas's gaze returned to mine. "I found her in Carleen."

Carleen had been one of Central's five satellite cities, and it had been the last city destroyed in the war. These days it was little more than a vast space of broken, vine-covered remnants that was filled with shadows, even on the sunniest of days. But it was also a town filled with ghosts.

Ghosts who just *might* have seen what had happened to Penny.

I frowned, but didn't chase the thought or repeat it out loud. "And is Carleen the reason you thought my night sight might be of use?"

"Yes," Nuri said. "Darkness remains a stain on that city, and it is far too big for Jonah to search it alone."

Jonah looked none too pleased about that particular statement, which made me suspect that whatever reasons Nuri might have for wanting my eyesight, searching Carleen wasn't one of them.

"That same darkness is one reason why the vampires haunt it," I commented. "It's not exactly a safe place for a cordon of rangers. One ranger and a half-breed more skilled at running than fighting won't exactly last all that long."

"A cordon of rangers will attract far more attention than two versed in the art of walking silently," Nuri commented. "That is what is needed in a situation such as this."

So I'd been wrong—Carleen *did* play a part in her plans. Even so, I still very much doubted searching that entire place was what she had in mind.

I rubbed a hand across my eyes. Guilt and the instinctive need to help children weighed against the desire to keep safe, to not do anything that might jeopardize my home and all the ghosts who lived within it. In the end, it wasn't a contest—I came down on the side of safety.

"Look," I said resignedly, "I'd like to help, but I really can't. It's too dangerous for me."

Nuri studied me for a moment, her gaze slightly narrowed

and expression intent. Reading me again—or, at least, attempting to.

"I'm sure it is," she murmured eventually. Then she blinked and half smiled. "Ah well, it was worth a shot. You may go."

Surprise rippled through me. "And just like that, you're releasing me?"

"Yes." She folded her arms across her ample breasts. "There'd be no point in trying to restrain or force you to help us, now, would there?"

"No." But that generally didn't stop anyone—and I had a feeling it normally wouldn't have stopped her.

"Then go." She hesitated, and her half smile grew. "But be aware, though I release you, fate may not."

I pushed to my feet, then met her gaze and frowned. "Meaning what?"

"Meaning fate brought you into our sphere of existence for a reason." She shrugged. "You are haunted by guilt. I do not believe you can or will walk away from the plight of those still caught in whatever web Penny escaped from."

"Then you've seriously misjudged me." I paused. "What about my weapons?"

"The knives you can have." Nuri produced them from somewhere within the folds of her skirt. I immediately strapped them on and felt safer for it. "The guns we shall keep. They have some interesting alterations we might replicate in our own weapons."

Which was damn annoying, but I guessed I should be thankful they'd at least given my knives back. I stepped toward the door. The shifter pushed away from the frame but didn't stand aside, forcing me to stop abruptly.

Once again my gaze met his. The vivid green of his eyes

reminded me very much of a deep forest; they were filled with shadows and danger. Yet, as I stared into them, an odd sensation of space and calm flowed over me.

This ranger was not what he seemed.

His nostrils flared, ever so slightly, as he drew in my scent. Pheromones stung the air, his and mine, mixing enticingly. Desire flared between us, fierce and bright.

"Jonas," Nuri said softly. "Let her go."

His gaze left mine with an abruptness that startled and, with a cool half smile, he stepped to one side and waved me on. Leaving me wondering just who'd been seducing whom. And why.

I frowned and walked out of the cell. Neither of them moved to follow, but as I made my way down the small lane, Nuri said, her voice soft but carrying clearly, "I'll see you soon, Tiger."

I shivered but didn't reply. I just got the hell out of Chaos.

Her words haunted me, plucking at my subconscious and making it impossible to sleep. Guilt, anger, suspicion, even desire—it all formed an emotive soup that burned through every fiber, tearing me apart, making me toss and turn and question my decision as much as their motives.

In the end, I gave up, got dressed, and—once I'd grabbed a coffee and the last of the protein bars I'd stolen from Central last month—headed up into the old tower to watch the stars and the remainder of the night roll by.

Dawn came and went, but it found me no less restless. I leaned against the old metal railing and glared across at the park, wishing I could see beyond the trees and the lingering shadows. Wishing I could see Carleen and whatever truths might lie there.

But there was only one way I was ever going to discover those, and that was by going there.

I had no doubt that *that* was exactly what Nuri wanted me to do. Had no doubt she was hoping that one step would lead to two, then three . . . and in no time at all, I'd be incarcerated within the walls of Winter Halo, investigating the disappearances for them.

I wearily scrubbed a hand across my eyes. I needed to sleep, needed to rest and recharge after the stress of the last twenty-four hours, but that was unlikely to happen any time soon. There were many things in this world I could and did ignore—but a child in danger? No matter how much I might tell myself otherwise, I just wasn't capable of walking away from something like that.

And if Nuri was telling the truth, then there was more than one child in danger here.

I swore softly, then thrust away from the railing and headed back down the stairs. The ghosts danced around me as I made my way to the weapons stash, their excitement stinging the air. Not that any of them would accompany me—they were content to explore vicariously through Bear and Cat.

I snapped two small guns onto the thigh clips, then grabbed a couple of sheer knives, strapping them onto my wrists as I headed down to the main kitchen to add a small water bottle and some of the old jerky bars that had been around forever to my day's supplies. They were about as tasty as eating cardboard, but I could survive well enough on them. Not that I actually *wanted* to very often—not when Central was so close, and it was easy enough to steal more palatable food.

I headed for the South Siding exit. It would have been quicker to exit through the dome, but Central's drawbridge was down, and there were people in the nearby rail yards, waiting to be shunted to work. I couldn't risk anyone seeing the museum doors opening and coming to investigate. They probably wouldn't see me, but they just might be tempted to run a more complete test on the system and discover my override codes.

The closer we got to the exit, the cooler and sharper the air got. Goose bumps chased one another across my skin, and I half wished I'd stopped to grab my coat. Beams of sunlight filtered through the upper levels of the thick grate protecting the tunnel entrance, but the lower part was packed with the rubbish that had washed from Central's drains after last night's rain. I stopped, wrinkling my nose against the soggy scent of refuse.

"Bear, Cat, could you check that no one is close?"

They hummed in excitement and whisked through me, forming a light connection before heading outside. As their ghostly forms disappeared into the bright sunshine, images began to filter into my mind. Chaos lay wrapped in shadows, and no one had yet stepped beyond its shipping container boundary. There was no way beyond actually going into the place itself to tell whether anyone on the upper levels was looking this way—although it wasn't as if anyone beside Nuri and Jonas had a reason to. Cat and Bear continued on toward Central. There were plenty of people on the drawbridge, and more still on the rail platforms or crowding into the caterpillar pods. There were also about a dozen guards—stiff, green-clad figures bristling with all sorts of weaponry—standing in the various guardhouses dotted between the curtain wall and the museum. Thankfully, none of these posts had a direct line of sight down the remains of the river—a curious mistake, given the close proximity of the rift. But maybe because they'd clas-

sified it as inactive, they'd decided it was of little threat—
although given how little anyone really knew about the rifts,
I wouldn't have been taking that sort of chance.

Still, their decision made it a whole lot easier for me.
I'd have to wrap myself in sunshine to get past the rail
yards, but at least they wouldn't see me exiting our hide-
away. Once Cat and Bear returned and broke our connection, I kicked the rubbish away from the grate, then stepped
out into the sunshine. Just for a moment, I raised my face
to the sky and let the sunlight caress my skin. I might be
genetically adapted to night and shadows, but there was
still a part of me that loved—even needed—the sun. Which
made sense, I guess, given it was *that* part that enabled
me to disappear into light—which was what I now needed
to do.

I took a deep breath and drew in the heat and energy of
the day, letting it flow deep into my body, into every muscle,
every fiber, until my entire being burned. Then I imagined
that force wrapping around me, forming a shield through
which none could see. Energy stirred as motes of light began
to dance both through and around me, joining and growing,
until they'd formed the barrier I was imagining. To the outside world, I no longer existed. The sunshine that played
through me acted like a one-way mirror, reflecting all that
was around me but allowing no one to see in. Thus protected
from casual scrutiny, I moved out, following the old riverbed
toward the railway yards.

My two little escorts spun around me, their excitement
becoming tinged with trepidation as we drew closer to the
rail yards. A pod slid silently into the station, its inte-
rior lighting coming to life as it stopped and the doors slid
open. The men and women crowded onto the platform
pressed inside and, in very little time, the pod doors closed

and the train whisked its occupants off to whatever factory or farm they'd been allocated for the day.

I ran across the lines, jumped onto a platform, and made my way through the complex, moving swiftly past stony-faced guards, then out onto the old road that ran between the museum's dome and Central's drawbridge. There was little traffic here, aside from those making their way to the pods and the occasional private vehicle taking its occupants to who knew where.

Pain began to crawl into my head. It was a warning I dared not ignore. I ran on, deep into the shadows of the trees, stopping only when there was no possibility of either the guards or any passersby on the street seeing me.

"Cat, Bear, keep an eye out," I said, then released the sunshine. Motes of light danced around me, slowly at first, then faster and faster, as they seeped from my body with increasing speed. Then, with a sound that was almost a sigh, they slipped away into the shadows. I fell to my knees with a grunt, my body aching and my head booming.

For several minutes, I did nothing more than kneel on the hard soil, sucking in air and trying to ignore the pain. This was the price all lures paid for using the sunshine shield. Even shadowing had its cost, although it was far easier to gather shadows and disappear into them, simply because, like the vampires, I could physically become smoke. It wasn't a psychic skill, but rather part of my nature—a magic that came from my soul and the darkness within it. But it nevertheless drew on our strength, and in the heart of a battle, it could certainly be deadly. I often wondered how many of my kindred had been destroyed during this brief period of helplessness—more than a few, I imagined.

Once the stabbing pain had eased to a dull ache, I

pushed to my feet and looked around to check my bearings. Central lay off to my left, as did the clearing where we'd found Penny and Jonas. I had no idea where exactly they'd entered the park, but given that the vamps had come from a southerly direction, that was probably the way I should head. I spun on my heel and marched through the trees, keeping an eye out for movement—not that anyone in Central made use of this park. Not until the sun had reached its peak in the sky and the remaining shadows had fled, anyway, and that was a few hours away yet.

It took an hour to reach Carleen's southern border. I stopped at the edge of the park, my gaze sweeping the remnants of the old curtain wall and the broken buildings beyond it. Though the old city was little more than a vine-covered mass of rusting metal and disintegrating concrete, it had once been home to over twenty thousand people, most of them families. In a way it still *was* home to many of those people, as the evacuation order had come far too late. Over a third of Carleen's population had still been here when the last bombs of the war had hit it.

Maybe it was the presence of so many ghosts that caused the pall of darkness that seemed to hang over this place, no matter what the time of day. Or maybe it was the existence of over a dozen rifts, many of which were still active. I didn't know, and I don't believe anyone in Central did, either. All I knew was that, even now, those in Central avoided this place like a plague, and it wasn't just because the vampires were more prevalent here. There was something very wrong about the feel of this place. Something slightly off center, almost otherworldly.

It was almost as if the rifts that drifted through this ruined city had leaked far more than magic—had spewed forth far more than demonic creatures.

All of which made it even more odd that Penny had somehow ended up here.

Hopefully, the ghosts here could provide an answer. Or, at the very least, point me in the direction from which she'd actually come. *If* they were feeling communicative, that was. I'd been here only a couple of times—and then only in the first ten or so years after the war, to scrounge through the wreckage in a somewhat useless search for parts for my old machines. While the ghosts had never been hostile toward me, they hadn't exactly been welcoming, either.

I swept my gaze across the long, broken wall one more time, though what I was searching for I couldn't actually say, then moved forward. The sunshine bathed me briefly, and I breathed deep, trying to capture and keep the warmth for as long as possible as the shadows crept toward me.

I resisted the urge to flick a knife down into my hand and leapt up onto a low section of wall. I hesitated, taking in the ruptured remnants of buildings and—farther to my left—the remains of what once had been a main road through the city. It was littered with building rubble, weeds, and trees that had twisted into odd shapes thanks to the eddying magic of the rifts. Plastic of various shapes and sizes—rubbish that had survived the destruction far better than Carleen itself— added spots of bright color in many darker corners, but otherwise this place was still. Quiet.

Yet not unoccupied.

Unease slithered through me. There was a watchfulness here that went beyond the displeasure of ghosts. It was almost as if something had crawled into this place and infested it with evil.

I shivered and shoved my imagination away. It wasn't like déchet were even supposed to *have* imaginations, let alone feelings. But while it *was* true that in those déchet designed purely to be soldiers or assassins, the limbic system—or at least the parts of it that controlled emotions and sexual responses—had been medically "curtailed" upon creation, the same had not been done to those of us who were created as lures. We'd been designed as bait, and a being without feeling, one who couldn't respond to emotional cues and who felt no emotion—be it pleasure or fear—wouldn't have survived long in *any* sort of culture, let alone been sexually attractive to those we were sent to seduce.

Could I love? That was a question I'd often pondered, and one I'd never found an answer to. I certainly couldn't breed; our creators had ensured *that* right out of the box. Or test tube, as was the case.

I swept my gaze across the ruins again, then—ignoring my increasing reluctance to enter this place—jumped down from the wall and headed for the remnants of the road. There was no immediate response from the Carleen ghosts, though a sudden sharpening in the tension that ran through the air suggested they were well aware of me.

Cat and Bear pressed close as I picked my way through the rubble. It seemed they disliked the feel of this place just as much as I did. We finally reached the road, though walking here wasn't really any easier, given what little remained of the asphalt after one hundred years of weather eating at its surface was pitted with yellowed weeds and mutated trees. At least there weren't any rifts in the immediate area—though that didn't mean there soon wouldn't be. There didn't seem to be any logic—or, indeed, any compliance to the laws of gravity or nature itself—in their movements. Neither wind nor gravitational pull had any influence on them, and they could just as easily drift against a gale-force wind as they could leap upward to consume birds, shifters in winged form, or even whole aircraft. I had no idea what happened to humans or shifters caught in rifts, but I'd seen the magic within them mangle the DNA of the flora and fauna they passed over, creating monstrosities that were neither and yet both. I very much doubted such a thing was survivable. Certainly the poor beasts who'd become part stone or tree hadn't lasted long.

Central—and presumably other cities in the proximity of the rifts—had made several attempts to destroy them, without success. These days they just attempted to track them, providing evacuation warnings where necessary— though, given the erratic nature of the things, those warnings were often useless.

A large tree loomed in the middle of the road, its gnarled trunk covered in a moss that glowed with an odd luminescence. I edged around it, taking care not to touch the moss, knowing from past experience that as pretty as the stuff looked, it leaked a substance that acted like acid when it touched your skin. Unpleasant and painful didn't even *begin* to describe the few hours that had followed that particular exploration.

We walked on, moving deeper into Carleen. The watchfulness grew, crawling across my senses, itching at my skin. But the Carleen ghosts made no move to approach me, and that was unusual. It was almost as if they were afraid . . . but what did the ghosts of this place have to be afraid of? It wasn't as if there was much in this world that could threaten them, and while there *were* vampires who lived off energy rather than flesh, they wouldn't be active in the middle of the day. And the rifts certainly couldn't affect them . . . could they?

Given what I'd seen rifts do to plants and animals, it was certainly possible.

The broken road began to slope up toward the center

of Carleen. If the ghosts were anywhere, they'd be there, gathered in the vast remains of the shelters under city hall. It was the place where most of them had found their deaths.

Energy of a different kind crawled across my skin, its touch dark and somewhat unpleasant. It wasn't the energy of a rift, not exactly, and yet it felt somewhat similar. I paused and looked left, scanning the shattered building remnants that rimmed a bomb crater. The sensation seemed to be ebbing from the base of that crater. I walked across and stared down into it. It was so deep that all I could see was darkness—a darkness that seemed thick enough to carve. For no good reason, I shivered and backed away from the rim. I had no idea what lay down there, and it wasn't something I wanted to discover. Not unless I absolutely had to, anyway. Even Cat and Bear seemed reluctant to investigate, and given their love of a challenge and exploring new things, it spoke volumes about the wrongness of that darkness.

We continued on up the hill. The buildings around us fell into even more disrepair, until there was very little left but a sea of concrete and stone rubble interspersed by the occasional rusted metal strut that had been twisted into weird and wonderful shapes either by the force of the bombs, or by the rifts themselves. It was a somewhat surreal experience—almost as if I were walking on an alien landscape. Especially since the luminescent moss seemed to be more prevalent up here. I paused at the base of a monument to some forgotten general, and looked around. We were standing in the middle of what once had been a large city square. Government buildings and small eateries had lined this place, but all of them were little more than dust and memories now. To my right lay another cavernous crater—this one caused by the three bombs that had wiped out not only the government officials who'd taken refuge within the thick walls of city hall, but also everyone who'd hidden in the shelters underneath it. The ghosts were there. Their energy crawled across my senses, a touch that was as dark as it was dangerous.

I frowned, but nevertheless continued on. The Carleen ghosts stirred restlessly, but made no move to either attack or flee. They were waiting. Judging.

I stopped at the edge of the crater. This one, unlike the other, wasn't wrapped in shadows, although the bottom of it was so deep I couldn't pick out what lay there. But I could imagine, given the number of people who had died here. Their bones, even after a hundred years, would probably be meters deep.

"People of Carleen," I said softly, "I need your help."

Their energy stirred, tinged with disbelief.

"A little girl was found here several days ago," I continued. "A ranger was with her. I need to know how she got here."

Anger exploded, fierce enough to knock me back several feet. Cat and Bear flung themselves around me, but the attack didn't happen. The ghosts of Carleen might be angry— murderously angry—but they weren't angry with *me*.

Not yet, anyway.

But to know what was happening here, I needed to be able to garner more than just emotion. I needed to see these people, talk to them properly, and that meant joining forces with little Cat. I might have an innate ability to hear the whisperings of the dead, but it would take more than that to talk to those who'd once lived here. Carleen had been a human city, and that one fact placed these dead beyond both my seeker and communication skills. Lures might have escaped most of the DNA interventions and restrictions that had been placed on our soldier brethren, but our creators had certainly made it impossible for us to read their thoughts. I had no idea if they'd also made it impossible for us to kill a human, because I'd never had to try. But in the five years our world had been at war, I'd never heard of a lure turning on their creators. Given that soldier déchet had been rendered incapable of harming a human, it was likely similar restrictions had been placed on us.

But Cat had been created in the months before the war had erupted, when the rush to create more rifle fodder had led to greater use of growth accelerants and all sorts of other shortcuts. While she'd been destined to become a soldier, neither she nor Bear—nor any of the other, littler ones who'd been in my care that day, in fact—had had their limbic systems altered in any way. Which meant, thanks to her tabby-cat heritage, she was highly attuned to all things supernatural. These ghosts might be little more than energy and emotion to me, but for her, they were fully fleshed beings.

"Cat, I need your help to communicate."

A mix of excitement and trepidation spun around me. What we were about to do was dangerous—for me, more than her. To converse with the *human* dead, I had to immerse deep into Cat's energy, all but becoming a ghost myself—and if I stayed in that state too long, I *would* actually die.

Still, the need for answers was far deeper than the fear of death. "Bear, keep watch."

I sat cross-legged on the stony ground, then closed my eyes and held out my hand. Cat's energy settled into my palm, then began to seep into my skin, into my body, creating a connection so strong that it was hard to tell where my energy ended and hers began. At the same time, a chill touched my outer extremities and began to creep slowly inward. It was the chill of death; when it claimed my heart I would die. The clock had begun its countdown.

I opened my eyes and saw what Cat saw. Thousands of people—men, women, and children—were gathered within the crater, some of them so solid they almost looked flesh-and-blood real, others little more than insubstantial scraps of frosted air. I scanned them until I saw a small group standing slightly apart from the others. *The officials,* I thought grimly. Leaders then, and leaders now, if the body language in the two groups were anything to go by.

My gaze settled on the tallest of the separated dozen. "I need your help, as I said."

"And why would you expect any help from those who have been abandoned and forgotten?"

"You've not been—"

"Then why has no one come to bury our bones? Why has no priest ventured here to bless our spirits and help us move on?" His voice was low but oddly rich and definitely not unpleasant. "You cannot expect to receive what you cannot give."

"There is nothing any of us alive today can do for you now," I replied. "The time for enabling you all to move on peacefully to your next life has long gone—just as it has for my little ones."

His gaze flickered slightly—regret, sorrow, it was hard to say. "Your little ones didn't have to die the way ours did. No child, then or now, should ever have to face such a fate."

"My little ones," I said, unable to help the edge of anger in my voice, "faced a death far worse than anything you could *ever* imagine. Trust me, the death that came with the bombs—however horrible—was nothing compared to what we faced."

"'We'?" He raised an eyebrow. "You live. The two little ones are as we are."

"I live by a quirk of fate." And the genetics that made me immune to all known poisons. "But I am not here to talk about our fate or yours. What can you tell me about the child who was here a few days ago?"

The air tightened around me. The deep-voiced man scowled. "And why would you be interested in *that* one?"

I frowned. "Why are you so . . . scathing about such a young girl?"

"It is not so much her—or any of the others who come through here, though there is much about them that speaks of the rifts that ravage this place," he replied, "but rather the one who accompanied her."

My frown grew. "The ranger?"

"No, not the ranger," he all but spat, "although one such as he has no right to enter Carleen. Not when his people are the reason we are bound here."

Vehemence stung the air, so sharp it snatched my breath and made breathing impossible for several seconds. "If you hate the ranger so much," I said, "why did you allow him entry?"

"Because the ranger was tracking *it.*"

The creeping sensation of ice had reached both knees and elbows. I needed to hurry this along, and yet, that was the one thing I couldn't do. It would offend the ghosts and possibly shut down the lines of communication. "'It'?"

"The creature who always accompanies the children."

"Creature?" A dead weight began to form in my stomach. "What sort of creature are we talking about?"

"The thing with few features." The hate and revulsion in his words were amplified a thousand times by the rest of the ghosts, creating an emotive wave that just about blew my senses apart.

I blinked back tears and tried to ignore both the pain induced by that wave and the strengthening creep of death. "Was this creature tall and thin in build, with a gray skin tone?"

"Yes."

I closed my eyes and swore softly. Part of me had hoped that Penny and Nuri had been wrong—that it *wasn't* the wraiths taking the children. I guess I should have known that a child with a strong enough seeker skill to understand what I was would not be wrong about who her captor was.

I took a deep breath and released it slowly. "Where did this creature take Penny and the other children?"

"Into the false rifts."

I frowned. "False rifts?"

He nodded. "The rifts that do not drift. The ones that hide within the shadows."

The image of the crater, with its thick, threatening darkness, swam through my mind. I shivered. I didn't want to venture into that darkness; I really didn't.

"How many rifts are there like this?"

"Six," he replied. "But only two are used when they are accompanied by the children. The large one you inspected, and one down the other side of this hill."

"Can you show me the one Penny came through, the day she was rescued by the ranger?"

Fear slithered around me. It seemed the Carleen ghosts feared the rifts, though what danger *any* rift presented to ghosts I still had no idea.

The deep-voiced man considered me for a moment and then nodded. "Follow me."

"I'll have to break our communication off. I cannot walk when linked to my little one."

"Unless you wish to join us here in Carleen, that is probably wise," he said, with a half smile. He would have been a good-looking man in life, because that smile transformed his ghostly features. "I can see death's claws gaining hold in your flesh."

And I could feel it. "Thank you very much for your honesty and your help. I really appreciate it."

He half bowed. "Perhaps, one day, you could return the favor."

"It would be my pleasure." I wasn't sure there was anything I could do to help these ghosts, but I couldn't see the harm in agreeing to the request, either.

"Then go. The little ones can follow our lead."

"Cat," I said as I closed my eyes. "It's time to leave."

Warmth spun through me, a sensation not unlike a featherlight kiss against skin, then her energy began to bleed from my body and condensed once more into my palm. The hands of death similarly began to retreat, but they left me shaking, weak, and colder than I'd ever felt in my life.

For several minutes I did nothing more than rub my arms with numb fingers in an attempt to get both blood and heat rushing back through my muscles. My toes ached as life flushed back into them, the sensation not unlike the pins and needles that flowed when I tried to walk after my foot had fallen to sleep.

I cursed again, then pushed upright. Carleen did a somewhat mad dance around me, and it took every ounce of concentration *not* to fall right back down again. It had been too long since I'd pushed myself like this; my strength—both physical and mental—was not what it should be.

I took another long, deep breath, and then said, "Okay, lead the way."

My two ghosts leapt off to the right. Thankfully, we headed down the other side of the hill, away from the crater with the unsavory darkness, not toward it. This section of Carleen was even more ruined, though, and there was little here but drifting flurries of metal and concrete dust. Luminescent moss covered the few oddly shaped mounds of building rubble that did remain. Its stench stained the air and lent the shadows a sickly green glow.

The Carleen ghosts led us down the steep hill and into a flatter section. In the distance I could see the vine-entwined remnants of the curtain wall and, beyond it, more trees, these ones healthy, untouched by the magic of the rifts. Did that mean the rifts within Carleen were as restricted to this place as the ghosts? That seemed strange, but then, given how little anyone knew about the rifts and their movements, maybe it wasn't. And there was little hope of getting the Others to tell us anything about the things. Beyond the fact none of them appeared to have any form of recognizable speech, all attempts to capture one of them alive had so far failed.

Bear's energy tugged at my left hand. I followed his lead off the path, picking my way carefully through the moss and the dirt. Dust puffed up with every step, filling the air and making breathing difficult.

Dark energy began to crawl across my senses, and my steps slowed. Ahead was another crater, this one unrimmed by anything more than dust. The Carleen ghosts stopped, but I moved on until I was standing on the edge of the crater. It wasn't as deep as the other one I'd seen, but the darkness was just as thick and unpleasant. I shivered. I really didn't want to go into it—but if I wanted to find out what had happened to Penny and the other children, then I really had no choice.

I swallowed heavily, then glanced back at the waiting energy that was the Carleen ghosts. Their reluctance to come any closer stung the air. I couldn't say I blamed them. "Thank you again for your assistance—and wish me luck."

Amusement spun around me, but with it came the urge to be cautious. As if I needed *that* sort of warning.

I took another of those deep breaths that did little to curb the fear crawling inside my stomach, then resolutely stepped into the crater and made my way down into the heart of that creeping darkness.

CHAPTER 5

The shadows thickened, became a real and solid presence that pressed down upon me like a ton weight. Every step became an effort; all too soon my leg muscles were quivering and my breath was little more than short, sharp jabs for air. It was almost as if I were climbing the sides of a very steep mountain rather than sliding into a crater.

Fear swam around me, fear that was both mine and that of my two little ghosts. As slow as my progress was, they couldn't keep up with me. This darkness, whatever it was, was pushing them back, refusing them entry. No matter how hard they tried, they were falling farther and farther behind.

I stopped and looked back, my breath little more than a wheeze as I sucked in the putrid air. The rim of the crater couldn't have been all that far above me, but it was barely visible through the ink that surrounded us. My two little ghosts were caught in an area between the thicker shadows and the murky light of day—sparks of energy that glowed brightly against the gloom of this place.

"Cat, Bear, you'd better go home and wait for me there."

Their sparks moved in agitation, and I smiled. "I know you want to help, but I don't want to risk your safety, and we have no idea just what this stuff might do to you if you continue to press against it." Especially given the Carleen ghosts' reluctance to enter this place. Maybe there was a reason; maybe they'd tried—and died—in the process.

No matter what humans might believe, ghosts *could* die—the fact that energy vampires could feed on their energy and thereby destroy them was evidence enough of that. I had no idea whether the darkness that inhabited these craters—or anything else, for that matter—could kill them, but it simply wasn't a chance I was willing to take. Carleen's ghosts feared something here, and if not this darkness, then what?

Both Cat and Bear's concern and reluctance spun through my mind. "It's okay," I said, keeping my voice as calm and even as I could—a hard task given the weight of this place and my own growing fear. "I'll be okay. I'll call you when I figure out what this place actually is or where it goes. Go home, and protect the little ones." I paused, then, as intuition itched at the back of my mind, added, "Don't let Penny into our home. I don't care what you have to do, don't let her—or anyone else—inside."

Their energy briefly danced about—they were happy to have something to do, someone to protect—then they pulled themselves free of the shadows and disappeared from my sight.

It was the first time in ages I'd been without them, and it felt oddly lonely.

I resolutely turned and continued pushing my way into the crater. By the time I reached the base, I was covered in

sweat and trembling from head to toe. I paused again, sucking in the air, hating the thick foulness of it. Hating the taste
of death that lay all around me.

Although I couldn't see them, there were ghosts here.
Ghosts whose energy felt as odious as the darkness itself;
it was almost as if this place had infected them, made them
into what it was.

Which made very little sense at all.

I frowned and took another step forward. The heavy
darkness slid around me, a sensation not unlike the caress
of silk against bare skin, but somehow unclean. Then, with
little warning, it gave way and lifted.

I blinked and looked around. The crater's base was
strewn with rubble, bones, and refuse. And, in one corner,
spinning on its axis, was a small, dark globe of shimmering, sparkling energy.

The fear crawling in my stomach exploded through the
rest of me. That globe was a rift. Stationary, visible, and
outputting a different sort of energy from the other rifts I'd
come across, but a rift nevertheless. Penny had come through
here, through *it*, if the Carleen ghosts were to be believed—
and I did. There was no other reason for her to be here. No
other way for her to *get* to Carleen without their having
seen her.

But a rift . . . I backed away but hit the thick wall of
shadows and was forced to stop. I hissed and tried to remain calm. Penny had come through this place. Where she
had come, I could go.

But Penny had been stained by darkness—possibly *this*
darkness. I didn't want that darkness in me. Didn't want
it to even *touch* me.

I closed my eyes and weighed the terror of approaching—
entering—that rift against the need for answers. I could walk

away now and no one would ever know—no one but the Carleen ghosts. *If* they'd remained around to witness my retreat, that is.

It was tempting—very, *very* tempting.

But then I saw the disintegrating features of my little ghosts, heard their screams as the Draccid gas that was fed into our air systems ate at their little bodies. Could feel the weight of them in my arms as Cat, Bear, and I tried—and failed—to get them out of the nursery and save as many as we could.

We hadn't known it was useless, that there was no safety to be found anywhere in the bunker. Not until the Draccid began eating at me, anyway, and Cat and Bear had crawled into my arms to die.

But I'd sworn, in the long months of my recovery, to never, ever let another child suffer if I could at all help it, and that was a promise I had no desire to break—not even now, faced as I was with whatever terrors might wait on the other side of that rift. Besides, I might have been called many things during my years as a lure, but "coward" had never been one of them. It wasn't a title I wanted to earn now.

I clenched my fists and forced reluctant feet forward. The rift's energy slashed at my skin, its touch sharp enough to draw blood. I bit my lip and drew a gun, flicking off the safety as the whips of power wrapped around me, drawing me closer, hastening my steps into that spinning orb.

I couldn't have stopped now even if I'd wanted to.

The orb began to rotate faster and faster. Air spun around me, thick and foul and filled with dust, growing stronger and stronger, until it felt like I was being pulled into the heart of a gale. A dark gale, from which there was no light, no life, and possibly no escape.

Only the fact that Penny had somehow escaped not only

from wherever she was being held, but from the orb itself, kept me from panicking, from fighting to be free.

The darkness of the orb encased me. Energy burned around me, through me, until it felt as if it were pulling me apart, atom by atom; it studied me, moved me, then, piece by piece, put me back together again.

Then the energy died, the whips holding me disintegrated, and I was spat out into an entirely *different* type of darkness. One that had a wooden floor, and where the air held the thick scent of perfume and sex.

Then pain overwhelmed everything else, and I shuddered, gasping for breath and kneeling on all fours, unable to move, sweat and blood dripping from my face and streaming down my arms to puddle on the floor beneath me.

The wounds on my arms, I reflected absently, looked like knife cuts—just as the scars on Penny's arms had.

She *hadn't* been attacked with a knife. Those scars had come from traversing the false rifts many, many times.

What the hell was going on?

To understand *that*, I needed to move. To explore where I'd been dumped. But moving was going to hurt; hell, even *breathing* hurt. It wasn't like I had many other choices, though. Kneeling here, bleeding and sweating, wasn't going to get me much in the way of answers.

I gritted my teeth and pushed to my feet, my breath a hiss of air as the shadowed room did several mad laps around me. For a few minutes, I did nothing more than stand there, battling to keep my knees locked and my body upright.

Then, as the pain eased, I looked around. The room was large and rectangular, with no windows and only the one door at the far end. Even from here, I could see the heavy padlock. Oddly, the lock was on *this* side, not the other, meaning it was designed to keep everyone else *out* rather than something in.

There was little else in this room beyond dust and cobwebs, and certainly no indication that anyone had come through here recently, much less a little girl.

I frowned and looked over my shoulder. The globe hovered above the floor, but it was less obvious in the shadows of this room. Its energy was muted, indistinct, as if all the fire had gone from it. A result of my using it, perhaps? Or was it naturally muted on this side—wherever the hell this side was? *That* was a question in urgent need of an answer, but first I needed to recover my strength.

I sheathed my weapon, then staggered over to the wall and leaned against it. After closing my eyes, I focused on my breathing, on slowing every intake of air as I reached the calm and peace of my healing state.

I have no idea how long I remained there. Healing could take minutes or it could take hours, and in this silent place of dust and cobwebs, it was rather hard to judge the passage of time.

When I finally opened my eyes, I felt renewed. The wounds on my arms—and no doubt those on my face—had healed, leaving no trace of the scars that had littered Penny's body. I still stank of sweat and blood, but there was little I could do about that. Not until I got back home, or at least stole some clothes from somewhere.

The aroma of perfume spun around me again and on a floor above, a woman laughed. It was followed by the squeak of bedsprings, and a low sound of pleasure—though this time the voice was male rather than female.

I frowned. Had I somehow landed in the basement of a house? And where was that house situated, given I obviously wasn't anywhere in Carleen anymore? I *couldn't* be. I had no idea if it was possible for ghosts to have sex, but there was no way in hell they could do so in a place like this, simply because no such place existed in Carleen anymore.

I pushed away from the wall and walked to the far end of the room, my steps little more than a whisper on the dusty wooden floorboards. The lock on the door was thick and old, the chain thicker still, but newer, shinier. It would have been easy to shoot either the lock open or the chain apart, but that would warn whoever was having sex that someone was down here.

Unfortunately, lock picking *wasn't* one of my skills, so I looked at the door instead. The frame was metal, as was the door, so even without the chain in place, it was doubtful I could kick the thing open without alerting the building's occupants.

My gaze fell on the hinges. They were the old-fashioned type with hinge pins. If I could knock them out, the door would open. Of course, I wouldn't be able to get them back in, not from the other side, anyway, but it was either that or go back through that sphere.

And there was no way in Rhea I was about to do that.

Before I escaped this place, however, I needed to change my appearance. I had no idea who or what waited outside, or how well guarded this building might be. The last thing I needed was my real image caught on some security camera. Better by far to conceal the truth and have them searching for a person who didn't exist.

At least I'd taken the time to recover from the trip through the rift, because I was going to need my strength. Rearranging my features—becoming someone else, at least on the outside—wasn't easy, nor was it pleasant. From what I'd witnessed over my years in the shifter camps, a shifter wanting to take on their animal form simply had to reach into that place inside where the beast roamed, and unleash the shackles that bound it. *This* type of shifting was more complicated. Not only did I have to fully imagine all the minute details of the body I wanted, but I had to hold it firm in my thoughts as the magic swirled through and around me. Easier said than done when the magic that changed me was anything but pleasant. Still, better *that* than someone recognizing me at a later date.

As I had with the healing state, I took several deep breaths and slowly released each in an effort to calm the tension running through my limbs. Then I closed my eyes and pictured a face in my mind. A face that was sharp, almost gaunt, with pale skin, green eyes, and a thin, unhappy mouth. She had a cleft in her chin, curly brown hair, and was slender. Flat-chested but strong. It was similar enough to my own build—aside from the flat chest—that it hope-fully wouldn't be quite as painful to change.

Then, freezing that image in my mind, I reached for the magic. It exploded around me, thick and fierce, as if it had been contained for far too long. It swept through me like a gale, making my muscles tremble and causing the image I desired to waver. I frowned and held fiercely on to the like-ness. The energy pulsed as the change began. My skin rippled, bones restructured, hair shortened, curled, and changed color. It burned, *hurt*; I gritted my teeth against the scream that tore up my throat, my breath little more than sharp hisses as pinpricks of sweat broke out over altering flesh.

When the magic finally faded, I collapsed back against the wall, sucking in air and feeling very different. I opened my eyes and looked down. My breasts were *definitely* smaller, meaning the rest of the image had probably stuck as well.

I wiped the remaining beads of sweat from my forehead,

then, ignoring the tremble still running through my muscles, slipped one of the knives from its wrist harness and knelt down. After sliding the edge of the knife under the hinge pin, I moved the blade along until the pin was jammed against the hilt, then hit the hilt with my hand. Unfortunately, I did little more than bruise my palm. I frowned, then sat down and dragged off a boot. A few decent *thump*s with the solid heel later, the pin came free. I repeated the process with the top pin, then grabbed the door and pulled it sideways, separating it first from the knuckles, then from the main lock. All that was now holding it in place were the chain, the old-fashioned padlock, and my grip on it.

I carefully peered out. The room was at the end of a long, somewhat shadowed hallway, and there were several other rooms leading off it. I couldn't hear anything other than the couple in the room above me, and the air was thick with dust and disuse. Whatever this area was, it was all but abandoned.

I slipped through the gap, then maneuvered the door back into place so that the main lock was holding it upright again. At least it would look closed from a distance.

I padded down the hall, checking each of the rooms as I passed them by, but, beyond some ancient-looking beds, found little more than dust and cobwebs. It didn't make sense. Why would the wraiths use a rift to transport themselves into a place like this? Why leave those above alive to go about their business when—up until now—all they'd ever done was destroy anyone and everyone who got in their way?

I reached the stairs at the far end. The basement door—if that was indeed what this place was—was locked, but this time by a fingerprint scanner. I cursed softly. There was no way I could get past that, not unless the damn power went out. And even if it did, they probably had a backup system . . .

meaning there was only one thing I could do if I wanted to get out.

I pressed my ear against the sturdy-looking door but couldn't hear anything on the other side. I raised the knife and thrust it, as hard as I could, into the unit. The knife was made from a specialized glass, and was harder than steel without the conductivity, so it presented little danger to me. There was a short, sharp explosion, and sparks flew as the system short-circuited. A second later I was through the door and in another corridor. This one was flooded with light, and the air was filled with warmth, perfume, and the tangy scents of men, desire, and sex.

I closed the basement door and quickly scanned the corridor. There were eight doors leading off the hall—most of them occupied, if the noises within were anything to go by—and an exit down the far end. Thankfully, none of the people in any of the rooms appeared to have heard the explosion, but I couldn't count on my luck lasting.

Instead of moving on, I glanced at the control panel. Though I'd short-circuited the system, the panel on *this* side looked intact. It might be better if whoever owned this place believed that someone had been trying to get *in*, rather than out.

I shoved my knife into its electronic heart, making more obvious the destruction I'd already wrought, then padded quickly toward the exit. But as I approached, so, too, did steps from the other side. I cursed, spun around, and ran for the nearest unoccupied room. I'd barely entered when two people strode into the corridor. With no time to close the door, I simply pressed my body against the wall and hastily wrapped the bright light of the room around me. The footsteps drew closer. I didn't dare move because I had no idea how secure my screen was, but I could hear and smell, and that was enough.

It was, surprisingly, two humans—one male, one female. The woman was heavily scented and heavier on her feet; an older woman, I thought. The male's movements were much lighter, and he smelled faintly woody. He also emitted a vibe that was watchful, tense. A guard of some sort, not a companion. They stopped near the far end of the hall, near the door I'd shorted.

"Deliberate destruction, from the look of it." The voice was gruff, masculine.

"So someone wanted to get in?" The woman's voice was pleasant without being memorable.

"I can't see any other reason to destroy the system like they have," the male said. "You want me to check if there's anyone in there?"

The woman hesitated, and her uncertainty and fear washed over me. "No," she said eventually. "We're being paid to ignore the basement, so ignore it we will. I'll just notify them that something has happened. If they want to check it, they can."

Them. They. Not he. Not she. There was more than one person involved in all this, whatever "this" was. But were they also involved with the wraiths? Or did we have two separate events happening here?

The two strangers retreated. I waited until they'd left the corridor, then released my light shield and looked around. The room held little more than a bed and a large wooden chest. Curious as to what the chest might contain—and whether it might offer any clue as to where I was—I walked across and opened the lid. Inside there was a variety of not just clothes, but sex toys.

I was, I realized suddenly, in a brothel. Which was a great

place to hide something like the rift, because it wasn't like visitors were going to be overly curious about what might lie beyond the rooms in which they were entertained. But that still didn't answer the question of who. Didn't answer the question of why the rift was here in the first place. Surely the authorities had not become so blasé about them that they'd allowed a building to be constructed around it?

I fished around in the chest and found a silvery gray cape and a gauzy white shirtdress. It was somewhat see-through and would probably reveal more than it covered—especially given that I now wore the clear under-breast shape-tapes, which were not only more comfortable than the old-fashioned bras the HDP had made us use, but far more supportive without in any way restricting movement. But it wasn't like I had a whole lot to worry about in this form, anyway. I quickly changed, then bundled my clothes and my weapons together and shoved them into a bag I found near the bottom of the chest. Once I'd put the cape on, I headed out.

In the hallway beyond, a buzzer sounded. The rooms around me suddenly bustled with activity, and, in short order, a small group of men and women were filing out of the rooms and heading for the exit. I quickly joined them, keeping my head down, avoiding looking at anyone as the group made their way through the lobby beyond the door, past a reception area, and out onto the pavement. Pavement that was crisp and clean and filled with people going about their business, not taking any notice of those of us exiting the brothel. The sun was fierce and bright, and its position in the sky suggested it was midafternoon, at least. I'd lost a fair chunk of time traversing that rift. I jogged across the road, dodging air scooters and electric cars, then turned and looked back.

The building was small and narrow—little more than five

stories high and four windows wide. Its rooftop was washed with the light of the UVs that lined the slightly taller buildings on either side of it, and it was nestled against a shiny metal wall that towered far above any of the buildings in this street. It was a curtain wall. And not, I suspected, *any* old curtain wall, but Central's itself.

The wraiths had a direct line of transport into the city. No wonder so many children had gone missing without the populace ever realizing monsters prowled in their midst.

I shivered and scanned the building again, looking for the brothel's name. Eventually I spotted a small, discreet sign that simply read DESEO. No doubt Nuri and her motley crew would be able to run a check on the owners of this place, as well as keep an eye on the comings and goings . . . *if* I contacted them about it, that was. I wasn't entirely sure *that* was a wise move—given they hadn't exactly denied a link to the government.

I turned and headed down the street. I had no idea where I was, but if this *was* Central, then this road would intersect the main thoroughfare soon enough. Central's internal layout consisted of a dozen roads; the outer roads were semicircular like the wall itself, but the inner ones were full circles. Victory Street—the only street that ran straight through the heart of the city—intersected each of these roads, which also acted as delineation among the twelve districts within Central. Those near the wall were the poorer sections; the closer you got to Central's heart—where the main business district and government centers were situated, as well as the only green space available within the city—the more exclusive and richer the community.

I found Victory Street—a spacious avenue that, despite the tall buildings lining either side of it, was still wide enough to allow real sunshine to bathe the street rather than just the UV lights—and headed north, toward the exit drawbridge.

The entire avenue at ground level was a mix of retail premises. At this end of town, closer to the walls, the shops and cafés tended to be smaller, and their contents—be it clothes, food stalls, or tables for the various cafés—spilled out onto the wide pavement, filling the air with a riot of scents and giving the street a wild, almost gregarious feel. It was these areas that I generally stuck to when I came here on ration raids.

The closer I moved into Central's heart, the more sterile the street and air became. Even the people in this section of the city seemed to have undergone some sort of purity process, I thought, as my gaze roamed across the gently moving sea of people ahead of me. While they didn't look anything alike physically, there was a common sense of serenity they all shared—an odd, almost superior air. And the fact that they were nearly all clad in white and gray outfits didn't help the feeling that in these streets, there was an entirely different level of living. One I would never understand or be comfortable with. But at least in my stolen clothes, I didn't stand out too much . . .

The thought froze as my gaze came to a halt on the wide shoulders of a man. A man who towered above the rest of the populace by a good foot, and whose short hair was the color of blue steel. My heart began to beat a whole lot faster and my footsteps quickened. Blue steel was a very rare hair color, and it was one that was very hard to reproduce in dye. I'd only ever seen that color five times in all the years I'd been alive, and all five instances had been during the war, on the head of a déchet. Not any old déchet, but rather, specialist assassins.

And *that* surely could mean only one thing.

I *wasn't* the only déchet to have survived the war.

CHAPTER 6

No, I thought, *it can't be*. Surely if other déchet had survived, I would have come across them sooner rather than later. Granted, assassins—like lures—were bred with specific skills and abilities built into their DNA, but that didn't explain the fact that in just over one hundred years of running regular supply raids into Central, there'd never been the slightest suggestion of another déchet living within her walls.

I tried to hurry without being obvious about it, desperate not to let the stranger get too far ahead of me.

Could he be an assassin déchet? Was it possible? Or was the goddess just teasing me? Like us, they'd been an extremely small group—far more lures and assassins had died in the tubes than regular déchet and, of those who *did* survive, more than eighty percent had not made it to puberty. When it came to the assassins, this high attrition rate was due in part to the fact that they'd used not only shifter and vampire DNA, but actual *animal* DNA. And the death rate within the blue-steel program—or grays, as they'd become known, thanks to the fact that their salamander blood had given their skin a silky smooth but slightly gray tone—had been ninety-eight percent. Only five had survived past puberty, and I knew at least one of those had died during the war.

Up ahead, the man with the blue-steel hair disappeared into one of the many walkways that made quick access from one street to various others possible. I broke into a run, desperate not to lose him, weaving my way through the crowd with little of the decorum expected in this part of Central.

I turned into the walkway. It was a three-meter-wide canyon between two high-rise buildings and was bathed in UV light. My steps slowed as I desperately searched the crowd moving between Victory and First Streets for any sign of the stranger. There was nothing.

I cursed softly and ran to the end of the walkway, stopping again when I reached First. Still no sign, but a scent teased the air. A scent that spoke of deep forests, dark satin, and something else. Something unexpected and icy.

But there was enough familiarity within that mix of aromas to stir memories of long nights of passion spent in the arms of a man with blue-steel hair. A man I'd been assigned to instruct in the arts of seduction and sex once he'd hit adulthood, and with whom I'd become closer than perhaps was ever wise.

A man who'd saved my life when I'd all but given up hope.

I followed the fragile, teasing scent through several more walkways and came into an area I wasn't familiar with. I paused, looking around, and caught sight of the stranger up ahead just before he disappeared around Fourth Street's gentle curve.

But I'd barely reached the spot where I'd last seen him when someone grabbed my arm and hauled me—rather unceremoniously—through a doorway and into more muted light. Before I could react in any way, a hand clamped over my mouth, then a velvety voice whispered, "If you do not wish to be caught by the ranger who follows you, make no sound."

It was definitely *his* voice.

Even after all this time, it was as familiar to me as the touch of the sun. I swallowed heavily, then nodded. Confusion, hope, and disbelief churned through me, all fighting to come to the fore and dominate. None of which was surprising, given I'd spent so long believing I was the sole survivor of my race.

His grip slipped down my arm to my wrist, and his large hand clasped mine. His skin was like silk, cool to the touch, but his palm was calloused. It hadn't been, when I'd known him.

He tugged me forward, through the semishadows, weaving in and out of various rooms and up several sets of stairs. I couldn't say anything. I could barely even think.

"This way." He flashed me a brief but all-too-familiar smile that had my senses dancing and desire stirring. "We're almost there."

"Almost where?" I somehow managed to say, part of me still unwilling to believe that this was happening, that *he* was real.

"To our transport, of course." There was amusement in his tone. "The ranger may be able to trace your scent through the streets, but he cannot fly."

He opened another door and we entered a small parking area that housed half a dozen short-hop vertical takeoff and landing vehicles—or VTOLs, as they were more commonly known. He waved a hand to the small red one. "Your chariot awaits, dear Tig."

So I *wasn't* mistaken. It *was* him. His silvery gaze, when it met mine again, was as filled with wonder and disbelief as mine had to be.

"Sal?" I whispered, still fearing to believe, despite everything my senses and my memory were telling me.

"Yes, and I have to tell you, I'm finding it just as difficult to believe it's actually *you*. That disguise of yours is rather repellant."

I smiled. "So how did you know it was me?"

"Because I would know your scent anywhere, even after all these years." He briefly touched my face, something close to wonder in his. "It is so good to see you again."

"But how did you surv—"

He placed a finger against my lips, stopping my question. "I'll explain later. For now, get in, as we're not safe from the ranger's pursuit just yet."

I climbed inside the small two seater. He jumped into the driver's seat and, with little ceremony, secured the canopy and started the VTOL's engines. Dust whipped around us as the vehicle rose. Then Sal pressed the steering stick forward and the craft shot out of the parking lot and into the bright light of day. I gripped the side of my seat somewhat fiercely and resisted the urge to look down. It had been a long time since I'd been in a VTOL—and I'd never been overly keen on them in the first place. I'd always been of the belief that if I'd been meant to fly, I would have been designed with wings.

Thankfully, short-hops were designed for just that. Sal steered the VTOL into another midbuilding parking lot, then stopped.

"And that," he said, opening the canopy, "should be the end of the ranger following you. However, we'll still head somewhere he cannot go, just to be sure." His gaze met mine. "Then, dear Tig, you can tell me why it's taken you so long to arrive in Central."

Meaning he'd been here all the time? Surely *not*. Surely the goddess would not have been so cruel as to put us so close to each other and yet never allow our paths to cross.

But I nodded and followed him back down to Victory Street. He caught my hand again, guiding me across the road to the building that was all glass and delicate steel. Given its proximity to both Central Park and Government House, even the bathroom in this place would come with a very high price tag. It certainly wasn't the sort of building where the likes of me would be welcome.

"I'm not sure I'm exactly dressed—"

"Actually, you're probably *over*dressed, given Hedone is, at its core, a very high-end brothel." Amusement touched his lips as he opened the ornate glass-and-metal door, and waved me through. "Please, inside, so that our scent doesn't linger."

"You work in a brothel?" I asked, though it wasn't entirely surprising. Assassins, like lures, had been designed to be sexually attractive to shifters, even though seduction wasn't often on their agenda. If Hedone catered to shifters, he'd be in high demand.

"No," he said, the amusement sharper. "I own it."

My gaze shot to his. "You *own* it?"

"Let's just say I have made the most of my escape from near death." He caught my hand again and led me through a foyer that was crisp and white. Sofas and comfortable chairs filled the huge expanse, most of them occupied by men and women as crisp and white as their surroundings. Some were sipping champagne, some were eating canapés, and others were flicking through electronic catalogues, no doubt trying to decide who might be the morning's entertainment.

A petite blond woman looked up from the large white desk that dominated one wall of the foyer, a smile touching her perfectly painted silver lips as we approached. "Mr. Casimir, I wasn't expecting to see you again this morning. Is there a problem?"

"No," he said evenly. "But I have a meeting at six, so could you give me a call at five thirty? We'll be in my private suite."

"Not a problem, sir." The woman's gaze flickered to me, her curiosity evident. But she didn't question my presence, and Sal made no move to explain it.

We walked into a lift that was all glass. Sal pressed his thumb against the scanner, then said, "Tenth floor."

I raised my eyebrows. "Just how many floors do you own in this building?"

He caught my hands in his and stared at me for several seconds, as if he still couldn't believe his eyes. "Just ten," he said eventually. "Although I am planning to buy more in the next few years."

I laughed softly and shook my head. "Only ten? Good grief, Sal, real estate in this part of town is worth a fortune. How on earth have you managed to buy ten floors?"

"It's not hard to do when you're as good at seduction as I am." It was immodestly said and actually quite true. He'd certainly practiced his seduction techniques on me often enough, both when I'd been assigned to teach him such things, and later, in the few times we'd met out in the field. "And I've had a hundred years to gather a fortune."

In a hundred years, I'd barely dared to venture outside my bunker. I stepped closer and gently traced the outline of his luscious lips with a finger. "How did you survive the cleansing?" I asked softly. "I thought I was the only one."

"So did I, for a very long time." He pressed a kiss against my fingertip. Desire surged between us, familiar and fiery. "You have no idea how glad I am to discover that you survived."

"And I you." It came out husky. Lord, it had been far too long since I'd been in the arms of another, let alone felt the touch of someone I actually *cared* about. To say my body was humming with eager anticipation was something of an understatement.

The elevator came to a halt and the doors slid open. The room beyond was vast—it ran the entire breadth of the building, in fact. Windows lined two sides, and sunlight burned in, so bright it was almost eye-watering. The space was divided into various zones by furniture, and somehow managed to feel more intimate than the sheer size of the room should have allowed.

Though the apartment's walls were as white as anything else in this section of Central, the furnishings were a riot of color and brightness; reds, greens, purples, golds, even the occasional splash of black, filled the room and no doubt added to the feeling of intimacy and homeyness.

It was a vastly different way of living from my old bunker.

"Drink?" He released my hand and moved across to a bar that dominated one corner of the kitchen zone.

"Yes." I stopped in the middle of the room and dropped my bag and cloak onto a nearby chair. And couldn't help feeling very out of place and somewhat awkward in all this opulence.

He poured two glasses, then walked back and offered me one.

"To survival against the odds." He touched his glass against mine. "To the renewal of a very old friendship."

"To friendships and renewals," I echoed, then took a sip. The bubbles teased my nose, and the liquid burned my throat, tart but refreshing.

For several minutes, neither of us moved. We simply drank the champagne and stared at each other. Then his gaze left mine and slid down my body, becoming a sensual and yet excruciatingly slow exploration that had pinpricks of sweat breaking out across my skin. It was all I could do not to pluck the glass from his hand and wrap my arms around his neck. To kiss him. Touch him. Make love to him.

He smiled at that moment, and I knew he'd sensed exactly what I was thinking.

"We have so much to catch up on," he said softly.

"We do," I agreed.

He placed a fingertip against the base of my neck, his touch light and cool. "So much to talk about."

"Definitely." I took another drink. It didn't do a whole lot to ease the fire growing inside me.

His touch slid down and, one by one, he deftly undid the buttons of my dress. "And yet," he murmured when the last button came free, "talking is the very last thing I want to do right now."

"I'm gathering that," I said, unable to keep the slight trace of amusement from my voice.

"What gave me away?" His touch slid back up and gently circled one nipple, then the other.

A shudder of delight ran through me. "Call it an educated guess."

"You always were a very smart individual." He brushed his lips across the base of my neck. "You were my teacher, my lover, and my friend, and it has been such a long time since I have experienced anything close to what we once shared."

"I've *never* experienced it, Sal. Not in more than one hundred years." I closed my eyes, drawing in the silky dark yet oddly corrupted scent of him, tasting in it enough familiarity to chase away fear and warm my senses.

"No other lovers?" he murmured, as his kisses trailed up my neck.

"No lovers. Just sex."

"Me, too."

His lips finally claimed mine. Our kiss was a long, slow exploration that was both familiar and new.

"I need you, Tig." His breath caressed my mouth and his gaze burned deep, the force of his desire so strong it singed every part of my being. "As you are, in this form, here and now."

"Then take me," I said simply.

He plucked the glass from my hand and placed both on the nearby coffee table. "It will be my great pleasure."

"And mine, I hope."

He chuckled softly, then his lips claimed mine again, although the urgency I could feel in him was still leashed, still restrained. He slid his hand around my waist, his fingers cool as they pressed against my spine and pulled me closer. His body was warm, hard, and so very familiar. I wrapped my arms around his neck, drawing us closer still. Restraint gave way to passion, and the kiss became fiercely erotic.

After what seemed like hours we finally parted. My gaze met his, and in the bright silver of his eyes both lust and memories gleamed. The rapid pounding of my heart was a cadence that filled the silence, and desire—both his and mine—was so thick and fierce it burned my throat with every breath.

I undid the buttons of his crisp white shirt, pushed it free from his shoulders, and ran my hands over the muscular planes of his chest and stomach, refamiliarizing myself with his body. His muscles quivered under my touch, but when I went to undo his pants, he slid his hand across mine and stopped me.

"Not yet," he murmured, "or this will be over in a second flat."

I laughed softly. "Has it been that long for you?"

"No. I just never did have much in the way of control when it came to you."

His fingers splayed against my rear end. Heat pooled wherever skin met skin, and flared across my flesh like fire. Lord, his touch was even more intense than I remembered.

With little effort, he lifted me, then carried me across to the dining table. My rump had barely touched the glass when he slid his hands up to my breasts, teasing and pinching my engorged nipples. Delight spun through me, but I had no intention of being a passive recipient of pleasure. Ignoring his earlier warning as much as his halfhearted attempt to stop me, I undid his pants and pushed them down, then proceeded to caress and explore him as thoroughly as he did me. For a very long time, we did nothing more than renew our memories of each other, teasing and enticing familiar responses, until tiny beads of perspiration covered our skin and all I could think about, all I wanted, was him. Until the two of us were trembling, hovering on the edge of climax and aching for release.

Finally, his fingers slid through my slickness and entered me, even as he pressed his thumb against my clit. He began to stroke, inside and out, and I shuddered, writhed, until it felt as if I were going to tear apart in sheer pleasure.

Unable to take any more, needing a *whole* lot more, I wrapped my legs around his waist and pulled him closer. A heartbeat later, he was in me, thrusting deep and hard, claiming me in the most basic way possible. Then he gripped my hips, his fingers bruising as he held me still for too many seconds.

But, oh, it was *so* glorious, being held motionless while my body throbbed with need, his body deep inside mine, heavy and hot with the same sort of need. I loved the feel of him. Loved his size and his shape and how insanely good it felt when he was in me.

Then he cursed softly and began move. Not gently, but fiercely, urgently, all control gone and nothing left but need. I was right there with him, wanting everything he could give. The deep ache blossomed, spreading like wildfire across my skin, becoming a kaleidoscope of sensations that washed through every corner of my mind. I gasped, grabbing his shoulders for support as his movements grew faster, more urgent, my body shuddering with the fierceness of his movements. Then everything broke, and I was unraveling, groaning with the intensity of my orgasm. His movements became almost savage, and, a heartbeat after me, he came so very deep inside.

For several minutes afterward, neither of us moved. Then he rested his forehead against mine, his breath warm and rapid against my skin.

"Dear god," he murmured. "That was a whole lot faster than I'd intended, but it was as every bit as good as I remembered."

"Dear *god*?" I repeated, amusement running through me. It was basically the human equivalent of the shifter term "by Rhea." "Since when did you start using human terms so freely?"

He grinned. "Since I began fucking them for a living. Shifters may have won the war, but there are still plenty of wealthy humans about more than willing to part with large amounts of cash in return for a good time. And they are far easier targets than most shifters."

There was something in his voice—an odd edge—that made me frown. "Calling them 'targets' makes it seem like you were doing more than merely seducing them."

"Maybe I was, but who really cares? We're talking about a race that stood by and did nothing while shifters erased our kind. We owe allegiance to no one but ourselves."

"Humans lost the war, Sal. They couldn't have done anything else *but* stand by and watch." Besides, it wasn't like humanity hadn't suffered losses. Millions had been killed; not just those who'd created us, but all those who'd fought behind déchet front lines, and all those who hadn't evacuated the cities in time.

He snorted. "It's their damn fault the war started in the first place. You cannot continually squeeze an entire race of people into ever-decreasing parcels of land and not expect a backlash."

"I'm not here to argue the rights and wrongs of the war, Sal. I'm just saying we're not the only race that suffered. Everyone lost in that war—even the shifters."

He raised an eyebrow, a touch of—not contempt, but something close to it in his gaze. "You're defending them?"

"No, I'm not. I'm just pointing out fact." Besides, I'd had a long time to think about the war. I couldn't hate the humans because I owed them my existence, and while I will never forgive the way shifters had destroyed us, I couldn't really hate them, either. Not when shifter blood ran through my veins and I'd spent so much time in many different shifter camps. I understood them far better than I did humans.

I unwrapped my legs from his waist, and he stepped back from the table.

"Another drink?" He turned and walked across the room. The afternoon sunlight caressed his skin, giving it a lovely silvery sheen.

"No, but I wouldn't mind something to eat."

He glanced over his shoulder. "Bacon and eggs okay?"

"Divine." I couldn't even *remember* the last time I'd had them. He continued on into the kitchen. I trailed after him, gathering my clothes but not bothering to put any of them on. "So how did you survive the cleansing, Sal? And what have you been doing these last hundred years?"

He selected our meals on the autocook, pressed a button, and then swung around to face me. His expression had lost much of its glow. But then, talking about the cleansing was enough to wipe the smile off anyone's face. Anyone who'd been there and survived it, at any rate.

"It was pure luck." His voice was soft, but I could see the shadows in his eyes, feel the pain and the anger in the emotive swirl surrounding him. "I was in Carleen when they bombed it. They wrote me off as dead and dumped me in one of the craters, along with everyone else who hadn't made it to the shelters." He grimaced. "By the time my body had repaired itself, the base had been all but razed, and all within murdered."

Including the children, I thought, and tried to ignore the bloody images that flitted through my mind. I swallowed hard, and wondered why humans seemed to believe that time erased all wounds. It didn't. It couldn't.

"What about you?" he asked.

"Same really. Just pure and utter luck."

The lie slipped off my tongue easily enough, though I wasn't entirely sure why instinct was warning me not to remind him about the genetics that made me immune to poisons. This was Sal: a déchet, just like me, and the man I'd once trusted with all that I was. But a hundred years had passed since I'd last seen him, a hundred years in which I'd done little more than protect my little ghosts and our home. I wasn't about to endanger them, even when it came to someone like Sal. Not until I knew beyond doubt that he was worthy of holding such a secret. People could change in a matter of years. In one hundred, anything could have happened.

"How long have you been in Central?" he asked. The autocook *ping*ed and the door opened. He removed two plates, then walked across and handed me one. It smelled so good my mouth began to water.

"A few weeks." I picked up a crisp bit of bacon and munched on it. Damn, it was almost as good as sex. Almost. "But I'm officially out of credits, and I'm looking for work."

The words were out before I'd even thought about them. *So much for not wanting to get involved with Nuri's investigations,* I thought resignedly. Instinct, it seemed, had far more sway over my actions than common sense.

He slid some cutlery my way, then perched on the stool beside me, his arm brushing mine as he tucked into his own meal. The brief moments of contact sent warm awareness surging through my body. I may have started out as the teacher when it came to all things sexual, but in subsequent years, he'd certainly taught me a thing or two. And even now, one hundred years later, that awareness and connection still burned bright and fierce between us.

He paused, his expression amused as he looked at me. "As much as I would love to offer you a position at Hedone,

I'm afraid I'd much rather keep you in *my* bed than have anyone else in yours."

"Nor would I wish to make money that way." My smile faded. "These days, sex is something I have because I wish to. I have no desire for it to become a task again, in any way, shape, or form."

"An understandable, if somewhat antiquated view."

I frowned. "What's antiquated about wishing to choose who I have in my bed rather than being told?"

"Perhaps 'antiquated' was the wrong word to use." He shrugged. "I merely meant that we were designed with specific skill sets, and it's a shame not to use them for our own gain."

"Which is what you've been doing for one hundred years—using sex and assassination to feather your own nest?"

He raised an eyebrow, amusement lurking around the corners of his eyes. "It sounds rather tawdry put like that."

"It wasn't meant—"

He raised a hand, stopping me. "I know. And no, I haven't spent the last one hundred years fucking and killing my way to a fortune. It's only been in more recent years that I returned full-time to the task for which I was created."

My gaze rose to his rather individual hair color. "And no one has ever said anything? Suspected you were far more than the front you present?"

He reached out and tugged at my hair. "Your deep orange-and-black hair is rather unique, missy. Has anyone ever said anything to you? Or do you wear this rather dowdy disguise full-time?"

Orange and black? Had he forgotten I was a white tiger rather than regular? I opened my mouth to remind him, then stopped, that odd warning to keep silent raising its head again. So I simply said, "Not full-time, but whenever I'm in Central, then yeah."

"And yet it is not as if there aren't plenty of shifters in Central. Your natural color—and mine—is mild compared to some of theirs."

That was certainly true. I guess I'd just been so caught up in the need for safety that I'd gone totally over the top. I mopped up the remains of the eggs with the last bit of bacon, then placed my cutlery on the plate and pushed it away with a sigh.

"That was lovely. Thank you."

"You are *most* welcome." He paused. "I know plenty of influential people, thanks to this place. It might be possible for me to at least get you a job interview. What are your qualifications these days?"

"Beyond theft?" I asked, amused. "Not a whole lot, to be honest."

He snorted softly. "There's not many calls for thieves, I'm afraid."

"Hence the reason I'm still unemployed." I hesitated. "I heard on the grapevine that someplace called Winter Halo was recruiting night watchmen, but I have no idea where or how to apply."

"I believe they are." His eyes narrowed as he studied me for a moment. "Do you have ID?"

"Of course." Or would have, if Nuri came through with her promise.

"Good." He pursed his lips for a moment. "I know the man in charge of recruitment, and I'm afraid he's very particular about the type of guard he employs."

"Particular how?" I hesitated. "He sleeps with them?"

"As far as I'm aware, no. Even in Central, such harassment is frowned upon."

"'Even in Central'? What's that supposed to mean?"

"It's nothing more than an acknowledgment that even with Central's somewhat lax employment laws, overt sexual harassment is not allowed."

Meaning it was allowed—or at least ignored—if it was done covertly?

"Anyway," he continued, "all of those chosen as guards are curvaceous in build, with large breasts and orange hair. It would appear the owner of Winter Halo has something of a fetish for the color."

As fetishes go, that was definitely one of the minor ones—and while my natural hair color was white and black tiger stripes and I couldn't exactly be described as curvaceous, as a body shifter it wasn't a hard form to attain. "Which isn't actually a problem, as you know."

"No."

I frowned, sensing an odd . . . not reluctance, not really. But there was definitely some sort of background resistance to the idea of my applying for the job at Winter Halo, and I couldn't figure out why. "Do you think you have enough swing with the recruiter to get me an interview?"

"Possibly. I should warn you, though, that the night watch has a very high turnover. Women do not seem to last very long in the position."

And did the reason have something to do with harassment of some kind? Or was something else going on?

My frown deepened. "Any idea why?"

He shook his head. "But there are few here in Central who are comfortable at night. The fear of vampires is fierce, even with the UV lights and the wall keeping them at bay."

"Then why would they apply for the job in the first place?"

"You really *haven't* been in Central very long." There

was amusement in his tone, but the shadows were deeper in his eyes. "It's not all sunshine and roses, believe me."

"For you, it must be." I waved a hand around his apartment. "You have all this, after all."

"Yes, but I didn't always live and work on First Street. I started on Twelfth—and believe me, it's a very long, very steep road to get from there to here."

I guess it would have been. Certainly Deseo was a far cry from Hedone—and if I ever *had* to work in a brothel, it would be at one like Hedone. I hadn't seen much of the place, but the foyer alone suggested the rooms where the transactions took place would contain far more than merely a bed and a box of toys.

"Anyway," he continued, gathering the plates, then rising and walking them over to the dishwasher, "I'll see what I can do. Of course, you do know it means you'll have to see me again."

I raised my eyebrows. "You say that like you expect me *not* to."

"Oh," he said, his grin cheeky, but the shadows even stronger in his eyes. "I can smell *exactly* how much you want to. I was merely giving you the option to walk away if you so desired."

I smiled. "I haven't seen another déchet for a hundred years. That, I believe, is answer enough."

"Well, then how about dinner? Somewhere fancy to celebrate our reunion?"

"I don't think I have the clothes to do fancy—"

He held up his hand, stopping me again. "Then it will be my pleasure to supply you a dress. Shall we say six tomorrow evening, in the lobby?"

"Sure." It would give me time to gather courage and

head back into Chaos. Hopefully, Nuri would be as good as her word when it came to getting me an ID.

"In the meantime," he said, spinning my chair around so that I faced him. "I have forty-five minutes before I must leave for my appointment. Shall I fill you in on some of my missing years, or shall I simply fill you?"

"My, my," I murmured. "Haven't we lost some finesse over the years."

He smiled. "Finesse, I have learned, doesn't always get what I want. And you didn't answer the question on the table."

I placed my finger on his chest and gently followed the faint line of hair down his stomach. His cock leapt, as if eager for my touch. I obliged.

"You could do both," I murmured, then leaned forward and ran my tongue across the tip of him, tasting sex and eagerness.

"No," he said, shuddering, "I don't believe I can."

From there on in, there was no talking, and I had absolutely no complaints. I might have spent many an hour longing for adult conversation, but sex and silence with a man I was so familiar with—and one of the few I'd trusted during the war—was far, *far* better.

And it was certainly far better than I remembered.

I left Sal's place at six, well satiated, well fed, freshly showered, and wearing my own clothes—which had been laundered and repaired. If I'd had tabby rather than tiger in my DNA, I probably would have been purring right now.

Dusk was just beginning to settle across the skies, though the streets of Central were still as bright as day, thanks to the UVs kicking into full action as the night approached. I hurried down Victory Street, heading for the drawbridge and hoping like hell it hadn't already been raised for the night. My little ghosts would worry if I wasn't back by night-fall, and if I didn't get out of this place before the drawbridge went up, I *would* be stuck here for the night.

The huge gatehouse came into view, and relief ran through me when I saw it was still down. But the guards were out of their houses, prowling about like beasts con-tained, their anxiety stinging the air. Obviously, the last pod of the day was late, and they weren't happy. And they *would* stop me from exiting if they saw me.

I ducked into the nearest walkway, waited impatiently for several people to pass, then, when the coast was clear, drew the light around me. It would dissipate as quickly as the remaining sunlight once I moved beyond Central's UVs, but that didn't matter. I doubted anyone would chase me even if they saw me at that point, as they generally feared the dark far more than they feared losing one citizen to night and the vampires.

I continued on to the exit. The ends of the silver curtain that Central used in place of the more conventional port-cullis gleamed brightly thanks to the lights that lined the gatehouse, but the sensors fitted into the thick metal walls didn't react to my presence, though they would have, had I been full vampire. It had taken ten years to completely rebuild Central, and, by that stage, all HDP bases had been well and truly destroyed, and the déchet population deci-mated. It never occurred to them that some might have survived—hell, it hadn't occurred to *me*, and I was one of the survivors—so they never built that possibility into their security systems. For which I was extremely grateful. Feeding myself would have been far more problematic had I not been able to make regular raids into Central.

I moved through the gatehouse and out onto the draw-bridge. The last pod of the evening finally pulled into the station, and people began streaming toward the city, forcing me to duck and weave to prevent collisions. While the sun-light shield prevented anyone seeing me, I hadn't physically disappeared; they *would* feel me if I collided with them. Once I was over the bridge, I jumped down into the rail yards and quickly traversed them. The farther I moved away from the lights, the faster the shield unraveled, until it had completely disappeared and I was visible to anyone looking my way. Pain flitted across my senses at the shield's loss, but I kept running until I finally reached the Barra's old watercourse. Though the possibility of being seen by a too-alert guard was now unlikely, I didn't relax. Night had all but settled in, and the vampires would be rising. And while I was close to the South Siding exit and there were, as far as I knew, no enclaves in this immediate vicinity, that didn't mean anything. There were who-knew-how-many old sewer-age and transport tunnels under Chaos, and Chaos itself was within easy running distance. Just because I'd never seen any vamps near here didn't mean they couldn't get here altogether *too* fast if one or more of them happened to be close enough to smell my scent or catch the sound of my heartbeat.

Which meant I had better get a move on.

But I'd barely taken three steps when Cat appeared. Her energy whipped around me, filled with fear and panic and images of darkness on the move.

The vampires weren't under Chaos.

They were attacking the South Siding exit, trying to get into our home.

CHAPTER 7

I reacted instinctively and without thought. My knives were in my hands before I knew it, and I was all but flying over the rocky, barren ground as I headed for the South Siding exit.

"Cat," I said, "I need flares. And weapons."

She raced away, leaving me alone with the night and the shadows. I half thought about dragging a veil around my body and becoming one with it, but I was heading for vampires, the one creature on this planet that could see through such veils—mainly because they were creatures of night and shadows themselves.

The closer I got to the exit, the more evident the sounds of fighting became. It was mixed with the sensation of fear and panic—my little ghosts were doing as I directed and protecting our home, but they were neither equipped for fighting nor very proficient at it. And if the hisses and snarls filling the air were any indication, then there was at least a score of vamps trying to gain access.

A score. And me armed with only knives and two small guns until Cat managed to get some more weapons . . . *Movement, to my right.* I swerved sharply but not fast enough. A body crashed into mine, sweeping me off my feet and down to the ground, where we rolled for several meters before coming to a halt. I raised a knife, but my hand was caught and held firm in a grip that was fierce and strong.

"Are you *insane*?"

The words were hissed, but the voice was nevertheless familiar. Jonas.

"What in hell do you think you're doing?" I bucked as hard as I could, trying to get him off me.

"Rescuing you from stupidity, that's what. Do you know how many vampires are down there?"

"Yes, but—"

"But *nothing.*" His legs tightened around me as I bucked again. "Don't be a damn fool. It would be nothing short of suicide to go down there right now."

I snorted and twisted my arms, trying to break his grip on them. "What do you care? You want me dead anyway, don't you?"

"What I want is neither here nor there. Nuri wants you alive, so alive you will remain."

"Damn it, you don't understand! The ghosts are down there!"

"The ghosts are already *dead*. The vampires *cannot* hurt them, but they can and will tear you apart."

"You're the one who doesn't understand!" The panic emanating from the exit was growing, as was my desperation to move, to get down there and help my little ones. "There are vampires who consume energy or souls, not just blood."

"I still don't see—"

"What do you think ghosts are?" I cut in. "An ectoplasmic force, that's what. And it *can* be consumed by some vampires."

He glared down at me, his green eyes bright and fierce despite the night. "I think your two little ghosts are clever enough to avoid—"

"That's the whole problem!" I spat back. "It's not just two ghosts. It's *hundreds*."

And with that, I lurched forward and smashed my forehead against his. It was a move he wasn't expecting, and it knocked him sideways. I pushed him the rest of the way off and, despite a spinning head and blooming headache, scrambled to my feet and ran on.

He cursed and all too soon was running after me. But my fear was fierce, and it gave my feet greater speed even if he had longer legs. Cat and Bear reappeared, carrying several larger guns and a couple of flares between them. Not much, and certainly not enough, not by a long shot, but better than nothing. I sheathed my knives, caught the weapons, tossed a flare back to the shifter, then clipped the other one to my pants. I raced over the slight hill that ran down to our bunker. Below me, vampires milled around the exit, scrambling over one another in their efforts to get through the ghosts who were valiantly attempting to hold back the tide. The scent of burned flesh stung the air, suggesting that at least some flares had been lit before I'd gotten here, and vampires were still being tossed left and right. But some were getting through . . . and it was at that point I realized that the exit was *open*.

By Rhea, how had *that* happened? Why were they even here, when in one hundred years they'd never come within sniffing distance of this tunnel?

They *wouldn't* come here. Not unless they were being

forced. I couldn't feel that dark, oddly mutated energy that I'd felt the last time I'd encountered the vampires, but that didn't mean that it wasn't near.

Not that it mattered. Not immediately. First I had to secure and clean out our bunker before I began to worry about the hows and whys of the exit being open.

I raced down the hill, my weapons gripped tight. As several vampires turned to face me, I began to fire, mowing some down, missing others. Behind me, Jonas unleashed his own weapons, the soft sound of rifle fire almost lost in the hissed snarls of the vampires.

"Bear, flare," I said. His energy spun around the flare, and an instant later it was lit. I snagged one gun onto a belt loop, then grabbed the flare and threw it into the middle of the vampire pack. They fled, creating a temporary clearway in the middle of the doorway.

"Cat, light the other one."

Her energy ran past me, and, a second later, light flared across my back. The shifter swung his flare back and forth threateningly, keeping the vampires momentarily at bay. But they ran along the edges of the light, ready to attack—*desperate* to attack—the minute the flares died.

I ran into the bunker, the shifter two steps behind. My flare began to sputter and fade. As Jonas threw his on the ground just in front of the entrance, I hit the EMERGENCY CLOSE button. The grate slammed home, but that didn't mean we were safe; this gate wasn't protected by either silver or a laser screen, and the vampires merely had to shadow to get through it. We needed to get to light, and that meant getting out of this tunnel and into the bunker itself—the one place I had no desire to take the ranger.

But it was either that or die, because we simply didn't

have enough weapons and there were still far too many vampires.

"This way," I said, voice tight. The ghosts fled before me, happy to see me, but their collective energy was so depleted and fear-filled it made me want to cry.

We ran down the tunnel, leaping over the bodies of the vamps who'd made it into the tunnel, our steps echoing in the silence—or mine did. The ranger's were whisper quiet. Darkness fell behind us, and the ghosts screamed a warning—the vampires were in the tunnel and coming after us.

"Bear, Cat, get those lights on up ahead."

They surged past us. A second later, the lights came on, the sudden brightness eye-watering. I blinked away tears and ran on, desperate to reach that room before the flood of darkness behind us hit. I ran into the light but didn't stop until I was at the far end of what had once been a nursery. Or one of them. This one happened to be empty at the time of the cleansing; the other one hadn't.

Jonas stopped beside me, radiating tension and a readiness to fight. I gripped my weapons, waiting, as the flood of darkness drew closer. They were shadowed, so they made little sound, but I could feel them. Feel their evil, hunger, and desperation.

I shivered, even as I wondered at that last emotion. There were plenty of easier pickings in Chaos, so why come here, after me?

Or were they, perhaps, still after Penny? They'd certainly prowled around the museum long enough last night, attempting to find a way in. Was this just an extension of that search?

Maybe. Maybe not. And it wasn't like I could ask them.

Shadows flickered across the edges of the light; then vampires re-formed. I raised my gun, as did Jonas, and together we picked them off, one by one, until the doorway was packed with smoldering bodies and we couldn't see the vampires beyond it.

Which, again, was odd. Vampires usually consumed their dead. "Waste not, want not" seemed to be their motto when it came to flesh and blood.

I stopped firing and lowered my weapons. Jonas kept his at the ready, his expression grim as he stared at the dead blocking the door.

"So," he said, voice holding just a hint of anger. No surprise there, I guess, given anger seemed to be his go-to emotion. "You're *not* the kind of shifter we'd presumed."

"It's not my fault you presumed wrong." I leaned against the wall and briefly closed my eyes. Now that we were relatively safe, reaction set in, and it was all I could do not to collapse on the floor in a trembling, crying mess. Some of that reaction came from the ghosts milling around me, their collective energy so close and thick my skin tingled and jumped in reaction. I reassured them the best I could, praising them for the bravery and their skill in handling the vampires and protecting our home. After a few minutes, their fear began to ease and a few even gathered enough courage to drift closer to the pile of vampires. But they didn't step beyond the light, and I can't say I blamed them.

"What were you doing in Central?" Jonas asked. He'd finally lowered his weapon but hadn't slipped the safety back on. Can't say I blamed him for that, either.

"What were you doing following me?" I countered. "And how did you even know it was me, given the body shift?"

He half snorted. "I am—or was—a ranger. Following scents is something we do."

And it was a generally accepted fact that a person's scent never changed. Only it wasn't exactly true—not for those of us created as lures. I *could* change scents if I so desired, but it took a lot of effort, and it made retaining the altered form all that much harder. Which was why many of us were simply relocated to a completely different area every new mission; it was easier than attempting to hold full body and scent transformations over weeks, or even months.

Of course, *not* altering my base scent was something that had almost killed me, after I'd been placed in a shifter camp that contained refugees from a camp I'd previously infiltrated. In fact, that mission going so wrong had been the reason I'd been here with the little ones when they'd unleashed the gas.

I thrust the bloody memories from my mind, then pushed away from the wall and stalked over to the smoldering mountain of flesh blocking the tunnel exit.

"Why were you following me in the first place? And how the hell did you even know I was going to be in Central?" I paused, looking over my shoulder, meeting his wary, angry gaze. "Nuri?"

He nodded. "She said you'd appear on the corner of Victory and Twelfth sometime after noon. She's rarely wrong."

Which made her far more than just a mind seeker. It meant she was a witch—a proper witch. One of the earth witches, who could not only read the future in the play of the world's natural forces and energy, but control the magic within it as well. And *that* made her, as I'd guessed, far more dangerous than any of the shifters she seemed to command.

"And why would she order me followed when I made it perfectly clear I wanted nothing to do with either of you or your mission?"

I grabbed a body on top of the pile and dragged it down into the light, where it immediately erupted into flame. As the smell of burning flesh began to stain the air, a shadow lashed out from the space created, forming claws that slashed at my face. I jerked back, watching as the vamp's arm exploded into fire the minute the light touched it, the ash of his skin swirling as he snatched the disintegrating limb back into the darkness. Grimly, I raised my weapons, aimed them through the small gap I'd created, and shot the hell out of the remaining vampires—or, at least, those who were too stupid to immediately run.

When both weapons clicked over to empty, I turned to find Jonas watching me, his usual angry expression touched by a hint of curiosity. It disappeared almost immediately, but it was, perhaps, a glimpse that there was more than anger to this man.

"You didn't answer my question, ranger."

I glanced up as Cat brought me fresh ammo unasked. I silently thanked her and reloaded the weapon before clipping it back onto its loop and heading for the exit. Jonas was here now, and short of throwing his ass back out into the night, there wasn't a whole lot I could do about it. Nor was it practical to pretend I only lived in this small section of the base. Penny would have no doubt mentioned the medical center and kitchen facilities. I might be able to get away with saying she'd been mistaken when it came to a museum entrance—they could search all they wanted, but they'd never find the tunnel I used; it was all but invisible when closed, and Penny had gone through it only when it was open—but there was no way they were going to believe everything she'd described had been little more than shock and imagination. Better to reveal the safer truths, while keeping others secret.

"She ordered you followed simply because she didn't believe you'd let the matter lie." Though I heard no sound of movement, his closeness pressed against my spine, an energy that was both unsettling and enticing. "That because of Penny, and because there were other children involved, you *couldn't* let the matter lie."

Nuri had understood altogether *too* much about me in the brief time I'd been in her presence.

The sensor light flashed as we approached the door, but it took several seconds for it to actually respond. With night upon us, all three generators would have now kicked in to fuel the main defense systems, lights, and air, but the secondary systems, like these doors, had power diverted to them only as required.

"How are you powering this place?" Jonas asked, as the door finally opened.

I shrugged. "I managed to get the old generators going. Finding parts was the hard bit."

"Considering how old the technology here is, it must have taken quite a while." There wasn't suspicion in his voice, not exactly, but it was pretty obvious he wasn't buying all that I was saying.

I met his gaze, seeing in the green depths the distrust I could feel. Seeing the awareness, however much he might be attempting to contain it. "It did."

"And the medical scanners Penny mentioned? Did you get them up and running also?"

I smiled, though it contained very little in the way of humor. "No need. Once I got the power going, most of the remaining systems came online, although the kitchen and food facilities were pretty foul. It took a hell of a lot of scrubbing before I could even *contemplate* using them."

His smile was an echo of my own, but, after a moment,

he pulled his gaze from mine and looked around. A slight frown creased his weatherworn but handsome features as he studied the dusty old metal beds lining either side of the long room. "What was this place? Some kind of bunk-house?"

An innocent enough question but one that could prove my downfall if I didn't watch how I answered it. "According to the ghosts, this was the nursery."

His gaze shot back to mine. "Nursery?"

I raised my eyebrows, surprised by his response. "Who did you think my little ones were? They're all the ghosts of the children who were murdered in this place."

"No one was *murdered*," he refuted. "Least of all children."

"And you were here to witness that, were you?" I snapped back. "Because these ghosts *were*, and they tell a very different story from the rewritten history currently presented as truth in today's schools."

"My, my," he said, voice mild but that dark anger of his sharper. "You're awfully vehement about a situation that supposedly happened long before you were born."

I flexed my fingers, trying to keep calm. He was trying to force a slip on my part, trying to uncover the truth, no matter what Nuri herself might wish or order. I had to be careful. Had to watch what I said.

And I couldn't, simply *couldn't*, let emotion get the better of me.

"You'd be pretty worked up if you could listen to their story and could experience the pain and the horror they went through." I tore my gaze away, my eyes stinging. "Their death wasn't pretty and it wasn't fast. No one who had been quartered in this place at the end of the war died easily. Believe *that*, if nothing else, ranger."

We walked through another doorway and I led the way left, into another of the main tunnels that allowed access to the next two floors. I avoided the sixth floor—which contained not only my sleeping quarters, but the bunk rooms, main medical facilities, and the crèche and training areas for young déchet—simply because they required ID and blood work to access them. And doing *that* would only confirm his suspicions. Instead, we continued on to the fourth floor, which was the area Penny had seen.

"Children aren't always the most reliable of narrators," Jonas said softly. "And it has been a very long time since the war."

"I agree, children aren't always the most reliable of narrators. And yet here you are, believing every word that comes out of Penny's mouth despite the fact Nuri herself said the child had changed."

"Touché." The hint of amusement in his voice was both surprising and oddly warm. Or maybe it just seemed that way simply because of the brief absence of suspicion and anger. "But that still doesn't negate the fact—"

"There's more than children haunting this place," I cut in. "There's the ghosts of all the adult déchet who were here at the time, and *their* story matches those of the younger ghosts."

He blinked. "There's déchet here?"

I smiled, though again it held little humor. "And ghosts of scientists, doctors, nurses, clerical staff, and probably a whole lot more that I've never even talked to. When your people cleansed this place, they cleansed it of *everybody* involved, be they human *or* déchet."

"Perhaps," Jonas bit back, no doubt reacting to the trace of anger that had ebbed into my voice despite my best efforts, "they figured it was the only sure way to rid this world of the perversion that was the déchet."

Perversion. Travesty. A foul corruption of nature. We'd been called all those things and more, both during the war *and* the years immediately after it, before the shifters had begun altering history. It still had the power to sting, even now. Just because my creation had happened in a tube rather than as a result of intercourse between two people didn't make me any less of a being. It didn't make me a monster.

Granted, there were déchet who *had* been monsters, especially in the ranks of those who had been first assault soldiers and either designed or medicated to feel nothing. But could the same not be said of humans and shifters?

Somehow, I kept my voice even as I noted, "There's an awful lot of hate in your voice for a race that disappeared over one hundred years ago, ranger."

"I lost a lot of family in that war." The dark anger in his voice was even stronger. But I guessed that was no surprise, given a shifter's life span was far longer than a human's. While Jonas himself didn't look old enough to have lived through the war, his parents surely would have. "It's not something time can erase, no matter what some might have you believe."

Given I'd echoed those sentiments not so long ago, I could hardly disagree.

We finally reached the fourth level, and I led the way toward the same small dispensing kitchen I'd taken Penny to. I was aware of Jonas looking around, silently taking everything in, just as I was aware of his every move. His every intake of breath.

It was damn annoying, that awareness.

"Coffee?" I said, increasing the length of my stride to pull away from him. "Or perhaps something to eat?"

"Coffee, one sugar if you have it."

Thankfully, he stopped in the middle of the room rather

than following me over to the machine, and looked around. "What was this place?"

I shrugged as I ordered two coffees. The machine, like the doors, was extremely slow to respond. "From what the ghosts have said, this floor contained secondary medical facilities, kitchens, and training for pubescent déchet."

His gaze came to mine, green eyes giving little away, but his energy watchful. Full of distrust. "How many areas can you access?"

The first coffee appeared. There was a hint of sweetness entwined through its bitter scent, so I handed it to Jonas. His fingers brushed mine as he took the cup, the brief caress electric.

"There's six floors that aren't filled with concrete," I said, resisting the urge to clench my fingers and keep hold of that electricity for a little bit longer. "But not all six are accessible. Some areas require eye scans and blood-work tests to enter. I haven't figured a way around them yet."

"You seem awfully proficient at working with old machines," he commented.

I shrugged and collected my coffee. "Mom was something of an electronics wizard. She used to find and repair old machines, and then sell them. That's how we survived."

Once again the lies slipped easily from my tongue. But it wasn't as if I could tell the truth—that with eternity stretching before me and little else to do, I'd read not only every scrap of material left behind in the bunker, but whatever I could find and steal from Central.

"So where did you live?"

"Everywhere. Nowhere. We moved around a lot, and most of it is a blur, to be honest." I gave him a thin smile. "Thanks to me, we weren't made that welcome in most places."

His gaze slipped down my length, a brief, judgmental

caress. "You do not have the scent of a human, so even if you *are* what you say you are, that should not have been a problem."

"'Shouldn't' doesn't equate to 'didn't,' ranger." I walked across to one of the padded benches lining the wall and sat down.

He considered me for a moment, then moved across to the bench along the wall opposite mine. Wanting to keep not only an eye on me, but distance also. It perhaps suggested he was well aware of the attraction flaring between us, even if he seemed to be controlling his reactions far better than I.

He took a sip of the bitter black liquid I called coffee and grimaced at its taste. But he didn't put it down, as Penny had with her water. "What were you doing in Central?"

I raised my eyebrows. "Nuri didn't tell you?"

His smile held little humor. "She cannot control what she sees. In this case, she saw where you would be, not what you were investigating."

Which was something, I guessed, and hopefully meant she would not "see" through my veil of lies and uncover what I was.

I leaned back against the wall and took a sip of coffee. "I didn't start off in Central. I actually started in Carleen."

He frowned. "What were you doing in Carleen?"

"Talking to the ghosts there."

"I didn't even *know* there were ghosts there."

"There are ghosts everywhere, ranger. You just have to be open to seeing them." I hesitated but couldn't help adding, "There's several déchet sitting with you right now."

He reached for his weapon with one hand, coffee splashing across the other, the action instinctive, automatic. *Fast.* As would be my death if he ever confirmed his suspicions about what I was. Then his gaze met mine and realization dawned. "*That* wasn't nice."

I couldn't help smiling. "No. But it was amusing all the same. Ghosts generally won't hurt you, ranger. Not unless you do something to hurt them, or someone they trust orders them to."

"Someone like you," he said, voice flat.

"Yes." It couldn't hurt to remind him I wasn't alone in this place.

He switched his coffee cup to his right hand and shook the remaining droplets of coffee from his left. "So what did the Carleen ghosts tell you?"

"That they left you alone only because you were tracking the wraith."

"Nice of them."

"Trust me, it was. There is a lot of hate in that place for your kind. I wouldn't advise going there without a damn good reason, because next time they might not be so generous."

"I will go where the investigation takes me, ghosts or not."

Then he was either very foolish, very brave, or had absolutely no experience dealing with the wrath of ghosts. "They said the wraiths were using what they called false rifts—rifts that are stationary and covered by that ill-feeling darkness that hovers over most of Carleen."

Jonas frowned. "What did they mean by 'false rifts'?"

"I'm not really sure, but their energy felt different from the energy I feel when I'm near the other rifts. Darker, dirtier, if that makes sense." I shrugged. "Anyway, I asked the ghosts to take me to the one the wraith and Penny last used."

Surprise flitted across his features. "*That* was a very

courageous step, given there are few who survive an encounter with a rift."

"Penny did, and more than once if the slashes on her arms are anything to go by." I frowned, suddenly remembering how quickly mine had healed. "Is Penny full shifter?"

"Yes," he said. "Why?"

"Because as I went through that rift, energy lashed at me. It left me with cuts similar to the scars Penny bears."

His gaze slid down. The small hairs on my arms rose, as if touched by electricity. Everything about this man, even his damn gaze, seemed to cause a reaction in me. "You don't have scars."

"No, because I heal quickly thanks to my shifter half. Penny should have the same healing abilities, and yet she bears scars."

He hesitated. "We suspect the drug program she and her family underwent might have made changes to her physiology."

Perhaps, but there was more than that going on with Penny. But I guessed I could understand his not wanting to tell a stranger, even if that stranger was someone he wanted to use. Or, at least, his boss wanted to use.

"The rift is the reason I was in Central. It spat me out into the basement of a brothel called Deseo on Twelfth Street."

"A brothel?"

"Yes. And you have to admit it's the perfect place to hide something you don't want anyone to find. It's not as if Deseo's customers would be too interested in exploring the premises when they're paying good money for other services."

"Yes, but surely the owners—"

"The owners," I cut in, "were scared to death of going

into the basement. But they were being paid to ignore it, anyhow."

"And you know all this how?" He studied me critically. "Via your seeker skills?"

I shook my head. "I had to smash the scanner to get out. The owner and a guard came to investigate. Apparently several people are renting the basement. You and Nuri need to uncover who those people are."

"As a seeker, you might be better placed to—"

"Sorry," I cut in, "but my skills lie in fixing old electronics and talking to ghosts, and that's as far as I'm willing to go."

For now, at least. What happened if Sal managed the impossible and got me a job was another matter entirely.

"Even if," Jonas said, "it might make the difference between saving those other kids or not?"

"Even if," I snapped back. "And *that* is a dirty card to play, ranger."

His smile held little in the way of mirth. "But it is nevertheless the truth."

"You and Nuri have resources I can only guess at. You're far better placed than a nobody living in an old military bunker to trace who Deseo's owners might be in contact with, or to place electronic surveillance on the brothel."

"Not electronic," he murmured, expression thoughtful as he drank some coffee. "Most businesses in Central do regular sweeps, even those on Twelfth. Information is a valuable commodity and can be bought and sold for vast sums."

And a brothel would be a perfect place to garner such information—especially for someone with seeker or reader skills. Was that how Sal had come to own a brothel on First? "Then how?"

He raised an eyebrow. "By placing someone inside, of course."

Of course. There was no better way than to garner secrets during the sexual act—it was what we lures had been designed for, after all. "Would that be Ela? The brown-haired shifter in the bar?"

He raised his eyebrows. "For someone who was only in that bar a few minutes, you seem to have done a very thorough sweep of its occupants."

"I'm a seeker," I said bluntly, "but in that particular case, anyone with half a brain would have sensed the tension in the air and taken note of who was where in case a fight broke out."

And now that I was actually thinking about it, that tension had been rather odd. If Nuri had been expecting me, believing I could help her, why had the shifters kept their hands close to their weapons—and even closer once I'd arrived?

"Who were the other people in the bar that day?" I added, "Were they from Central?"

"Yes." He half shrugged. "They were potential clients, but we got into something of a disagreement just before you arrived. It happens."

I wondered if the potential clients had anything to do with Penny's case. I suspected they might, if only because everything seemed to be aligning in an effort to force these people and me together on this investigation.

"And they left after I'd been darted?"

"Yes."

"Meaning," I muttered, "they're probably back in Central telling anyone who'll listen that there's a real, live déchet running around. Who cares if its the truth or not?"

"I doubt it," Jonas said. "Those particular shifters have

no desire to get involved with Central's authorities. If they're going to do anything, it'll be investigating the disappearances themselves. Besides, they won't find you in Chaos, and given Penny never mentioned this place in their presence, it's unlikely they'd find you even if they did search."

"I hope you're right, ranger, because the ghosts and I quite like our current situation."

"It is certainly more peaceful here than in either Chaos or Central," he agreed. "Who was that man you met there?"

I raised my eyebrows. "What business is it of yours who I meet?"

"Nothing, except for the fact that you led me on a merry dance almost immediately after meeting him, and yet up until that point showed no awareness of even being followed."

"Given I *wasn't* aware of your presence, it was hardly a deliberate attempt to lose you," I replied evenly. "We simply used a VTOL."

"I gathered." His expression was back to disbelief and anger, but I supposed that wasn't unexpected given we'd deliberately lost him and we both knew it.

I finished the last of my coffee, then tossed the cup in the nearby recycling slot and rose. "As lovely as this little chat has been, ranger, I need to sleep. You are welcome to claim whatever bench or bunk takes your fancy."

His eyebrows rose. "You trust me to roam around your sanctuary alone?"

"You are never alone. Not in this place." I gave him another humorless smile. "The ghosts will tell me if you attempt anything that endangers our home."

"Warning heeded." A slight trace of amusement warmed his lips and his eyes. "Enjoy your sleep."

"And you your investigations." I hesitated, remembering

my conversation with the adult déchet earlier. "But I *would* avoid the ninth level if you value your life. That is where the bulk of déchet bones lie, and they will not allow a shifter anywhere near them."

With that, I walked out and headed for the secondary medical center. The soft foam on the mediscan beds was comfortable, and there was no other bedding on this floor, as most of it had once been the training and teaching grounds for pubescent déchet. Some of the ghosts came with me—mostly the younger ones, as well as Bear and Cat. The rest remained to keep an eye on—and gossip about—Jonas.

Once in the medical center, I switched off all the monitors, then climbed into the bed the farthest from the door and closest to the wall. In very little time, I was asleep . . . and, rather annoyingly, dreaming of a shifter with a body of a warrior and fury for a heart rather than the lover I'd only just been reunited with.

Ghostly chattering woke me many hours later. I didn't immediately move or open my eyes, but simply let the small noises of the place envelop me. Beyond the ghosts' excited whispers about their adventures following Jonas last night, there was the soft sound of breathing. The ranger, in a nearby bed. His crisp, sharp scent spun around me, reminding me of the evening storms that came after a long, hot summer day. It even had the same sense of darkness and violence lying underneath it. Beyond Jonas, little else seemed to have changed. Silence stretched through the bunker's corridors, though the air was touched by the stench of the vampire I'd burned last night. Outside our bunker, dawn had stirred across the skies and, if the electricity in the air was anything to go by, it was going to be an unpleasant day.

I opened my eyes and met Jonas's bright gaze. He'd been watching me sleep, and the thought stirred through me enticingly. "Enjoy your investigations last night, ranger?"

"I did." His voice was a pleasant rumble, the anger within it briefly absent. "This place is vast."

"It was." I swung my feet off the bed and rose. "But much of it is now either unusable, inaccessible, or under concrete."

"Indeed." He sat up. "I didn't find much in the way of bathroom facilities in this place. Where do you shower?"

In the main bunk rooms, that's where. But given I couldn't admit I had access to that area, I simply raised an eyebrow and said, "Why? Are in interested in sharing one?"

His gaze slipped down my body and a smile briefly teased his lips. "Not when you wear that form. Your true self is much more pleasant."

"Pleasant" was such a nonword when it came to compliments. "How do you know the form you saw was my real one, and not this?"

"It's something of a talent." He shrugged. "What are your plans today?"

"Why are you asking?"

His smile lost its humor, and the warmth fled his bright eyes. "Because if you plan to go back to Carleen and investigate those other rifts, I very much intend to go with you."

Rather than respond to *that* declaration, I headed out of the room and walked back down the hall to the kitchen. Jonas followed, not willing to let me out of his sight, not even for a moment, it seemed. After ordering two coffees and several protein bars, I turned and said, "And if I don't?"

He shrugged. "Then I will wait until you do."

"Again, I have to ask, why?"

"Because *that* is what I have been ordered to do."

My eyebrows rose. "And do you always do what you're told?"

"It depends on the order." His gaze was heated, angry. Determined. "But in this case, my niece is involved. And I will do everything in my power to bring down those who are responsible for the change in her."

And heaven help anyone who got in his way, obviously. "What about the information I gave you on the rift in Deseo's basement?"

"Nuri has been informed, and will act on the information today."

I raised an eyebrow. "How? Communication devices don't work down here."

"We don't need them."

Meaning I was right—he and Nuri *could* share thoughts. The dispensing unit dinged a reminder. I handed Jonas both a coffee and protein bar, then picked up mine. "I guess we'd better get moving, then."

Surprise briefly touched his otherwise set expression. "This early?"

"The earlier the better, as there's not so many people about to catch me coming out of the bunker." I headed for the tunnel that would take us down to the seventh level and the South Siding exit. "Besides, I have plans to meet a friend tonight."

I could feel his gaze on me—a quicksilver caress that sent goose bumps flitting across my skin. And they weren't the result of fear or cold. Far from it. "Do these plans involve the same man you met last night?"

"That, ranger, is none of your business." I glanced over my shoulder. "And no, you cannot come with me, nor do I want you following me. In this case, three is most definitely a crowd."

One dark eyebrow rose. "Never fear, I'm not into voyeurism."

Maybe, I thought, *and maybe not.* Because if he gained even the slightest inkling that my meeting with Sal was anything *other* than pleasure, then watch he would.

"What about the vampires?" he added as we moved through the sixth-floor cross-link. "How do you intend to dispose of their bodies? Burning them under lights will make this place rather odorous."

I shrugged. "I can't risk dragging them out into the sunlight, as the smoke might attract unwanted attention. I'll just have to hope the ventilation system will have taken the worst of their smell from the air by the time I get back."

By the time we'd reached the pile of vampires—which were still smoldering thanks to the closeness of their carcasses to the wash of light—I'd finished my coffee. I placed the cup near the wall to recycle later, shoved the protein bar in my pocket, then determinedly walked to the pile of dead and began tossing them into the middle of the room. Jonas joined me and, in a very short time, the vampires were little more than disintegrating ash. But the smell of burned flesh was sharp and rank, and my stomach churned. Thank Rhea I was going out for the day.

I walked over to the room's control panel and set the lights to come on automatically with dusk. Then I ordered the ghosts to stay within its protection and not to approach the vampires should they attack again tonight. They were more than happy to comply.

With Cat and Bear dancing in front of me, I headed down the tunnel to the South Siding exit.

"Why do all the ghosts not come with you?" Jonas asked. "I would have thought they'd enjoy the break from the monotony of this place."

I shrugged. "Cat and Bear were closest . . ." I stopped abruptly. *To me when they gassed this place and we all died,* I'd almost said. I really *did* have to watch myself.

"Closest to what?" Jonas asked.

Though he was behind me, I could feel the weight of his gaze. Feel the force of thoughts as he tried to read my mind and pry free my secrets. But lures could not be read by anyone other than the strongest seekers—and there were few enough of those around.

"Closest to training age, from what they said. I guess it's natural for them to be more adventurous."

"But you said there are adult déchet in this place. Why would they be restrained?"

I shrugged. "I don't know. It's not like they talk to me all too often. It's usually just me and the children."

We reached the South Siding exit. The day was, as I'd sensed, crisp and cool, and overhead thunder rumbled ominously.

"Sounds like rain isn't very far off." His gaze swept the rubbish and ash-strewn dirt beyond the grate. "You might want to grab yourself a coat."

I might, but it involved going back to the restricted floors, and that still wasn't going to happen when he was near. "With the look of those skies, any coat I have will be next to useless inside of five minutes."

I opened the grate, then reset the lock code. I had no idea how the vampires got the grate open last night—or why they even needed to, given all they had to do was shadow to get in—but it wasn't going to happen again if I could help it. Once Jonas was out, I hit the lock switch, ensured the grate did come down, then guided the ranger around to the left, away from the rail yards.

"Why are we taking the long way around?" he asked as we walked up the hill to the back of the museum buildings.

"Because it's a good way of avoiding the guards and any chance of being questioned." I glanced at him. His skin was a warm, sun-kissed gold, even in the cool light of a storm-clad day. "I don't know about you, but I generally prefer to avoid the interest of officialdom."

"A point I totally agree with, so lead on."

We made good time around the museum and across the park, and in little more than an hour were approaching our goal. Rain splattered down, big fat drops that sizzled as they hit the broken road surface that divided this part of Carleen from the park. The battered curtain wall opposite us was covered in moss and vines, and there was nothing unusual to be seen—nothing other than the pressing darkness that was now forever a part of this place. And yet . . . energy crawled across my skin. An unnatural energy.

"There's a rift near here." Jonas's voice was heavy as he gazed thoughtfully to the left. "It's on the move."

I frowned. "How do you know that?"

His gaze came to mine and, just for an instant, the darkness I'd seen glimmering in both Penny's and Nuri's eyes shone in his. "I'm sensitive to them. It moves toward us, so if this false rift of yours is near here, we had better investigate it quickly."

I hesitated, my gaze scanning the wall again, wondering if the energy I felt was the approaching rift, the false one, or something else altogether. I couldn't tell, and that worried me.

At least I still had my guns and knives—not that they'd do much good against the force of either rift.

"Tiger?" Jonas prompted. "We need to move. Now."

I forced reluctant feet forward. The rain hit my body, slithering down my neck and plastering the thin shirt to my body, but it wasn't the cause of the chill that was growing in the pit of my stomach. The closer I got to the false rift, the more that chill grew. My two little ghosts crowded close, their energy bright sparks that shivered and danced across my skin.

I leapt onto the broken wall and paused to get my bearings. We were farther north than where I'd entered yesterday, but, after a moment, I saw the gnarled giant tree covered in moss and swept my gaze left. The hill wasn't too far away . . . neither was that crater, and its heavy darkness.

I jumped down and led the way through the tangled mess of destruction and regrowth. But the farther we got up that hill, the more the darkness stung my skin, until it felt as if my whole body burned with its presence. Something was different. Something had happened between yesterday and today. I looked around, suddenly aware of the ghosts who watched, and stopped.

"Is there a problem?" Jonas asked immediately, one hand on his weapon.

"That's what I'm about to find out. Keep an eye on that rift." I found somewhere safe to perch, then held out a hand, palm up. "Cat?"

She settled on my hand, then seeped down into my body. The creep of death immediately began to assault my limbs, faster and sharper than before. Doing this two days in a row was dangerous, but it wasn't like I had many other choices. The tall ghost I'd spoken to yesterday stepped forward.

"The gray creature was here last night," he said. "He moved one of the rifts."

"The real ones, or the false ones?"

"False. The one that was in the crater you went down yesterday now stains our resting place."

Why would he move a rift? Was it a result of my using it yesterday, or the subsequent destruction of the security panel? Either way, it just might mean they would be keeping a closer eye on their devices. "Is this the first time they've moved the rifts?"

"Since they made them, yes."

"'They'?" I frowned. "There's more than one?"

"There are three," he replied, anger in his expression. "Two men, one woman. You must stop them. That rift cannot be allowed to remain where it is. It stains our bones and ashes with its malevolence."

"I'll do what I can." I paused. "Can you give me a description? Were they all wraiths?"

"Wraiths?" he said, frowning.

"The gray beings with few features."

"Yes. Though two wore clothes of *this* world, and one wore pants similar to what you have on."

While that last bit matched what Penny had already said, it was odd for wraiths to be wearing clothes at *all*.

"Thanks again for your help."

He bowed. "My name is Blaine."

"Thanks, Blaine." Then I added silently, *Cat, time to leave*. Her energy seeped from me and the world spun, thick and dark and cold. A hand gripped me, holding me steady.

I drew in a shuddering breath; my hands and feet were heavy with the chill of death, and its frost lingered far too close to my lungs.

"Thanks," I said after a moment.

"What in hell just happened?" Jonas said. The warmth of his grip seeped into my body, flushing the chill from my skin.

"I was talking to the ghosts."

"Which ghosts?" His gaze briefly skated the immediate area, then came back to mine. "Carleen or yours?"

"Carleen." I gently pulled my arm free, though the heat of his touch lingered, continuing to warm me. "They said the wraiths were here last night, and that they moved the false rift I went through yesterday."

He raised his eyebrows. "Meaning they're likely aware someone used it."

"Or—given I destroyed the security panel in the brothel's basement—they're simply being cautious." My gaze swept the shadows that inhabited this place. "The ghosts also said there were three of them."

"Three wraiths?"

I nodded. "And all of them wearing clothes."

"Odd behavior for wraiths." He frowned. "It's not as if clothes would hide what they were."

"No." I took a deep, steadying breath, then waved a hand. "This way."

We walked across to the crater that contained the second of the false rifts, but stopped on its rim. The blackness within it crawled across my senses; it was a thick, gelatinous evil that stole my breath and made me want to run. The very *last* thing I wanted to do was go into that darkness, but there was no other way to discover where this rift might lead.

"The false rift lies at the bottom of this crater, below the shadows."

"What shadows?"

My gaze shot to Jonas. "What do you mean, 'what shadows?'" I waved a hand toward the blanket of darkness that lay only inches away from my fingertips. "I mean *that*."

He glanced down at the crater, then his gaze came to mine

again, his expression curious. "I see nothing. Nothing beyond a weather-torn bomb crater and a sea of white bones."

"But . . ." I hesitated, glancing at the thick shadows, seeing nothing beyond it. Feeling nothing beyond it. "You really *can't* see it?"

"I can't see whatever it is you see, obviously." He considered me for a moment, then moved forward, down into the crater. Within three steps he'd disappeared. The ghosts stirred around me anxiously.

"What about now?" he said. "Can you see me, or is there nothing more than shadow?"

The timbre of his voice hadn't changed. There was nothing of the stress, or the sheer, depressive weight of the darkness that made every step a struggle, in his words.

"Nothing but shadow."

"Odd. Wait there, and I'll investigate the base of this crater to see if there's anything more than old bones."

"The owners of those bones are watching, so be respectful."

"As much as I can be. Tell them I mean no disrespect."

"You just did."

"Oh." His voice was farther away. I waited, tension gnawing at my belly, wondering what was going on, why he couldn't see the darkness, and why it wasn't reacting to him.

"Okay," he said a few minutes later. "I've reached the bottom. There's nothing here but the dead. There's certainly nothing that resembles a false rift."

"I'm coming down." I hesitated, glancing at my ghosts. *Wait here.*

Concern whipped around me, but when I stepped toward the inky soup, they didn't follow. In three strides I was within it. It folded around me, thick and heavy, a weight so fierce every step was a battle. Only determination kept me moving forward.

"Tiger?" Jonas said. His voice seemed to be coming from a long way away. "You still there?"

I stopped and tried not to breathe too deeply or too fast. The last thing I wanted was to draw in any more of the thick air than necessary. "Yes. Why?"

"You took three steps into the crater and disappeared. There's something very strange happening here."

"Obviously. I'll meet you back at the rim."

I retreated. Leaving was a hell of a lot easier. Cat and Bear zipped around me, happy to have me back so soon, then settled near my shoulder, their energy caressing me as I sat on my haunches and waited for Jonas to return.

He appeared out of the gloom like a ghost becoming solid. His gaze ran past me, his green eyes narrowing as he studied some point to the left. "The rift is but a few minutes away. It has slowed but not yet stopped."

"Why is it you can sense the real rift and not the false one?"

His gaze came back to mine, his expression thoughtful. "I do not know. But we need to decide what we're going to do soon if we do not want to be caught in the true rift's mesh."

"There's only one thing we can do." I waved a hand at the inky blanket. "You can't see what I see, and I'd wager that means you won't be able to use it, either."

"Why don't we test that theory out?" He held out a hand.

I hesitated, then placed my hand in his. His warm fingers enclosed mine as he turned and tugged me forward. Only this time, there was no darkness, no weight, nothing but the eroded walls of the old crater and the bleached, white remnants of the dead at its base.

"There is definitely magic of some kind at work here,"

I muttered, "because when I'm holding your hand, I can't see anything but what is physically here."

"One more test, then." He released my hand. Instantly, the darkness descended and the light disappeared. I swore softly, but a heartbeat later, Jonas caught my fingers and once again the shadows fled.

"Whatever magic it is," he said, expression grim as he tugged me back toward the rim, "it appears you can both see it and react to it, but I cannot—even when we touch."

"Unfortunately, as I said earlier, that also means you're unlikely to be able to use the false rift that undoubtedly lies at the base of this place."

"Yes." Frustration fairly sizzled through that one short word. His gaze met mine. "What do you intend to do?"

"Go down there, of course. We need to find where the other children are, and this might just take us—or me—to them."

His smile was grim. "I do not think it'll be that easy."

Neither did I, but that didn't stop me hoping. "It might be worth getting Nuri down here. She may be able to unravel the threads of magic within this crater, or at least tell us where it might have originated from—here, or from the other side of the rifts."

He nodded and cast another glance over his shoulder. "We're out of time. The rift will be here in two minutes. I cannot stay. I will wait for you by the grate tomorrow morning." He paused, his expression hinting at anger again. "It would be advisable to let me in if you do not wish me to create a ruckus and draw unwanted attention to your retreat."

"Don't be early," I warned. "I'm meeting a friend tonight, remember."

"I remember." He took a step away, then paused again, meeting my gaze as he added, "Be wary."

"I will."

He walked away. I watched him for several seconds, admiring his lean outline and purposeful strides, then said softly, "Bear, Cat, follow him. Let me know everything he does, but make sure you get home by dusk." The other little ones would worry, otherwise, especially after last night's attack.

Their excitement kissed the air as they spun off after Jonas. I took another of those deep breaths that did little to calm the fear deep inside, then reached once more for the shifting magic. I had a bad feeling I'd need all the strength I could get; holding a form that wasn't mine was little more than a waste. At least until I knew what waited for me beyond the darkness of this rift.

The magic rose like a storm. I held my own image steady in my mind as my skin rippled, bones restructured, hair shortened and changed color. It still hurt, still burned. It always did, no matter how often I'd done it in the past. I gritted my teeth against the scream and did my best to ignore the sweat pouring down my altering flesh.

Then, finally, when the magic faded and I was once more as I was made, I stepped into the darkness. It felt ten times worse than it had only moments before. It was almost as if the magic sensed that *this* time, I intended to go all the way through it. It seemed heavier, more gelatinous; its thick strands resisted every step forward before they snapped, their fractured ends tearing at my flesh as they fell away. I have no idea how long it actually took to get through the barrier, but it seemed like forever. Even when I finally came to the base of the crater and broke free from the darkness, my sense of time and daylight was still scrambled. Whatever the magic was, it was playing merry havoc with that instinctive part of me.

For several minutes I did nothing more than stand there, sucking in air and waiting for the weakness in my limbs to retreat. The dark energy behind me crawled across my spine, but it was the energy in front of me that was sharper, more dangerous.

There was, as I'd suspected, another false rift here, and it was bigger than the one I'd gone through the previous day. It spun slowly on its axis, shimmering in the shadows, its surface regularly crisscrossed with jagged spears of lightning. The energy of them slashed the air and littered my skin with angry-looking welts. The cost of traveling through this rift was going to be far higher than yesterday's, but if I wanted answers, then I had to go in.

I drew my gun, flicked off the safety, and strode forward. The jagged lightning peeled away from the surface of the slowly rotating sphere and struck at me, drawing blood as it wrapped itself around my arms and my legs, first capturing me and then dragging me toward the sphere. Dust spun around me, thick and foul and filled with bone and jagged metal pieces—the remnants of the people and the buildings that had once stood here, no doubt. As the sphere encased me, its energy burned around me, touching every part of me before it slowly, carefully, tore me apart, atom by atom. It was agony itself, and if I could have screamed, I would have. There was no sense of movement this time, just blackness in which there was no light, no sound, no sense of life. Just pain and the feeling that my particles were being stretched to the breaking point. Then, piece by piece, the energy put me back together, the lightning holding me died, and I was ejected into darkness.

I stumbled for several steps, then, as my legs gave way, fell full-length onto a surface that was hard, gritty, and cold. And that's where I stayed, panting, groaning, my body on fire and the scent of blood thick in the icy air. I don't know how long I remained there, desperately trying to ease the inferno of pain sweeping through me, before I heard it.

A whisper of sound.

A footstep.

My breath caught in my throat and my fingers clenched around my gun. The thick darkness was again still, silent. But it was not without scent, and that scent was old and rank.

And filled with vampires.

CHAPTER 8

If the richness and depth of that scent was anything to go by, there weren't just a few vampires here, but a whole lot—maybe even a nest full. Most weren't close, but one, at least, must have caught the smell of my blood and had come to investigate. He was off to my left, in the deeper shadows near the filth-covered walls.

So why wasn't he attacking? If he'd been close enough to smell my blood, then he was close enough to have caught the beat of my heart and sense my humanity. Restraint was *not* something I'd ever associated with vampires before, and it filled me with foreboding.

But it also gave me a fighting chance of survival. *Not* that I intended to fight. If there were as many vampires here as the scent stinging the air suggested, then *that* would be nothing short of stupidity. I drew the darkness deep into my lungs and let it filter through every fiber, until it felt as if my whole body was vibrating with the weight and power of it.

The vampire within me rose swiftly to the surface, embracing that darkness, becoming one with it, until it stained my whole being and took over. It ripped away flesh, muscle, and bone, until I was nothing more than a cluster of matter. Even my weapons and clothes became part of the night and the darkness. In this form, at least, I'd be harder to pin down and nigh on impossible to feed on—or so my makers had said. It was a theory I'd never actually tested.

And, as I'd said to Jonas, there *were* vampires who fed on energy. I just had to hope there were none of *those* in this place.

I pushed away from the hard, grimy floor and moved forward. Though I had good night sight in my normal form, as matter the night was as bright as day, though it was a day without color. Everything was black and white, and inverse to what it normally would have been.

The room the false rift had spat me into was long and thin, reminding me somewhat of a corridor. I had no idea what lay beyond the rift itself, because it gleamed with a fire that was almost blinding. At the opposite end of the room lay the bent and broken remains of a metal door. Between it and me waited the vampire. In the inverse light, he was little more than a cluster of softly gleaming particles. He didn't move, didn't react, though I had no doubt he was as aware of my presence as I was of his.

It was a weird situation—and one that could change for the worse at any moment. For whatever reason, this vampire was restraining his instinctive urge to attack, and I had to make use of it.

I moved forward purposely, as if I had every right to be here. Anything else could be my downfall.

The vampire stirred. *Mistress?* His voice was scratchy, guttural, and something I sensed through my particles rather than actually heard—telepathy rather than spoken words. But the mere fact I was hearing him at all had shock rebounding through me. Never once had my makers—or anyone else, for that matter—ever suggested that vamps were capable of *any* kind of legible, intelligent speech. *You wish accompaniment?*

Why would he call me "mistress"? Who was he mistaking me for? Surely *not* another vampire? He'd been in this room when I'd shifted from flesh to shadow, and would be aware that I wasn't a true vampire.

Then I remembered the dark force I'd sensed when I'd rescued Penny, and the feeling that the actions of the vampires were being controlled. This "mistress," whoever she was, might be the force I'd sensed.

But the Carleen ghosts had said wraiths used these rifts, not vampires, and *that* suggested that the two might be working together. It was a possibility that had chills racing through me. If it was true, Central was in deeper trouble than we'd initially thought. Although, how in hell had the wraiths learned common tongue—a language that these days was used in all but a few provincial outposts? I had no doubt wraiths were intelligent, but why would they bother learning our language when we were nothing but prey to them?

And how were they even speaking when they had no mouths to form words?

But then, everyone had believed vampires incapable of speech, too, and that was very obviously wrong.

Maybe *that* was what they'd wanted the children for. Maybe they were somehow siphoning language skills from them. But if that was the case, why choose children? Why not adults?

The vampire's matter stirred, and I realized he was

waiting for an answer. *No*. I kept my mental tones low and scratchy, and kept mental fingers crossed it was a close enough imitation of whomever he was mistaking me for. *I wish aloneness*.

So be it. He melted away into the whiteness.

I didn't relax. One vampire might have let me be, but there were many others out there in the inverse night, and who knew what they might do?

I contemplated the broken door for a moment, then moved toward it. It was aeons old, thick with rust and slime. It also looked military grade—the same grade and design that was everywhere in my bunker.

Only trouble was, there *were* no other bunkers near Central, so where the hell was I? And why had the wraiths brought the children through here? Surely they hadn't been kept here—with the vampires present that would have been a little too like tying down a lamb and expecting the wolves not to attack.

I flowed over the broken door and moved into the whiteness beyond. The room again resembled a corridor, but this time there were various doors leading off it. Some were closed, some not. Most were empty, but from several came the thick sensation of vampire. There was no sense of awareness coming from their direction, which, I guess, was another point in my favor. While it was darker than night down here, it was still day above. Vampires generally slept when the sun was up. Given I could feel nothing *other* than vampires close by, I quickly moved on, anxious not to incite the interest of the vamps that slept here.

The corridor ended in a T intersection. There was a sign on the wall, but the writing had long given way to grime and was all but indecipherable. Only the tip of an arrow pointing to the left stood out. I followed its lead and headed that way, if only because the bulk of vampire scent seemed to be coming from the right. The corridor widened and the walls on either side gave way to thick windows. The wide rooms beyond them were filled with the broken remnants of uterine pods, tiny medibeds, and various other machines. My stomach—or what there was of it in this form—began to knot. This was looking more and more like the laboratories in my bunker. The laboratories in which they'd taken samples, testing and retesting the DNA of their latest batch of freshly birthed creations to ensure the health and viability of each before all were sent on to postnatal care.

This *had* to have been a déchet bunker—but which one? I knew of only three: Central had been the smallest, with the biggest near the port town of Crow's Point, and another deep in the Broken Mountains. I couldn't imagine vampires haunting *that* place, as there wasn't much in the way of hunting up there—not when it came to easy pickings, anyway. There *were* shifter communities living there now, but they tended to be nomadic in nature, and therefore had little need of the sewerage and service tunnels that had made life so much easier for the vampires in many human communities, even in this day and age. There might be plenty of cities as protected as Central, but not everyone lived in such places, and many of these smaller communities were as ill prepared as Chaos when it came to the vampires.

I continued on. Up ahead, the darkness began to grow, which in this inverse lighting meant *actual* light rather than darkness. Which was confusing, as any sort of light was dangerous to vampires.

And if the wraiths were working with the vampires, at least in some capacity, why would they have *any* part of this place lit up so brightly? They hated it as much as the vampires.

As I drew closer to the light, the darkness within me
began to unravel. Muscle and bone found structure and
re-formed, until I was once again fully fleshed. The scanner to the right of the heavy metal door *beep*ed as I
approached, then slid open. What it revealed was a fully
functioning laboratory.

I stood outside the door for a moment, scanning the wide
room, letting the feel of it wash over me. There were no
ghosts in this place, no scents other than antiseptic. Metal
examination tables gleamed, and the medibeds that lined
the far wall—six in all—made mine look like something
out of the Stone Age.

I took a step, then froze as red light flared from either
side of the doorway and scanned me. A heartbeat later an
alarm went off, the sound sharp and strident in the silence.

I spun and raced back into the darkness, gathering it
around me as quickly as I could. Ahead, in the corridor
beyond the T intersection, vampires began to stir. I couldn't
risk staying here. Couldn't risk having them realize I was
not one of them. There had to be at *least* two score of them
here, if that stirring sense of evil was anything to go by.
I'd barely survived an attack by one score—and even then
only with the help of my little ghosts. Two score was death,
pure and simple.

I came to the T intersection and surged to the right. The
vampires in the long corridor had come to life; their energy
milled, and their confusion and uncertainty stained the
air. I controlled my own fear and slowed my headlong
pace. To get through, to survive, I had to make them
believe I belonged here—that I *was* whoever that first vampire thought I was.

Mistress? A different tone, harsher and scratchier than
the first. *Problem?*

Alarm fault, I growled back. *I go get others.*

The energy of them parted slightly, leaving me a slender pathway to the room with the false rift. I took a deep mental breath and moved through them, feeling their wrongness slither through every part of my being.

If I could feel them, they could undoubtedly feel me.

Tension ran through my particles, and all I wanted to do was run—the one thing I couldn't do when in the midst of them.

I was midway through when the energy around me began to change. Their confusion deepened, hardened. Became dangerous. I didn't alter my pace; any move, any suggestion of fear, would have them all over me. Yet fear stepped into my heart nevertheless, and its stain ran through my matter.

Wrong, a voice at the back growled. *Not mistress.*

Rhea save me, I thought, and bolted, with every ounce of speed I could muster, for the false rift. I tore through the energy of several vampires, felt their matter slash at me—through me—a sensation not unlike sharp claws tearing at flesh. Particles ripped and spun away, and I realized the true depth of the situation I was in. They didn't *have* to force me into flesh. They could render me dead by simply tearing me apart, piece by energy piece.

I bolted over the broken door and streamed toward the false tear. There was no reaction as I drew close. The sphere showed no awareness of my presence and no jagged bolts of energy leapt out from the brightly lit surface to snag me.

Flesh, I realized suddenly. It was set to react to flesh, *not* matter.

I swore and began unraveling the shadows. Halfway down the room I hit the floor running, even as the darkness continued to bleed from my torso. The vampires screamed and claws lashed at me, biting deep, drawing blood. One arm re-formed; I was still gripping my weapon, so I fired it. The wooden stakes tore through shadows to the left and the right and bounced harmlessly off the walls. Hair re-formed; hands snagged at it and yanked me backward. I fired over my shoulder, heard the squawk as the wood tore into flesh and the taint of blood stained the air. The scent seemed to incite greater fury in the vampires, but they didn't tear their fallen comrade apart. Didn't eat his flesh and drink his blood. They simply ran over the top of him and continued to tear at me, their desperation and fury so fierce I could barely even breathe.

The surface of the false tear began to rotate. The lightning stirred, flickered, as I drew closer. One jagged bolt speared out, wrapping around my ankles, capturing me. I stumbled, swore, then caught my balance, trying to move faster than that burning, biting lash seemed to desire. More claws tore at me as another jagged piece of energy snared my other leg. The vampires were close—far too close.

With no other choice, I stopped running, twisted around, and raised both weapons, firing nonstop as I was drawn purposefully—but far too slowly—toward the rift. There were at least twenty vampires fighting to get at me, and more pouring through over the broken door as I watched.

I needed space. I needed time. Needed to get into the false rift and hope like hell I had the strength to survive its agony. Because no matter what, I wasn't about to stay *here*.

Some vampires fell under the barrage of stakes, but others spun into darkness, re-forming once the bullets had torn past. Their screams filled the air, their fury and desperation to stop me evident in the bloody glow of their eyes.

Dark energy lashed my back. Whips snaked out and

snared my upper arms, its touch biting deep. Blood stained my shirt, and the scent fueled the vamps into a greater frenzy. One gun clicked over to empty. I tried to snag it back onto my belt and reach for a knife, but the sphere's energy had pinned my upper arm to my body and severely restricted my movement. I swore and kept firing the second.

The vampires lunged at me from all sides. I screamed and thrust backward—straight into the fierce energy of the false rift. It sucked me in, then ripped me apart, and I hung in the darkness for I don't know how long, silently screaming, unable to do anything else. Then, with agonizing slowness, my particles were reassembled and, with little finesse and a whole lot of force, I was ejected.

I didn't even stumble. I just fell flat on my face and, for who knows how long, I stayed there.

After a while, I somehow found enough energy to roll onto my back. All I could smell was my blood, and it felt as if every bit of me had been beaten and bruised. Even my soul ached.

I took a deep, shuddering breath that did little more than fling a dozen fresh arrows of pain across my torso. I ignored them, closed my eyes, and reached for the healing. It took a while, but eventually, calm descended and my body began to repair itself. Unfortunately, the healing state didn't last anywhere near long enough. While I could heal just about any wound short of limb, head, or heart removal, the depth of the repairs depended on my strength. I'd pushed myself hard today, and all with little more than bitter coffee in my belly. It wasn't enough.

But at least blood no longer poured from the multitude of slashes caused by both the vampires and the false rift. It was better than nothing, I supposed.

I rolled onto my hands and knees, then slowly pushed

upright and stared at the wall of darkness that stood between me and getting home. The thought of going through it again churned my stomach, but there was no other option. Not if I wanted to get out of this place—and I did. Desperately.

I forced my feet forward. The darkness soon enveloped me, its thick strands resisting every step forward but not as fiercely as it had on the way down. Nor did it tear at my flesh as it snapped away—which was good, because I doubted I had a whole lot of unmarred skin left.

I came out of it so suddenly I stumbled and fell on my hands and knees. Energy whipped around me, filled with concern, and it took me a moment to realize it was Bear and Cat. Then the little bit of strength I had left fled, and I fell into unconsciousness.

I woke to shadows and noise. There was warmth around me and comfort underneath me rather than the chill of the weather and the cold bite of ground. The air smelled murky and was thick with so many scents it was hard to pick one from the other. Obviously, I was no longer in Carleen.

I frowned and opened my eyes. The room in which I lay was small and neat, with little more than the bed, a side cabinet, a somewhat grimy mirror, and a washbasin beside which rested two small but clean-smelling blue towels.

Cat and Bear whisked in from wherever they'd been, the force of their excitement making me smile even as their energy seeped into my skin, allowing me to share their adventures and explorations. Images flowed through me, around me, in dizzying succession, filling me in on all that had happened even if in a somewhat confused manner. We were not only back in Chaos, but also at Nuri's. Jonas, from what I could gather, had carried me here—over his shoulder, like a bloodied sack of potatoes. He was in the room next to mine, stripping off clothes stiff with my blood—which suggested we had not been here very long at all.

And Jonas? I asked them. *What did he do while I was away?*

More images flooded my mind. Jonas had retreated as far as the park, but once the rift had passed, had come back to the rim of the crater to wait. Nuri had joined him a few hours later, and while she'd prowled around the edges of the crater, she hadn't entered it. The Carleen ghosts, Cat noted, had been wary of her.

I frowned again. *Why are ghosts afraid of her?*

Their uncertainty filled me, then Bear's energy touched mine more deeply and he said, *It is the darkness, as much as her power, that they fear.*

I guess I could understand their fearing her power, because witches traditionally had control over the dead and she could, if she so chose, banish or destroy them.

Before I could question them further, the door opened and Nuri ducked into the room. "Ah, you're awake," she said, not sounding the least bit surprised. She held a large jug in one hand and clothes in the other. The room was almost too small for someone her size, though it wasn't so much her weight but rather the sheer amount of power radiating from her. It overwhelmed this tiny space. Was it any wonder the Carleen ghosts feared her? They surely wouldn't have come across many like her, even when they'd been alive.

"I'm afraid your clothes were a little beyond repair," Nuri continued, "so you'll have to make do with this tunic. Your weapons are in the shoulder bag at the base of the bed. Once you're washed and dressed, come downstairs and join us. We've fresh bread and stew ready, if you're up to eating."

"How long have I been here?" I said as she poured the hot water into the small basin.

She glanced at me, brown eyes shrewd. "Worried about that date you have this evening, are you?"

Jonas obviously didn't feel the need to be restrained in *any* of the information he passed on. I raised an eyebrow. "And what business of yours is it if I was?"

She smiled, though there was very little humor in it. "No business of mine at all, though I cannot help but be curious as to what is so important about that date you would rush off so soon after near death."

Near death? I'd been depleted and bloody, for sure, but I doubted I'd been anywhere near death—though, given what Cat and Bear had showed me, I'd certainly *looked* it.

"Perhaps I merely desire the company of the man I'm intending to meet." I paused. "How long was I out?"

"Not long enough by half." She finished pouring the water, then turned to face me. All sorts of speculation was evident in her sharp gaze. "Come downstairs and tell us what you found. You owe us that much, at least."

I owed them nothing, and we both knew it—especially after their initial attack on me. But this mystery was already far bigger than I could handle. I needed help, and Nuri and her shifters were the logical choice—even if a dangerous one, given their undenied government links.

"Fine," I said. "I'll be down in ten minutes."

She nodded and left, closing the door behind her. I listened to her retreating steps, then flicked the blanket off and rose. Muscles twinged, but there was little in the way of true pain. Most of the lash marks had disappeared, but there was a cut on the inside of my left wrist that was raised and angry-looking. It was, I suspected, where the vampire had slashed through my particles, spinning some of them away. And maybe that meant it wouldn't—couldn't—heal any more than it already had. Dried blood stained most of my body, as well as matting my hair, if the itchy state of my scalp was anything to go by.

Grimacing, I grabbed one of the towels and the flowery-smelling soap, and cleaned myself up. Then I dunked my head into the bowl, scrubbing my short hair, freeing as much of the gunk as I could, even as I wished I was back at the bunker and in one of the hydro pods.

The tunic Nuri had left for me was full-length, and made of a soft gray wool. It was V-necked and split to the thigh along one side to allow easier movement. I'd worn this type of garment many times in the various camps I'd been assigned to during the war, and knew from experience they were not only extremely comfortable, but also sexy, as the flowing nature of them accentuated rather than hid curves. It was the sort of garment I could easily wear to meet Sal tonight, and couldn't help wondering if I'd been given it for that very reason. There was a pair of leather sandals with the dress, and they also fit perfectly.

I glanced at a mirror and frowned at my reflection. As much as I rather liked the startling contrast of white and black stripes in my hair, I'd seen no tiger shifters in Central for a while, which meant I'd stand out a little too much in that place. And given I needed to be orange if I were to have any hope of getting the job at Winter Halo, maybe it would be better if I started wearing that form to get comfortable with it. I pictured what I wanted in my mind, then reached for the shifter magic. It swept through me, fierce and fast, and in very little time the stripes were replaced by orange and my naturally lean form was a little more curvaceous.

Which meant it was time to go downstairs and face

Nuri and her crew. I slung the hessian bag holding my weapons over my shoulder, took a deep, steadying breath, then said, "Let's go get this over with."

Bear whipped around me, excited we were on the move again, and headed out. Cat, as usual, stayed close, though there was little in the way of concern in her energy.

Jonas waited in the corridor beyond our door. His muscular arms were crossed and he leaned one shoulder against the opposite wall, his stance casual yet oddly guarded. His dark hair was damp, and he smelled fresh, clean, and wild. His gaze swept down my length, a leisurely caress that sent delight skittering across my skin. Desire stirred, its scent stinging the air, his and mine combined. But when his gaze finally rose, there was little of that heat evident in either his expression or his eyes. This man might want me, but he still didn't trust me, and that, right now, held greater sway over his actions. His restraint should have pleased me—he was a ranger, after all. The war had been a long time ago, but it seemed that—for him—it might well have been only yesterday. I had no doubt sex with Jonas would be good, but it would also, given that hate, be dangerous. It would take only one tiny slip on my part, and that would be the end of me. And yet I also knew that none of it would have made any difference had he shown an inclination to act on desire.

But then, I'd been bred to seduce shapeshifters such as he—shifters who were not just warriors, but leaders. Jonas might not be in control of this little lot, but I had a suspicion he could have been. That once upon a time, he *had* been. Maybe not of this group, but another. There was just something in the way he moved, something in the way he reacted, that reminded me of the shifters who'd been my targets so long ago.

"This way," he said, and pushed away from the wall.

I followed his easy strides along the short corridor, then down a set of stairs. The room we entered was the small one I'd seen when linked to Bear the first time I'd been in this place—the one with the small electric stove and half a dozen motley-looking chairs. Only one of those was currently occupied—unfortunately by Branna, the thickset, golden-haired man who'd darted me with Iruakandji. I flared my nostrils as I neared him, drawing his scent. It was sharper—dryer—than Jonas's, reminding me more of grass and sand rather than the wildness of storms.

His golden gaze swept me, enticing little in the way of reaction, then lifted, lingering longest on my hair. He didn't say anything; he simply rose and walked to the other side of the room, as far away from me as was possible without actually leaving. Where he could watch, and react if needed, I very much suspected.

Bear, you want to keep an eye on him? He'd already acted once without thinking—I had no doubt he'd do it again if I so much as twitched the wrong way. It was a somewhat common occurrence among male lion shifters, who tended to be fiercely protective of friends and family. Bear whisked off to stalk the grim-faced Branna, but Cat stayed close.

"Stew?" Nuri asked, holding a metal spoon over the divine-smelling pot of meat and vegetables.

"Definitely," Jonas said. He grabbed the bowl she offered him and headed for the small table tucked behind the stove.

"Tiger?" Nuri glanced at me and raised an eyebrow. I had no doubt she'd noted the change of color, but she made no mention of it. But then, Jonas had no doubt informed her I was a body shifter, so it wouldn't have come as a surprise.

"Yes, thanks." I tried not to sound like I hadn't eaten

fresh meat for the best part of a year. Stealing fruit and veg was one thing, but meat was expensive and not so easily snatched. And wildlife was rare in the park these days, thanks to the vampires. Jerky—my main meat source—was definitely a poor substitute.

She handed me a large bowl, and I followed Jonas to the table. It had been set for four, and there was a large loaf of bread sitting in the center.

I slung my bag over the back of the chair opposite Jonas and sat down. Nuri sat to my right. Branna stayed right where he was. Maybe he wasn't hungry. Or maybe Nuri thought putting him in close quarters to me wasn't such a good idea, and had ordered him on watch.

"So," I said, figuring I might as well get the conversation happening, "what did you make of the magic that lies within that crater?"

Nuri picked up her spoon and ate some stew, considering me as she munched. "It is unlike any magic I have come across before."

I scooped up some of the stew, and briefly closed my eyes in utter enjoyment.

Amusement crinkled the corners of her eyes. "Good, huh?"

"The best stew I've tasted in years." Hell, it was the best stew I'd tasted since the war, but I couldn't exactly say that. "So the magic *is* wraith in origin?"

Nuri slid the bread across to me. "No, it's not, though there are parts of it that definitely have their feel."

I tore off a chunk of bread, then pushed the loaf over to Jonas. "Meaning what? That the wraiths have learned our magic?"

"No, rather the other way around. Someone here has learned theirs."

I frowned. "How is that even possible? The wraiths

don't speak our language, nor do they hang about long enough to learn it. They just appear, kill, and leave."

"That is the truth as far as anyone is aware," Nuri said. "But that doesn't mean things haven't changed."

"Something certainly has," Jonas commented. "The mere fact the wraiths are getting into Central to steal children is evidence enough of that."

"They could be coming through that rift I found in Deseo's basement. It may not be a direct line from their world into ours, but there are plenty of rifts in Carleen. At least some of them would have to be active entry points for the wraiths."

"Even if they *were* using the rift in the brothel," Jonas said, between mouthfuls of stew, "it still doesn't explain how they're getting from that basement and into the children's homes without being either seen or crisped by the UVs."

"Unless, of course, they have help from someone in Central," Nuri commented. "And I'm afraid I believe that to be the case."

I munched on some bread. It was still warm, and as delicious as the stew. "But how would the wraiths even make a deal with someone from Central? As I've already said, they don't speak our language, and it's not like they can advertise."

Nuri half smiled. "True. And I don't think that's what's happening here, anyway. The magic is more a bastardization from both worlds, and there is something very volatile about its feel. It's almost as if the two were fused together by force rather than desire."

"Meaning what?" Jonas asked.

She shrugged. "I don't know yet. I need more time to study that barrier."

"And the false rift in Deseo?" I said. "What's happening with that?"

"Ela—the other shifter your little ghost saw in the bar—has just acquired a job there. She'll keep an eye on who goes into—or comes out of—that basement."

"She can hardly be there twenty-four/seven. And Jonas said electronic surveillance is impractical."

"Which it is," Nuri agreed. "And that is why Ela is not the only one going in."

I raised my eyebrows. "How many people do you have working for you?"

"*With* me, not for me." Amusement touched her lips. "The core group is four, but we have half a dozen shifters we trust who we can call on in times of need."

"Are those shifters the same ones you were having the disagreement with when I first arrived with Penny?" I paused. "How is she, by the way?"

"No. And Penny . . . she's okay." Nuri hesitated. "We're currently keeping her isolated, as I can't break past the darkness that clouds her thoughts, and I do not trust it."

"There *was* something about her manner that disturbed me." My gaze swept from Nuri to Jonas and back again. "But I figured it was the same shadow that I sometimes sense in both of you."

"Did you, now?" Nuri shared a brief glance with Jonas. "But you're wrong. Whatever you sense in our auras, it is not the source of Penny's current problems."

Which didn't tell me a whole lot. "Then what do you think is?"

She hesitated. "I'm not sure, but it has the same basic feel as that barrier in the crater."

"Meaning Penny is linked to the barrier somehow?" Even as I asked the question, a very bad feeling began to grow deep inside me. *That* barrier had ultimately led to a rift that had taken me to a laboratory guarded by vampires—and if the darkness of that barrier had infused Penny's aura, what were the chances that whatever was happening to her also somehow linked her to the vampires?

"Either that, or she's linked to whomever created that barrier." Nuri paused, and her power surged briefly, burning across my skin, tasting, testing. "What is it?"

I swallowed my mouthful of stew and met her gaze. "Is it possible the darkness within that barrier also has the taint of vampire?"

She frowned. "Vampires are not capable of magic."

"No, but they *do* share a collective consciousness."

"Yes, but I don't see how that connects to the barrier and Penny."

"The false rift I went through today took me into some sort of old military bunker," I said, "within which was a new and fully functional lab. It was protected by lights, but the vampires were protecting the lab itself."

"Which explains the mess you were in when you appeared back in Carleen," Jonas murmured. "It's a wonder you managed to get out if you appeared in the middle of a nest."

"It wasn't a nest." I met his somewhat skeptical gaze evenly. "And they were initially asleep."

"I'm still not seeing why you think Penny and the vampires might be linked," Nuri said, with another of those warning looks to Jonas.

I hesitated. "Last night, when the vampires attacked my bunker, they also raised the grate that protects it. Aside from the fact they didn't need to, no one but myself and my ghosts know the code for that gate. No one but Penny, who saw me key it in."

"That's a bit of a stretch," Jonas commented. "For a start, the technology is so old it would probably take someone with an electronic lock pick all of three seconds to crack."

"Did you see a pick on the vampires? I didn't." Not that a pick would have been easy to see given the situation, but that was beside the point. "And, as I said, why would they want the grate open when they could shadow and flow through it?"

"They wouldn't," Nuri said. "Unless, of course, they were checking the code for someone else."

I nodded. "Hence my asking whether that darkness contained any hint of vampire. It might be possible that we face not only a coalition of wraiths and someone in Central, but vampires as well."

"*Not* a possibility I wish to contemplate," Nuri murmured.

"We may not want to, but we can't ignore the possibility, either."

Nuri leaned back in her chair, her expression thoughtful. "Any idea where this vamp-infested lab might be?"

"No." I tore off some more bread and scraped the remains of the stew out of my bowl. "But, as I said, it was an old military bunker, and there were several disused labs that reminded me an awful lot of the labs within my bunker—though I was under the impression the humans of Old Central had only the one déchet base near here."

"They did. The others were in Crow's Point and in the Broken Mountains." She pursed her lips. "There *were* several satellite military installations, of course. It's possible we're dealing with one of those."

"There were old uterine pods and neonatal medibeds in the disused labs," I said. "Not something the regular military would need, I'd imagine."

"No." Her gaze met mine. "Are you sure it wasn't some

part of your own bunker, a section you haven't uncovered yet?"

"I'm sure." My reply was a little sharper than necessary. "Aside from the fact there didn't appear to be any ghosts in this installation, my bunker isn't infested with vampires."

"That you know of," Jonas said. "It's possible the inaccessible areas could be."

"No, they're not, because the ghosts don't have my restrictions, and they'd tell me if the vampires were there."

He raised an eyebrow. Though there was little in the way of expression on his face, in the bright depths of his eyes curiosity, distrust, and desire all burned. It was a mix that was oddly compelling. "Yet you yourself said not all the ghosts talk to you."

"The adults don't." He was still baiting me, still trying to trip me up, even if the question was a logical one. "But the children have been there for over one hundred years, and they know that place inside out. They'd tell me if vampires had suddenly become a feature."

"Which means it must be one of the other déchet facilities." Nuri tapped the table lightly, the sound echoing. "Although it seems odd that if the people behind this are based in Central, they would have their lab facilities so far away."

"But it's not that far away. Not when they're using the false rifts to transport there and back."

"Yes, but the rifts are hardly practical if they cause so much damage to the user." Jonas crossed his legs under the table, but his calf brushed mine in the process and sent warmth spiraling through the rest of me.

This attraction, I thought, as I edged my legs away from his, was getting ridiculous.

"Just because the false rifts harm me doesn't mean they

similarly affect those who created them. If they have the skill to make them, then they also have the skill to program their DNA into them. I doubt they would suffer the same sort of difficulties I did when using it."

"Penny suffered much the same type of wounds," he said.

"Yes, but why would they bother programming the DNA of the children into it? The number of them alone would make it too hard."

"It would also take too much time and energy, for little gain," Nuri agreed, voice heavy. "From what I could glean from Penny, they're using these children as test subjects and don't exactly care whether they live or die."

"And yet," I said, "they're not truly mistreated. Penny is undernourished, but she isn't ill."

"That might only be due to the authorities finally seeing the pattern in the disappearances. Best to take care of the test subjects you have if getting new ones is increasingly more difficult." Her sharp gaze came to mine, and again her power swept me, intense and oddly filled with expectation. "The question is, what's *your* next step?"

I leaned back in my chair and contemplated, once again, the wisdom of trusting these people. Cat stirred and her emotions washed through me, urging me to trust, to help. To find the children and make them safe. And it was that, more than anything, that remained the controlling factor here. If not for the fact there were children involved—children who might yet be saved—I definitely would have walked.

I scrubbed a hand across my eyes, then said, "That depends."

"On what?" Nuri asked evenly.

"On how fast you can get me working ID for Central. The friend I'm meeting tonight said he might be able to arrange an interview with the recruitment officer at Winter Halo." My gaze flicked to Jonas as I said it, though I'm not entirely sure why. It wasn't like he was going to show any reaction given we were strangers and he refused to even acknowledge the attraction between us. "He'll tell me tonight if he was successful or not."

"ID is not a problem. In fact, we could do it now. Branna, get the scanner." As Branna made a noise not unlike a growl before he walked away, Nuri added, "Who is this friend of yours?"

I raised an eyebrow. "Why?"

She half shrugged. "I'm curious, because the timing seems . . . fortunate."

"Fortunate how?"

"When you first came here"—she gestured at the room with one hand—"you reminded me somewhat of a feral cat—fierce, skittish, and distrustful of both Chaos and us. You had the air of someone who kept very much to herself, and who socialized little. With the living, anyway."

As summations went, she'd pretty much nailed it. But then, she was a seeker, and no matter how much I'd tried to control my emotional output, she would nevertheless have caught the odd unguarded moment. Especially given she was also a witch of some power.

"And now?"

"The distrust remains, but there is more life in you. More . . . awareness and warmth, in a sense. It is as if a long-ignored part of you has come to life."

Another good summation. Part of me *had* come to life, and the more time I spent with Sal, the harder it was going to become to get that part of me under control once this all ended.

The thought made me frown. Sal lived in Central—had

for some time—so why did it have to end? I really didn't know. Intuition might be part and parcel of being a seeker, but weaving together emotions and images and coming up with judgments was something so ingrained it became a subconscious activity rather than a conscious one. And sometimes, those judgments *remained* at a subconscious level.

So what had I picked up on Sal that made me think my association with him would not be long-term? Was it the change I sensed in him or merely caution?

I didn't know, and that was worrying.

"I don't see how all *that* relates back to my meeting."

"I'm not sure myself," she admitted. "It's just a feeling. You, us, the missing children, the sudden appearance of an old friend in your life. I think they're all linked, even if I can't yet see or find the connecting threads."

"I never said his appearance was sudden."

She smiled. "There are some things in this world you don't *have* to say. So, what is his full name? I think we should have him checked out, if for no other reason than to ensure he *is* the man you remember."

I hesitated, but as much as I didn't want to admit it, she was right. Meeting Sal might be nothing more than a coincidence, but when combined with that odd itch that Sal and I were not destined to be long-term, then yes, I needed to be careful.

"It's Sal Casimir. He runs the Hedone brothel on First."

Jonas's eyebrows rose. "You *do* have some high-flying friends. Especially for someone who generally lives like a hermit."

"Preferring the company of my ghosts is more a matter of caution rather than reclusion. And with welcomes like the one you gave me, can you blame me?" Though I tried to keep my voice mild, a touch of anger crept through regardless.

Maybe Jonas's attitude was catching. "And it certainly *doesn't* mean I can't enjoy the occasional dalliance. Sal's appearance was certainly fortunate in more ways than one."

Amusement fleetingly touched his lips, and it transformed his weatherworn but ruggedly handsome features, lending him a warmth and vibrancy that was almost breathtaking. It was gone just as quickly as it appeared, but the memory of it lingered deep inside.

Branna returned, thumped some sort of scanner onto the table, then stomped off.

"Pleasant sort of chap, isn't he?" I murmured, not sure whether to be amused or concerned about his continuing suspicion. It was deeper—angrier—than the disbelief I sensed in Jonas, and far more dangerous. And yet he seemed very much leashed. Nuri might have said she worked with these men, but when it came to Branna, she was at the controlling end of his chain.

"It is not in his nature to trust. It never has been." Jonas reached for the scanner and pressed a small button. The scanner came to life, blue light gleaming softly from the device's small screen. "It was a year before he began to speak to me with any degree of civility."

"A year? I'm surprised you put up with that sort of attitude for more than even a few days."

He smiled, but it was filled more with sadness and memories than warmth or humor. "That's not something any of us really had any control over."

I frowned. "Meaning you were forced into each other's company? How?"

"That," Nuri said heavily, "is a story for another day. We've already set up an ID for you. All we have to do is scan in your image and physical attributes, and it will be good to go."

I frowned. "What name did you give me?"

Amusement teased her lips. "Ti Zindela."

"Interesting choice," I murmured. Especially given "zindela" meant "man's defender."

"I thought it was appropriate," she said, voice mild.

Leaving me wondering yet again just how much her seeker skills had picked up on me. Obviously not *too* much, otherwise I doubted they'd be sitting near me so calmly.

Jonas rose, the scanner in one hand. "Let's get this done, then you can head off for your meeting with the lover. You want to stand over near the wall?"

I rose and walked over there. Jonas followed me, a presence that washed heat across my spine despite the fact he wasn't close.

"What address did you give me?" I asked as I turned around. "Here?"

Nuri shook her head. "You're not likely to get a job anywhere in Central if you list Chaos as your address. They tend to ignore us at the best of times."

I frowned. "Then what did you put?"

"Smile," Jonas said. "Unless, of course, you want a frown to be your ID comparison picture."

I flashed a brief smile. "Better," Jonas said, and hit a button. Blue light scanned me, running my length several times before *beep*ing.

I glanced at Nuri, eyebrow raised.

"There's an inn called Old Stan's on Twelfth run by friends of mine. We've used them for cover purposes before. They'll run interference on any queries you might get, or pass them on to us."

"Okay," Jonas said. "It's done. Give me your right wrist."

I held it out. He wrapped his fingers around my hand, his grip warm and strong as he pressed the unit against the underside of my wrist. The machine emitted another *beep*, then there was a short, sharp sting as the RFID chip was inserted under my skin.

"You're now officially one of them," Jonas said, his grip lingering perhaps a little longer than necessary.

"Great," I muttered, glancing down at my wrist. The skin was slightly red where the chip had been inserted, but other than that, there was little sign of its presence.

"You'll need to learn these points off by heart." Nuri slid a piece of paper across the table toward me. "It's your birth date, where you were born, et cetera. They will ask you, even if they can get the info from the RFID."

Jonas stood to one side. I brushed past him, my skin tingling at the brief but luscious contact, and picked up the piece of paper. "Newport?" I glanced at Nuri, eyebrow raised. "It's a back-of-nowhere town—why choose that as my birthplace?"

"Because fifteen years ago a virus voided the town's RFID system, rendering all birth and death records up to that point irretrievable."

"How fortunate." My voice was dry.

"It was, rather. And no, we didn't do it. We do, however, make use of it. Central won't check your records because they can't."

"Surely they'd have to be aware that such destruction would be open to abuse by . . ." I hesitated, searching for the right word, not wanting to give offense.

"Less-than-savory types?" Nuri prompted, with a smile. "And yes, they are. Which is why we've also given you a work history that *can* be checked."

I frowned. "Your organization is sounding bigger and bigger."

"We're mercenaries," Jonas commented, moving back

around to his side of the table. "And there's a large network of us who work on a quid pro quo basis. We back their histories, they back ours, as necessary."

"And," Nuri added, "the relevant people have already been informed of your new ID."

Huh. These people didn't muck around any. I folded the piece of paper and tucked it into my pocket. "There's one other thing I need."

"That being?" Nuri asked.

"I want to talk to some of the women who worked the night security but quit."

"We already have," Jonas said. "They couldn't tell us much."

"Maybe they couldn't tell *you* anything," I said, "but maybe they'd talk to me, as another applicant."

"I'll see what we can arrange," Nuri said. "But right now, you'd better leave if you want to get into Central before they close the gates for the evening."

As I picked up my weapons bag, my gaze drifted to Jonas. "I'll see you tomorrow."

"You will." There was so little inflection in his voice I wasn't sure if it was a threat or a promise.

I hesitated, then, with a nod to Nuri, turned and left. Cat and Bear shot ahead, excited to be on the move again. We made our way down through the various levels, the air thick with scents and sounds, filled with oncoming shadows and the pressing weight of everything above us. My skin crawled and my stomach twisted, and it was all I could do to maintain my pace, to not run like hell out of the too-close confines of the place.

A feeling I oddly *didn't* get when I was at Nuri's.

The late-afternoon air was cool and sweet, and I sucked it in, cleansing my lungs of all that was Chaos. Then I pulled out the piece of paper, quickly memorizing it before tearing it into tiny pieces and releasing it on the breeze. Bear chased several of the pieces, his laughter running across my senses and making me smile.

We followed the old river's course and, in very little time, reached the South Siding exit—where a rush of excited, worried little ghosts met us.

While we'd been away, someone had tried yet again to get into our home.

CHAPTER 9

It took me a good ten minutes to calm them down enough to get any sort of clear imagery. What had tried to get into our home was gray-skinned, flat-faced, with large eyes and little in the way of other features. A wraith. A *female* wraith.

In the middle of the day.

Either Nuri was right, and wraiths had gained the ability to move around in daylight, or something else was going on.

But what? Why would a wraith—or anyone else for that matter—want to get into our bunker? As far as anyone else knew, aside from the museum section, the place was filled with concrete.

Only Nuri, her crew, and Penny knew otherwise.

And if Penny *was* connected to either the wraiths or the vampires—or to whoever or whatever the force was behind the vampires—then why come here today? They'd have to know she wasn't here, but rather in Chaos . . .

No, I realized suddenly, *they* wouldn't. Nuri had mentioned she was keeping Penny isolated. Maybe she didn't mean physically as much as *mentally*. And *that* meant that while the wraiths hadn't succeeded getting in today, they might well in the future. It might have been only one hundred years since the end of the war, but technology developments had far outstripped anything I had here in the bunker. While in some ways that might be a blessing, it could also be a curse. I had no real idea how easy it would be for someone possessing the right code-breaking equipment to get past my current system.

Which meant I'd have to risk firing up another generator for daytime use, and installing full security on the South Siding exit, at least until we'd sorted out what was going on.

I scrubbed a hand across my eyes, then punched in the security code and headed into our bunker. Dusk hadn't yet fallen, so the lights weren't on yet. Not that it really mattered, as I didn't need them. After all my years of living in this place, I could have walked around it blindfolded. I headed for the main generator panel room and coded in new exceptions, bringing the South Siding exit and its corridor back into the security net. While the tunnel had no weaponry of any sort, bringing it back into the system meant that if someone broke in, we'd at least have time to react.

A few minutes later, with a rattle and a cough, the spare generator kicked into gear. I kept my fingers crossed it held up—and that we sorted out what was going on sooner rather than later.

With that done, I headed for the hydro pods and quickly

cleansed myself. Once I'd re-dressed, I ordered Cat and Bear to keep an eye on things and headed back out.

The last caterpillar pod for the evening pulled into the station just as I reached it. People piled out and their sharp scents—human, shifter, sweat, and perhaps a touch of fear at the oncoming of night—filled the air. Other than the sound of their hurried steps, there was little other noise. There were no conversations, not even whispers. Everyone seemed intent on moving forward as swiftly and as economically as possible.

I kept to the middle of the crowd until we were through the gatehouse, then eased to one side and made my way into First Street. Five minutes later I was entering Hedone.

The receptionist—another blonde—looked up as I entered and gave me a wide smile. "Welcome to Hedone," she said, voice warm and pleasant. "How may we help you this fine evening?"

"I'm here to see Mr. Casimir. He's expecting me."

"Of course. And your name is?"

"Ti Zindela."

"Please, take a seat while I give Mr. Casimir a call."

"Thanks." I moved across to one of the plush white leather armchairs and idly picked up one of the catalogues. The screen instantly came to life and began scrolling through a selection of athletic men, making me wonder if gender preference had been one of the details inputted into the RFID.

"Ms. Zindela?" When I glanced at the receptionist, she added, "Mr. Casimir will be down in twenty minutes. He apologizes for the delay, but has a business call he has to finalize first."

"Thanks."

I spent the first ten minutes scrolling through the catalogue, amusing myself by picking various men and trying to guess their fees. I didn't get *any* right. To say the prices here were exorbitant was putting it mildly.

After that, I switched to reading the history of Hedone, noting with interest that while Sal had registered the business five years ago, it made no mention of his previous experience in the industry. No mention that Hedone was merely the latest purchase in a long line of brothels. No mention of the fact that he'd spent years gradually moving his business through the various districts, until Hedone became a reality.

But maybe that history wasn't a plus. Maybe here on First Street, you just *didn't* admit to a past that involved anything other than being bred and born in this area. As people kept noting, I didn't know much about Central, so it could have been a real possibility.

Sal strode into the waiting area just as I was placing the catalogue back on the table.

"Find anything you like?" he said, smile wide and infectious.

"One or two." I rose. "The prices are little out of my range, however."

"Not surprising, given the prices here are out of the range of most of Central's occupants. Such exclusivity is very sought after by those who can afford us, however." He caught my hand and tugged me into his embrace. "You smell and look very pretty tonight."

He smelled like cold, dark silk, but there was something else, something I'd noted—and dismissed—yesterday. That odd note of corruption was much stronger today, and it crawled unpleasantly across the back of my senses.

Uneasy, and not knowing why, I raised an eyebrow and said, "Suggesting I smelled less than pleasant yesterday?"

He laughed softly, then lowered his lips to mine, the kiss firm and demanding but surprisingly brief. "We have a six thirty appointment with Nadel Keller."

"And he is?"

"The recruitment officer at Winter Halo. As promised, I contacted him today to see if he was still looking for security personnel. He is."

"And he's interviewing at night? Isn't that a little odd?"

"He's doing it as a favor to me." Sal stepped back and studied me. "I think he'll like what he sees."

"I thought you said he didn't sleep with employees."

"He doesn't. But he does have to cater to his boss's tastes, even if it goes against his own."

Which didn't exactly sound like Keller was above sexual harassment; he just wasn't attracted to the personnel he was paid to employ. "So you know him fairly well?"

"He's one of our better customers." He half turned and offered me his arm. "Shall we go?"

No, I wanted to say, *definitely not.* And yet I had no idea why I was so reluctant. Intuition was crawling, but it wasn't telling me *why.* I forced a smile and linked my arm through his. "I'm gathering, then, that the dress is suitable."

"Totally. But a simple gray tunic would never be considered inappropriate in this district."

A point that only made me wonder yet again just how much Nuri had sensed about me. Dusk had settled in by the time we stepped outside, the darkening skies streaked with fading ribbons of red and gold. Not that you could tell night was approaching, because here in the streets of Central, it was as bright as day.

"How do you stand it?" I said as Sal guided me to the left.

He glanced at me, eyebrow raised. "Stand what?"

I waved my free hand toward the UVs perched atop the nearest building. "Twenty-four hours of daylight. Don't you ever feel the need for darkness?"

After all, it ran in our blood, even if it didn't control or restrict us like it did the vampires.

He shrugged. "After living in Central for so many years, I'm probably more comfortable in the light than I am in the darkness."

Something within me very much doubted that. "How long have you been here?"

"Seventy years, give or take."

And we'd never met in all that time? Central was a large city, but if he'd spent most of those years working his way up from the twelfth district, I should have at *least* scented him before now. "How did you get around Central's insistence that all its citizens have RFIDs?"

His gaze met mine, and there was something in them that chilled me to the core. As a déchet assassin, killing wasn't just his job but part of his nature, and it was something I'd accepted without question. But the coldness I'd just glimpsed—it wasn't the dispassion of a killer, it was something else altogether. Something darker. *Meaner.*

"When you can shape your form into any desired image," he said, "acquiring RFIDs is not a problem."

"Yeah, but getting rid of the body *is.*"

"Not really. It's just a matter of choosing the right time and location for the kill. The vampires will take care of the rest." A somewhat disbelieving smile teased his lips. "Don't tell me you've never stolen another's identity?"

"I can honestly say I haven't."

"Then how the hell have you gotten by? Most of the major population centers have insisted on RFIDs since the war."

"I didn't live in major cities." I shrugged. "And did I mention I'm a very good thief?"

We turned left, onto a side street, and moved toward Second. "But you do have an RFID now, haven't you?"

"I said I did." I glanced around as we crossed Second Street and moved toward Third. "Where are we going? I thought we were eating in first?"

"No. Nadel could only spare half an hour, so we're meeting him at a place on Sixth, which isn't far from where Winter Halo is situated."

"Is he likely to ask me many questions about the company? Because I don't know a whole lot about it."

"Not really. They'll test for fitness and aptitude if he considers you an appropriate candidate, but you're there to guard the place, nothing more."

"So what sort of research do they do there that needs such a specific type of guard?"

He shrugged. "As I said, the owner appears to have a fetish for a certain look, but I can't really tell you more than that."

Won't, not *can't,* instinct whispered. The unease deep inside me was growing, but short of actually coming out and asking him why he was lying, the only way I was going to get any sort of truth was by unleashing my full seeker skills on him. And I could really only do that while we were having sex. He knew well enough what I was, and if he *was* holding secrets he had no desire for me to learn, he would be guarded against me. But he also had no idea how strong my seeker skills were during sex, because I'd never used them on him.

"Here we are." He released my arm and moved his hand to my back as he guided me through a doorway and into a small foyer. It was bright and white, but there were splashes of red and gold among the white of the furniture, and a wall of rich brown wood to one side of the desk.

A petite woman with pale brown hair glanced up as we entered. "Welcome to Rubens," she said, with a smile. "How may I help you?"

"We have a table booked under the name of Casimir," Sal replied, his voice cool.

She checked, then said, "For three?"

"Yes."

"This way, please." She picked up three menus, then moved toward the wall of wood. It split apart, revealing a dining room that was not only intimate, but also surprisingly shadowed—or at least as shadowed as anything in Central seemed to get. Tables were well spaced, and the air rich with the scents of humans and shifters. Underneath all those ran the delicious notes of roasting meat. I might have eaten just over an hour ago, but it seemed my stomach was more than happy to consume more, if the somewhat noisy rumble was anything to go by.

The woman guiding us moved easily through the tables, heading toward the rear of the room. As we followed her, another scent teased my nostrils—a scent that was deep forests, dark satin, and, oddly corrupted. Sal's scent. Except it was coming from up *ahead*, not behind.

I stopped so abruptly Sal ran into me, and would have sent me flying if he hadn't immediately grabbed me.

"What's wrong?" His grip on my arms was almost too firm.

"Nothing." My gaze roamed the rear shadows, but the scent had faded almost as quickly as it had appeared, and it was now impossible to pin down where it might have come from. *Who* it might have come from. Maybe I'd imagined it. Maybe the air-conditioning had simply caught

Sal's scent and made it appear as if it had come from the front rather than from behind.

"Then why did you stop?"

I hesitated as instinct warned me not to say anything. "Sorry." I glanced back at him and smiled. "I just caught a whiff of roast. It's been a while since I've eaten anything that smells *that* good."

"Your thieving skills are severely lacking if the mere smell of roasted meat can stop you so abruptly."

Though there was amusement in his voice, there was an odd gleam in his eyes that spoke of . . . not distrust, not even disbelief. Just . . . uncertainty. As if he wanted to trust me, but wasn't entirely sure he could.

That distrust was new. I'd had no sense of it yesterday, so what had happened between then and now? Surely it couldn't have been anything I'd said, because I hadn't really said all that much.

Had he been checking up on me? He wouldn't have discovered anything if he had. No one in Central knew me, and, unless he had spies in Chaos, he wouldn't have gathered much intelligence there, either.

"Have you ever tried to steal a haunch of beef?" I said, with an ease that belied the turmoil inside. "It's not exactly something that fits under your shirt."

"True."

The woman paused and glanced back at us, an eyebrow raised in query. I forced my feet forward again and added, "And hunting isn't exactly easy these days, not unless you go deep into the mountains."

"Again, true." He paused. "Have you ever been to the Broken Mountains?"

"No." Not since the war, at any rate. "Why?"

He shrugged. "I've heard the ruins of the old base have been infested by vampires."

It was an interesting statement given my recent discovery of a vampire-infested base. But did that mean he was involved in whatever was going on? I wanted to believe not, wanted to believe his question was nothing more than coincidence.

But I just couldn't.

"Why would vampires infest the abandoned ruins of an old military base?" I feigned confusion. "There's nothing there for them to hunt."

His gaze searched mine for several seconds, and then he shrugged. "Just curious. I thought you might have had some experience up there. You were stationed up there once, were you not?"

"I'd hardly call it 'stationed,' given I was only there for a few days while I was waiting for reassignment. But I doubt . . ." I paused as the scent teased my nostrils, sharper than before. I glanced left, my gaze roaming across the half shadows. There were several tables nearby, all of them filled with couples, but again, the scent disappeared before I could pin it down.

"Doubt what?" Sal prompted.

"Doubt the shifters would allow such an infestation to survive if they *have* made it up there." I drew in a deeper breath, but once more there was nothing.

But I wasn't imagining it—and *that* was scary. Because while it was an undisputed truth that a person's base scent *didn't* change, it was simply impossible for two people to have the *exact* same scent. There were always differences, no matter how slight. Even identical twins smelled different—I knew that for a fact.

Yet Sal's natural scent *had* changed, however subtly, and now there was someone here in this room who shared the same smell.

What the hell was going on? Was this really Sal, or had someone, somewhere, taken over his identity? But that didn't make sense, either, if only because he knew me, and knew about our past. Body shifters might be able to attain someone else's image, but they couldn't take their memories. Even *I* couldn't do that, and I'd been bred to not only take over the identity of female shifters to infiltrate the various camps but also—at least for a short period—their lives.

Besides, an identity snatch didn't explain why there was someone else in this room who smelled exactly the same as Sal. Granted, some lures—like me—could change their scents to match their identities, but Sal wasn't one of those. None of the grays had been given that skill, because it wasn't really an ability assassins needed. If they did their job well enough, they were in and out before anyone could scent them, let alone see them.

So, did we have yet another lure survivor on our hands, or was something else—something weirder—going on?

I swept my gaze across the room again as the woman stopped at a table set for three. There was no one even remotely resembling Sal here, so that cut out the possibility of a clone. Though why Sal would want a clone given his Salamander blood enabled him to regenerate to the point of limb regrowth was beyond me.

Sal pulled out my chair, seating me, then moved around to the chair directly opposite. The woman handed me a menu, but my smile of thanks was somewhat absent. My neck prickled with awareness. I was being watched, and it was all I could do to resist the temptation to turn around and meet my watcher's gaze.

"Ah," Sal said, the sharp sound of his voice making me jump slightly. "And here's Nadel, right on time."

I glanced around as a tall man with receding blond hair approached the table. He shook Sal's hand, his manner more formal than usual for friends, then glanced at me.

"And you would be the young woman who is interested in the security position at Winter Halo?"

His scent swirled around me, an interesting mix of old paper, vanilla, and something furred. Not Sal's scent. Not the scent of the unseen man who watched from afar. I rose and offered my hand. "Ti Zindela, at your service, sir."

His grip was warm and soft. It wasn't the grip of a man who'd ever worked hard for a living—and it certainly wasn't the grip of a soldier. Though why I'd thought it might be was a mystery.

He looked me up and down, then said, "And have you had any experience in the security industry?"

"Yes, but mostly in smaller establishments. I've never worked for any company as large as Winter Halo."

"You're chipped?"

I raised an eyebrow. "Isn't everyone?"

"Not if they come from Chaos." He paused. "You don't, do you?"

"No." I waved a hand at the empty chair. "Please, sit."

He hesitated. "I'm afraid I can't. There've been problems at the company, and I have to get back."

"I hope it's nothing major." Though Sal's tone bordered on disinterested, I had a suspicion that was anything but the truth.

Nadel gave him a somewhat wary look. "Nothing that I can speak about, I'm afraid."

"No, I imagine not," Sal replied. And again, I sensed his interest even though all outward signs suggested otherwise.

The older man frowned and returned his gaze to mine. "I'll scan your details, if you don't mind. If your references and history check out, we'll be in contact about the position."

"Any idea how long that will take? I'm afraid I'm running low on credits."

He shrugged and pulled a small scanner from his jacket pocket. "It should take only a day or so. Where are you currently staying?"

I raised my hand, wrist side up. "A place called Old Stan's on Twelfth."

He sniffed as he scanned the RFID. "Not one of the more favorable establishments in Central."

"Maybe not, but it's one of the few I can afford given the credit situation."

"I shall see if I can hurry the process along." He glanced at Sal, nodded, then turned and walked away.

I blinked. "Well, that was short and sweet."

"As I said, they are in desperate need of security personnel. If your references check out, you can expect to be contacted by tomorrow evening."

"Huh." I sat back down. "Why were you so interested in what was happening at Winter Halo?"

He smiled. "I'm lucky Nadel is not as perceptive as you."

"That you are. And stop avoiding the question."

His smile grew. "Information is better than credits in Central. Remember that if you wish to succeed in this place."

A tall, brown-haired waitress appeared and, after a quick glance at the menu, I ordered the roast beef and vegetables. Sal made it two, and ordered wine for us both.

I leaned back in my chair as she left and kicked off one sandal. "And is that what you're doing at Hedone?" I raised my toes to his leg and slowly slid them upward. His gaze darkened, became hungry. "Gathering information?"

"There is no better place to collect information than those few vital moments postcoitus, when the mind is completely relaxed and the guard down. You, of all people, should know that."

I did know that, but knowledge and action were often two very different things. Warriors who'd been at war most of their lives sometimes didn't relax, even during sexual acts. That had always made attempting to read the complete road map of their emotions and put together a picture of plans and possible outcomes very dangerous—especially when a lot of shifters were sensitive to any sort of mental intrusion. Even something as noninvasive as seeking could be a death sentence if it was tried on the wrong target.

Using my skills on Sal *would* be dangerous. Even if he had nothing to hide, discovery might very well signal an end to our friendship. I was both breaking the trust between us and betraying our friendship by attempting to read him, and the loss of both would be a very high price to pay given I'd only just found him again. And yet, while I very much hoped I'd find nothing to implicate him *and* that he wouldn't discover what I'd done, I couldn't *not* do it.

I studied him for a moment, then said, "But you're not a seeker yourself, so I take it you're employing men and women who are."

"Seekers or telepaths, although that is something we look for rather than advertise for," he said. "Hedone has a good reputation, our pay rates are good, and so are the conditions. I have a long list of those wishing positions."

"And is information gathering the reason why the history of Hedone mentions nothing about making your way up from the twelfth district?"

He smiled, but again there was something very cool, almost inhuman, about it. Which was an odd thought given Sal and I had *never* been human in any common sense of the word. "Those who partake of our offerings would be less inclined to do so if they were aware of our history."

"Nadel is one of those customers?"

"He is indeed."

"And he's a shifter?"

Sal raised an eyebrow. "You couldn't tell?"

I shook my head. "His scent was a little strange—not human, but not really shifter."

"That's because he's only half-shifter, and a tabby at that." He smiled. "He has a preference for overly tall, dark-skinned women with bountiful breasts—"

"'Bountiful breasts'?" I cut in, with a laugh.

"His words, not mine. Luckily for me, I happen to employ a telepath who fits such a description. I've gotten some interesting information from him over the years."

"Anything about Winter Halo's owner? Anything I should be worried about, that is?"

"Other than his predilection for sleeping with his staff, no."

"Then why were you so reluctant about arranging this meeting?"

"Because I wish you in my bed, not his." He caught my foot as it reached his thigh, shifted it to the top of his leg, and began to knead it. I sighed in pleasure, closed my eyes, and enjoyed the massage.

Our meal arrived. We ate it leisurely, talking and joking and laughing. It almost felt like old times back at the bunker. Almost.

Because there was an underlying tension that ran between the two of us. A tension that was sexual in nature, and something else. Something that was almost—but not quite—wariness. Or maybe even suspicion.

It made me wonder about that call he'd received before I'd arrived. Made me wonder about the part he might play in all this—if he did, indeed, play a part.

When our meal was cleared, the last of the wine consumed, and the bill paid, Sal said, his expression guarded, "So, would you like to come back to my place?"

I raised an eyebrow, a smile teasing my lips. "That depends."

"On what?"

"On whether you actually *want* me to come back to your apartment." I cocked my head slightly. "I have to say, you don't exactly seem enthused by the idea."

A grin split his lips, but it wasn't quite as real as it should have been. "Oh, I am. I just didn't want to get my hopes up too far."

"Good." I placed my napkin on the table and rose. "Shall we go, then?"

He rose and caught my hand, his fingers brushing my wrist as he led me out of the restaurant. The night was cool and bright and, overhead, a storm rumbled—a sound that seemed at odds with the almost blinding light that bathed the streets. As we walked back to First Street, he said, voice nonchalant, "What happened here?"

He raised our joined hands and pointed to the ugly scar left by the vampires. I hadn't thought to disguise it, and that was a very stupid mistake on my part.

"Camouflage," I replied, with an easy smile. "I thought I might be a more believable security guard if I wasn't such a clean skin."

"Maybe." Though his expression gave little away, the threads of suspicion seemed stronger.

I hesitated, and then said, "You don't think it'll be a problem, do you?"

"That I don't know." He shrugged. "But if it's only camouflage, you can get rid of it easily enough, can't you?"

"Of course I can. It's only real wounds that cause a problem when body shifting." The lie slipped easily off my tongue. I frowned and squinted up at him. "But you know that."

He waved his free hand. "The war was a long time ago, Tiger."

It might have been a long time ago, but I certainly hadn't forgotten it. I couldn't, not when I lived with reminders of the war and the actions of the shifters every single day. Sal might not have those reminders, but even so, why hadn't he called me on the lie? Had he truly forgotten or was he was testing me? And if the latter, why?

I didn't say anything, however, and we continued on in silence—a silence that was edged with both desire and watchfulness. It was the latter that stirred alarm. I needed to be very, *very* careful tonight.

"Would you like some wine, or perhaps a coffee?" he asked as the elevator stopped on his floor and the doors opened.

He strode ahead of me, heading for the kitchen. I kicked off my shoes, then stripped off my tunic, dumping both on the nearest sofa as I followed him across the vast space of his home.

"Perhaps later," I replied. "Right now, I'm hungrier for something else."

He paused in the middle of reaching for a bottle of wine and glanced over his shoulder. His gaze swept me and that hungry light reappeared. "So it would seem," he murmured, and closed the fridge again.

He reached for my waist, but I caught his hand instead

and led him toward the bedroom. "This time," I said, my voice low, "we do it my way."

"More than happy to," he murmured, his free hand sliding sensuously down my spine before coming to rest on my butt. His touch was cool, especially when compared to the fire that raged inside of me. And while his salamander blood meant his touch would never contain the heat of mine, it nevertheless seemed . . . odd. I frowned but thrust away the curiosity and questions that inevitably stirred. I'd get answers soon enough if I did this right.

I stopped when I reached the bed and turned to face him. "Don't move," I said. "And most certainly don't touch."

He raised an eyebrow, amusement and expectation warring for precedence in his expression. "Where is the fun in not touching?"

"You've been around humans far too long if you cannot remember the simple pleasure of receiving rather than sharing."

I began to strip him, taking my time, exploring each new bit of flesh as it was revealed, touching and kissing and tasting. By the time his shirt fell to the floor, he was breathing fast and the smell of desire was so thick in the air that it filled every breath. I kept going, kept teasing, my fingers playing around the waist of his pants but not undoing them. Not releasing him.

When I finally did, his groan was one of sheer pleasure. His cock jumped free, thick and hard and quivering with expectation. I ran my tongue over its tip and he groaned again, the sound almost desperate. I smiled and kept on tasting him, kept teasing him, until he was quivering with the need for release and his body was tense with the effort of control. Then I rose, my nipples brushing his chest as I kissed him. Softly, gently.

"I presume you have massage oil?" I murmured, my lips brushing his as I spoke.

"In the bathroom." His reply was little more than a husky growl.

"Then I'll go get it while you lie on the bed." I brushed a final kiss across his lips, then stepped away. "Lie on your stomach, not your back."

"I don't think—"

I placed a finger against his lips and silenced him. "This isn't about thinking. This is about pleasuring. Lie on the bed."

He took a deep, somewhat shaky breath, then did as I bid. I retrieved the oil, warming the small, pliant bottle between my hands as I climbed on the bed and sat astride him. His skin quivered where our flesh touched.

When the heat of my hands had warmed the oil enough, I undid the top and slowly dribbled it onto his skin, starting at the base of the spine, then moving upward to his shoulders. Once the bottle was recapped, I moved back to the base of his spine and began to work the oil into his flesh, alternating long sweeping strokes with more circular ones, my hands not leaving his skin as I worked my way up his spine, then across his shoulders and down each arm. Then I made my way back down his body. After dribbling more oil onto my hands, I continued on, over his firm rump and down the muscular length of his legs, concentrating on his feet for a while before moving back up his legs. When my fingers slipped between his thighs and brushed his balls, he jumped slightly and groaned.

"God, don't," he murmured. "Or I may not last."

I chuckled softly. "This from the man who once boasted he could make a woman come a dozen times before he himself felt the need to release."

"That was a long time ago." He jumped again as my fingers brushed him a second time. "The need for control is not especially prized in a world that values time over quality."

"Then that is this world's loss." I moved to one side. "Turn over."

He obeyed. Precum gleamed on the tip of his cock, and I leaned across, my hair brushing his belly as I swirled my tongue around the tip of him, drawing in his salty taste. His hips instinctively arched upward, silently urging me to take more of him. I didn't.

Instead, I poured some more oil over his body, then sat astride his legs and began to massage him again, slowly exploring every inch of his well-defined stomach and muscular chest, gradually working my way upward until my breasts were pressed against his.

"By god," he said, his words little more than a puff of agonized air, "All I want to do is take you in my arms and plunge myself inside you."

"But you can't," I replied. "Not yet."

I kissed him, gently at first, then deeper, harder, our tongues entwining, exploring. When I pulled away, he groaned again. I smiled but held his gaze as I kissed and licked my way back down his body. When I licked the base of his cock, he jerked in response, groaning, quivering. He was close to his breaking point—close, but not quite close enough. I needed him to be nothing but emotion and need and desire. So I teased him, played with him, alternating between taking him in my mouth and running my tongue around the base of his cock and balls, until every inch of him was quivering for release and the smell of his desire stung the air, thick and heavy and desperate.

Only then did I sit astride him. I didn't let him enter me, but rubbed myself up and down the length of him.

He made a low sound of desperation, then grabbed me and quickly changed our positions. He hovered above me for several seconds, his gaze on mine, his body shaking with the fierceness of his control.

"No more," he growled. "From here on in, I'm in control."

And with that, he thrust inside me. I groaned in pleasure, but the sound was automatic, as were the responses of my body. Because the minute he entered me, I released the gate on my seeker skills, allowing my energy and aura to merge with his, letting it entwine as intimately as our bodies, until emotions and thought became something I could see and taste. I ran swiftly across the surface images, sensing within them a hunger I couldn't explain—a hunger that was fierce, icy, and alien. I plunged deeper, seeking the darker recesses and hidden places. Saw, in rapid succession, fragmented images from his past—his actions, his lovers, those he'd murdered and become, and those he'd simply murdered. Then, deeper still, felt the anger, the desperation, and the fear of a world determined to destroy us. Saw four humanoid forms—two male, one female, and one that was something else altogether—become trapped by a bitter, alien, darkness that swept around and through them, merging their particles, making them one. Saw the four become three as one was killed and its blood and flesh consumed.

There was nothing more beyond that. Nothing but that bitter, alien darkness. It was as if he'd been reborn in that moment and everything that had gone on before then—everything he'd been and everything he'd done—had been erased. All that remained were vague, fragmented memories that made little sense.

Slowly, carefully, I withdrew from his energy and aura. As awareness of the here and now resurfaced, I reimmersed myself into the sensations flooding my body. Became aware of the fierceness of his thrusts, and of pleasure, spiraling ever tighter. His lips, hard on mine, demanding and desperate.

I wrapped by legs around him, pressing him tighter, harder, against me. His breathing became harsher, his tempo more urgent. The burn of desire built and built, until the need that pulsed between us became all-consuming and the air so thick with desire I could barely even breathe.

We came together, his roar echoing across the silence, his body slamming into mine so hard the whole bed shook.

When I finally caught my breath again, I took his face between my palms and kissed him long and slow, even as my gaze searched his, looking for any sign of suspicion, of doubt. There was nothing but languid contentment.

I wished I felt the same.

I had no idea what had happened to Sal, or what indeed those images truly meant, but one thing was clear.

This man—this déchet—wasn't *my* Sal. He might have his scent, he might have his form, but the Sal I'd known had all but died just after the war's end, when that oddly bitter darkness had combined his spirit and his flesh with that of three others. It was an event that had left him irrevocably changed, and in ways I couldn't even begin to guess at.

The biggest problem, though, was not what he might have become, but rather the connection he now had with the other two who had survived.

Because Sal knew exactly what I was.

And that meant, somewhere out there in Central, two other people were also aware of it.

Or did it?

Because if the slate really *had* been all but wiped clean when they'd been caught in that alien darkness, then maybe he actually couldn't remember much more than my name and the fact I'd been a lure—just like him.

Which in itself was telling, because the grays had *never* been designed as lures, and it certainly wasn't a position Sal had ever been placed in. They were assassins, pure and simple, even if they sometimes used seduction to get closer to their targets. And while they could shape-shift in much the same manner as us, it was simply a means of making escape easier once they'd completed their assignment.

I really hoped the theory was true, because I didn't need those other beings fully aware of my capabilities.

Sal rolled off me, then propped his head on one hand and studied me for several minutes. I returned his gaze evenly, even as I sensed the shift in his mood—the need for pleasure and release moving subtly to the need for answers.

It was a need that *wasn't* coming from him, but rather from those who were now forever connected with him.

Sal might be inclined to trust me, but the other two were not. Which meant I could never, *ever* wear my true form. Not when I was with Sal, anyway. He might remember my scent, but there'd been no indication in the reading that he actually remembered what my true form was. And even though he knew I was a tiger shifter, he obviously thought my coloring was the more standard orange tiger. It did, at least, give me some leeway if I ever did have to resort to my own form here in Central.

"So when did you actually arrive here?" he asked eventually.

I waved the arm containing the chip and smiled. "According to my newly jigged chip, five days ago."

"Retouching chip information is expensive—I thought you didn't have any credits."

My eyebrow rose. "Since when were credits the only form of payment?"

He grunted. "Where were you before Central?"

"Officially *and* unofficially, in Newport." I paused, feigning a trace of confusion. "Why all the questions, Sal?"

He shrugged. "Just curious as to why I hadn't come across you before now."

A question I wanted answered in regard to him, as well. I mean, how could we have spent so many years sharing the same city and *not* come across each other before now? I might mostly be a recluse, but I still had to make regular runs into the city. And it wasn't *just* for supplies, but to cater for those occasions when the desire for sexual contact overwhelmed the need for safety—something that happened every few months. What were the odds of both of us being in this city for so long, and never coming into contact? Or even catching the slightest scent clue?

Little to zero, I thought grimly.

But with suspicion so evident in his aura and his eyes, I dared not open the gates again to my deeper seeker skills. I just had to run with instinct—and ignore the fact that instinct was telling me to get the hell out of Hedone and away from Sal. To return to the safety of my bunker and my ghosts, before my life irrevocably changed.

Not wanting to think about the reasons behind that warning when I could do so little about it without further raising Sal's suspicions, I leaned forward and kissed him. If there was one thing that obviously *hadn't* changed, it was his high sexual appetite. And in this situation, I had no qualms about using it, just as I'd used it countless other times when an assigned target had begun to ask difficult questions. There was little talk for the rest of the night, just exploration and pleasure, until we were both fully satiated and our bodies weak with exhaustion. Then we slept.

Or at least he did. I spent the night staring up at a ceiling lit by the never-ending brightness of the UV towers outside the building, wondering what the hell my next move was going to be.

CHAPTER 10

The sharp ring of Sal's com unit broke the silence. I closed my eyes, pretending sleep as he grunted and rose from the bed. His gaze swept me, a cool caress that sent prickles of unease down my spine even as he moved away.

I remained still and listened to his retreating footsteps. After a moment, he said, "Sal Casimir."

A deeper, darker voice—also male—said, "Pick up."

Sal did, basically ending any chance I had of overhearing the conversation. I might have the genes of a tiger, but they weren't helping in this instance. Sal was speaking so softly I could barely even hear *him*, let alone the man at the other end of the com unit.

With no reason to pretend I was still sleeping, I yawned, stretched, then got up and headed for the bathroom. Sal had the latest in air showers, which actually used small amounts of water mixed with air—a rarity these days, as water conservation had been a priority since before the war had begun. I wasn't entirely sure why, given it seemed to rain regularly lately, but maybe it was simply a hangover from the many years of drought this area apparently once faced.

The call had ended by the time I padded out to the living room to find my tunic and get dressed. Sal's expression was forbidding, and his gaze, when it met mine, was hooded and angry.

I paused and raised an eyebrow. "What?"

He waved a hand, the movement short, sharp. "Nothing. There's just been a problem at another business I own. I'm afraid I'm going to have to bundle you out sooner than I'd expected or wanted."

He was lying. I was certain of it, though there was nothing in his voice or actions to give that impression. "I hope it's nothing major."

"So do I."

He strode toward me, all dark and dangerous energy, and it took every ounce of will to remain where I was. He wrapped his arms around my waist and kissed me fiercely, but it was a desperate thing, absent of hunger or true passion. Then he released me with a suddenness that had me staggering back a couple of steps.

"I'd like to see you again." He swung around and stalked across to the kitchen. "Shall we say tomorrow night?"

I frowned, unsettled by his abrupt change of mood and the lack of passion. That call, I was suddenly sure, had been something to do with me. Something he hadn't wanted to hear.

I shivered and rubbed my arms. Of course, it was more than possible the certainty was nothing more than paranoia, but even so, I wasn't about to ignore it. Similar such insights had saved my life more than once during the war.

"Sure," I replied, keeping my voice even. "But you can leave a message at Old Stan's if you can't make it. I'll understand."

"I will. Until tomorrow night, then."

He didn't turn around, didn't offer to see me out. After staring at his back for several moments, I headed for the lift and left.

Once I reached the street, I paused and breathed deep. The air was crisp and cool, and it chased the scent of dark silk and wrongness from my nostrils. I wished it could do the same to the scent that lingered—however lightly—on my skin. There was something about it that just rubbed me the wrong way.

Or maybe it was simply the knowledge that the Sal I'd known—the Sal I'd once trusted with all that I was, and all that I'd dreamed of—was no more.

I took another breath and discovered the teasing, electric aroma of a summer storm. Jonas was near. As I looked to the right, he stepped out from the entrance of the next building. He shook his head minutely, his gaze flickering briefly past me before he turned and walked away.

I yawned, then waited for a gap in the traffic and crossed the street, my gaze sweeping the glass fronts of the building opposite. I couldn't see the threat Jonas indicated, but then, maybe I wouldn't. If there *was* someone following me, it was a fair bet they'd be more practiced at concealing their presence than I was.

I paused as I reached the other side of the road and glanced up. Sal stood near the window, watching me. I gave him a smile and a wave, but couldn't escape the notion that something was very wrong, that I needed to find out what he was involved in, and *fast*.

I silently called Cat and Bear, then turned and walked away, keeping Jonas in sight but staying half a block behind. My two little ghosts appeared within five minutes, happily dancing around me for several seconds before calming down. I asked them to keep an eye on Sal without getting too close, and to report back to the bunker by sunset. They immediately dashed off, excited to be doing something new and interesting—another sentiment I wished I shared.

Jonas turned right onto a walkway heading toward Second Street but, as he did so, flicked a hand to his left, seeming to indicate I should keep going straight. I did, only turning right when I reached the next one. There was no one else in the walkway, and my footsteps echoed in the vast, empty canyon between the two streets. When I reached the end of the walkway, I turned left onto Second Street and casually glanced over my shoulder. There was no one there . . . and yet my skin crawled with awareness.

I wasn't the only one who could wrap myself in sunlight in this city. Whoever followed me was also capable of it.

Tension wound through my body. I flexed my fingers and fought to keep my pace even. Running would be the worst thing I could do right now; it would only further raise the suspicions of whoever was behind me.

"Head to Old Stan's," Jonas said behind me. "It's close to the market on Twelfth, between the main gate and the first walkway. I'll meet you there."

I didn't acknowledge him, just immediately headed across the road and into the next walkway. The crawling sense of awareness never went away, but it never drew any nearer, either. I wondered if the person following me was one of the two people Sal had merged with, or if it was someone else entirely. Sun shielding was an extremely rare talent, and while I had no idea if it could be found in anyone outside those created in the déchet labs, it wasn't hard to imagine that if someone *did* possess the ability, they'd be shuffled into either the public or private army.

I continued moving through the various walkways until I reached Twelfth, then paused, looking left and right to get my bearings. I knew the market section well enough—it was where I pilfered my supplies of fresh fruit and veg—but I'd always come at it from outside the city rather than inside. After a moment, I caught the sound of stallholders promoting their prices and goods, and headed left again. The market soon came into sight. It was a riot of color, sounds, and mouthwatering aromas. A sea of tents and temporary stalls stretched across the entire street, blocking the road and forcing all those needing to get farther down Twelfth through the many higgledy-piggledy rows. I resisted the instinctive urge to snag some fruit and knobs of crusty bread as I wove my way through the market, and walked on.

The curtain wall stretched high above me now, a rusting silver monolith that under normal conditions would have cast this whole area into deep shadows. Old Stan's was a four-story timber building that was barely more than two windows wide. The myriad of antennas and satellite dishes that lined its roof gleamed warmly in the bright light of the nearby UV tower, and the small lane between it and the next building was filled with overflowing bins and old men in even older chairs. I gave them a nod as they glanced my way. I had no idea who they were or why they'd sit in a refuse-filled lane, but for as long as I'd been coming to Central to steal food, there'd been old men sitting in that lane, smoking and drinking and talking.

I opened the inn's somewhat battered blue metal door and stepped into slightly shadowed coolness. A wrinkled, gray-haired old man looked over the edge of the tablet he was reading and gave me a grin that was missing a few teeth.

"You'd be Ti Zindela, then," he said, voice gravelly and warm.

"And you'd be Old Stan, I'm guessing," I said, with a smile.

"I am, lass, I am." He waved a hand toward a somewhat rickety-looking set of stairs at the back of the small entrance hall. "Your room is ready—it's on the top floor, number 4C."

"Thanks."

He tossed me a key, then got back to his reading. I took the stairs two at a time; room 4C was at the rear of the building and one of two on the top floor. I opened the door and stepped inside. The room was small, consisting of little more than a bed, a washbasin and tap, and probably the smallest autocook that ever existed. I couldn't imagine there'd be too much in the way of food options within it, but I guessed it was better than nothing. And it wasn't like I was going to stay here very long, anyway.

Jonas leaned a shoulder against the window that looked down into the small alley, but turned as I closed the door. "Did she follow you here?"

I raised my eyebrows. "She?"

He nodded. "There was a slight feminine overtone, though her scent was extremely tenuous. You never saw her?"

I shook my head. "I did sense a presence behind me, but I never actually spotted her. Whoever it is, she's damn good."

Mentioning the fact my follower was probably using a sun shield certainly *wasn't* an option, given very few people alive today would even know what it was.

"She was so damn good she wasn't even visible." His voice was flat. Suspicious, though whether it was aimed at me or not I couldn't say. "I'd suspect magic, except for the fact I couldn't smell it."

I raised my eyebrows. "You can smell magic?"

"Some." His nostrils flared slightly and a slight trace of distaste briefly crossed his otherwise enigmatic expression. "Just as I can smell your friend. He has a very odd scent."

"Sorry, but there's not a lot I can do about that right now." I walked across to the autocook and studied the menu. As I suspected, there wasn't much. I opted for a cheese-and-vegetable omelet, hoping that at least with the market being so close it would be fresh, then turned to face Jonas. "Odd in what way?"

He hesitated. "He's no vampire, and yet there are undertones of night and death in his aroma that speak of those creatures. But there's also something else, something I can't really place—it reminds me a little of the scent of the Others, but it's wrapped in humanity. Which makes no sense at all."

No, it didn't, although it did make me wonder if perhaps the fourth figure I'd seen in Sal's memories had been one of the Others. But if it *had* been, surely he and his two companions would not now be alive, not when there'd been reports of just one of the creatures taking out entire units after the war.

I thrust the question away and said, "How long were you following me last night?"

Jonas's expression gave little away. "From the moment you and he walked out of Hedone to the moment you returned. Why?"

"Were you in the restaurant at all?"

"Yes."

And I hadn't even seen him, let alone sensed him. He was living up to everything I'd ever heard about the rangers—which made me even more thankful my job during the war had generally kept me away from them. "And did you sense another in that room who smelled the same as Sal?"

He frowned. "No two people can have the same scent. There are always differences, even in close-knit family units."

Well, while that was true enough, those of us created to be lures certainly *could* both change our scents and match them to others'. But it was never an ability given to the grays, and I really hoped it was one of those facts Sal didn't remember.

"I thought that, too, until last night," I said. "I couldn't pinpoint who the second scent belonged to because of the air-conditioning, but he or she was watching me and Sal from the moment we arrived until the moment we left."

"Meaning someone suspects you are not who you say you are."

"Or they suspect I might be behind the break-ins at both Deseo and that military base."

Jonas frowned. "Why would they suspect that? You're not even wearing the same form, and the olfactory senses of a vampire are, as far as I'm aware, even duller than a human's. They smell life and blood but little else. Even if that *weren't* so, there is no way they could have reported your scent to anyone here in Central."

"Except for the fact that they're obviously working with someone here in Central."

His gaze narrowed. "What makes you so certain of that?"

I hesitated. I needed to be *very* careful about what I said and what I didn't. He was already suspicious that I was keeping information back; I didn't need it exploding into full-blown certainty. "The fact that, when I appeared in the military bunker, one of the vamps called me 'mistress' and asked if I needed any help. He obviously mistook me for someone else—someone who looks very similar to the form I was wearing last night. I suspect it was the only reason they didn't immediately attack."

He swore softly. "You should have mentioned this to Nuri earlier."

"I didn't *remember* earlier," I snapped back. "And what does it matter anyway? You can simply telepath the information across to her now, anyway."

"That I can." His smile was grim. Cold. "What else have you failed to mention?"

"Ranger, it might be wise to remember I'm *not* working for you and Nuri." My voice was surprisingly soft given the anger surging within me. "I'm *only* doing this because I want to help those children, so don't take that tone with me or, by Rhea, I'll walk away and leave you milling around in uselessness."

"And the mouse will rise, and woe betide those who oppose her," he murmured.

I blinked. "What?"

He shrugged. "It's a line from an old fairy tale. I'm surprised you haven't heard it before."

"Mom was human and didn't do shifter fairy tales." And our handlers and educators certainly hadn't. It had proven problematic more than once.

He gave me another of those cool smiles. "Anything else?"

"Yeah, finding whoever is interacting with the vampires won't be easy, as I suspect they might be a shifter of some kind."

"My type of shifter, or yours? And why would you suspect that? The vampires certainly couldn't have told you."

"Because I'm not the only body shifter in Central. Sal's one, and so is whoever shares his scent."

The autocook *ping*ed softly. I opened the unit and took out the plate. The omelet not only looked fresh, but smelled divine. I ferreted around until I found a knife and fork, then moved across to the small table. All the while, Jonas watched me.

Eventually, he said, "Do you believe Sal is involved with this other person?"

"Well, I don't think it's a coincidence that they smell the same." I ate some of the omelet and then met his gaze. "I did a reading on him last night."

His eyebrows rose. "Meaning?"

I hesitated. "Nuri's a seeker herself, so you're obviously aware what we can and can't do."

He simply nodded, his arms crossed and expression giving little away.

"Well, *some* of us are capable of going deeper than merely reading surface thoughts and emotions. We can delve into past memories and gain insight on all that that person might have seen and done." I hesitated. "But it can only be done during sex."

"In that case, remind me never to have sex with you."

My smile was as cold as his voice. "I don't think there's any danger of that, ranger."

"No."

And yet, even as he said it, desire rose between us, tainting the air with its rich, heady aroma. I dropped my gaze from his and steadfastly ate the omelet—even as my skin prickled with awareness and heat flushed my body.

"So what did you discover during this invasion?"

"It's not an invasion. It's nothing as crude as that," I snapped, then took a deep breath and added, a little more calmly, "He got caught in some sort of weird darkness with three others, and it merged their DNA. I'm pretty sure they can communicate telepathically. Sal got a call this morning, and I think it was one of the people I saw in his mind."

"If they can communicate telepathically, then they wouldn't need to use standard coms."

"True." I bit my lip for a moment. "Perhaps it's not a true form of telepathy, but rather something like the seeker skill, in that they share impressions rather than thought."

"It's possible." There was an odd edge to his voice that had me frowning. But before I could say anything, he added, "Can you describe the three he was caught with?"

I shook my head. "They were little more than silhouettes. All I can tell you is that there was one man, one woman, and someone else. Someone that felt unnatural, maybe even alien."

"So the woman who followed you here is very possibly one of those three?"

"Possibly." Or it could be one of Central's rangers, alerted to my presence thanks to the other lot of shifters who'd been at Nuri's when I'd first arrived there. Anything was possible at this point.

"What about the darkness itself?" he asked.

That edge was deeper. "It was unnatural and also very alien. Why?"

"Because what you're describing is probably a rift." He scrubbed a hand through his short hair. "This is not good news."

I frowned as I rose and walked across to the autocook,

depositing my plate in the slot before ordering two coffees. "But if he was caught in the rift, he'd be dead. People don't survive them."

"People do," he snapped back. "It's rare, but it happens. But if he was caught in a rift with those others, then they now all share not only a form of collective consciousness, but possibly many of the abilities they had individually."

Because rifts chewed up the DNA of whatever they encountered and spat it out in a completely different form. But if that was the case, why did Sal look the same? He shouldn't, given the terrible results I'd seen of plants and animals caught in rifts. Or was it simply a matter of his using his shifter skills to maintain a form he was more comfortable with?

"That would explain how Sal and the person in the restaurant could share the same scent," I said eventually.

He nodded. "The other three will also hold the same scent."

"Other two," I corrected. "The fourth person caught in that rift didn't actually survive."

"At least that means there's one less for us to track down." His voice was grim. "What else did you catch?"

"Nothing during sex."

He raised an eyebrow again. "And afterward?"

"Again, nothing. But for no reason at all he brought up the Broken Mountains and asked if I'd been there recently."

"Interesting."

"More so given he also mentioned that he'd heard they were now infested by vampires."

The autocook *ping*ed and two steaming mugs of coffee appeared. I picked them both up and walked across to Jonas, handing him one but making sure our fingers didn't brush.

He raised an eyebrow at my actions, and amusement briefly teased his lips. It made me wish he'd smile more often. Unfortunately, it fled as swiftly as it had appeared.

"There are no vampires in the Broken Mountains. I have kin up there; they would have mentioned it."

"But there *is* an old military base, isn't there?"

"Yes." He took a sip of coffee, his expression thoughtful. "You think he was deliberately trying to get a reaction out of you?"

"I think it's more than possible. If Sal, his two unknown friends, and the vampires *are* somehow all connected to whatever is going on, then they'll be aware that someone raided that base last night."

And really, why else would he suddenly mention the Broken Mountains if he wasn't involved in some way? Coincidences happened, but there were just a few too many occurring now for it to sit comfortably.

"Then perhaps our task today should be to go investigate that old base."

I hesitated. "I don't know—"

"It's daylight," he cut in. "Even if the place *is* infested with vamps, they should be out. And all we really need to do is confirm whether that base is the one you stumbled into."

"And what about my follower?"

He smiled, but this time, there was nothing nice about it. "Let me worry about your follower."

I hesitated again. "How will we get up there?"

"I'll grab an all-terrain vehicle and meet you at the rear of the museum in two hours."

I nodded. That would give me time to go home, change, and grab some weapons. I wasn't about to go anywhere near an old military base that might or might not be infested with vamps without being fully kitted up.

"How will I know when it's safe to leave?"

"You're not leaving by the front door. Another reason we use this place is because it has an escape hatch. If you pull the bed away from the wall you'll uncover a small trapdoor; it leads to a set of stairs that'll take you to the roof. Jump across to the next building, then shimmy down the drainpipe. It takes my weight, so it won't be a problem. The back of that building has fallen into disrepair—go through it, then move back onto Twelfth."

"What about the occupants of other buildings? What if I'm spotted?"

"This is Twelfth Street," he said, a trace of sarcasm in his voice. "People don't care what you're doing, as long as it's not affecting them."

"Fair enough." I downed my coffee in several gulps and just about burned my mouth. "I'll head off now, then—"

He caught my arm, his grip firm and oh so warm. Desire rippled through my body and spun through the air, entwining with his, creating a storm that threatened to overwhelm self-control—his as much as mine, if the darkening of his eyes was anything to go by. I licked my lips, torn between the need to keep safe and the desire to press closer, to breathe deep the scent of him, to let it flush through my body and claim me, as I suddenly wished he would claim me.

What in Rhea was going on? I'd never felt an attraction this fierce before. I might be designed to attract and be attracted to shifters, but this was something that had *never* happened.

"Not yet. Leave it for ten minutes."

His voice was little more than a husky growl, and even more alluring than the desire that spun around us. I wanted to lean forward, to taste the lips that were so close, but such an action could only end badly. He might want me, but he didn't trust me and he *certainly* didn't like me. I wasn't that desperate for intimacy that I'd take such a risk with such a man.

"Fine." I pulled my arm free from his grip and stepped away from him. Cool air rushed between us, chilling the smattering of sweat that beaded my skin. This man was dangerous in more ways than I'd ever imagined.

I walked across to the autocook and ordered a second cup of coffee. I didn't offer him one. I didn't dare risk getting that close again.

When I finally turned to look at him, he was just finishing his drink. His gaze was enigmatic when it met mine, the desire long gone, even if its scent still stung the air. "Two hours. Make sure you're there."

"I will be."

He left, and a huge sense of relief swept me—though why it felt like I'd dodged a bullet when every bit of me still thrummed with need I have no idea.

The sooner I found those kids, the sooner I could get away from him and Nuri, the better, I thought resolutely.

And ignored that annoying inner voice that snorted in disbelief.

I took a sip of coffee, then placed it on top of the autocook and walked across to the bed. If the various bits of welding evident on the metal framework were any indication, the bed had been repaired more than a few times. It made me wonder just what went on in this room. Sex, however strenuous, usually wasn't enough to break such a sturdy-looking bed, even if many shifters tended to be vigorous lovers.

Would Jonas be? Even as that thought entered my mind, I thrust it away impatiently and lifted the end of the bed.

Dragging it away from the wall revealed a thick rope tied to one of the bed's metal struts and the trapdoor. It was close to the floor and looked barely wide enough to squeeze *my* shoulders into, let alone Jonas's. Still, he'd obviously used this exit; if he could fit, so could I.

Especially given I could shadow if there was no source of light.

But the rooftop and the street were nothing *but* light, and there was no way I was going to be seen in *this* form. I didn't care how much he believed no one in the area would care; I'd learned the hard way that people would and could do the unexpected.

I finished my coffee, then took a deep, calming breath and called to the shifting magic. I imagined dark hair and eyes, and a thin, unpleasant face. I also changed my scent, giving it sour overtones. Jonas might have said he'd deal with whoever was following me, but if for some reason he didn't, then the caution would pay off. Especially if it was one of Sal's companions.

With that done, I squatted down beside the trapdoor. There were two small holes on either side of the panel; I hooked my fingers into them and pulled it free. The space beyond was tight and dark, with barely enough room to maneuver. I lay on my belly and peeked in; a ladder led upward into a deeper darkness, and it didn't exactly look in the greatest state of repair.

Still, it wasn't like I had another choice. I squeezed into the small space, tucked my knees up, then grabbed the rope and pulled the bed back against the wall. Once the trapdoor was secured, I called to the night and the shadows, and became one with them. I flowed up the ladder, my particles brushing against its cool metal surface. Within a few minutes, slivers of light began to flicker through the darkness above me. I gained flesh once more, but the ladder wobbled alarmingly under my sudden weight, forcing me to hang on grimly for several seconds.

Once I was certain it wasn't about to break, I slowly climbed up the rest of the way. As the shadows grew dimmer and the light stronger, a small, circular hatch became visible. I hooked an arm around a rung, then reached up and carefully turned the wheel. There was a slight groan—the sound of metal grating against metal—then it spun and the hatch popped. I blinked against the influx of bright light and cautiously peered out. The rooftop was a sea of technology—there wasn't just an odd assortment of antennas and satellite dishes, but a battery of solar units, some of them almost as old as the ones on the tower at the museum—and might, in fact, provide spare part possibilities if I ever got desperate enough.

I climbed out of the hatch, ensured it was locked, and then rose and scooted across to the building's edge. The gap to the next building was only six feet and really didn't take much effort. I found the drainpipe easily enough, and a few seconds later was back on the street.

But I didn't take the route Jonas had pointed out. I simply walked out onto Twelfth Street. Even if my follower was still out there, she would see and smell someone other than me.

It didn't take long to get back to my bunker, and I was almost immediately surrounded by ghosts, who weren't just happy to see me, but anxious to pass on their news.

For the third time in as many days, someone had tried to get into our bunker.

I swore softly and tried to concentrate as they excitedly relayed all the details—all of them doing so at the same time. Our would-be intruder was a gray-skinned man who wore military pants—not déchet pants, but something similar, if the images the little ghosts pressed into my mind were anything to go by. It wasn't Sal—aside from the fact he was with me all last night, this man had an unusual scar running down his left cheek. It reminded me somewhat of the slashes rangers used to signify their rank and unit, but the scars on *this* man were thicker, uglier, and certainly not a result of a knife or claw—or not the claw of any creature in *this* world, anyway.

At least whoever it was didn't get in, but next time it might be another matter entirely. I praised the little ones for their vigilance, even as I wondered what the hell I could do to further protect this place. I had no doubt whoever it was would try some form of code breaker next—it was, after all, a logical step. It might take some time to crack open this grate, but they would eventually get through.

And while this tunnel was now a part of the bunker's secure system, there were no laser curtains within it to drop down if a break-through occurred, and no automated weaponry, either. It was alarmed, and that was about it.

And I couldn't ask the little ones to keep on defending it, simply because I had no idea what other technology or magic these people had access to. If they could make false rifts, then they might just have a way of dealing with ghosts, too.

I bit my lip as I punched in the code, then stepped into the tunnel. I hesitated as the grate closed, my gaze settling on the control box. I could fuse it; that would certainly stop them—at least until they got a laser torch and simply cut the bars open. Hell, that might even be their next option—it would certainly be quicker than using a code breaker.

But fusing the control box would also stop me exiting the bunker during daylight hours, as I couldn't use the riskier museum exit. Right now, the last thing I wanted was to trap myself.

I moved on. Maybe there was something in the weaponry store on the sixth floor I could use. While I was familiar with most of the items stashed within the vast room, there were boxes in the rear I hadn't opened for decades.

The ghosts trailed ahead of me, dancing along to the beat of my footsteps, their little forms faint wisps of fog in the tunnel's darkness. But it was a beat that made me feel oddly lonely—though how I could *ever* feel that way in a place filled to the brim with people I had no idea. I guessed it was just the fact they weren't *living* people.

It was, I thought somewhat bleakly, going to be a tough few weeks getting used to it just being me and my ghosts again. I might fear others discovering what I was, but I really couldn't deny that—despite everything—it had been nice to have flesh-and-blood company for more than a few hours at a time.

We reached the sixth floor, and I made my way across to the security door that divided the corridor section from the bunk rooms, the stores, the main medical facilities, and what had been the training grounds for prepubescent déchet.

"Name, rank," Hank's gruff metallic voice said.

"Tiger C5, déchet, lure rank." I pressed my thumb against the blood-work slot and waited until the system geared up and took the required sample. It took even longer than usual for the door to open, which wasn't a good sign when it came to the generators. When it finally did open, I immediately headed toward the main generator room. The backup generator was making an alarming amount of noise and was shaking so badly I'd swear it was attempting to shear free from the bolts holding it down. I checked it and couldn't see anything obviously wrong, but hit the maintenance switch, anyway. It would take the generator offline for an hour, but that wasn't much of a risk given I had no intention of leaving to meet Jonas until the last possible minute.

With that done, I made my way to the weapons store, and searched through old boxes stacked at the rear of the room. A few of these were even older than me, with the date stamped on some indicating they'd originated from the years before the war. I had no idea if the equipment within those boxes would even be usable this far down the track, but old guns weren't what I was looking for, anyway.

I began moving the various crates and dust bloomed, catching in my throat and making me cough. The ghosts laughed and dashed through the clouds, their little forms briefly gaining substance before the particles fell away. Eventually, I found something I could use: movement-activated electro-net devices. They'd been designed to capture both shifters *and* vampires, and while they wouldn't kill either, they'd certainly incapacitate them for several hours, long enough for the ghosts to deposit them in the holding cells, out of harm's way until I could get back and take care of them.

I went back to the South Siding exit and set them up, ensuring the deactivate switches were well hidden. With the tunnel as protected as I could possibly make it, I headed to the hydro pods to clean up. Once I'd changed back to the orange-haired, sweeter-smelling form that matched the RFID information in my wrist, I dressed in fresh clothes, then headed for the weapons store to kit up. When I came to the box of flares, I hesitated. My supply of them was running low, but it would be stupid not to have some with me if the bunker in the Broken Mountains *was* infested with vamps. I grabbed a backpack and threw a couple in, then headed back to the south tunnel.

After giving the ghosts instructions on what to do with anything or anyone we caught, I switched on the electro-net modules and walked around the back of the museum to meet Jonas.

The sky was dark and the air thick with the scent of rain. I grimaced and half wished I'd brought a coat with me . . . although if the mountains *were* infested with vampires, then getting wet would be the least of my problems.

Jonas was waiting at the far end of the museum's grounds. He leaned against an ATV that had definitely seen better days, although the treads, at least, were thick and new-looking.

"Did you dig this thing out of a garbage dump or something?" I stopped several yards away from him. Despite being upwind, his scent still washed across my senses, oddly electric. It was as if the oncoming storm were somehow echoing through him.

"It's called camouflage." He pushed away from the vehicle. "We don't need to be drawing attention to ourselves."

I snorted. "What you call 'camouflage' we used to call 'rust.'"

"Oh, there's plenty of that, too." He swiped a hand across a sensor, and the doors rose. "Your carriage awaits."

"Shame my prince doesn't," I muttered. Not that there were any real princes left these days, as the royal family had been decimated in the earliest years of the war. I slung my rifles and backpack onto the rear seat, then climbed in.

He raised an eyebrow as he got in beside me and closed the doors. "You do not look the type to be searching for a prince."

"I'm not. It was just a random comment." I did, however, love stories about them, both real and fictional. I might not have had anyone read me such things growing up, but in

the years since the war I'd had enough time to read whatever I liked—and I certainly *hadn't* just read technical
manuals. I added, "What did you do to my follower?"

"Nothing. She'd disappeared by the time I got down
there." He started up the ATV and the big engine's roar
shattered the silence.

"Yeah," I commented, voice dry. "We're really going
to be unnoticed in this thing."

He flashed me an all-too-quick smile as he typed our
destination into the GPS, then switched to autopilot mode.
"Once we near the Broken Mountains, I'll throw her into
stealth mode. At the moment it doesn't really matter."

I guess. I waited until the ATV had cleared the trees
and reached the main artery away from Central, then said,
"Did you try to track her?"

He nodded. "Her scent led to the market, but I lost it in
the myriad of other smells."

Which had no doubt been intentional. I had no idea who
this woman might be, but if she now shared Sal's DNA
and some of his memories, she'd have an idea of how to
lose any possible tail.

I was silent for a few minutes, watching the roadside
gradually become a blur as the ATV picked up speed, then
twisted in the seat and studied Jonas. "How did you and
Nuri meet?"

He crossed his arms, his expression enigmatic. "Why?"

"Because you just seem an odd combination."

"That's true enough." He shrugged. "We were thrown
together by circumstances beyond our control."

"When?"

"More than a few years ago." He glanced at me. "If you're
going to ply me with questions, expect the same in return."

"You and Nuri have done nothing but question me," I replied evenly. "And you certainly don't believe me."

"That's because you're not telling the truth."

"Says who?"

Another of those cool smiles touched his lips. "Nuri."

Her seeker skills were a whole lot sharper than mine if she was pulling *that* sort of information from me without intimacy. "It's rather unusual for a human witch and a shifter to be capable of linking telepathically, isn't it?"

"It is, but Nuri is an unusual woman."

That certainly wasn't a statement I could argue with. "I have a suspicion the same could be said of you, ranger."

He shrugged and didn't answer. No surprise there.

"Are you lovers?"

He blinked, then laughed, the sound short, sharp, containing little in the way of humor. "No, we are not."

"But you're obviously close."

"That we are."

I was beginning to think it'd be easier to get water from a stone than information from this man. "And the others?"

He raised an eyebrow. "What about them?"

"How did you meet them? It's obvious that Branna isn't exactly on friendly terms with anyone."

"No, he's just not on friendly terms with you. And he hates liars."

I raised an eyebrow. "Which doesn't exactly gel with what you said earlier about him not trusting you for a year. Does that mean he thought you were lying about something?"

"No, but as I also said, he's a lion shifter, and they tend to take a long time before they trust."

"Why does he hate déchet so much?"

"His family was killed by them."

My stomach sunk. That *wasn't* the news I'd wanted to hear. "So he was born during the war? He doesn't look that old."

"Most shifters tend to hold their age better than humans, and their life spans are generally double."

"Yes, but if he was born during the war, then he's at least a hundred years old. He should be showing some signs of age, and he's not."

Jonas shrugged again and reached behind the seat to snag a backpack. "Hungry?"

"In other words, question time is over."

His gaze met mine, green eyes glacial. "When you start telling your secrets, I might. Fruit or trail ration?"

"Fruit."

He tossed me an apple, then ripped open the plastic surround on what smelled like beef jerky and began eating. Silence fell, but it certainly wasn't an easy silence. It was too filled with awareness.

When I finished the apple, I tossed the core out the window, then crossed my arms and stared at the countryside whizzing by. It had been ages since I'd been this far out, and it was good to see that the scars of war had all but disappeared into a sea of green. Here and there the remnants of a human city jutted skeletal metal and concrete fingers toward the sky, but as we got farther away from Central, the forests and ruins gave way to the vast tracts of farmland that were Central's lifeline.

It took another hour to reach the Broken Mountains, and as the ATV began to climb, Jonas switched to stealth mode and silence fell around us. The shadows got deeper and the air colder, until I once again began wishing I'd brought a coat with me.

"Here, wear this." Jonas pulled an old military coat

from the floor behind his seat and handed it to me. It smelled vaguely of oil and musky male; it wasn't Jonas's scent, but someone else's. Someone I hadn't met yet. "It belongs to Micale, our mechanic, but I'm sure he won't mind you borrowing it."

I raised my eyebrows as I pulled the coat on. It was about two sizes too large, but right then I wasn't caring, given it was also thick and warm. "You own this thing?"

"We do. It comes in handy if we are hired for work outside of Central."

"And does that happen often?"

He flashed me another of those all-too-fleeting grins. "Often enough to warrant owning an ATV."

I half smiled. "So where do you keep it? Obviously not in Chaos."

"No. Aside from the fact it's too wide to get through the lower-level streets, leaving any piece of technology unguarded in that place is just an open invitation for scavengers to help themselves."

"So you keep it in Central?"

"Maybe."

Frustration rolled through me, but I could hardly complain about his not directly answering questions when I was doing exactly the same thing. The GPS began to *ping* softly, and I glanced down as the screen came online. Our destination was a little circle of red we were rapidly approaching. Jonas switched back to manual mode, then pulled off the road and drove into the scrub. The ATV's treads crashed their way through the undergrowth, leaving a thick trail of destruction behind us.

"There's little point of remaining in stealth mode right now," I commented. "Anyone with decent hearing is going to hear this thing ripping through the forest a mile away."

"Which is why," he said, hitting the kill switch, "we walk from here."

The ATV came to a halt and the doors raised. I grabbed my pack and climbed out. The air was thick with the scent of eucalyptus and freshly churned dirt, and the light uneven. I glanced upward; all that was visible was a sea of mottled green. Bright shafts of sunlight stabbed through the canopy, spearing downward but not really lifting the deeper gloom of the forest floor.

Jonas locked down the ATV, then shouldered his rifle and said, "This way."

"Have you been to this base before?" I had to run to catch up with him. He was moving fast, and with all the stealth of a hunter.

It was a stealth I *didn't* possess.

"Once."

"When?"

He glanced over his shoulder, his eyes bright in this shadowed place. "Does it matter?"

"It does in that it gives us pointers as to when this place was infested." If it was infested, that is.

"It wasn't when I was here. Not with vampires, anyway."

That odd edge of anger was back in his voice, and I frowned. "Meaning what?"

"Nothing." He paused, then added, "The ATV might have made a bit of noise, but you're not exactly quiet yourself."

"Given I'm not a trained soldier or ranger, that's not surprising," I snapped. "If you want me to be quiet, then we need to go a bit slower."

"A vampire's deepest sleep cycle hits at midday; if they are in that bunker, then that's our best time to explore." His voice was grim. "That gives us fourteen minutes to get there."

"And how many miles do we have to traverse?"

"Only two."

I swore softly, caught a glimmer of amusement in his eyes, and motioned him on. He instantly disappeared into the forest. I followed as fast and as silently as I could.

We made it to the base in thirteen minutes; it wasn't the stuff of world records, but it was still pretty damn fast.

I stopped beside Jonas, my breath a harsh rasp that seemed to echo across the shadowed silence. The mountain slid away from our position under the trees, sweeping down into a low, cleared valley. The building that stood in the center of it was squat, long, and unremarkable. It was little more than an ugly concrete rectangle with no windows and very little in the way of distinguishing features. There was certainly no evidence that this place had once been a large and active military base.

And yet it had been from here that the humans—with several battalions of déchet—had brought the war to the shifter's homeland in a last-ditch effort to defeat them on their own turf.

It was a move that had gone very badly not only for the déchet and the humans stationed here, but for the war itself. The base had lasted only five months before a retreat had been ordered, and that retreat had signaled the beginning of the end for both human hopes of winning, and for my kind.

"Is that the place?" I asked, feigning ignorance. "It doesn't look like much."

"Not on the surface it doesn't," he said. "But like most human military bases, the business end is mostly underground."

"How do we get in?" There were two exits that I knew of, one at the far end of the building, and another in the trees on the opposite side of the valley. But given I wasn't supposed to know anything about this place, I could hardly admit to knowing about either.

"Certainly not through the main entrances," he said. "They'll have security on those for sure."

"Then how?"

"Through an old blast break." He shifted his rifle from his shoulder to his left hand; the safety, I noted, was now off. "Keep an eye out. If someone in Central is working with the vamps, then it's possible they've set up additional security around the perimeter."

"Surely the shifter communities would have picked something like that up." I unslung my own rifle and followed him down the hill. "They still do regular patrols around here, don't they?"

He shook his head. "Not really. The packs and prides that call these mountains home tend to avoid the old bases, be they human or shifter."

"Why?"

He shrugged. "They are a reminder of a past most would rather forget."

"If you forget the past, you only end up repeating it," I said. "History is evidence enough of that."

He glanced at me. "So you have nothing in your past you would rather forget?"

My smile held little in the way of humor. "Haven't we all?"

He half shrugged. "I suspect you and I have more than our fair share, though."

That was undoubtedly true. "I was speaking generally rather than personally."

"I know." He motioned to the right of the building. "The blast shaft is over this way."

We made our way down the hill. The grass was still

dew-kissed despite its being close to ten, meaning we left a very clear trail behind us. But as Jonas didn't seem worried about it, there was little point in my being so.

The grass gave way to gravel as we neared the base. The pitted concrete walls loomed above us, thicker and higher than they'd seemed from the valley's rim. We kept to the shadows of the wall, moving in single file toward the western edge. The silence seemed heavy and oddly uneasy this close to the building, and I had a feeling we were not the only ones awake and aware in this place.

I flexed the fingers of my free hand and tried to relax. If there were watchers here, then surely Jonas would be aware of them. He was a ranger, after all, and trained for this sort of thing. Given that he wasn't reacting in any way, either I was imagining things or our watchers were friendly.

He stopped about ten feet shy of the end of the building and motioned upward. "We can access the break from here."

"And just how are we going to get up there? Neither of us have wings, and you didn't bring any ropes."

"Cats don't need ropes, and I can boost you up."

I had cat genes and I certainly couldn't have leapt that high—the top of the wall was a good twenty feet or more away. That was one hell of a boost up.

"Come on," he said, hunkering down and cupping his hands. "We're running out of time."

In more ways than one, I suspected. But I slung my rifle back over my shoulder, then placed a foot into his hands and lightly touched his shoulders for balance.

"Ready?" he said.

I nodded, my gaze on the building's edge high above us. Without warning, he thrust up, and I was suddenly soaring into the air. A heartbeat later, something sleek and

black raced past me, seeming to defy gravity as it ran up
the pitted concrete wall and disappeared over the edge.
An edge, I suddenly realized, I wasn't going to make . . .

I made a grab for it anyway, but missed and, just for
an instant, I seemed to hang in midair, going neither up
nor down. Then gravity reinforced itself, and I began to
drop. I slid my fingers against the concrete, trying to find
something to grab on to, but there was nothing . . . then
another hand wrapped around mine and my fall came to
an abrupt halt.

"Got you," Jonas said and, with a grunt of effort, hauled
me up and over the edge.

The minute I was safe, he released me and rose. "Wait
here. I'll go check the break."

I nodded, not about to admit that I really couldn't have
done anything else right then. While I'd never been afraid
of heights, I wasn't a fan of falling from them, even if my
genes generally meant I landed on my feet.

I took several deep breaths to calm the butterflies in my
stomach, then pushed to my knees and looked around. The
roof was concrete like the rest of the building, but it was
mostly covered with long drifts of leaves and other forest
debris. At this end of the building, however, the concrete
that was visible was black and riddled with cracks and
large potholes. Bomb damage; obviously, though, the
bombs used here had not been the ones they'd used on
Carleen and the other satellite cities. This place would not
be standing here in this condition if they had.

"Okay," Jonas said. He was squatting next to what
looked to be a particularly large fissure near the other edge.
"It looks like we're in the clear."

I rose and walked over. The break was about three feet
wide and double that in length, and it dropped down into

a darkness that was thick and foul, but free from the scent of vampire.

"Are you sure this leads into the main base?"

"Yes." He glanced up. "You ready?"

No, I wasn't. Although I was well aware that we needed to figure out whether this place was the base I'd discovered earlier, I had no desire to enter it. And it wasn't just the fear of the vampires. There was something within the darkness, an awareness that edged toward anger.

There were ghosts here, ghosts who were not only resentful but, I suspected, violent.

"Tiger?"

My gaze rose to his. "Vampires are not the only things we have to worry about in this place."

He raised an eyebrow. "Ghosts?"

I nodded. "They're filled with anger. We need to step lightly around their resting places and make sure we do not disturb their bones."

"I'll be as respectful as possible. Are you ready?"

I nodded. He gripped the edge of the fissure and dropped down. After a moment, he said, "Okay, your turn."

I took a deep, somewhat shuddering breath, then gripped the edge of the fissure and fell into the heavy darkness.

CHAPTER 11

I landed in a half crouch and swept my gaze across the deeper shadows beyond the small puddle of light filtering in through the fissure. The air was thick and foul here, and entrenched with the scent of death. Old death, not new. There was no indication of vampires, however, nor did there appear to be anyone or anything else in the near vicinity.

I rose and stepped away from the light. The room was large and square and contained nothing more than forest and concrete debris. There were no furniture remnants, no evidence that there had ever been power or light in this room, and only one door—a big sturdy metal thing that had been torn away from its hinges and now lay on its side to the left of the doorway.

It wasn't a room I was familiar with. But then, as a déchet, I'd been escorted into this place via the tunnel in the woods, and kept to the lower service and medical areas.

"Where are we?" I unslung my rifle and held it ready.

"The gas chamber." His voice was soft, but it held a note that chilled me to the core.

"The gas chamber?"

"That's what we called it." He glanced at me. His expression was set—cold—but his eyes gleamed with a rage as old as the scent that surrounded us. "We lost a lot of people in this place the first time we breached it."

I frowned. That had almost sounded as if he'd been here . . . and yet, he *wasn't* that old. He *couldn't* be that old. It would make him easily more than one hundred years old, and even shifters didn't hold their age *that* well. "We?"

He waved a hand dismissively and moved to the doorway. "It was a historical 'we,' not me personally."

That made sense, but I had a feeling it wasn't exactly the truth. That he'd actually meant what he'd said, impossible or not.

"So why was it called the gas chamber?" I followed him across the room and peered over his shoulder. His rich scent filled my nostrils and provided brief relief to the foulness otherwise filling my lungs.

The hall beyond was about four feet wide and seemed to roll on endlessly, with no other exits evident. It was a perfect place to trap someone if ever I saw one.

"Because that's what they did, both in this place and in that hall." He moved forward cautiously.

I went with him, watching every step, being careful not to stand on or kick any debris that might give away our position if there was someone hiding within the bowels of this place.

"Gas only works once," I said. "Wearing masks the second time would surely have fixed that problem."

"Except they used Draccid, and we had no protective gear against that drug at the time."

Draccid. I shuddered and briefly closed my eyes. Tears stung my eyes as the screams of the little ones once again echoed through my memories, and I clenched my fists against the urge to lash out at the man moving so silently in front of me. He wasn't responsible for that destruction, even if he belonged to the race that was.

But at least I now knew how the shifters had gotten hold of that gas—when they'd finally defeated this place, they'd obviously found stores of it.

"How was base taken, then, if not through this breach?"

"We found the secondary tunnel. It was protected with more traditional methods, but a few well-placed mortars soon fixed that."

"I'm guessing by then, the humans had evacced."

"The humans had, but not the déchet."

Of course, I thought bitterly. Rifle fodder was what déchet had been designed for, after all.

"There's another door up ahead," he continued, "and an exit into the main bunker not far beyond it."

"If this is the bunker I discovered, then the vamps will be in the lower service levels, where the labs and regimental bunks are."

He briefly glanced over his shoulder. "You know this how?"

I gave him a thin smile. "I live in a human military bunker, remember? I have no doubt they were all built along similar guidelines."

He grunted but didn't look convinced by my answer. No surprise there, given he generally didn't believe anything I said.

We finally reached the door at the far end of the long corridor. Like the one behind us, it had been torn off the hinges and now lay several yards away in the next corridor—but this time the damage looked new rather than a product of a war long past.

Jonas ran a finger across the frame that held the string-like remnants of what once had been thick industrial hinges.

"Are vampires strong enough to do something like that?" I asked, frowning.

"No, but some of the Others can."

"Then I can only pray to Rhea that I never come across one of those creatures."

"You wouldn't know much about it if you did." He rubbed his fingers together, and a look of distaste crossed his features. "Thankfully, the thing that did this is probably dead."

"How can you tell?"

"There's blood on the hinges and sprayed across the wall to our right. Their blood, like a vampire's, has acid-like qualities; you can see the path of its spray by the stained pitting in the concrete."

"The Others would only enter this place if there was something to hunt. That might be all the proof we need that this is the base at the end of that false rift."

"Hardly, given there's more than one old military base in the country."

"But it wasn't mine, and the only other base within reasonable distance to Central—"

"We go *nowhere*," he cut in, voice flat and edged with finality, "until we're sure this *is* the bunker you discovered."

We did things his way, or else, it seemed. "And if it is?"

"Then we arrange a little cleansing party."

There was a note of . . . not anticipation, but something close to it, in his voice, and it sent a shiver down my spine. "I'm not going to be a member of that party. I'm not a soldier, Jonas, and I want no part of that sort of action."

He raised his eyebrows. "Even if it helps free the missing children?"

"The children weren't at the base I discovered."

"You can't be sure of that, given you only saw a small section of it before you set off the alarm and the vamps attacked."

"The Carleen ghosts said the children had been moved. Besides, the only scent in the air was that of the vampires, and that wouldn't have been the case if the children had been there recently."

"Maybe they're being held on another level. The ventilation system isn't active, remember, and even I couldn't smell the scent of humanity through the thick layers of concrete in this place."

The ventilation system might not be working, but there *was* fresh air getting to the lower levels. Even vampires couldn't survive forever on foul air.

But I didn't bother pointing it out. Jonas had moved on, anyway.

We walked silently through the network of corridors and stairwells. Four levels down, we began to find the bodies. Or rather, the battered remnants of what once had been bodies. The ghosts of those who'd died here flitted across the edges of my vision, and though they made no move to stop us, their fury and bitterness grew, until it became a physical weight that made both my body and heart ache.

We mean you no harm, I said, in an effort to ease the force of their emotions. *We merely seek information about the children who were recently stationed in this place.*

Images flooded my mind—images of death and destruction, of the blood that had soaked the walls of this place and flooded the floors. Images of the fallen who, even after death, had been given no peace, no final resting place, but rather had their bodies hacked to pieces and their parts scattered, simply because the shifters had falsely believed that déchet could rise even after death.

My stomach rose and I stumbled several steps, scattering leg bones as I battled not to lose everything I'd eaten for breakfast.

Jonas immediately swung around. "What's wrong?"

"The ghosts," I somehow said, in between huge gulps of air. It didn't ease the need to be violently ill, given the air was as foul as the images flooding my mind.

He frowned. "Are they projecting?"

"And how." I pressed a hand against the wall, but it was slick and cold, despite the blood that oozed warmly across my fingertips . . .

It was all I could do not to jerk my hand away. It *wasn't* real, it was memory. *Their* memory, not mine. And memories couldn't hurt me.

But the ghosts *could*. If their anger got strong enough, if the energy they were creating got fierce enough, they could very easily tear me—tear us both—apart.

"You need to get out of here," I said abruptly.

"Not until we're sure—"

"Now," I said, cutting him off. "Before they decide to do more than simply flood my mind with images."

"But why would the ghosts . . ." He stopped, and understanding dawned in his eyes. "We did this to them."

"Yes," I said. "You did. And your presence in this place, where what is left of them rests, is very unwelcome. Retreat while you can, shifter; I'll continue on alone."

"That may not be wise—"

"What other choice have we got?" Another wave of anger and imagery flooded my mind and made me shudder. "Contact Nuri once you get back to the surface. If this *is* the bunker I found, then she will have to appease these ghosts before any of you are able to deal with the vampires."

He hesitated, then nodded and resolutely moved toward the stairwell. I waited to see if the ghosts followed, but they seemed content to remain here, where death had found them.

I am not shifter, I said. *I am what you were—déchet. I'm sorry you were murdered in a manner such as this, but I do not deserve to bear the brunt of your bitterness.*

Their anger, if anything, increased. My surviving when they hadn't was not a point in my favor, apparently.

I swore softly and called to the shadows within me, letting them wrap around my body and make me one with the darkness rather than flesh. It didn't ease the force of their empathic attack, but it at least allowed me to move with greater speed through the place.

I flowed down through the levels quickly and silently, finding no hint of vampires or, indeed, anything or anyone else. Just a lot more bones and ghosts. Thousands had to have died there in an effort to hold that place; no wonder the war had gone ill for humanity after its fall.

Two more levels down, I found the vampires.

There were only eight of them in this section, and they were curled up on the floor in what looked like an old storeroom. Scattered around their sleeping bodies was not only the debris of the dead, but boxes and furniture remnants from the base itself.

I didn't stop; I didn't dare. Not when doing so risked one of them sensing my presence and raising the alarm. Besides, I needed to discover whether this was the place the false rift had deposited me.

Nuri and Jonas could uncover whatever else might be here. If this *was* the base of operations for whatever they were doing to the children—and the newness of the lab

I'd found certainly seemed to indicate that was the case—
then surely there'd be files to find, at the very least.

I moved down to the next level and quickly explored it.
The metal walls of the corridor and rooms became slick
and rusty, reminding me of the ones I'd seen beyond the
room that had held the false rift. My heart began to race
a little faster; this might be it.

I moved cautiously through another doorway, and
encountered a sea of unmoving flesh. Vampires, at least
two score of them. I hesitated, but really had no choice but
to keep exploring. Just because there were more vampires
here didn't mean I was in the right place.

But the next level down, I found both the corridor and
laboratory I'd seen earlier. Relief spun through me, but it
was mixed with trepidation. I'd already had to fight for my
life in this place once; I had no desire for a repeat session.

Even so, I hesitated at the T intersection, looking toward
the room that held the false rift, tempted to go check if it
was still there. But there'd been far too many vampires clustered in the rooms leading off the corridor, and the thick
sensation of them certainly hadn't eased any since then.

In the end, caution won out. I spun and retreated, as
fast as I could. My task here was done. Everything else
was now up to Nuri and Jonas.

When I'd reached the upper levels and had finally moved
beyond the fury of the ghosts, I regained flesh form and ran
up the final few flights of stairs until I reached the fissured
room. Jonas wasn't here, but I could hear him moving
around above. I slung my rifle over my shoulder, then leapt
up and gripped the edges of the fissure. A heartbeat later,
hands grabbed mine and I was swung up onto the roof.

"Well?" he immediately said. "Is this the place or not?"

"It is." I pulled my hands free from his, but the warmth

of his touch seemed to linger as I stepped back. "But there's at least fifty vampires between this point and those labs."

He grimaced. "*That* is not so good."

"No." I glanced at the sky. Given the position of the sun, it was already well after two in the afternoon. And it was going to take us several hours, at least, to get back to Central. "You're not going to have the time to do anything this afternoon, anyway."

"No. Nuri's ordered us back to Chaos, anyway. She's gathering reinforcements and equipment for a raid tomorrow morning."

"As I've already said, I'm not taking part in that raid."

"Because you're not a soldier?" He snorted and shook his head. "I've seen you fight, so forgive me for not believing that. I doubt there's many a trained soldier as good as you."

That's because I *had* been trained to fight—it just wasn't my primary purpose. But I couldn't exactly admit that. "Just because I've grown adept at fighting vampires doesn't mean I've had any meaningful training."

"Agreed, but it's vampires and ghosts we face here, and you're very good against one, and can sense—if not reason with—the other. Both of those skill sets are bonuses on this sort of mission."

"I'm not coming back here with you, Jonas—end of story."

"I could leave you here."

"You could, but even then you can't force me inside. Not if you want to avoid alerting the vampires." I hesitated, then added, "Besides, I need to keep close to Sal, given there's a damn good chance he's involved in all this."

Jonas didn't immediately comment, and his expression, as usual, gave little away. I had an odd feeling he was once again conversing with Nuri—and that meant their connection was very strong indeed. Telepathy usually had distance limits, which was why, during the war, lures had been assigned "monitors" who relayed the information back to base. Eventually he said, "That *is* a logical step, I suppose."

"You don't know how glad I am that you and Nuri agree with me," I said, rather sarcastically.

Amusement flirted with his lips, and it briefly lifted the unforgiving shadows that seemed so prevalent in his bright eyes. It made me wish, once again, that he'd smile for real, and more often.

But maybe it was a good thing he didn't. I was attracted enough to the damn man now, despite the layers of distrust he aimed my way. I didn't need the ice between us melting, not in any way, shape, or form.

"Given we plan a raid tomorrow, it ultimately makes sense we keep an eye on the players. Or at least the one we're aware of at this point." He spun his heels and headed for the end of the building.

"Which is why I asked the little ones to keep an eye on him today," I said, following him. "They'll report back to me at dusk."

"Good idea," he said, "but why not keep them on him twenty-four/seven?"

"Because while they may be ghosts, they aren't adults. Bear was right on puberty at death, and Cat was only seven. Ghosts don't grow and they don't age, they just remain as they were when they died. I don't know how shifters bring up children, but I don't let my little ones roam around after dark, especially given the vampires' recent attacks on our home."

"Neither do we." He paused at the edge of the building and glanced at me. "Do you need a hand down?"

I shook my head, turned around, and—ignoring the butterflies taking flight in my stomach—slowly lowered myself over the edge. Once I was at full arm stretch, I let go and dropped the rest of the way, landing lightly. Jonas just leapt down, his fingers barely brushing the soil as he quickly balanced and moved on.

"But," he added, "your little ones are ghosts. There's not much that can hurt them."

"Maybe, but they *are* still little, even if Bear likes to think himself more of an adult than barely a teenager. And like all kids, they get scared."

"It's hard to imagine ghosts capable of emotions and fear," he said, "especially when those ghosts were déchet."

"Then maybe déchet aren't what the rumors and fairy tales would have you believe."

He snorted. "Oh, they are, and that's coming from experience rather than reading material."

"Meaning you were in the war? You may look a little battered around the edges, shifter, but I doubt you're *that* old."

"My father was in the war, as was my uncle, and both encountered déchet more than a few times. It scarred them more than just physically."

There was a note in his voice—a hint of ice and utter hate—that sent chills across my skin. If he ever confirmed his suspicion that Penny was right, that I was déchet . . . I shivered and thrust the thought away. He wouldn't find out.

But Nuri, as an earth witch and seeker, certainly *could* if I wasn't very careful in her presence.

"The humans didn't actually start the war, shifter. Your people did. Humans just made sure they had a reasonable chance of fighting back."

He snorted again. "So creating unfeeling monsters was a reasonable response, was it?"

"There were monsters on both sides," I snapped back. "Shifters were hardly saints themselves, even if history has been rewritten to state otherwise."

He cast me a look that could be described only as contemplative. "It almost sounds as if you were there."

I raised an eyebrow. "Do I look that old to you?"

"No, but you're a shifter capable of full-body transformation—who actually knows what you look like?"

"I was wearing my true form when I brought Penny to Chaos—"

"A form I didn't see as I was unconscious," he cut in.

"But you saw it later, when you and Nuri questioned me in the cell. As I said, do I actually look that old to you?"

"No. But then, we've established the fact you're not exactly telling us the whole truth. This could be just another of a long line of subversions and half lies."

"And I'm not the only one doing that, am I?"

"We have told you nothing *but* the truth."

"Except for those times when you avoid it. Like when I asked just how connected you are to the government."

"We aren't."

"Liar."

He half shrugged. "You are free to believe what you wish."

"And I will, just as you may, shifter."

"At least we have reached agreement on something," he muttered, and, from there on in, increased his pace.

I didn't actually care, because walking at such a fast clip meant I had to concentrate on the path and gave me less time to actually think about the stubborn, angry man in front of me. The trip back to Central was also done in silence, which at least meant I wasn't running the risk of saying the wrong thing and possibly outing myself.

He stopped at the back of the museum and opened the ATV's door on my side. I climbed out, then hesitated and met his gaze. "Contact me when you get back from the raid. And good luck."

"Hopefully we'll have the raid planned well enough that we won't need luck."

I hoped he was right, but a whole lot could happen in the time between now and their raid tomorrow. I stepped away from the ATV as he hit the door-close switch, and watched until it had disappeared through the trees before spinning around and heading for the bunker's exit.

Dusk was just beginning to drift pink-and-lemon fingers across the sky by the time I arrived. Thankfully, the grate was still in one piece, and no ghosts waited for me, which meant nothing untoward had happened during the day.

I entered the tunnel, deactivating the electro-nets as I approached each one, then resetting them once I'd passed. With that done, I headed for the bunk rooms. I needed to wash the day's grime from my body, although all I really wanted to do was drop into my bunk and sleep for a good ten hours. It had been a long day today, and an even longer night last night, and I was running close to exhaustion.

The ghosts rallied around me as I exited the nursery sections, and began bombarding me with images of everything they'd done during the day. Mostly they'd spent the time in the museum, following the visitors and gossiping about them, but occasionally they amused themselves by moving items placed in one spot by museum staff to another.

"Are Cat and Bear back yet?" I asked once they calmed down a little.

A wash of negativity ran through my mind, rapidly

followed by worry. "They're okay," I added quickly. "They're just on a mission for me. Keep an eye out for them."

Some of the older youngsters rushed away immediately to return to the main tunnel and keep watch, but most of the littler ones stayed with me, happily filling me in on everything else they'd seen and done during the day.

I was out of the shower and just pulling on a tank top by the time Cat and Bear arrived. Their excitement and happiness stung the air and I couldn't help smiling. They'd not only enjoyed their assignment, they wanted to do it again tomorrow.

I sat cross-legged in the middle of my bunk and patted the blanket on either side of me. "Tell me what he did."

Their images began to flow through my mind. Sal hadn't immediately left Hedone after he'd bundled me out the door, but had instead gotten back on the com unit and made a rather long phone call.

"To whom?" I cut in. "Did you catch a name?"

Cat's energy ran across my skin, briefly connecting us on a more direct level. *No,* she said, her voice soft and sweet, *we didn't get close, in case he sensed us. But it was a woman.*

Meaning it was more than likely the woman who'd been caught in that rift with him. "Thanks, Cat."

Her energy retreated, and the images ran on. After the long conversation with the woman, Sal changed and headed downstairs to Hedone, spending several hours doing paperwork and talking to customers and personnel.

It wasn't until the early afternoon that he'd left and walked directly to a glass-fronted, ten-story building. The name Winter Halo flashed into my mind, and I swore and briefly closed my eyes. Despite everything, part of me had hoped I'd been wrong, that he wasn't involved, that he and I could go on as we always had, as friends and lovers.

But I guess surviving the war and remaining undiscovered was all the good luck the goddess Rhea was going to extend my way.

"Did he see anyone while he was in there? Talk to anyone?"

The image of a tall, thin-faced man with dark hair, shadowed skin, and oddly magnetic blue eyes flashed into my mind. With it came a thick sensation of uneasiness. My ghosts hadn't liked this stranger's feel or presence.

"Why?" I asked. "What was it about him you found so unsavory?"

This time it was Bear who touched my skin and formed a deeper connection. No surprise there, given the toll it took on them to initiate contact like this. My initiating it—as I had when I'd talked to the Carleen ghosts—drained me, not them, though why it worked that way I had no idea.

He feels strange. Bear's voice broke slightly, a physical sign of puberty and one he was eternally stuck in.

Like a vampire feels strange?

No. Vampires feel like the dead. This was . . . He hesitated, and I felt his mental shrug. *Alien. It was almost as if he didn't belong in our world.*

Jonas had said that the darkness I'd seen in Sal's mind—the one that had caught all four people and forever changed them—had been a rift. And while some rifts simply did nothing more than rip apart anyone or anything unfortunate enough to get in their way, many were gateways by which the Others entered our world.

And Jonas had also said that Sal's scent had undertones that reminded him a little of those creatures.

Which more than likely meant I'd guessed right—the

fourth person I'd seen *had* been one of the Others. It would also explain why they'd killed him so quickly. But it meant Sal now had that creature's DNA in him, and surely to Rhea I would have sensed a change as big as *that*.

Or would I?

Over one hundred years had passed since I'd last seen him, and that was more than time enough for memories to become rose-colored and unreliable.

Bear's touch retreated, and the images resumed. Whoever Sal had seen inside Winter Halo had not been happy. Neither of the ghosts had been close enough to catch the conversation, but the other man had certainly been animated. On body language alone, it looked like he'd been laying down some ground rules, and that meant Sal wasn't in charge—not if what I was now seeing was any indication. But why would he be, when we'd been bred to follow rules rather than give them? He may now run several successful brothels, but that didn't mean he'd entirely escaped his DNA programming—even if it was programming those other two people now shared.

When Sal finally left Winter Halo, he didn't—as I'd half expected—return to Hedone, but had instead headed straight down Victory Street, away from the first district and toward the twelfth. I had a bad feeling I knew exactly where he'd gone, and the very next image proved me right.

I closed my eyes for a moment and swore softly. Cat's energy patted my arm, offering sympathy even though I doubted she really understood my anger.

The images rolled on. Sal, heading into Deseo, walking unchallenged through the establishment and down into the basement. He punched a code into the newly fixed security control panel, walked down the steps, and disappeared into the false rift.

There really *was* no doubt now. Sal was involved with whatever was happening to the children.

"Cat and Bear, you did a great job," I said. "Thank you very much."

Their pleasure at being able to help was so strong I could almost see their smiles. They danced about me, eager to repeat their adventure tomorrow.

"Maybe," I said, "but the first thing we'll do tomorrow is head to Carleen. We need to find out what Sal was doing, or where he went from there."

Bear's energy settled against my skin again, briefly renewing that stronger connection. *Why not tonight? Tomorrow gives him too much time to escape.*

"He's not escaping. He can't." Why I was sure of that, I couldn't say. But he and the others seemed very tied to Central, and not only because the businesses they ran were all very successful—a point that made me wonder just what their female partner was involved in. "Besides, we can't risk moving at night, Bear. The vampires are aware of our presence now, and I have no doubt they'll be watching our bunker even if they can't get in."

Bear wasn't happy with this decision, but, despite his grumbles, I knew he understood. Just as I knew he had no more desire than me to confront vampires at night, when they were at their strongest. "Tomorrow we'll head to Carleen and see what the ghosts say. In the meantime, could you keep an eye on the electro-nets I set up in the tunnel? And let me know the minute one of them activates?"

He zoomed off, happy to have something to do. Cat also drifted off, but I could her chattering to the other little ones, no doubt filling them in on their adventures over the day. Smiling, I climbed into bed, shut down the lights, and slept the sleep of the dead.

*　*　*

I woke just before dawn and headed to the main weapons cache. I had no idea what I might find in Carleen now that Sal and his partners were clearly aware that someone not only knew of their activities, but also was actively trying to stop them—and that meant I had to be prepared for any eventuality. So I strapped on as much weaponry as I could physically carry—it was better to be overprepared than underprepared.

The city's drawbridge was still closed as we made our way through the rail yards, but many of the pods were already humming to life, powering up for the day's activities. I crossed the main road quickly and moved into the park. Shadows still haunted the more densely treed sections, but Bear assured me that—no matter what my imagination might be saying—there were no vampires lurking in the undergrowth, ready to jump out at us.

It took us a little under an hour to reach Carleen's broken curtain wall. I scrambled over it and once again moved carefully through the clumps of luminescent moss, avoiding the darker energy of the rifts as I headed toward the road that climbed up to the remains of the town's main center.

But the Carleen ghosts met me halfway up the hill, and their anger was so fierce it felt as if I'd slammed into a physical wall. I gasped and bent over, suddenly battling to breathe.

"Blaine," I somehow managed to croak, "the force of your anger is too overwhelming—you need to tell everyone to tone it down."

The emotive output immediately pulled back. I took several quivery breaths, then dropped the rest of the way to the ground and crossed my legs. The fastest way to find out what had been going on since I'd last been here was to connect directly to them via my ghosts, but it would have to be fast. Creating this type of connection so often in a short space of time was a severe drain on my strength, and I had a *bad* feeling I would need to be at peak abilities to cope with the crap that was heading my way.

Of course, that same intuition didn't illuminate exactly what it meant by "crap," which was damn frustrating.

"Cat, I need your help again."

I held out my hand. Cat's energy immediately began to seep into my body and, just as quickly, the chill of death began to creep into my outer extremities.

With the countdown to death begun, I ran my gaze across the figures clustered in the middle of the road until I found Blaine. He was standing to one side of the main group and was accompanied by several others. No matter what the crisis was, it seemed the leaders of this place still preferred to hold themselves apart from the general public.

"What's the problem?" I said.

"The wraiths came back," he said. "This time they did more than just shift a false rift. This time they created a wall we cannot get through."

My gaze jerked to the top of the hill. All I could see were the skeletal remains of once-grand buildings. Certainly there wasn't any sort of barrier visible—not even that of a false rift. I frowned. "What sort of wall?"

"Magical," Blaine spat back. "It banned us all from our resting place, and it burns at our bones."

If it felt as if the magic was burning at their remains, then it was probably some sort of earth magic. But witches capable of using the energy of the earth to power the creation of magic were few and far between, and those capable of twisting that energy to evil purposes even rarer.

But it was scary knowing the people behind the false rifts were apparently capable of doing just that. "How many wraiths were there?"

"Two—one male, one female. It was the latter who performed the magic."

The chill of death was reaching past my knees. I had to hurry this along. "And they were both wraiths?"

"In appearance, yes, although they were speaking common tongue."

If they were speaking, then despite appearances they certainly weren't wraiths, as wraiths had no mouths. But then, I didn't really expect them to be. Not after everything I'd learned over the last day or so.

I imagined Sal's facial features in my mind, superimposed the larger eyes and grayer skin of a wraith, and then pushed the image out to the ghosts. They immediately began to stir and mutter, answering my question before I even asked it. But I asked it anyway, just to be certain. "And is this one of them?"

"Yes," Blaine said immediately. "You know him?"

"I thought I did." My voice was grim. "Did they do anything other than raise the wall and boot you out of your resting place?"

"Yes. They moved the children."

"They *what*?"

"Moved the children. Five were taken by the male into a rift; the other eight were taken by the women into the vehicle she arrived in."

I could understand their splitting the children to help prevent a total disruption of their plans in the event of discovery, but why split them so unevenly? "What sort of vehicle?"

He shrugged. "It was a large ATV, military in design but not holding military registration."

Why would they take five through a rift, and the others in an ATV? None of this was making any sense—unless, of course, they were preparing a trap. "What sort of registration did it have?"

"Government."

"Government?" I couldn't help the surprise in my voice. "Are you sure of that?"

His smile was thin. Humorless. "Yes. I was an official here in Carleen, remember. Military vehicles were often used to ensure our safety, especially in the latter parts of the war."

The ice had reached my thighs and was beginning to leach through my torso, making it difficult to think, to move. To breathe. I needed to end this.

Fast.

And yet I couldn't. There were still too many things I needed to know. "Which direction did the ATV go when it left here?" I hesitated, then added, "I'm presuming it did leave?"

"Yes. It went toward Central."

For the second time in as many seconds, shock ran through me. "Central?"

He nodded. "We followed them to the boundary, but no farther. They were heading through the park, moving toward your city. Whether they actually continued in that direction, we cannot say. We prefer not to leave the boundary of our home."

Most ghosts didn't. Bear and Cat were a rarity in that regard, and it was undoubtedly due to the fact that they'd died in my arms.

"And the . . ." My breath caught in my throat and froze the rest of the question in place. Panic surged, but a heartbeat later, I sucked in a breath and quickly said, "Other three—which rift did they go through?"

"The one that remains outside the barrier the gray witch raised." Concern crossed his expression. "You had best end this conversation, unless you have a sudden desire to become one of us."

"I don't, but thanks for your help."

He bowed and, as Cat's energy began to pull away, quickly added, "Find these people. Stop them."

It was all I could do to say, "I plan to."

With Cat's connection gone, I slumped backward and stared up at the matte gray skies, sucking in air and waiting for the chill of death to leave my body and for feeling to creep back into my limbs. My two little ghosts pressed against me, offering the comfort of their presence as much as their energy, but I had no intention of pulling on their strength to restore mine.

After what seemed like ages, the shivering stopped and I felt strong enough to stand. I stared up at the long road rising ahead of us, then resolutely pushed myself on.

It was a tedious climb in my weakened state, and I was sweating heavily and shaking with fatigue by the time I got to the top. I seriously had to take time out to heal myself; I might have had a good night's sleep, but it wasn't enough to restore me at a cellular level, and that's what I needed right now. If I *didn't* heal, I was going to be in big trouble—especially if I *hit* trouble.

I paused at the top of the hill and looked around. The dark energy of the false rift that hovered around the resting place of the ghosts was easy enough to spot, but I couldn't see or feel anything that indicated there was any type of magic at work here. Certainly there didn't appear to be anything that would prevent my moving closer.

But as I tried to step forward, Bear spun in front of me, stopping me in my tracks. Red flashed through my mind—a warning of danger.

I frowned and raised a hand, carefully pressing one finger forward. I was almost at full stretch when a thin strip of green light leapt up from the broken road surface and snatched at my finger. I jerked it away quickly, but the sliver followed, reaching for me, its feel foul and somehow corrupted. I ran backward, afraid to turn my back on the thing, and, after several steps, the sliver faded away. I sighed in relief and said, "Thanks, Bear."

He whisked lightly around me, seemingly amused that he could see what I could not. "How far around this hill does it go? Could you check?"

He was off in an instant. "Cat, do you want to check how high the barrier reaches? Just be careful not to get too close."

Her energy kissed my right cheek, and then she was gone. I crossed my arms and stared at the foul darkness that now dominated Carleen's main square. Why would they put it here? Why not simply leave it where it was and just erect another earth-fueled barrier around it?

I rubbed my forehead wearily. I didn't understand these people, but then, that wasn't really surprising given I had a hard time understanding anyone who could hurt children.

Which made my attraction to Jonas all the more troubling. It was *his* people who'd used the worst possible method to destroy everyone in my bunker. I should be so repelled by him that I couldn't stand to be in his presence rather than the opposite being true. And while I'd like to blame my DNA programming, I suspected there was a whole lot more going on than just that. I'd spent a lot of time in shifter camps during the war, and no shifter had snared my interest this way. Nor had any of those I'd chosen to lie with afterward. So why was he different? Was it the darkness within him? Or was it simply a matter of wanting someone I knew I could never have?

Bear returned and the image of a green wall surrounding the entire top part of the hill flashed into my mind. A couple of seconds later, Cat joined us. The wall was apparently two trees high. Which maybe meant I *could* get over it, but not in daylight. It would have to be done at night, when I was able to shadow and move as easily as the vampires—and that was something I was loath to do when they were so very aware of our presence in the area.

Which meant there was nothing more I could do here. Not at the moment, anyway. But the day wasn't a total waste—I now had proof Sal was involved, and that surely meant my next move had to be questioning him.

And once I'd questioned him . . . I closed my eyes against the slither of pain that ran through me.

Once I'd questioned him, I would have to kill him. I couldn't release him, because he would then come after me. He and his partners were already far too uncertain about my part in the break-ins at their facilities.

Of course, given what they'd been doing here today, it was totally possible that he *wouldn't* meet with me. But even as the thought crossed my mind, I brushed it away as nonsense. Sal was a gray—a cool, calm assassin. He wouldn't flinch at killing me any more than he had the hundreds he'd killed during the war, and who knew how many after. He might regret the loss of our friendship, and he might briefly miss the sex, but his emotional center, like those of the déchet soldiers, had been chemically altered.

Perhaps not to the same degree, but it had nevertheless been done.

He wouldn't miss me as I would miss him.

But before I did anything, I had to get back to full strength. To have any hope of being able to question and kill Sal, I had to be at the top of my game physically *and* mentally.

I spun on my heel and headed back to our bunker. It took just over an hour to get there, by which time Central's drawbridge was down and the rail yards buzzed with life. I switched direction and took the long way around, preferring to walk through the dappled light of the small park behind the museum to the crowded confines of the pod platforms.

I finally made it to the tunnel and headed for the main kitchens on level five. The machines were running low on anything resembling fresh food, so I settled on several protein packs, a somewhat less than appealing-looking orange, and a large black coffee. Once I'd consumed those, I returned to the bunkhouse and made myself comfortable on my bed. After asking the ghosts to keep watch, I closed my eyes and focused on nothing more than my breathing, on every intake of air as it washed through my nostrils and down into my lungs. Eventually, the calm healing state began to descend. It took a while, but the persistent, niggling chill that had settled deep into my bones began to ease, and the tiredness that had plagued me over the last day or so began to ebb away.

Eventually, I took a deep breath and pulled myself from the trancelike state. The bunk room was silent; none of the ghosts were near, not even Cat and Bear.

Frowning, I pushed to my feet and walked over to the exit, pressing my thumb against the scanner and waiting with some impatience for Hank to do his bit and open the doors.

The ghosts appeared as I walked into the corridor heading down to the next level. They swirled around me excitedly, everyone chattering at the same time, creating a whirlpool of sound and color and concern.

But not for me.

For the two people who were now standing at our exit grate.

"Guys, calm down." I waited several seconds for them to do so, then added, "Who is at the grate?"

Images flashed into my mind. One was Nuri, the other was Branna. Both of them were bloody, but Branna looked in particularly bad shape.

I swore softly and ran down into the tunnel, switching off the electro-nets as I went.

"Tiger," Nuri said, relief in her voice as I appeared. "You need to let us in. You need to help us."

"Why?" I asked bluntly. "What can I do that you can't get from Chaos or Central?"

"We can get many things in Chaos, but there's no working mediscan beds, and Branna will die without one."

My gaze went to him. There was a rough bandage around his waist, but it was dark and dripping with blood. His left arm had also been bandaged, and even from where I stood it was obvious it had been broken in several spots. And there was a truly vicious-looking wound peeling open on his forehead.

I returned my gaze to Nuri's. "Central has mediscans, probably far better than the ones I have here."

"Yes, but Branna, like the rest of us, is outcast."

"I thought you said no one in Chaos was outcast."

"Except for us, and those like us. Or, at least, those of us they know about."

"Meaning what?"

She waved a hand. "That is not important right now. The only thing that matters is the fact that those in Central will let him die rather than treat him."

I have to admit, I was more than a little willing to let that happen myself, especially given what he had already done to me, and what he no doubt would do if he ever found out what I was.

"Please, Tiger, this is important."

I hesitated, then said, "Okay. But we keep him sedated even after he's healed. The ghosts will not appreciate his presence and may well react."

"Deal."

Her fast response had me worrying. Was it really wise to let these two into our sanctuary? Was there even a choice now that they were here? They couldn't remain outside without attracting the sort of attention I wanted to avoid, and there was something in her expression that suggested she wouldn't leave even if I refused entry. I punched in the code and stepped back as the grate opened.

"Follow the ghosts," I said, offering Nuri no help. She was a strong woman, and an earth witch besides. If she needed help bearing Branna's weight, she could pull it from the earth. I had no intention of getting within arm's reach of the man, even if he was bloody and momentarily broken.

I reset the nets and followed a safe distance behind the two. Nuri hauled Branna into the mediscan nearest the door, then stepped back and eyed the unit somewhat dubiously. "They really are ancient, aren't they?"

"I did warn you." The light screen shimmered to life as the bed's thick foam enveloped Branna. A soft *beep*ing filled the silence; his body might be broken, but there was nothing wrong with his biorhythms, aside from an accelerated pulse rate—no doubt due to his body's natural healing abilities trying to cope with both his broken bones and the blood loss. I set the scanner into motion, then glanced across to Nuri. "So where's the third musketeer?"

"Musketeer?" She raised an eyebrow. "I take it you mean Jonas."

"Yes." I glanced at the screen as the scanner finished and began listing recommended actions. Despite outward appearances, no major organs had been damaged, and the only real danger he was in was that he was still losing blood too fast.

"I'm afraid he's the other reason we're here."

"Really?" I pressed a couple of buttons; restraints wrapped around Branna's ankles and wrists. While the scans suggested he was truly out of it, I wasn't about to take chances. "Why? What has he done?"

"The fool has gone and gotten himself captured."

My gaze shot to hers. *"What?"*

Her expression was grim. "Our infiltration of the bunker did not, as you might have guessed, go according to plan."

"The ghosts?"

She shook her head. "They were easy enough to deal with, despite the fury in their hearts."

There was something in her expression that had unease crawling through my gut. "Meaning you destroyed them?"

"Those who did not accept the offer to move on, yes." Her voice held an edge of unexpected ruthlessness. She might be an earth witch, but there was a steeliness in her— a coldness—that was very uncommon. "Our concern right now is for the living. The dead have had their time; they cannot linger here."

"And is that the fate you plan for those who haunt this place?" My voice was soft, my hands clenched. I had no weapons, but I had the ghosts. And while I had no wish to put any of them in harm's way by asking them to attack this woman, I *could* draw on their power. It might not be as powerful or as all-consuming as the force she was capable of, but it was nevertheless deadly.

A cool smile touched her lips. She was well aware of what I could do—and obviously wasn't concerned.

"What happens to *them* very much depends on what decisions you make in the next few minutes."

The ghosts—the warrior ghosts—were gathering. As was their fury. This situation could very easily run out of control if I wasn't very careful.

"Meaning what?"

"Meaning, I want you to go back to that bunker and rescue Jonas."

I snorted. "If the vampires have him, he's long dead. They tend not to be able to resist the urge to feed when fresh blood is in the offering."

"He's not dead," she said. "He hasn't even been fed on."

The certainty in her voice made me frown. "And how can you be sure of . . ." I hesitated, then added, "You're linked, and it's more than just telepathy, isn't it? Because, as far as I know, telepathy has distance restrictions."

"Yes, it has, and yes, we are. And I will not leave him to whatever fate these bastards have planned for him."

"Then raise an army and raid the place. You're living in the middle of Chaos's mercenary section, for Rhea's sake—there's plenty of vampire fodder available there for the right sort of credit."

"True, but mercenaries are not the answer in this situation. You are."

The tension in me—around me—continued to build. Energy crawled across my skin, thick with fury and the need to attack. The ghosts didn't, but I doubted the restrictions of their programming would hold if they truly felt threatened. I drew in a deep breath, knowing I needed to keep a lid on my own emotions if I was to have *any* hope of controlling that of the ghosts.

"And why would you think that?"

"Because you are what they are."

Her gaze met mine, and my blood ran cold. She knew. Rhea help us all, she *knew*. Part of me wanted to run. Part of me wanted to kill her where she stood.

I did neither. I simply said, "And what might that be, Nuri?"

"You are vampire," she said, voice flat. "Or rather, you are a déchet whose blood runs with the stain of their darkness."

The energy and fury stinging my skin sharpened abruptly, snatching my breath and making my own seem minute by comparison. Just for an instant, I saw an answering spark run across Nuri's fingertips—it was fierce and thunderous, and it was warning enough of the power that was hers to unleash. I silently begged the older ghosts for calm—for restraint—and said, "That does not make me invisible to them. That does not mean I could pass through their ranks any more easily than you. The injuries I received when I stumbled into their nest the first time was evidence enough of that."

"Yes, but it will enable you to get in with some hope of being undetected, and it will also enable you to get Jonas out."

"And how do you think I'm going . . ." I stopped. She was talking about shadowing. Or, more specifically, shadowing with Jonas. "I don't even know if something like that is possible."

"It is, because I've seen vampires do it."

"Just because they can—"

"You are what they are," she repeated. "And I have read the future in the breeze and the earth, and you are Jonas's only hope. You *will* do this. You *must*, for your sake as much as ours."

For my sake? Then I thrust the thought aside. Now was not the time to examine such an odd comment.

"Or what?" My voice was flat. Without emotion. Without hope. I knew the answer, because it was the same one that had echoed down through time and history.

"Or," she said, her voice as emotionless as mine, "I will not only destroy all that you hold dear, but I will send them to a very special kind of hell—one that is usually reserved for the vilest of souls. The choice, dear Tiger, is yours."

CHAPTER 12

The urge to leap over the bed and rip her throat out with my bare hands was so fierce I actually took a step forward. It took every ounce of willpower to not only restrain that urge, but to contain the answering surge of energy from the older déchet still gathering around us.

Nuri, I noticed, hadn't moved, even though I had no doubt she was aware of both my fury and that of the ghosts.

"I'm guessing," I said, voice low and flat, "that my fate will be the same?"

"Oh no, you'll be free to remain here—alive, alone, and fully aware that you could have saved them and failed." Her gaze narrowed a little. "Just as you failed to save them once before."

Shock ran through me. She'd read me altogether *too* well. I clenched my fists and said, "You have *no* idea what went on in this place after the war—"

"And at this point," she cut in, "I don't *care*. Make your choice, Tiger."

There *was* no choice, and we both knew it. But I couldn't go down without a fight, even if it was only a war of words.

"If you could do such a thing to the young ones who haunt this place, then you are no better than those we hunt."

"I seek to save the lives of the *living*." Though her voice remained calm, the flash of darkness and fury in her eyes suggested my words had hit a nerve.

And so they should have. Murder was murder, whether we were talking about the living or the dead.

"What happens afterward?" I asked. "If I manage to survive—and bring Jonas back—what then?"

"You will help us find the children."

"And after that?"

She frowned. "After that, you are free to go on as you always have."

I laughed. It was a harsh and bitter sound, and both the little ones pressed closer to me, their energy both comforting and confused. Not so much about this situation or even the woman in front of us, but rather both by my anger and that of the older déchet around us. Not since the gassing of this place had any of us felt so furious, and yet so helpless.

"You will have to forgive my reaction," I said, when I could actually speak, "but someone who would threaten the existence of so many innocent ghosts to save one living soul is not someone I'm inclined to trust."

"It's more than just one soul," she snapped back. "Or have you forgotten the other thirteen missing children?"

"I haven't forgotten *anything*." Not the children, not the war, not the worthlessness of promises. After all, had not the shifters assured all those caught in—or herded back to—the bases after the war that rumors of eradication were untrue? That places would be found for us in a world broken by war?

"You have my word . . ." She caught herself, making me wonder if she'd read my thoughts, then continued, "I swear, on the heart of the earth goddess herself, that if you do your utmost to help us rescue both Jonas and those children, I will do nothing to threaten either you or those who haunt this place."

I crossed my arms. Making such a vow was the next best thing to signing her own death warrant if she didn't follow through. Her goddess was not benevolent when it came to such things.

Still . . .

"What happens if I don't rescue him? What happens if we rescue some, but not all, of the children?"

"If you fail, we all fail. That much I have seen."

"Answer the question, Nuri."

"Nothing will happen. A vow was made, and it will be upheld."

"By you. What of those you work with? We both know you have some sort of government connection—just as we both know standing aside while others seek to cleanse this place of us would not make you a vow breaker."

The mediscan *beep*ed, and I jumped. I took a slow, deep breath in an effort to calm my nerves and glanced at the screen. In my anger at Nuri and her threat, I'd forgotten to give the go-ahead for all recommended actions. It was tempting to do nothing—to deny Branna the treatment that would help save his life. *Very* tempting. It might also be the safest course of action and one that would undoubtedly save me future grief. But if I did and he died, then I would be no better than them. *Not* that I was, anyway. I might have been

bred as a seductress, but killing my targets after their usefulness had ended often came hand in hand with that.

I accepted all the machine's recommendations, then
met Nuri's gaze again. "Do you deny government links?"

"If this place is attacked, it will not be from anything
we have said or done."

An assurance that didn't sit well, especially given she
hadn't answered the actual question. And, I judged, had
no intention of doing so.

"Fine," I snapped. "I'll try. But you do realize that if
Jonas is still alive, it's because they have plans for him. Or
because they are using him as bait."

"I'm aware of those factors, and that is why you must leave
now. They will not be expecting a response so quickly."

I wasn't so sure about that. "And just how do you expect me to get up there? No matter what the rumors are
about vampires, they can't fly, and neither can I." Or, at least,
not when there was any light about.

"Our ATV is parked behind the museum. Use it." She
tossed me a control disk. "Bring him back to us alive,
Tiger. It's just as important to you as to us that this
happens."

I frowned. "Meaning what?"

She waved the question away. "Go. Your ghosts will
come to no harm."

"When it comes to the ghosts, it's probably you who
should be worried, not me. They *will* fight you if you
attempt anything untoward."

"I won't, not as long as you uphold your end of the
deal." She half shrugged. "And Branna has neither the skill
nor the knowledge to harm them. He is fury and bluster,
nothing more."

I seriously doubted *that*. None of these people were

what they appeared on a surface level—they all had deeper depths, and certainly deeper secrets. I hesitated a moment longer, but my innate awareness of night and day told me the sun was on the march through the afternoon sky. If I was to have any hope of pulling this rescue off, then it had to be done before dusk set in and the vampires woke.

Cat, Bear, stay here and keep an eye on her. Make sure she doesn't release Branna. Warriors, stand down. Do not attack them. With that, I spun on my heel and walked out.

And prayed like hell that by trusting Nuri, I wasn't making the biggest mistake of my long life.

I drove the ATV as close to the base as I dared, but made no effort to conceal its presence nor pull off the road. I simply turned it around so that we could jump straight into it and flee—presuming we actually made it out of the base alive, that is.

Besides, if there were watchers about, they'd spot the vehicle sooner rather than later. The canopy high above might be thick enough to reduce the fading daylight to mere flickers—and therefore stop any guards on the wing from spotting me—but there was no such protection here at ground level. The undergrowth was thick and crawling with shadows, neither of which was a deterrent when it came to vampires. And if they *had* set patrols around the perimeter of the base, they'd see past any attempt of concealment. The transport was too big—and chewed up the soil too badly—to escape detection. Which is why I was here, on the opposite side of the valley from where we'd entered last time. I was hoping against hope that Sal had forgotten about the déchet entrance into this place.

I slipped the control disk into my pocket, then reached

back to grab the large rucksack and climbed out. Though
I'd packed enough weapons to cater for a small army, I
still couldn't escape the fear it wasn't going to be enough.
But then, given Nuri, Jonas, and Branna—and who knows
how many others—had already failed to raid this place, it
was a fear that was well-founded.

I slung the rucksack over my back and scanned the
nearby trees, trying to remember where exactly the path
that led to the riverside entrance was. After a moment I
spotted the marker rock, although the faint path that should
have been evident just beyond it had long ago returned to
its forest roots.

I moved into the thick undergrowth. I couldn't hurry in
case I missed one of the markers, and yet I was all too
aware that time—and the night—were pressing closer.

It took twenty minutes to get to the river, and by that
time I was sweating with effort and fear. I squatted at the
base of a battered and fire-scarred old eucalyptus tree and
scanned the clearing before me. It really hadn't changed
all that much in over a hundred years and—despite the
forest's obvious attempts to reclaim its land—the rock-
strewn ground between here and the wide river remained
relatively open. My gaze swept upstream toward the waterfall that masked the entrance. The river still thundered
over the forty-feet drop and spray spun through the air,
rainbow bright in the day's last dance of light. I couldn't
see anything out of place and certainly couldn't smell anything other than earth, water, and eucalyptus.

If there were watchers here, they were well concealed.

I rose and headed upstream, keeping to the shadows
that were growing ever thicker along the tree line. I paused
again as the old path dipped toward the waterfall, prickles of unease crawling across my skin. This place was too

quiet—there wasn't even birdsong. It was as if this part of the forest had been stripped of all life and sound. Which, considering vampires now controlled the base, was entirely possible. They had to be eating something, after all, and given the numbers I'd seen and the lack of fresh bodies and bones, they obviously weren't dining on one another.

I scanned the shoreline as well as the ridge above, but once again couldn't see anyone—which didn't mean they weren't there. I eyed the faint path that disappeared behind the water, and wondered if the unease growing ever stronger within me stemmed from the certainty that this was a trap, or merely fear of what I was about to attempt.

Not that it really mattered. It wasn't like I could turn around and walk away.

I shifted the heavy bag to a slightly more comfortable position, then continued on. It would probably have been safer to call to darkness within and become one with the gathering night, but I really couldn't afford to waste the energy—not when I was going to need every scrap I could muster if I was to have any hope of getting us both out of here.

I carefully made my way down to the base of the waterfall. The air grew thick with spray that shimmered like a rainbow and clung to my clothes like silvery jewels. I kept close to the ridge wall and headed under the fall. The path was slick with moisture and thick moss, evidence enough that no one had been this way for some time. And despite Jonas's statement that shifters had blasted the secondary tunnel into the base wide-open, there was little in the way of damage to be seen here. But then, this was the déchet entrance. They'd no doubt had a completely separate entrance for human personnel.

I ran my hand along the wall, the rock cold and slimy under my fingertips, and eventually found the indentations

I needed. After flicking open the false rock panel, I brushed away the cobwebs and bits of slime, then pulled the old lever down. The machinery that powered this particular door was water-driven, so there was a fair chance it was still operational. If it wasn't, I could use the emergency exit on the top of the ridge, but that was another twenty minutes away and would erase any chance I had of getting in and out before the vamps woke.

For several minutes, there was no response; then, with a sharp *pop*, a gap began to appear as the otherwise solid rock wall slid open. It ground to a halt again before the door was fully opened, but a three-feet gap provided more than enough room to get through.

I dropped the rucksack close to the base of the wall and opened it up. After pulling out the last of the flares and shoving them into a smaller pack, I grabbed several modified rifles, some ammo, and a couple of pistols. Once I'd strapped on my knives, I slung the smaller pack over my shoulder and moved into the tunnel, leaving the bigger rucksack—and the bulk of the weapons—behind. I had no idea what shape Jonas was going to be in, and I couldn't carry both him and the rucksack. Not in shadow form, anyway. Hell, I wasn't even sure it was *possible* to carry him in that form. If I couldn't, all the weapons in the world weren't going to help. But if we did happen to make it back this far, we'd at least have a fresh supply of ammo and weapons to move on with.

As the deeper darkness of the tunnel enveloped me, I called to the shadows within and became one with the night. I rose upward, until my particles brushed the slick and slimy roofline, and then pressed on. The tunnel was long and angled steeply downward, but there was very little evidence of the desecration visible in the upper levels.

Maybe there'd been no need to come down this far—or maybe there'd simply been no one left to rip apart by the time they'd gotten down here. At least it meant there were no ghosts here.

I reached a cross-section and paused, looking right and left as I tried to get my bearings. The air was still, and I had no sense of life nearby. There were no vampires here; maybe they were all concentrated on the levels above, protecting the labs and whatever else was going on up there.

After a moment, I went left. The tunnel narrowed and burrowed deeper into the earth. I knew from the few times I'd been here that the two levels below this were a mix of déchet quarters and containment cells. In some sections, the only thing that had separated us from our prisoners had been the thick, silver coated metal bars that made up each containment cell—and sometimes they'd been woefully inadequate. Though I'd never witnessed it, I'd heard tales of bear shifters bending the bars as easily as butter, then running amok through the déchet ranks, taking out a dozen or so before being gunned down by humans. Déchet warriors might have been bred to be as fast and strong as shifters, but they'd also been chemically castrated—not just physically, but mentally. Free thought *wasn't* something the humans wanted—not when their creations were as deadly as the shifters they were designed to fight. As a result, most of those in these levels would have been in a sort of "holding pattern" and incapable of defending themselves. It was just another thing to hate about a war that had caused so much grief and destruction.

I did a thorough search of both lower levels, but didn't find Jonas in either. Not that I was surprised; breaking him out was hardly going to be *that* easy. I sped back up the tunnel until I reached the crossroads again, then scooted through the smashed remains of what once had been the main déchet-processing terminal for this bunker. I found the stairs and moved upward, checking the next two levels and still finding nothing. There was now only one more level before I reached the labs I'd discovered. If I'd had fingers and toes in this form, they all would have been crossed in the hope that I'd find Jonas on *that* level rather than on the floor above, where all the vamps were.

Except they *weren't* all there.

The second I moved into the next level, I sensed them. Their presence stung my particles, as did the thick sense of hunger and fury. They wanted to slash and tear and feed, but were being restrained, even in sleep.

I had to get Jonas out before that restraint broke—because it *would* break, if what I was sensing was any indication.

I moved on carefully, away from the vampires rather than toward them. I had no doubt they were clustered around Jonas's cell, but I couldn't leave the remaining sections of this level unchecked.

There was no one else here. I had no idea what this level had been used for when the base was active, but these days it seemed to be little more than a weird mix of rusting debris and more recent metal containers. Interestingly, those containers had government IDs. Someone had connections; either that, or Sal and his crew were in the pirate business as well as child experimentation.

With the remainder of the level checked, I had no choice but to move toward the vampires. The closer I got to them, the thicker the air became with their rank scent, and the more my fear grew. It was lucky I was one with the night rather than flesh, because they would have picked up the thunder of my heart from a mile away.

The first shimmers of white that indicated life appeared

in the darkness; several vampires were sprawled over one another in a doorway. I rose higher, until every bit of me scraped across the cold steel of the roofline and slowly crept past them.

The corridor beyond was a sea of white. There had to be at least a score of them here. Rhea help us both if they woke up before we got out . . .

A shiver ran through me, which was always an odd sensation when in particle form. I crept along the roofline, all senses centered on the sea of death sprawled below me. About halfway down, several stirred. I paused, hoping they hadn't sensed me. That it was just the natural stirrings of nocturnal creatures very close to waking up.

They settled down again, but it didn't ease my tension. Night was too close and time was running out. They would wake soon. I had to be out of here before that happened.

The end of the corridor came into sight. The door that barred my way was heavy steel that bore blast marks. That it was still usable, let alone able to contain a shifter while stopping the vampires from getting in, was a testament to how strong they'd once made these things. I paused and scanned the frame that held it. There wasn't enough of a gap between it and the door for even particles to get through at either the sides or the top of the door, but there was a good inch gap at the base. It would do.

I'd barely squeezed inside when the awareness of danger hit. I jagged sideways, and the thick metal bar that would have cut through the middle of my particles and done Rhea only knows what damage merely skimmed my side. But such was the force behind the blow that it sent me spinning away.

Another blow came at me. I cursed mentally and surged upward, out of reach, even as I called to my flesh form. As the second blow sailed underneath me, I regained form and dropped to the ground, hitting hard but feetfirst.

The third blow I caught and held, though the force of it shuddered up my arm and hurt like hell.

"If you want to get out of this place alive," I said, voice little more than a harsh whisper, "you'd better stop trying to kill me."

His shock was so fierce it hit almost as strongly as a physical blow. I really had no idea why I could sense this shifter's emotions so clearly—especially when I wasn't actively trying to read him—but I wished it would stop. Especially now, when the distinct lack of emotion in his expression belied the strength of that emotive swirl.

I swung the pack from my back and squatted down. "We have about five minutes before the vampires wake—"

"I've only ever seen one race other than the vampires able to do what you just did," he cut in, voice harsh. "I was right—you're one of them. You're a déchet."

I glanced up quickly. The fierce shock I'd felt only seconds ago had turned to anger. Anger and utter hatred. He hadn't moved, but every ounce of him quivered like a bow too tightly strung. One wrong move, and we would both be dead.

"But not a soldier, no matter what you think." My voice was calm, despite the tension rising within me. Tension the vampires closest to the door would sense if they were anywhere near consciousness. "And, right now, I'm your only means of getting out of here."

He snorted, and I couldn't help noticing his clenched fists. Even in the blackness, his knuckles glowed white, but somehow he was restraining the urge to lash out.

For now.

"Nuri would never—"

"Nuri sent me," I cut in. "There *is* no one else coming, Jonas, so you have a choice—me or death."

His expression very much suggested death might be a better option. I would have laughed if it hadn't been so dangerous. It seemed there were some prejudices that could never be breached, no matter how much time had passed.

Which made Nuri's comment that I had to rescue him for my own sake even more baffling.

I pushed upright, weapons in hand. "Choose, shifter."

"And if I choose death?"

"Then you are a fool. But if that is your decision, then you can have the weapons. At least you can go down fighting."

I offered him the shotgun and pistol. It was a dangerous ploy given the emotional turmoil and his obvious desire to kill, but there was no other option. To get out of here, I had to trust him.

And he had to trust me.

His gaze flickered to the weapons, then met mine again. After a moment, he took the shotgun, flipped it around, and pointed both barrels straight at my face.

"What if the death I choose is yours?"

The tension boiling through me sharpened abruptly, but I didn't let any of it show physically. It might have been a very long time since I'd used any of my seductress skills, but I could still control my emotional output if I really desired—although if he could read me as well as I seemed to be reading him, it was probably a pointless exercise.

"If that is your choice, then so be it." I shrugged. "But even if you somehow make it out of here alive, you will never find those children."

"Says who?"

"Nuri." I hesitated, then added, "And you might wish to know I have no more desire to be here than you have to be rescued by me. But Nuri threatened the lives of every ghost within my bunker. I cannot let my little ones die any more than you would choose to walk away from those still missing."

For several precious moments, neither of us moved. Outside the bunker, dusk was dying, and inside the vampires were beginning to stir. We had two minutes, if that, before all hell broke loose.

"Choose, shifter. *Now*."

"Then I choose life." He lowered the shotgun. "Yours *and* mine."

For now.

Once again, he might not have said those last two words, but they nevertheless hovered in the gulf between us.

"Fine," I said, to both what had been said and what had not. I handed him a pistol, then reached back into the pack and retrieved the remaining weapons, clipping them to my belt before slinging several ammo clips over my shoulder. I shoved three flares into my leg pockets; the other two and the remaining ammo clips I gave to him.

"How do you plan to get us out of here?"

His voice was so cold it sent frost down my spine. It was stupid to care given *this* was the very reaction I'd been expecting if he ever confirmed I was déchet. But I did, and I couldn't entirely blame my breeding—or rather, my innate attraction to shifters—because I'd never experienced this sort of reaction before.

I took a deep breath and called to the shadows within. As the darkness surged and began to change me, I said, "The same way I got in."

And with that, I leapt at him. He dove away, his reaction fast, but not quite fast enough. I caught him at hip level, and the surging energy swept past me and through him, tearing us both into particles. Feeling him in and around me—separate and yet not—was a weird sensation, but I had no time to dwell on it. The vamps nearest the door were so close to waking I could feel the rise of their alertness.

I surged under the door, then rose upward, hoping to escape detection for as long as possible. But my particle form was now double its weight, and it was already taking its toll. Especially given the particles that were Jonas were a seething, constantly moving mass of fury within me.

You'll kill us both if you don't quit it, I thought, though I wasn't certain if the combining of our particles allowed for that sort of communication.

He didn't reply, but his movements eased. I made it to the roofline and crawled along. Urgency beat through every inch of me, but I couldn't afford to hurry. Any sudden movement was likely to attract the attention of the vamps.

We were three-quarters of the way down the corridor when they finally sensed us. A scream of fury went up from those who'd been sleeping near the cell door, and, in an instant, the rest of them were awake and hunting. I gave up subtlety and surged forward, arrowing for the door out of this bottleneck. The vampires who'd been sleeping there were already on their feet, but they were searching for a threat at ground level. It was only at the last possible moment that they sensed us and leapt up. Their claws slashed at the air, and pain flared as several particles were snagged and torn away. Then we were through and fleeing fast.

They came after us, howling like banshees, no doubt to alert those in the levels above that there were invaders present. They leapt at us randomly, sometimes knocking one another over in their desperation to bring us down. The force of their movements buffeted me, and claws and teeth tore through me, sometimes causing damage, sometimes not. I ignored it and spun down the center of the stairwell, surging past the various floor exits as I headed for the processing level. There was little in the way of finesse in my movements now. I was basically free-falling, but it still had the desired effect—we'd gained distance. Not much, but maybe enough.

We finally reached the processing center. I fled through the fields of broken offices and furniture and headed for the déchet exit tunnel. The vampires were a howling wind all but snapping at our heels; they would overrun us in a matter of minutes.

We had one chance, and one chance only, to escape.

I hit the tunnel and—from Rhea only knows where—found the strength to go faster. Once again, we pulled ahead of the vampires. Light began to flicker in the distance, but it was moonlight rather than sun. It wouldn't help us, wouldn't stop the vampires.

The partially opened exit door came into sight. I called to our flesh forms as we neared and dropped lower; it would limit the damage of hitting the ground when we were moving so hard and fast. The darkness surged, and a heartbeat later, we were two rather than one, flesh rather than mere particles. In that form, we both tumbled through the doorway. It hurt—Rhea, how it hurt—but there was no time for the pain or weakness washing through my limbs. Acknowledging either would only get us killed.

I untangled myself from Jonas and leapt for the control lever, pushing it up fast.

There was no response.

I swore and ran to the door. Nothing seemed to be

jamming its movement, and yet it wasn't moving! In sheer frustration, I kicked the damn thing . . . and with a groan that oddly reminded me of an old man forcing himself upright, the door began to close.

But it was too slow. Too slow by half.

The vampires lunged for both me and the lumbering door. Bullets zinged past my ear and exploded into the face of the nearest vampire. Blood and gore ballooned, but it didn't stop his momentum, and he cannoned into me before I could unclip my weapons and sent us both tumbling. I'd barely thrown his body off me when another hit; he tore at me with teeth and sharp claws, and the scent of my blood mingled with his, stinging the night air with its sweet foulness. I swore and grabbed his arms, trying to stop him from slashing me even as I bucked to get him off. As he went sailing over my head and into the wall of water, I scrambled upright and grabbed both a flare and a weapon. But before I used either, light bit through the night. Jonas had thrown his two flares into the doorway.

It might stop the vampires long enough for the door to close, but it wouldn't stop them coming after us. There were other paths out of that place, and I had no doubt the vampires knew about them.

"This way." I grabbed the heavy rucksack, then spun and ran up the old path, away from the water and back toward the trees. Jonas followed close on my heels, as silent as the night itself, but undoubtedly more dangerous.

Behind us, the screams changed from fury to pain, and the stink of burned flesh began to steal through the air.

"They're throwing themselves on the flare," Jonas said, rather unnecessarily. "We need to get out of here—fast."

I cursed, but the reality was, I was already at top speed. Taking particle form always drained me, but carrying

Jonas had made it ten times worse. I was running on empty and fading fast.

Movement to my left: A vampire surged up the bank, dripping water as he came at us. I raised the shotgun and fired almost in the same motion, but the vampire faded. The bullets hit the stony ground, and sparks flew as they ricocheted into the night. A second later he was in flesh form again and leaping for my throat. Two more shots rang out, the sound so close it hurt my ears. What remained of the vampire's face exploded into a hundred bloody bits and covered me in goo. I ignored it, leapt over his falling body, and kept on running—into the trees, along the path, heading for the ATV and the hope of safety it offered.

Behind us, there was only darkness and death. I had no idea if the door had closed, or whether the weight of the vampires sacrificing themselves to protect those behind from the light of the flare had forced it to a halt, but it didn't really matter. They were coming. We'd run out of time.

"Faster," Jonas growled. "They're on the path."

"I'm *trying*!" I reached for more speed, but there really was nothing left in the tank.

Jonas cursed but remained by my side. I wasn't sure if that was by choice or practicality. There was safety in numbers—two against a score or more certainly had more hope than one.

I spotted the final marker, and a second later we were on the road. The ATV waited ahead, a big metal beast that would at least offer some protection from the howling horde now on our tails. I swung the rucksack out of the way and grabbed the control disk from my pocket. The minute my fingers touched it, the doors began to open.

"I'll drive." Jonas took the disk without missing a step.

"I've probably had more experience in this sort of situation than you."

Of that, there was no doubt. I'd driven it up here easily enough, but our chances of getting out of here alive could only be improved with someone capable of manually driving the thing at the wheel.

I threw the rucksack into the vehicle and leapt in after it. Jonas did the same, then hit the door release—but even as they began to slide shut, a boiling mass of hate and desperation broke out of the trees and came at us.

I grabbed the flares and ignited them. The fierce light blinded me as much as the vampires and I blinked rapidly, trying to get my vision back even as I threw two flares to either side of the ATV and the final one over the back, providing an uneven circle of light around the vehicle. It wouldn't be enough, but it would at least keep them at bay long enough for the doors to close and for Jonas to boot up the engine.

Once again, vampires threw themselves at the flares, covering the deadly light with the weight of their remains. It was an action I'd never witnessed before, and it spoke of their desperation—or at least of the desperation of those who now appeared to be in league with them.

The doors finally slipped into place and locked. At the same time, two of the flares were extinguished, and the vampires hit us—literally.

The sheer force of their onslaught was almost tornado-like; the big vehicle rocked with not only the impetus of their movements, but the weight of their blows. It might be military in design, but it was styled more like a troop carrier than an armored vehicle. It had not been designed to counter this sort of attack.

"For Rhea's sake, get us out of here!"

"I'm trying, but these things aren't race pods."

The rocking grew more violent and darkness reclaimed the night as the last of the flares became buried under a sea of burning, stinking flesh. Several vampires hit the windshield, their emaciated faces filled with desperate fury as they clawed and smashed at the glass. It held up, but I had to wonder for how long.

As the ATV's engine finally roared to life, something hit the roof so hard it actually buckled. I slid down in the seat and started loading weapons. There was another *thump*, then a metal strut speared into the cabin, the thick point barely missing my leg as it smashed into the center console. Hands clawed at the broken roof structure, peeling the metal back as easily as butter. I raised two guns and started firing. The sound was deafening, and metal ricocheted inside the cabin as much as outside, cutting everything in the near vicinity—the vampires, the ATV's innards, and the two of us.

It didn't matter. Nothing mattered. Nothing except getting out of here.

Jonas threw the vehicle into gear, and the ATV lurched forward. The vampires crowding the front of the vehicle were crushed under its heavy treads, but neither those clawing at the windshield nor those trying to squeeze through the peeled back roofline were shaken loose. I kept firing. There was nothing else I could do.

With an ominous *crack*, a multitude of hairline fractures began to race across the windshield's face, until they formed a thick web that was almost impossible to see through.

And still the vampires thumped it. A hole appeared, small at first but getting larger with each blow, until it was big enough for a fist to get through. Needle-sharp claws slashed left and right, desperately seeking a target. Steering one-handed, Jonas grabbed a gun, flicked off the safety, and began to fire. The windshield completely shattered and glass sprayed everywhere, inside and out, cutting whatever the metal shards had failed to touch.

One of my guns clicked over to empty. I threw it down and grabbed another. The second gun did the same. I grabbed the last of the loaded weapons and kept on firing.

The vampires seemed endless. They just kept coming at us as the ATV rumbled on. It was gathering speed as it bounced down the old road, but it still wasn't moving anywhere near quickly enough. At the rate we were going, the vampires would have it—and us—in pieces before it reached full speed.

"Has this thing got lights?" I had to yell to get over the tornado of sound created by the vampires, the guns, and the engine's clattering.

"Yes, but it's solar-powered, and while the batteries will get us back to Central, using the lights will drain them far too quickly."

"If we *don't* use them, we won't need to worry about getting to Central, because we won't get out of these damn mountains alive."

Fingers appeared along the nearest side pillar, and a second later, a vampire swung himself around like a rubber band and arrowed feetfirst into the ATV. I yelped and flung myself back, only to be stopped by the sturdy seat. He thudded into my chest, the force of the blow so great that the air left my lungs in a gigantic *whoosh*. I couldn't breathe; I could barely even think. He screamed and twisted upright, his hands grasping for my neck. Despite the burning in my lungs and the lights dancing in front of my eyes, I somehow flicked my knives down into my hands and slashed them across the middle of his gaunt body. He didn't immediately react, and, for a heartbeat, I thought the haze of pain and lack of air had caused me to miss. Then his hands slithered from my neck as the top part of his body fell one way and the bottom another.

I coughed and desperately tried to suck in air and ease the burning in my lungs. The effort caused red-hot lances of pain to shoot through the rest of me. I'd broken a rib— but right now that was the *least* of my problems.

More vampires came at us, from both the front of the ATV and the torn roof. I guess we were lucky in that the space was confined; only a few of them could squeeze into the holes they'd created, but that didn't stop the rest of them from trying. The sheer weight of numbers now on the ATV had to be at least partially responsible for the slow pickup of speed. I guess we had to thank Rhea that they all were more intent on getting their share of available blood rather than actually thinking; if they'd become one with the night and filled this space with the weight of them, they might very well have suffocated us.

My guns clicked over to empty again. A second later, Jonas's gun did the same. He cursed, threw it down, then hit a switch. Light bit into the darkness, clean and bright and deadly. The vampires in and around the vehicle became ash in an instant, and the ATV lurched ahead with a suddenness that flung me forward. I smacked a hand against the dash to stop my head from doing the same, and watched the black tide of vampires—some burning, some not—peel away from the vehicle, leaving the road clear.

We'd done it. Against all the odds, we'd actually gotten out of the bunker alive and managed to fight our way free from the vampires.

Now all we had to do was make it home.

CHAPTER 13

The ATV died five miles out of Central, but by then it didn't matter. The vampires had given up pursuit a mile or so after we'd left the Broken Mountains; on the wide-open freeway, the old ATV was simply too fast for them.

Once the vehicle had lumbered to a halt, Jonas forced the doors open, then climbed out. He didn't look at me or acknowledge me in any way, but simply stood in the middle of the road, sucking in air like a man on the verge of suffocating. Fighting the fury, I sensed. Fighting the need to lash out and kill.

I gathered the spent weapons and placed them all back in the rucksack, then climbed out. I might have an armory at my disposal, but there was only a finite amount of weapons within it. I couldn't afford to keep discarding them.

Jonas's shoulders twitched as my feet hit the tarmac, but he still refused to look at me. I shouldered the rucksack into a more comfortable position, then headed for Central. I had to get back to the bunker. The little ones would be worried about me, and I needed to be there in case the vampires hit it again. Ghosts might be dangerous, but they could only do so much before their energy faded. If the vampires attacked with the ferocity they'd shown when trying to stop the ATV, then Rhea only knows what would happen. And an attack was very possible given the vampires would undoubtedly inform Sal and his partners not only of the presence of a déchet in that place, but our consequent escape . . . I stopped abruptly and swore.

The minute Sal heard about the attack, he would come looking for me. If I couldn't be found in Central, then he would know, for certain, that I was the one infiltrating their bases. To have any hope of finding the missing children, Sal and his partners needed to remain *uncertain* about me.

"What?" Jonas's voice was harsh.

I turned around. He still wasn't looking at me. There were bloody rents down his powerful arms and a myriad of minor cuts everywhere else, but all in all, he'd come out of the attack far better than I had. "I need to get into Central—fast."

"The drawbridge is up; there *is* no getting in there at night."

"For you and the vampires, maybe." I dropped the rucksack to the ground. "Take that back to the bunker for me. Nuri is there, as is Branna."

"What the hell are they doing *there*?" His gaze finally met mine. All I could see were old prejudices and hatred.

"Branna was dying. They came to use the medibeds."

"And you let them?" Disbelief edged his tone.

"I healed you knowing what you were—why would I not heal Branna?"

"Because you're déchet—and *he* tried to kill you."

And Jonas was never going to get past my heritage. Sadness slithered through me. The fierceness of our attraction suggested we could have been good together, at least physically. Anything else—anything *more*—was beyond the realm of possibility for someone like me.

"I am not a monster, Jonas, no matter what the history books would have you believe."

"It's not just history that gives rise to that belief—it's firsthand experience. There are still some alive today who took part in the war."

"Yes, and I'm one of them. Shifters are responsible for just as many atrocities as humans and déchet. It was a war; right or wrong, these things happen." I studied him for a heartbeat. It was useless arguing with him. His mindset was never going to change. "I have to go—"

"Why?"

"Because the minute they hear of the attack, they'll come looking for me. I need to be found."

He frowned. "What does it matter when you can change form at will?"

"Sal won't take action against me until he's absolutely certain I'm involved."

Which was a lie. There was no true emotion in Sal, and I knew full well he *would* kill me if he in any way suspected my part in breaking Jonas out. But he'd at least question me first—and therein lay my chance. I was a lure, and I'd been bred to resist all manner of drugs and poisons. If that was one of the many things that had been erased from his memories when the rift had hit him, then I could twist the situation to my advantage.

It would be dangerous, but to save the lives of innocents, I had to at least try.

"Protect my home, Jonas," I added. "It is the very least you can do, given I've now saved your life twice."

And with that, I called to the darkness and became one with the night. Though I was bone weary and wanted nothing more than to collapse in a bloody heap, I drew on every scrap of energy I had left and headed for Central with as much speed as I could muster.

Thankfully, this form didn't have the limitations of my flesh form, and it took a little over fifteen minutes to get close to the bunker.

I sent a message to Cat and Bear, asking them to bring out washcloths, fresh clothing, and one of the purple vials still kept in the freezer units of the main med center. Then I reclaimed flesh form and collapsed in a quivering, aching heap in the trees behind the museum. As much as the need to keep moving—to get into Central before Sal or his partners came looking—burned through me, I couldn't. Not in this state. I needed to repair my body and erase most of my wounds before that happened. One or two I could explain away, but not a multitude.

I pulled myself into a sitting position and reached for the healing state. Eventually, the waves of pain began to fade away as calm descended and the healing began. It took longer than I might have wished, but it had to be done.

When I finally opened my eyes, Cat and Bear were waiting patiently. The cloths, my tunic and sandals, and the vial I'd asked for were sitting in front of my crossed legs.

I smiled and sent them mental kisses, but their relief at seeing me was tinged with concern. They knew what I was about to do; they knew it was dangerous.

"I'll be okay," I said softly. "And it's the only way to get the information we need about those children."

Cat drifted forward and patted my arm; Bear was not so

easily mollified. "I promise I'll come back," I added. "But this has to be done, and I have to do it alone. I cannot risk Sal or anyone else who comes after me sensing your presence. Besides, I need you to help protect the bunker."

Bear's energy combined briefly with mine, forming the link that allowed him to speak. *Nuri is there. She will not let us come to harm.*

"Not unless she needs to," I agreed. "But the vampires may well mount an attack, and you have to be there to help protect the little ones, Bear."

His energy withdrew. He wasn't happy, but he accepted the situation. I wrapped my arms around their little forms, feeling their particles in and around me; feeling their fears and concern.

"Go," I said, releasing them. "I'll be back tomorrow morning."

They went reluctantly. I pushed to my feet. Pain flared across my ribs, but it was little more than an echo of the pain that would have hit me had I not taken the time to heal myself. I picked up the small vial and studied it. It had been a long time since I'd used this stuff, and I wasn't looking forward to the aftereffects. But it was the only way I was ever going to get anything resembling the truth from Sal.

I uncorked the tube, quickly tipped the frozen liquid into my mouth, and crunched the ice before swallowing it. It would take little more than ten minutes for the fast-acting poison to leach into my skin; it wouldn't kill me, but it *would* kill anyone who came in contact with me. Even Sal, who could heal himself against any wound, but who didn't have the immunity to the more severe toxins that I did—and they didn't come any more toxic than Sueño. It was fast, and it was *very* deadly.

But before he died, he *would* talk.

I took a deep, quivering breath, then became one with the night again and moved toward Central. The haphazard walls of Chaos came into view, the bottom levels wrapped in darkness, the upper levels randomly lit by patches of bright light. I swerved away, keeping to the shadows that hugged the curtain wall between Chaos and the draw-bridge. Though I wasn't entirely sure where Old Stan's was from *this* side of the wall, I knew it was closer to the main gate than Chaos itself.

At the midway point between the two, I surged upward. The closer I got to the top of the wall and light of the UVs that poured over it, the more the shadows within began to unravel. As my flesh form began to reinsert itself, I made a last, desperate lunge for the top of the wall. My hands slid against the slick surface and suddenly I was sliding backward again. I cursed, scrambling madly, and, at the last possible moment, found a fissure big enough to hook my fingers into. My momentum was such that the sudden stop just about wrenched my shoulder out of its socket, and I hit the cold metal wall hard enough to force a grunt of pain. For several seconds I just hung there, my heart going a million miles a minute as I sucked in air and tried not to look at the long drop below me. If I did fall it wouldn't actually matter, as I could become night again and stop long before I got anywhere near the ground, but that knowl-edge didn't stop my irrational fear of heights asserting its ugly head once again.

But hanging here was wasting time, and I had a bad feeling that was something I was fast running out of. I lurched upward, grabbed the far edge of the thick wall, then pulled myself up onto the top of it.

Central stretched before me, bright and quiet. While there were guards stationed atop either drawbridge, they only did random patrols of the main wall if the vampires were notably active. The UVs had long ago been protected from any sort of standard weaponry taking them out, and, as far as I knew, the last of the bombs had been destroyed at the war's end. None had been made since. No one wanted to take the risk given the amount of rifts already rolling across the landscape.

I took another deep breath, then called to the sun shield. While the guards might not actively patrol, if they happened to be looking the right way and saw a shadowy human form running along the top of the wall, they *would* investigate. As light wrapped around me, I finally looked down, searching for a way off this wall. Old Stan's was only a few buildings away to my left, but I needed a building that was taller. I might have a tiger's sure-footedness, but I couldn't run the risk of breaking something with that sort of drop.

I padded along the wall, moving away from the inn and the markets. The ramshackle buildings that hugged the wall grew ever taller, and I soon found a building where the drop was only a couple of floors. I took another of those deep breaths to calm the butterflies and irrational fears, and jumped down. I landed safely, my fingers barely brushing the rooftop as I steadied myself, then moved toward the edge of the building and jumped to the next one, then the next, moving steadily downward each time.

As I neared the inn, I let the sun shield unravel and jumped down into the lane. The two old men sitting on either side of a fire burning in an old bin gave me a nod as I walked past them but made no comment. But there was a gleam in their eyes—an odd watchfulness in their expressions—that made me wonder if they were something other than just old men huddling near a makeshift fire.

Given what I'd discovered when moving the bed to get into the hidden stairwell, it was very possible that these old men were actually guards.

I pushed open the door and stepped into the cramped foyer. Old Stan still manned the desk and gave me a nod before returning to his reading. Something within me relaxed. If there'd been someone waiting upstairs, I had a feeling he would have warned me.

I took the stairs two at a time but slowed as I neared the top floor. While instinct might be suggesting Old Stan could be trusted to pass on a warning, I wasn't about to take chances. The fourth floor was dark and silent, but I couldn't sense anything out of place.

I stepped into my room, but again, nothing and no one waited. I relaxed and stripped off my clothes as I walked to the bed. I was as hungry as hell, but it was the middle of the night and the majority of Central was asleep. If Sal came calling—and I had no doubt that he would—then he at least had to find me in bed, if not asleep.

I crawled into the thick but scratchy sheets and tried to relax. But there was no getting rid of the tension, and I practically jumped at every little creak. It certainly didn't help that it now felt as if thousands of tiny ants were marching across my skin, making it prickle and sting. It was the first indication that the drug was taking hold.

I closed my eyes, willed myself to ignore the hostel's creaks and groans, and slept.

Only to be woken by the realization that someone was watching me.

Tension rolled through me, but a heartbeat later, Sal's seductive, satiny scent enveloped me, and I relaxed.

But only outwardly.

"Sal," I murmured, not having to feign the sleepy exhaustion in my voice, "what in Rhea are you doing here?"

"I came to apologize for my rather ungentlemanly manner yesterday morning," he said. "And to check that you were all right, given you didn't turn up for our dinner date."

That was because I'd totally forgotten about it. I opened my eyes. Though his smile touched the corners of his silvery eyes, he was watching me a little too carefully. Suspicion and regret stung the air, though I wasn't entirely sure whether the latter was his or mine.

"If there's one thing I have no expectations of when it comes to you," I replied, "it's gentlemanly behavior."

He laughed softly and reached out, hooking the edge of the blankets with one finger and pulling them away from my body. The cold air caressed me, sending goose bumps skittering across my skin and making my nipples harden. Or maybe *that* was a side effect of the sudden heat in his gaze. He might not trust me, but he sure as hell still wanted me.

His finger moved to my skin and began a long, almost tortuous journey from my shoulder to my hip, then back up again, until he paused at the long, barely healed scar under my left breast.

"I didn't notice this yesterday," he murmured, his fingertip following the scar's length, then journeying the final inch or so to my breast. My breath caught as he squeezed my nipple, his touch just an edge into the territory of pain.

"That's because it wasn't there yesterday." I shifted from my side to my back, presenting my full length to his gaze. His desire flared brighter, igniting the flame of my own. If this was to be our last time together, then I wanted it to be the best time.

"It almost looks like someone clawed you." His touch

moved to my other breast, again more forcefully than needed, as he caught and teased my nipple.

"Someone did." Amusement teased my lips. "How do you think I got the money for this room, Sal?"

His gaze leapt to mine and, just for an instant, something dark and almost predatory touched his gaze. "I thought you didn't sell yourself."

"Under normal circumstances, I don't, but I need to eat and I need shelter, and I have no desire to enter Chaos to find either." I shrugged. "It turned out he was after something more than just sex, but hey, I've done far worse in my time, and he paid well."

His fingers brushed the scar again, as if he could uncover my lies by mere touch. "You took a chance with such an action—the authorities do not approve of sex workers plying their trade beyond approved venues."

"I was careful, Sal." I caught his shirt and gently but firmly pulled him closer, until my lips brushed his, as I added, "So is an apology all you came here for?"

He smiled. "It certainly isn't."

Then his lips came down on mine and he kissed me. It was a fierce thing, a hungry and yet oddly desperately thing, but it nevertheless sung through me as sweetly as anything we'd ever shared before. Perhaps because this was the last time we would ever share this sort of intimacy.

Or perhaps it was because I wasn't the only one resorting to poison. It was there on his lips—I could taste the sourness of it.

I wrapped my arms around his neck and pressed tighter against him. I could feel the tautness in his powerful body, could sense the need for satisfaction warring with the urge for caution. I released one hand and undid his shirt and released the ties on his pants. His cock sprang free, thick, hard, and eager. I caressed it, and a shudder ran through him before he abruptly pulled away.

"My apology will be entirely too fast if you keep doing that." Amusement touched his lips. He rose and shucked off his shirt and pants. "Scoot over."

I obeyed. He joined me on the bed and pressed his length against me.

And in doing so, signed his death warrant.

In that moment, I hated myself—hated Rhea and fate and even my birthright. I was killing the only friend I'd had during the war—the only person I'd ever really trusted—and all I wanted to do was cry.

I blinked rapidly against the sting of tears and forced myself to concentrate on sensation. He slipped a hand underneath me, pulling me closer as his other hand cupped my breast and his thumb brushed my nipple. Pleasure shuddered through me and he chuckled softly, then repeated the process, again and again, first one breast, then the other, until I was aching with the need to be touched elsewhere.

I turned and pressed my butt against him. His thick cock speared between my legs, moving back and forth through my wetness, teasing but not entering me. He nipped my earlobe, an action that again bordered on pain, and a shudder ran through me. He chuckled quietly and ran his tongue across the lobe, a touch that briefly eased the ache before he nipped again. I moaned softly, unable to help myself. He continued to alternate between the two, moving from my ear to my neck and across my shoulder before moving down my body until he reached my hip. There, his movements stilled. His breathing was harsh, rapid, and it brushed my skin with heat. Desire—his and mine—stung the air, thick and sharp and luscious. He was fighting for control, I realized, fighting the need to plunge

himself into me, to take me hard and fast and furiously.
And I knew why; he needed time for the poison on his lips
to start reacting on me.

Given that I needed the very same thing, I didn't move.
Then his hand slipped between my legs and caressed my
clit, and I forgot about the poison, forgot about killing, and
just enjoyed. He kept touching me, teasing me, until I was
slick and desperate and shuddering with need. When he
plunged his fingers inside and began to pump them in and
out, I came, hard and fast and gloriously.

It was his undoing.

With a groan that was all desperation, he flipped me onto
my stomach, lifted my ass, and plunged into me. His grip
on my hips was as fierce and as desperate as his strokes,
pulling me back against him after every thrust. I closed my
eyes, becoming lost in the rough pleasure, moaning softly
every time his thick cock speared deep inside me. His movements became faster, harder, until the whole bed was shaking under the force of it.

Pleasure rose and tightened, until my entire body felt
ready to break. Then my orgasm hit again and I fell so
deep and hard that for several seconds I couldn't even
breathe. A heartbeat later, Sal followed me over that edge,
his groan loud as he came deep inside of me.

Neither of us immediately moved. I struggled to
breathe, struggled to come down from the high and think.
All I wanted to do was collapse on the bed and feel the
warmth of Sal's body wrapped around mine as we both
drifted to sleep.

But that was not to be.

Not ever again.

Again tears stung my eyes. Again I blinked them away.
With a soft sigh of satisfaction, he released me, then

rose from the bed and walked across to the autocook, punching the button and ordering coffee.

I swung my legs off the bed and sat down, watching him. As the rich aroma of coffee began to fill the air, I said, "What did you use?"

He glanced at me, surprise evident. "Veritite."

I nodded. "A good drug." It was one that killed slowly, without pain. It also forced the recipient to tell the truth, although it was nowhere near as powerful as the drug I'd used. He would be dead long before the Veritite truly began to react on my body.

The autocook *beep*ed. He retrieved his coffee, took a sip, then said, "How did you know?"

"I tasted it when you kissed me."

"And by then it was already too late to do anything about it."

I nodded. "For both of us, I'm afraid. Because Veritite is not the only poison I've ingested this evening, and the vial *I* took began working on you the minute you touched me." My voice was soft and edged with sadness, but it nevertheless contained a hint of command as I added, "You will keep your voice low and you will not call for help, either physically or mentally. You will not move unless I order it."

He tried. His body trembled with effort as he attempted to move his arms, then his legs. But he couldn't even drink the coffee from the mug he held close to his lips. His fury and need to kill washed over me, so fierce it snagged my breath for several seconds.

"Bitch," he eventually muttered. "But at least I have the satisfaction of knowing that you will die beside me."

I didn't disabuse him of the notion. It was far better for him—and his partners—to believe that was the case. "Sit down on the chair, Sal."

He fought the order with all that he had, but his body had been mine to do with as I wished the minute he'd pressed his length against me. He might still have free thought, but he couldn't refuse any order I gave him.

And soon he wouldn't even have free thought, let alone breath or life itself.

I pushed away the tide of remorse and watched him move somewhat stiffly to the old chair and sit down. I rose, plucked the coffee from his grip, then sat back down on the bed again. After taking a sip of the hot but bitter liquid, I said, "What are you doing with the children, Sal?"

"I'm doing nothing with them. Were you the one who raided the bunkers?"

I half smiled. The compulsion to answer beat through my brain, thanks to the Veritite, but it was a desire I could have successfully fought if I'd wished. But there was no point in wasting energy that way. "Yes. How did you find out?"

His smile held very little in the way of humor. "Deseo is the first brothel I owned. I'm still a silent partner."

Which perhaps explained his odd reluctance to set me up for an interview with Winter Halo's recruitment officer. Maybe he'd suspected that I was behind the break-in at Deseo; he'd certainly never been one to believe in coincidences.

"What are your partners doing with the children?"

"Developing immunity. How did you find the false rifts?"

"The Carleen ghosts told me about them." I paused, frowning. "Why do you need children to develop immunity? And immunity against what?"

His smile was cold and humorless. "We need them because they are either survivors of the rift doorways, or the children of such survivors, and that makes them special."

"So it's not all rifts we're talking about?"

"No. Most kill. But those that are doorways bleed not only magic into this world, but also the matter—the very atoms of creation—from the other side."

My gaze widened a little as the implications hit. "Meaning those who survive such rifts are neither of this world or the next, but a mix of both?"

He nodded. "And the perfect subjects to use in our attempts to develop immunity serums."

I frowned. "Immunity to what?"

"To light, of course."

"But why do you need that? You can walk in light easily enough."

"I can, but those with whom I now share DNA cannot." He paused, and life seemed to leach from his eyes, leaving them cold and hard and alien. "Did you use your seeking skills on me?"

"Yes. I know you were caught in a rift with three others, one of which was a wraith." His breathing was becoming harder, faster, a sign that the drug was beginning to shut down his system. I doubted he was aware of the problem just yet, but he would be, very soon. I had to get my answers while he could still speak. "Why are you doing this, Sal? The wraiths will kill us all if they ever get hold of something like that."

He smiled, but it held little in the way of warmth or humor. "They won't kill all of us. And it's not just the wraiths we seek immunity for, but also the vampires."

His words hit like a punch to the gut, and, for several seconds, all I could do was stare at him. Then I licked my

lips and said, voice a little hoarse, "I can perhaps understand the drive to develop light immunity for wraiths given
what has happened to you, but why in hell would you want
it for the *vampires*? Are you insane?"

He half shrugged. "It's not me who seeks such a thing."

"Meaning it comes from one of your partners? Why?"

"Because he is a rare survivor of a vampire attack. He's
one of them, at least in part."

I'd heard tales of vampire survivors over the years—or
dhampirs, as they were more commonly known—but I'd
never actually believed them. It was said while they were
unable to walk in light, they were not afflicted with the
need of blood. It went some way to explaining not only
why they were making the serum for vamps, but also why
the vampires seemed to be taking orders from his female
counterpart. The rift had muddled their DNA, so they were
all now part vampire—although Sal and at least one of his
partners was still able to walk in sunlight.

"Surely even your vampire partner cannot want the total
and utter destruction that will be wrought on our world if
either—"

"Why do you even care?" he cut in harshly. "What have
humans ever done for the likes of you and me?"

"They gave us life—"

"And then made no move to help us when we had outlived
our usefulness." He snorted softly. "The vampires, at least,
I can understand. They live to eat and breed and destroy, and
is that not what you and I were also designed for?"

His breathing was becoming harsher—more of a
struggle—and for the first time ever, fear flickered across
his beautiful face. The muscles of his strong arms became
taut, as if he were trying to force movement. I had no doubt

he was attempting the same with his legs, but there was
little evidence of response. The drug moved insidiously
fast through the body, freezing muscle response from the
outer extremities in. It was a swift and horrible way to die,
and had there been any other drugs on hand, I would not
have used it.

But even as remorse surged, I remembered that this
wasn't my friend. That rift had forever changed him, and
within his cool gray skin there now lurked monsters.

Monsters who'd kidnapped young children and were
even now torturing and experimenting on them.

It was all that mattered, all I had to concentrate on.

"What did you use?" His voice was harsh—furious—as
the realization of an inglorious death hovered in his bright
eyes.

And it was that, more than death itself, that angered
him, I realized. "Sueño. Where are the children, Sal?
Where are you keeping them?"

He hissed. It was an ugly, desperate sound. "Why the
fuck did you use such a dirty drug on me? What we had
deserved more consideration than that."

I smiled, but there was little in the way of warmth or
humor in it. "What we had died right along with the man
I cared about the minute he was caught in that rift and
became wraith and vampire and Rhea only knows what
else. Where are the children, Sal?"

"I cannot tell you where they all are, because I do not
know."

"Then where are the five you escorted from Carleen?"

He swore again, but he could no more refuse to answer
me than he could move or call for help. "Under Chaos. In
the very heart of the vampire nest there."

I blinked. That was one location I certainly hadn't been expecting. "Why the hell would you leave five children in such a place?"

"Because it would take a hundred déchet in peak fighting form to enter such a nest and survive. There is no such force alive these days—and the shifters lost the capacity for true fighting long ago."

I seriously doubted *that*. "But why waste the lives of five children when one or two would have achieved the result?"

He shrugged. Or at least attempted to. Again that wave of fury hit me. I took another sip of coffee, but my hands were trembling, and the liquid splashed over the rim of the cup, splattering across my bare thighs. I placed it on the floor, then met his gaze again.

"Because those five had already outlasted their usefulness."

I could only stare at him. He had basically given those children to the vampires, knowing what they would do to them, knowing how horrible that death would be.

Suddenly, I was *very* glad his death would be slow and agonizing. "Are they dead?"

He smiled, though only one part of his mouth responded. Sueño's creeping death was almost upon him. "No. The vampires are under orders not to touch them until after a rescue attempt."

"Who made the order? Who is the woman who controls the vampires?"

Again, that fleeting half smile. "We all can, because the minute the rift melded our DNA we became a part of the greater nest."

The greater nest? That wasn't something I liked the sound of. "What are the names of the two people who were caught in that rift with you, Sal?"

He opened his mouth, but no sound immediately came out. His chest was bellows-like as he struggled to suck in the air his body and brain was now being deprived of. Death was close, so very close.

"Samuel Cohen." He paused, then added, his voice little more than a harsh whisper, "Ciara Dream."

The glint in his eyes had my own narrowing. A second later, I realized what he'd done. "What names are they using in *this* time?"

Again he opened his mouth, but this time no sound came out. The Sueño had taken full hold. The end was near. I closed my eyes for a moment, then rose and walked over to him, catching his cold, lifeless hands in mine.

"May the goddess forgive your actions against these children, Sal, because I can*not*." There were tears in my eyes and on my cheeks, but fury in my heart. "You had a chance of new beginning at the war's end, and instead you chose the path of death. I will burn your body and spread your ashes on the wind so that you will never know the peace of the earth mother's arms around your decaying flesh."

And with that, I stepped away and watched him die.

It was a bitter, ugly thing to behold, but I nevertheless watched it, until his body gave up the struggle to live and the light of life finally died in his eyes.

Then I sat down, called to the healing state, and carefully chased every drop of the two poisons from my body.

Dawn was rising by the time I was done. I rose, my body stiff and sore from being held in one position for so long, and headed for the door.

I had children to rescue.

It was time to gather the ghosts.

CHAPTER 14

C at and Bear met me at the bunker's exit, but their greeting was muted, their energy filled with a mix of fear and trepidation. Because of their deeper connection with me, they knew what I intended to do—and were fully aware of the dangers involved.

I'd never called on the adult déchet for help before now, and I really had no idea how they would react—especially given their furious state the last time I'd been in our bunker.

I punched the entry code into the grate and slipped inside before it had fully opened. I hit the CLOSE button as I passed and fought the urge to run down the tunnel. The desire to get under Chaos and rescue those five children might hammer through every part of me, but the last thing I needed was to be caught in my own security measures. I switched off the electro-nets as I approached each one, and only broke into a run once the last was deactivated. My footsteps echoed lightly across the silence and almost felt like a call to arms. I wondered if the adult ghosts were listening. Wondered if they would respond.

I found Nuri and the two men in the medical center. Branna remained fully secured, but he was awake and fighting mad, if the anger that bloomed the minute he spotted me was anything to go by. Jonas was sitting on the bed to the right of Branna's, and Nuri had dragged in a chair from somewhere and was sitting to Branna's left.

Only Nuri showed any sort of relief at my arrival. "Did your Sal come looking for you, as you feared?"

"He did." My voice was clipped, cold. Cat and Bear crowded closer, but I could feel the rest of the children nearby. Their energy stung the air, electrifying it, making the hairs on my arms stand on end.

Nuri's gaze narrowed. She could obviously feel it, too, but all she said was, "And?"

"And I got the location of five of the children."

"What?" Jonas leapt off the medibed, a mix of disbelief and hope in his eyes. "How?"

I shot him a glance. "By doing what I was bred to do— seduce, drug, and question him."

The questions I could see in his eyes got no chance to surface, because Nuri cut him off with an abrupt gesture. "And the remaining children? What of them?"

"Sal didn't know where they were. He wasn't told."

"So they did—*do*—suspect you." She pushed up from the chair and began to pace, her dark skirts swishing almost angrily around her ankles. "This is not a good development. Where are the five?"

"In the sewers under Chaos."

Jonas swore, and Branna just looked angrier. Nuri stopped, her face going pale. "Sal told you this? And you believe him?"

"Yes, because the drug I used gave him no option but to tell the truth." I paused and half shrugged. "It is undoubtedly a trap, but they are nevertheless there."

She thrust a hand through her dark hair and resumed pacing. "That is one of the larger nests; I doubt we could ever muster enough people—"

"You won't have to. I'm going in with the ghosts."

She stopped again, her gaze narrowing as it swept me. "That is dangerous—for you *and* for them."

I snorted softly. "And who in this room is truly bothered about *my* safety?" I thrust my hand toward the two men. "Them? We both know they would dance on my ashes in glee if I was destroyed."

"I wouldn't risk staining the soles of my boots," Branna growled. "But the thought of the vampires tearing—"

"Branna, enough." Jonas's voice was flat, but it nevertheless contained the whip of command.

I glanced at him in surprise. His expression gave little away, but I had no sense of the fierce anger and distaste that had been so evident only hours before. Maybe he was simply controlling it better.

"You cannot go into that place alone," he said, voice now as neutral as his expression. "It would be both your death and that of the children. Yours *and* ours."

"I'm not foolish enough to take my little ones into that place." My gaze returned to Nuri. "You all need to leave."

"We can be of more help if we—"

"No," I snapped, "you can't. I'm calling to the soldiers who haunt the old corridors. I have no idea if they will actually answer my call to arms, but I *can* guarantee having two shifters so filled with old hatreds and prejudices standing at close quarters will only inflame an already dangerous situation."

"And the five children? If you manage to get them all out of that nest alive, where will you take them?"

"I'll bring them to you, in Chaos." I hesitated, then stepped back. There was so much more I needed to tell them, but, once again, time was of the essence. I had no idea how long it would take for Sal's partners to realize things had gone sour, but when they did, they would no doubt order the five children destroyed—especially given that, according to Sal, they'd outlasted their usefulness. Why that should be, I had no idea, and, right now, it wasn't important. I had to get to them—rescue them—before the vampires were unleashed. "Where is the best place to enter that nest?"

Nuri hesitated. "Any of the open sewer outlets within Chaos's lower level will get you into their tunnels, but the best place is probably the old main outlet half a click downstream from the drawbridge. It's the one they generally use."

I frowned. "If this is common knowledge, why has no one done anything to block it?"

"Because while the old sewer system was completely eradicated within Central to ensure the vampires had no point of entry, the government doesn't really care what happens beyond its walls." She shrugged. "Besides, any attempt to shut down *that* sewer exit would only result in their using the Chaos ones more. I doubt those forced to live on the lower levels would appreciate such an event."

"But surely an eradication program . . ." I cut the question off. Right now, the why behind allowing an active nest to exist so close to Central didn't matter. I waved a hand at the door. "Leave. All of you."

"You'll need to release Branna first," Jonas commented.

I hesitated, my gaze meeting his. "Only if you swear to control him. Otherwise, he can take his chances with the ghosts."

"He will not threaten you in any way or form when released." Jonas's gaze was on Branna rather than me. "Will you?"

Branna's expression was mutinous, but after several seconds, his gaze dropped from Jonas's, and he muttered, "I will do nothing to harm you in this place. You have my word."

I smiled grimly. In other words, once *out* of this place, he would do his utmost to ensure I was as dead as those who haunted these halls.

"Fine," I said, my gaze on his. "But just remember what is at stake."

A smile touched his lips. He knew what was at stake, and he didn't care. It made me wonder just what the déchet had done to his kin during the war. It had to have been bad for this sort of hatred to linger so many years after its end.

I walked around the bed, brought up the main screen, and then released his bonds. He sat up immediately and rubbed his wrists; his gaze, when it met mine, was lethal, but he kept his word and made no move toward me.

I glanced back to Nuri. "Follow Cat. She'll get you out of here."

She hesitated, then nodded, her skirts swirling as she spun and walked to the door. Branna cast me another dark look, then leapt off the opposite side of the bed and stalked after her.

Jonas didn't immediately move, but I could feel his gaze on me. It was a weight that did odd things to my breathing and, for no real reason, made me angry. At the attraction I couldn't control, at him for hating so much, and at fate for forcing me to destroy the only other good thing that had come into my life in the last one hundred years aside from my little ones.

Only he *hadn't* been good, I reminded myself bleakly. Quite the opposite.

"What happened to Sal?" Jonas asked eventually.

I closed my eyes briefly. "He's dead. He will never harm another child."

"To which I can only say, 'good.'" He paused. "I take it he was also déchet?"

"Yes. But an assassin, not a soldier."

"I wasn't aware there were different types."

"No, because the few mentions of us in the history books tar us all with the one brush even as they retouch the truth and paint the shifters in a glorious light."

He didn't say anything to that, but there wasn't much that *could* be said. It was the truth, pure and simple. I waved a hand to the door. "Go."

He hesitated. "Good luck."

"Thanks." I crossed my arms and refused to look at him, even though I could feel his silent command to do so. After several seconds, he walked out the door and didn't look back.

As the sound of his steps retreated, I released a breath and glanced to where Bear waited patiently. "I know you want to come with me, but I need you here. You're the oldest of the little ones, and the only one who has had any sort of combat training. I'm afraid it falls to you to protect this place—and them—from attack while we're all gone."

His energy caressed my skin. *You should not be alone with the others. They are dangerous.*

Yes, they were. But they were also déchet, and used to following orders. Maybe not mine, but I was hoping that after a hundred years of guarding nothing more than their bones and waiting for orders that would never again come, they would jump at the chance for action.

They are our only hope against such a large nest of vampires, Bear. I have no choice but to attempt this.

If it goes wrong, if death comes, call, he said. *We should be together at such a time.*

I closed my eyes against the sting of tears. They'd died in my embrace, and he was now offering the same comfort to me. *Thank you. I will, I promise.*

He pulled away. I took a somewhat shaky breath, then spun and headed for the weapons room. If I was to have any hope of surviving the next few hours, then I'd better be armed to the teeth. It wasn't just weapons that I grabbed, but a large roll of light tubing. It was as heavy as hell and would restrict the speed with which I could move, but when all else failed, the pack full of weapons and the attached tubing might be the only thing standing between certain death and us.

With that done, I headed down to the ninth level. The closer I got to them, the more their energy bit. I hoped like hell it wasn't a bad sign.

Cat returned, her energy briefly brushing my skin, her presence warm compared to the chill the adult déchet were emitting. *They have gone. The grate is closed again.*

"Thanks, Cat." I sat down and held out my hand. "I need your help to contact the adults."

That is dangerous.

I know. But I had no other choice given the adults seemed intent on keeping their distance.

Cat didn't hesitate, simply let her energy caress my palm and merge into mine. As I became one with that other realm and the creeping hand of death once again began to claim my flesh, I said, "Déchet soldiers, I need your help."

There was no immediate response, but the chill of death increased, and this time it came from without rather than from within.

Then a sharp voice behind me said, *We know what you want. Tell us, why should we help those who are responsible for our destruction?*

"Because you're not helping them. You're helping their children, who cannot be held accountable for the actions of their parents during a time of war."

No one helped our little ones. They were left to rot just as much as we were.

"I know *precisely* what was done to them. I was there, remember?"

And survived.

"Because of my genetics, and the fact I was made immune to all toxins and poisons, yes. That is not my fault."

We do not blame you for surviving.

Well, good, because there wasn't a whole lot I could do about it except die for real—and that was a possibility if I didn't get their cooperation and quickly end this conversation. Death was moving entirely too fast up my legs.

"Nor should you blame the offspring of humans and shifters for actions they took no part in."

Air stirred, then the speaker stood in front of me. He was a thickset, hirsute fellow, more bear than human. Death had obviously caught him midshift.

And what does this mission offer us other than the possibility of a permanent death?

"It offers you the chance to vent your anger and kill. The nest we raid is a large one, and, yes, there is a very real possibility none of us will survive." I paused, studying him. "But isn't going to battle and taking the chance of a true and glorious death worth such a risk?"

Other ghosts began to appear behind him. Their murmurs filled the air, but were so soft I had no idea whether it was assent or dissent.

The chill of death was getting stronger. If I didn't end this soon, I wouldn't have the strength to enter the nest and save those children.

It would appear the others agree with you, he said eventually. *We will accompany you and tear this nest apart.*

"And not harm the children? Or, indeed, those who come to claim them?"

Cold amusement touched his expression. *We made no move against the shifters, even when they entered this place. We cannot, unless ordered to do so. You know this.*

I knew, but it didn't hurt to check. "Thank you all for agreeing to help," I said. "Cat?"

Her energy immediately left me, but for several seconds, it was all I could do to suck in air. My entire body was trembling, and my feet and hands ached with the chill of death. I wasted precious minutes calling to the healing state to chase the cold from my flesh, then pushed upright and said, "This way."

I led the way down the levels until we hit the seventh, then headed for the South Siding exit. Once the grate was open, I paused, reaching out to Cat and Bear, sending them gentle kisses as the adult ghosts surged out into the sunlight. They were once again going to war, and their relief stung the air, making it shimmer and dance. Or maybe that was just a result of the sheer number of them who'd answered my call to arms. There had to be at least a hundred there, and it made me hope that Sal was right—that such a force *could* destroy the vampires.

I closed the grate and ran through the wasteland between Central and the bunker, not stopping when I hit either the rail yards or the station platforms. No one stopped us; in fact, everyone moved out of the way long before we got anywhere near them. It was almost as if the energy of the ghosts was a wave that brushed them aside; certainly some of their expressions were startled, if not a little scared.

I ran on, following the gentle curve of the curtain wall, my gaze scanning the riverbed as I tried to find the old sewer outlet. I eventually discovered it settled deep in the steep left bank of the old riverbed. It was taller than I was, a big semicircle structure made of red brick that had been stained almost black by time and weather. Once upon a time a thick metal grate had covered the outlet's opening, but the bars had been peeled back and rather resembled twisted, skeletal fingers reaching for the sky. Sad-looking shrubs clung to the sides of the outlet, and a wide, well-worn path led into it. The smell coming from within . . . I shuddered. It was thick with rot and death, and all I wanted to do was run.

I squashed the urge, freed the light tube from the backpack, then unfolded the slender but powerful solar panel and shoved it in the ground. Once I unraveled and activated the tube, it would provide enough brightness to keep the vampires out of arm's reach. Or, at least, that was the theory. I'd never actually seen these things in action.

I hooked the tubing to my belt so that it would unroll as I moved, then grabbed two weapons and said, "Right. Let's go kick some vampire butt."

The déchet surged into the darkness. I followed quickly, my body tense as the stinking darkness enveloped me. Nothing immediately jumped out at us. The sewer drain was wide and empty, and though moisture and slime dripped from the upper sections of the old brick arch, little water ran down the deeper middle of the drain. I stuck to the left bank and ran after the ghosts, my steps light but echoing softly across the silence.

The vampires would hear it. Even though the rising sun would be pushing them to sleep, they would hear my footsteps and wake. It was just a matter of how deep into this system we got before that happened.

I ran on, every sense alert and every muscle so tightly strung it felt like the tiniest blow would break me. But as we moved deeper and deeper into the sewer system, there was no sign of the vampires and absolutely no movement beyond the rats that scattered the minute they sensed our presence.

But the air was growing ever colder, and the scent of death and darkness had grown so strong every breath felt like an invasion.

The last of the light tube rolled out, and we still hadn't found the vampires. I swore softly, then unhooked it from my belt and attached the control box. *Here goes nothing,* I thought, and hit the activation switch. Light flared across the darkness, milky white and somewhat muted. I had no idea if this was it, or whether the tube took time to warm up, and I couldn't stick around to find out. Even a slither of sunshine was better than nothing.

I moved on. Ten minutes later, we hit the nest.

There was absolutely no warning that we were even near it; one minute I was following the ghosts down the tunnel, the next I was at a junction of six outlets and the reek of vampire was so thick and strong the air felt diseased. Fear slammed into my heart as my gaze swept the large, circular area. There were no structures here, and nothing that resembled accommodation, beds, or basic comforts. The vampires seemed content to sleep where they fell, be it on one another or the thick, slime-covered floors of the various tunnels. But there *was* something here other than darkness and vampires—bones. They were everywhere, inches thick, all over the floor. Some had even been used to form a macabre effigy of humanity in the middle of the junction. Bloodied bits of flesh and internal organs were scattered around the base of the structure, undoubtedly offerings to whatever god the effigy was supposed to represent.

What I couldn't see were the children.

The energy of the ghosts briefly surged upward, drawing my gaze in that direction. Two metal cages swung gently above the sleeping vampires, and inside them were the children. There was no movement, no sound, coming from them. Either they were scared witless, or they were drugged. I prayed for the latter, simply because it meant there was less chance of them making a noise and waking the nest. We were only going to get one shot at this, and there was no way in hell I was going to grab two or three and leave the others behind.

The vampires nearest me were beginning to stir. Why they hadn't woken before now, I couldn't say, but I had to move before they did. I quietly but quickly slipped off the pack and placed it on the ground. It left me with the six guns I carried and my knives, but if they got past the ghosts, then I very much suspected no amount of weaponry was going to help. I flexed my fingers, reaching for calm, and said, *Déchet, I need a score of you protecting this tunnel. The minute they wake, the rest of you attack. Use the weapons if you can—it won't take as much of your energy as attacking the vamps directly would.*

I could feel the discontent. They wanted to attack now, while the vampires still slumbered. That's sensible in wartime, but not here. Our greatest chance of getting those children out in one piece lay in freeing them from those cages before the vampires woke.

The ghosts weren't happy, but the vampires remained undisturbed. Relieved, I called to the darkness and surged upward, squeezing through the thick bars of the nearest cage, then re-forming inside. As the cage swung and creaked at my sudden weight, three sets of wide, frightened eyes stared at me from pale, gaunt faces. But they made no sound and, after a moment, I realized why. Their mouths had been sewn shut.

Anger ripped through me, so fierce it charged the air. Below, vampires sniffed and stirred, and the ghosts readied to attack.

Calm. I needed to be calm if we were all going to get out of here alive. But it was a hard state to achieve when I was staring at the bloodied, swollen mouths of the three little ones. The youngest was barely four . . .

I briefly closed my eyes, fighting the sick fury as much as the fierce and sudden joy that Sal had died as slowly and as painfully as he had, then forced a smile and whispered, "I'm going to use a little magic and get you all out of here, but you have to do exactly what I say. Okay?"

Wide eyes stared back at me. I had no idea if they understood me or not. I took another, somewhat shuddery breath, which did little to erase the fury, then gently motioned the two littlest into my arms. They hesitated, then shuffled close enough that I could wrap my arms around them both. I glanced at the oldest of the three. "I'll be back for you in a minute. Don't make any noise."

He nodded. I called to the darkness and let it wash through the three of us. Then I went back through the bars and dropped toward the exit tunnel, landing, rather ungainly, just beyond the ghosts guarding the tunnel. I re-formed us all, and then motioned the little ones to sit and wait. They nodded, eyes wide and somewhat glazed. I became darkness again and moved back out into the junction. Tension sung through the air and on the far outer reaches of the nest, vampires stirred and muttered, the guttural sound heavy in the silence. I spun upward and collected the third boy, but this time, when I re-formed, weakness hit and my stomach convulsed. I have no idea whether it was the stink of this place or sheer terror, but it was all I could do not to vomit. I glanced at the three children; wide, frightened eyes stared back at me. I forced a smile, held up a hand, signaling them to wait, then stepped back into darkness.

I was barely through the curtain of ghosts protecting the tunnel when the vampires finally became aware of our presence and all hell broke loose.

Their screeches and fury filled the air, but even in the bedlam of being torn from their slumber and attacked by the ghosts, they sensed my presence and surged en masse, their claws slashing at my particles even as others shifted to darkness and chased after me. But just as their energy began to lash around mine, the ghosts hit them, flinging them away and freeing me. I slipped into the second cage and found flesh. But there was no time to comfort these two, and no time to explain what was about to happen. I simply grabbed them, pulled them into my arms, and tore us all into darkness.

Ghosts rose to escort me into the tunnel. Vampires flung themselves at us, only to be sharply tossed back into the screaming, pulsating mound of flesh and fury. One of them hit the effigy of bones, and the whole structure cracked and began to tumble. The vampires screamed in despair and rose as one, forming a huge black wave that hit us hard, scattering the ghosts and sending me tumbling. I splattered against a sidewall and saw stars, but the surging mass had not finished yet. They hit me again, the force of the blow so strong that my particles were forced apart, until all that separated me from an inglorious death was the merest of threads. Somehow, I gathered myself together and shot forward, heading for the tunnel and praying to Rhea that the ghosts could hold them off long enough for me to re-form and get the children out of there.

Shots ricocheted across the darkness as the ghosts began to use the weapons. The scent of blood bloomed thick and heavy in the air, but the vampires didn't stop to feed on their fallen. They were too busy trying to get me, to kill me.

I shot past the barrier of ghosts and became flesh again. But I was going too fast, and I hit the ground hard. I curled my body around the little ones to protect them as best I could as we tumbled several yards past the other three.

When we finally stopped, I released my grip on them and pushed upright. The tunnel spun around me, and my knees briefly buckled, threatening to send me crashing back down again. I swore and reached back to grab my one and only flare. I lit it and tossed it toward the tunnel entrance. The flickering light revealed a growing wall of twisted, angry flesh, and no matter how many times the ghosts shattered that wall, it just kept rebuilding and growing.

We *had* to get out of there.

I glanced at the first three I'd rescued and made a come-here motion. They stared at me and didn't move. I can't say I blamed them, given I hadn't really done much more than fling them from the frying pan into the fire, but we couldn't remain here. I had no idea how long the ghosts could hold out against the black tide battering them, but it was very evident time was the one luxury we didn't have much of.

"We need to move before the vampires can reach us," I said softly. The two slightly older children I'd just rescued climbed to their feet and pressed against me. A small hand touched mine. I wrapped my fingers around hers and glanced down, giving her a quick, bright smile that felt every inch as false as it was. "It'll be okay," I whispered. "We just have to move. Just wait here while I get the others, okay?"

She nodded solemnly. I released her hand, then ran over to where three of them still sat. "Up we get." I caught the hands of the oldest two and hauled them upright, then squatted in front of the remaining little girl. "Can you climb onto my back and hang on really, really tight?"

After a moment, she nodded. I swung around and she climbed onto my back, her grip so fierce around my neck she would have choked me had she been any stronger. I clasped the hands of the others, then said to the remaining two, "Okay, keep close; grab my shirt if you have to. There's light up ahead, but we need to run through this darkness for a little bit."

They nodded solemnly; one of them grabbed my shirt-tails, but the oldest boy simply waited beside me. There was no fear in any of them; they were just all wide eyes and solemn faces. Maybe they'd seen so much they simply *couldn't* fear anymore. But Penny had also showed little in the way of fear or situational awareness. Maybe it had something to do with Sal's tests. Or maybe it was simply shock.

We went as fast as the little ones could, but it was slow, so damn slow. It brought back memories of the bunker, of the death I'd tried to outrun then, and the uselessness of the effort.

No. This time, I *wouldn't* fail.

This time, I *would* save the children.

Behind us, the flare died, and the ghosts gave way. The

tide was after us. I resisted the urge to go faster; to do so would risk losing the boy who clung to the back of my shirt. The ghosts weren't done yet. There were still weapons firing, and that meant there was still hope.

Then awareness surged—several vampires had gotten past the re-formed line of ghosts and were approaching fast. I didn't stop, simply shifted the little girl's grip from my hand to my shirt, then pulled the rifle free and fired randomly over my shoulder. One vampire went down, its guttural howl abruptly cut off; the other, however, was still very much in action.

The oldest boy reached up, snapped the second rifle free, then spun and shot. The vampire went down with a scream. The boy looked at me, and there was dark satisfaction in his eyes.

"Good shot," I said. "Now let's run even faster."

We did. Up ahead, light began to twinkle—the tubing offering a distant line of hope. The children saw it, and their speed increased. Behind us, the wall of ghosts broke again, and again the vampires surged after us. Their hate and desperation were so fierce they were wind that battered our bodies and nipped at our heels. I fired over my shoulder until the rifle clicked over to empty, then swiftly hooked it onto my belt, grabbed one of the smaller guns, and kept on firing. Vampires went down, but more came after us.

We hit the light; hope surged fierce and fast, but we were hardly out of the woods yet. The tide was still behind us, and I had no idea how long the light tube would hold them off. But given their actions in the Broken Mountains' bunker earlier tonight, I wouldn't have been surprised if a few sacrificed themselves for the safety of the greater nest.

I stopped. Five wide gazes immediately met mine. "I

need you all to run ahead while I stop the vampires behind us. Follow the light tubing—it'll lead you into the sunlight and an old riverbank. Wait for me there."

They nodded solemnly. The oldest of them held out the modified rifle he'd used. I hesitated and then shook my head. "You keep it, just in case one of them gets past me. It won't," I hastily added, to reassure the younger ones. "But it's always better to be safe. Go. And keep together."

They went. But their small silhouettes had barely disappeared around the tunnel's gentle curve when the vampires surged into the light. As they began to burn, I grabbed another weapon and fired—not at those who were becoming ash but at those who flung themselves at the light. As the bodies began to mount up and the stink of ash and flesh stained the air and churned my stomach, the ghosts reappeared, forming a somewhat ragged line in front of me. Less than half of them were left, and I had no idea whether the others had been killed or were merely depleted of energy and unable to help. Those who remained, however, radiated a fierce and utter joy. They were doing what they'd been bred to do, and they didn't care about depletion or even death.

I spun and left them to it. But I resisted the urge to bolt after the children. It was better if I kept some distance between us, just in case the vampires broke through again.

Which they did.

And this time, they also shattered the light tube. As the light in the immediate area went out and darkness began to chase its way up the rest of the tubing, I spun and started to fire. Vampires screamed and went down, only to be replaced by three or four more. I kept firing until the weapons grew hot in my hands and the low-ammo light began to flash in warning. One weapon clicked over to empty. I flung it away, but before I could grab another, they hit me. We went down in a mass of screaming, biting, clawing flesh. I swore and fought with everything I had, battling to get one arm free so I could at least flick a knife down into my hand. But they grabbed it, tore at it, chewing at my flesh like dogs do a bone. I screamed and became darkness, hoping in that form I'd at least have a chance of escape. But they felt it and changed with me, and the attacks were somehow worse because it felt as if they were tearing me apart from the inside out.

Damn it, I *wouldn't* die like this! I couldn't do it to Cat and Bear and all my other little ones. I forced a hand through the stinking mound of flesh, pulled a gun free, and began to fire. There was no finesse, no aim; I just pulled the trigger and kept on firing. Bloodied vampire bits bloomed into the air, and the weight holding me down shifted. Not much, but enough. Energy surged from Rhea knows where, and I forced my way upright. I flicked the knife free and kept on firing as I slashed left and right, cutting limbs and faces and bodies. But there was no end to them; I would die here if I didn't move.

The ghosts arrived, and vampires were picked up and flung away. "Thank you, thank you," I said, then leapt over the pile of bloody, broken bodies in front of me and ran like hell.

This time, the line of ghosts didn't hold very long at all. No matter how fiercely they wanted to fight, they were no longer flesh, and beings of energy could do only so much.

I kept on running. It was pointless doing anything else now. My trunk was a maze of bloody wounds, there were chunks out of my arms and legs, and my strength—like that of the ghosts—was ebbing. I needed to reach the sunlight. It was my only hope.

The vampires surged closer; the wind of their approach buffeted my spine, but I had no more strength, no more speed. I gripped my knife and gun so tightly my knuckles glowed. This was it . . .

They hit me. Again we went tumbling, but this time, I somehow twisted, firing nonstop at the stinking mass surrounding me. I hit the ground back first and slid several yards, firing all the while. Then the gun clicked over to empty . . .

Something whistled through the air, and a heartbeat later, light exploded into the tunnel. The vampires screamed and erupted into flame, their flesh becoming ashes that rained all around me.

Then a hand grabbed mine and hauled me upright. Jonas, I realized in surprise.

"What in Rhea—"

"Explanations can wait," he said, voice tight. "The children are safe, and *we* need to run. That light bomb is only going to hold them off for a couple of minutes."

As if to emphasize his words, the bomb's light began to flicker and fizz. It was all the encouragement I needed. I ran as hard and as fast as I could. Jonas kept behind me, his hand lightly pressed against my back, as if to encourage even more speed from my aching, weary body.

We pounded around another long, curving corner. Up ahead, like a distant star, sunshine beckoned. We were close, so close, to safety.

Behind us, the light bomb went out, and the black tide was once again on the hunt.

"Faster," Jonas growled. Despite the urgency in his voice,

the pressure of his hand against my spine didn't alter, though it must have been tempting to simply shove me.

But I had nothing left to give. My breath was little more than ragged gasps, every bit of me was bruised, bloody and sore, and I really had no idea how I was even managing to remain upright, let alone run.

But I didn't want to die. It hadn't been only my DNA that had kept me alive when the Draccid had killed everyone else—it had also been willpower. That same willpower was undoubtedly the only reason I was even functioning now.

Jonas began to fire over his shoulder. I kept my eyes on the ever-growing half circle of light, determined to reach it.

The wind of the vampires' approach began to batter us. Jonas hissed, a sound filled with fury and no small amount of fear, but he kept his hand on my back, kept pushing, even though he could have so easily left me and saved himself.

A silhouette appeared in the bright circle up ahead. A heartbeat later, several flaming arrows shot past us and buried themselves in the flesh of the nearest vampires. They immediately exploded into fire, creating enough light that the mass behind them hesitated.

It was enough.

Jonas finally shoved me, and I went tumbling, rolling, into the sunlight. I came to a jarring stop at the edge of the old riverbed, and for several minutes didn't move. I simply stared at the sun and sucked in its bright energy. Against all the odds, I'd saved the children *and* survived, and if I'd had the energy I would have whooped in sheer and utter delight.

Then a rush of dark air hit me, followed closely by the sensation of fury. The vampires had *not* finished with us yet. I somehow scrambled upright, my knives in my hand as I stood and stared at the sewer's entrance. Jonas and Branna stood twenty or so feet farther up the embankment but far enough away from the entrance that the sun shielded them. Their bodies were tense and their guns raised. Nuri was farther away to my left, and the five children were with her.

A black tide of flesh spewed from the tunnel. They burned almost as soon as they hit the sunlight, but one or two broke through the gathering cloud of ash and ran at me even as their bodies exploded into flame and began to disintegrate. These ones, Jonas and Branna coolly shot.

Eventually, the tide became a trickle, then died. As the final gunshot rang out, I said, "Is that the last of them?"

"Not quite," Branna said.

Then he looked at me and, in one smooth motion, lifted his gun and fired.

I threw myself sideways, but I was on the very last strands of my strength, and I simply had nothing left in the way of reflexes or speed. Even so, the bullet that had been aimed at my head tore through my right shoulder instead, spinning me around and throwing me to the ground. A second shot rang out, and I closed my eyes, waiting for the end to come.

It never did.

Confused, I pressed my hand against the bloody wound in my shoulder, trying to stop the flow of blood as I forced myself upright.

Branna was on the ground, blood pouring out of a hand that was now missing several fingers. Jonas bent and picked up Branna's weapon, his expression giving little away but fury marking every movement.

"You were *warned*, Branna," he said, voice flat. "Why do you not ever *listen*?"

"Because she's déchet *and* dangerous! She should be dead, not living so close to us or the damn city."

Something within me shattered and hardened. No matter what I said, no matter what I did, it was never going to make a difference to these people. If saving Jonas and the lives of five children had made no difference, then nothing would. I was déchet, and that was all they would ever see. Jonas and Nuri might overlook it long enough to use me, but their fear and prejudice undoubtedly ran just as deep as Branna's.

When all this was over, and I was no longer of use to them, they would get rid of me. That was as clear as the sky overhead.

"As the other children should be dead?" Jonas snapped. "Because you know full well that *she* is our only hope—"

"Then there *is* no hope," I cut in harshly.

Jonas's gaze jumped to mine. It was a weight I felt deep inside, and filled with a fury that was suddenly aimed at me. "What?"

"I said there is no hope." I clipped the empty gun to my belt, then looked at Nuri. Her expression was an odd mix of surprise and fear. "I can't do this. I won't."

"You are not the type to walk away," she said, her voice even despite the emotional turmoil I could feel in her. It wasn't me she feared but rather my walking away. She really *did* believe I was the only hope to save the remaining eight children. "You can't."

"Watch me." I took a step backward. Then another.

"The children will die, Tiger. I've seen this, just as I've seen that is something you do not want on your conscience."

"You're right, I don't. I have risked not only my own life to save these five, but the lives of my little ones *and*

those of the déchet. And in gratitude, he"—I flung a bloodied hand in Branna's direction—"has attempted to kill me
not once, but twice. There will *not* be a third time."

"I swear to you—," Jonas began, but I cut him off with
a harsh laugh.

"As you vowed only a few hours ago to control him?
As he vowed to do me no harm? No," I said. "You can save
your breath *and* your vows, because I no more believe them
than you can believe it is possible for a déchet to be anything more than a mindless killer."

"Tiger, you *have* to listen to me—"

"No, I *don't*." My voice was as grim as Nuri's was
urgent. "I'm done listening to you. I'm done helping you.
I've been drugged, interrogated, had the lives of my ghosts
threatened, and now I've been shot—and all by the very
people who want me to help them. Enough is enough."

"If you do not help us," she said, voice grim, "then I will
be forced to carry through with my threat and make you."

"That threat worked before because I had no warning
and no time to prepare. *That* is no longer the case. Believe
me, there are still weapons hidden in the bowels of our
bunker that have not been seen since the war, and I *will*
unleash them against both you and your city if you ever
attempt to harm my little ones."

She studied me, her arms crossed and determination
evident in her gaze. She wasn't going to let the matter go,
no matter what I said—and yet there was also a sense of
acknowledgment that I really *did* mean to walk away, and
nothing she or anyone else said would stop that.

The five little ones I'd rescued had gathered around her
skirts and were now staring at me, their wide eyes seeing
too much, understanding too much. Just like Penny. It

made me wonder if they, like her, were somehow connected to the people who'd kidnapped and tortured the children. Made me wonder if it meant that those behind all this would soon know of my decision to walk away. Would it make any difference? Would it mean the vampires would stop attacking our home and leave us alone?

Maybe. Maybe not.

I doubted such peace was worth the lives of eight children, though.

"What we need to do is report her damn presence to the authorities," Branna growled. "They can go in and raze the place, just in case there's more of them hidden there."

"There *is* no one else. With Sal dead, I am now the last of my kind. But go ahead and report my presence—it's undoubtedly what you planned to do once all this was over anyway." My gaze went to Jonas's. "Because, hey, I'm not human and I'm not a shifter. I'm just a monster with no feelings or thoughts of my own, and therefore undeserving of consideration or life."

There was no emotion visible on Jonas's face. No acknowledgment of my words. Why I even expected there to be, I wasn't entirely sure, given that I was only speaking the lies they wholly believed.

I added softly, "But if there's *one* thing you should believe, then it's the fact that I will do everything within my power to protect my home and my little ones. And anyone who enters that place with ill intent *will* regret it."

He didn't say anything. None of them did. My gaze flicked down to the weapons he still held. "Shoot me if you want. I really don't care at this point."

And with that, I turned and walked away.

They didn't try to stop me.

They didn't shoot.

But the weight of their gazes lingered long after I'd left them behind, and it made the guilt even harder to bear.

Because despite all my denials, Nuri was right about one thing—I couldn't ignore the plight of those children. It wasn't in my nature.

I just had to find a way to help them that didn't involve Nuri and her men.

There were ghosts in this place.

Most kept their distance, simply watching as I made my way through the broken remnants of their tombstones. One or two of the braver ones brushed my arms with ethereal fingers—caresses that reached past the layers of jacket and shirt to chill my skin. But these ghosts meant me no harm. It was simple curiosity, or maybe even an attempt to feel again the heat and life that had once been theirs. And while I knew from experience that ghosts could be dangerous, I was not here to disturb or challenge the dead.

I was here simply to follow—and maybe even kill—the living.

Because the person I was tracking had come from the ruined city of Carleen, which lay behind us. It had been the very last city destroyed in a war that may have lasted only five years but had altered the very fabric of our world forever. One hundred and three years had passed since the war's end, but Carleen had never been rebuilt. No one lived there. No one dared to.

Given that the figure *had* come from that city, it could mean only one of two things. Either he or she was a human or shifter up to no good, or it was one of the two people responsible for kidnapping fourteen children from Central—the only major city center in this region. No one else had any reason to be out here, in the middle of nowhere, at night. Especially when the night was friend to no one but the vampires.

Of course, vampires weren't the only evil ones to roam the night or the shadows these days. The bombs the shifters had unleashed to finally end their war against humans had resulted in the rifts—bands of energy and magic that roved the landscape and mauled the essence of anything and anyone unlucky enough to be caught in their path. But that was not the worst of it, because many rifts were also doorways into our world from either another time or another dimension. Maybe even from hell itself. And the creatures that came through them—collectively called the Others but nicknamed demons, wraiths, or death spirits, depending on their form—had all found a new and easy hunting ground in the shadows of our world.

These rifts were the reason Carleen had never been rebuilt. There were a dozen of them drifting through the city's ruins, and there was no way of predicting their movements. Neither wind nor gravitational pull had any influence on them, and they could just as easily move against a gale force wind as they could leap upward to consume whatever might be taking flight that day—be it birds, aircraft, or even clouds. Once upon a time I'd believed that being caught in a rift meant death, but now I knew otherwise.

Because the people responsible for kidnapping those children were living proof that rifts were survivable—although by calling them "people" I was granting them a humanity they did not deserve. Anyone who could experiment on young children for *any* reason was nothing short of a monster. That they were doing so in an effort to discover a means by which vampires could become immune to light just made them all the more abominable.

But it wasn't as if they could actually claim humanity in the first place. I might be a déchet—a lab-designed humanoid created by humans before the war as a means to combat the superior strength and speed of the shifters— but every bit of my DNA was of *this* world.

The same could not be said about those responsible for the missing children.

I'd managed to rescue five of them, but I had no idea how they were or if they'd recovered from the horrific injuries inflicted on them. Those who could tell me were no longer my allies; they'd tried to kill me. Twice. They would not get a third chance.

I continued to slip quietly through the night, following the teasing drift of footsteps. Whoever—whatever—it was up ahead certainly wasn't adept at walking quietly. Which suggested it wasn't a vampire, or even a shifter. The former rarely traveled alone, despite the fact they had very little to fear at night, and the latter were apparently night-blind. Or so Nuri—who was one of my former allies, and a powerful human witch—had said.

I tended to believe her—at least on that point. Even before the war, both shifters and humans had lived in either cities or campsites that were lit by powerful light towers twenty-four/seven. Vampires had always been a problem— the war had just kept them well fed and had allowed them to increase in number. It made sense that after generations of living in never-ending daylight, the need for night sight would be filtered out of humanity's DNA.

No, it was Nuri's promise—that no harm would befall the ghosts living with me in the old military bunker if I helped them find the remaining children—that I wasn't so sure about. While she might not hold any prejudices against déchet, the others in her group were all shifters and, from what they'd said, had all lost kin to déchet soldiers during the war.

While I wasn't by design a soldier, I could fight and had certainly been responsible for more than a few shifter deaths. Only my kills hadn't happened in open fields or battered forests, but rather in the bedroom. I was a lure—a déchet specifically created to infiltrate shifter camps and seduce those in charge. Once firmly established in their beds, it had been my duty to gain and pass on all information relating to the war and their plans. And then, when my task was completed, I killed.

I'd been a very successful lure.

And I still was, I thought bleakly. Images of Sal—and the brutal way I'd killed him—rose in my mind, but I pushed them away. Sal might have been the only friend and confidant I'd really had during the war, but he'd also been the third member of the group who'd kidnapped the children. And when I'd realized that, I'd had little choice but to take action. There were many things in this world I could ignore—many things I had no desire to be part of— but I could not idly stand by and watch children suffer. Not again. Not if I could help it.

It was thanks to Sal—to the information I'd forced out of him before he'd died—that those five kids were now free. Six, if you included Penny, the child I'd rescued from the vampires that had been tracking her in the park.

But that still left eight. And while I had no intention of helping Nuri and her crew, I also had no intention of abandoning those children to their fate.

Which is why I'd been in Carleen tonight.

Sal and his partners had created what the ghosts there called "false rifts": balls of dirty energy that resembled regular rifts but were—as far as I could tell—nothing more than a means of quick transport from one location to another. I'd gone there tonight to investigate one of them, which is why I was out here alone. Cat and Bear—the two little ghosts who normally accompanied me on such journeys—were back home in our bunker. We'd learned the hard way that ghosts could not enter the rifts and I wasn't about to place them in any sort danger if I could at all avoid it. They might be déchet, they might be ghosts, but they were also only children.

The graveyard gave way to a long slope that was filled with rock debris and the broken, decaying remnants of trees. Halfway down the hill lay a gigantic crater, its rim strewn with rocks, building rubble, and twisted, sick-looking plants. Weirdly, even though I was standing above it, I couldn't see into the crater itself. I frowned, my gaze narrowing. It might be the middle of the night, but the vampire DNA in my body had gifted me with—among other things— the ability to see as clearly at night as I could during the day. But the shadows that clustered just below the crater's edge were thicker than the night itself and they emitted an energy that was dark and dirty.

Rift, an inner voice whispered even as my skin crawled at the thought of getting any closer.

But the figure I was tracking had disappeared, and there was no place other than the crater he or she could have gone. If I wanted to uncover whether that person was one of my targets, then I had to keep following.

I started down the hill. Small stones and fragmented metal scooted out from underfoot with every step, the latter chiming softly as the pieces hit the large rocks in my path. The graveyard ghosts danced lightly to the tune, seemingly unconcerned about either leaving the graveyard or approaching the rift—which in itself suggested that whatever that darkness was, it wasn't dangerous. Either that or it was one of the few stationary rifts and, as such, posed no immediate threat to either them or me.

I wished I could talk to them. Maybe they could have told me if my target came here regularly, or even who he or she might be. But these ghosts, like those in Carleen, had been human, and that meant I couldn't directly talk to them as I could to shifter or déchet ghosts. Not without help, anyway. The scientists who'd designed us had made damn sure those destined to become lures could not use their seeker skills to read either their thoughts or their emotions. They may have created us to be their frontline soldiers against the shifters, but they'd also feared us. Mind reading wasn't the only restriction placed on us when it came to humans—killing them was also out of bounds. Not that I'd ever tested *that* particular restriction—it had never occurred to me to do so during the war, and there'd been no need in the one hundred and three years after it.

Energy began to burn across my skin as I drew closer to the crater. The ghosts finally hesitated, then retreated. Part of me wished I could do the same.

I stopped at the crater's rim and stared down into it. The darkness was thick, almost gelatinous, and lapped at the tips of my boots in gentle waves. It was unlike anything I'd ever come across before. Even the shadows that had covered the other false tears had not felt this foul, this . . . alien.

This wasn't magic. Or, if it was, it wasn't the sort of magic that had originated from *this* world. It just didn't have the right feel. So did that mean it had come from the Others? From wherever *they'd* come from?

Were they even capable of magic?

I really had no idea. I doubted there was anyone alive who *did* know, simply because anyone who'd ever come across one of them hadn't lived to tell the tale.

Except, I thought with a chill, Sal and his partners. They'd not only survived but—thanks to the rift that had hit them just as a wraith was emerging—Sal's partners now had its DNA running through their bodies.

I stared down at my boots, at the oily, glistening substance that stained the tips of them. Revulsion stirred, and the urge to retreat hit so strongly I actually took a step back. But that wouldn't give me the answers I needed. Wouldn't help find the missing children.

And it was that desire more than anything that got me moving in the right direction. One step; two. No stones slid from under my feet this time. Or, if they did, they made no sound. It was still and hushed in this small part of the world—almost as if the night held its breath in expectation. Or horror.

The darkness slithered over my feet and ankles, and oddly felt like water. Thick, foul water that was colder than ice. It pressed my combat pants against my skin as it rose up my legs, and the weapons clipped to my thighs gained an odd, frozen sheen. I crossed mental fingers and hoped like hell this stuff didn't damage them. I didn't want to face whatever—whomever—might be waiting at the bottom of this crater without any means of protection.

The farther I moved down the slope—the deeper I got into the darkness—the harder every step became. Sweat trickled down my spine, but its cause wasn't just the effort of moving forward. This stuff, whatever it was, scared me.

I reached back and pulled free one of the two slender machine rifles strapped to my back. I'd adapted them to fire small wooden stakes rather than bullets, as that was the best way to kill vampires. While there was a chance none of my weapons would work after this muck touched them, I still felt better with the rifle's weight in my hand.

The darkness washed up my stomach, over my breasts, then up to my neck. I raised my face in an effort to avoid becoming fully immersed for as long as possible. Which was stupid. It was just darkness, not water, no matter how much it felt otherwise. I wouldn't drown in the stuff.

But could I breathe?

I took one final deep breath, just in case, and then pushed on. The ink washed up my face, then over my head, and it suddenly felt as if there were a ton of weight pressing down on me. Every step became an extreme effort; all too soon my leg muscles were quivering and it took every ounce of determination I had to keep upright, to keep moving.

I pressed on, but I really had no idea whether I was heading in the right direction. Not only did the darkness envelop me, but it also stole all sense of time and direction. God, what if this was a trap? What if all along they'd intended nothing more than to lure me down here to get rid of me? Sal's partners *had* to be aware of his death by now, just as they had to be aware that I was the one who'd found and rescued the five kids—after all, those kids had been nothing more than bait in an attempt to trap and kill me. That it hadn't gone exactly as they'd hoped was due to good luck rather than to bad planning on their part. Or, rather, good luck and a whole lot of help from the adult déchet who haunted my bunker.

And while Sal's partners might have no idea what I truly looked like—and therefore could neither stop me from entering their businesses in Central nor hunt me down— they were well aware that I lived in the old underground military bunker outside that city. And they'd undoubtedly realize I would not abandon the rest of those children.

I *had* been expecting some sort of retaliatory attack, but against our bunker rather than out here in the middle of nowhere.

If this was a trap, then it was one I'd very stupidly walked right into. But there was nothing I could do about that now. I just had to keep moving.

But the deeper I got, the more crushing the weight of the darkness became. My legs were beginning to bow under the pressure, my spine ached, and my shoulders were hunched forward. It felt as if I was about to topple over at any minute, and it took every ounce of concentration and strength to remain upright. May the goddess Rhea help me if I met anything coming up out of the crater, because I doubted I'd even have the energy to pull the rifle's trigger.

Then, with little warning, the weight lifted and I was catapulted into fresh air and regular night. I took a deep, shuddering breath and became aware of something else. Or rather some*one* else.

Because I was no longer alone.

I turned around slowly. At the very bottom of the crater, maybe a dozen or so yards away from where I stood, there was a rift. A real rift, not a false one. It shimmered and sparked against the cover of night, and while the energy it emitted was foul, it nevertheless felt a whole lot cleaner than the thick muck I'd just traversed.

Standing in front of it were four figures—three with their backs to the rift, one standing facing it. The solo person was the dark-cloaked, hooded figure I'd been following; the other three . . .

I shuddered even as I instinctively raised my weapon and fired. The other three were tall and thin, with pale translucent skin through which you could see every muscle, bone, and vein. There was no hair on their bodies and they didn't really have normal faces—just big amber eyes and squashed noses.

Wraiths.

And they reacted even as I did. Though none of them had anything resembling a mouth, they screamed—it was a high-pitched sound of fury I doubted any human would be capable of hearing, and it made my ears ache. The two figures closest to me—the cowled man and the figure I presumed was the wraith's leader—leapt sideways, out of the firing line of my weapon. But the other two came straight at me. I kept firing, but the machine rifle's wooden bullets bounced harmlessly off their translucent skin.

I quickly sheathed the rifle, unclipped the guns from my pants, then turned and fled into the soupy darkness.

Just because I *could* fight didn't mean I had to or wanted to—especially not when it came to wraiths. And two of them at that.

The darkness enveloped me once more. My pace slowed to a crawl but my heart rate didn't. I had no idea whether this muck would affect them as it did me, and all I could do was pray to Rhea that it did. I didn't want to die. Not here, not in this stuff, and certainly not at the hands of a wraith.

I forged on, hurrying as much as the heaviness would allow, my breath little more than shallow rasps of fear and every muscle in my body quivering with effort. While I couldn't hear any sound of pursuit, I knew they were behind me. Ripples of movement washed across my spine, getting stronger and stronger as they drew closer.

Fear forced fresh energy into my legs. I surged on, desperate to reach the crater's rim. I might not be any safer there, but I could at least run and fight a whole lot better out in the open.

The ground slipped from under my feet and I went down on one knee. Just for an instant, I caught a glimpse of starlight; then a thick wave of movement hit my spine and knocked me sideways. Stones dug into my side as the air left my lungs in a huge whoosh. Claws appeared out of the black—they were thick and blue and razor sharp, and would have severed my spine had the wind of their movement not hit me first. Luck, it seemed, hadn't totally abandoned me.

I fired both weapons in a sweeping arc. I had no idea where the wraiths were, because the darkness had closed around those claws and the rippling movement seemed to be coming from several directions now. Something wet splashed across my skin and face—something that stung like acid and smelled like egg. I hoped it was blood, but I knew there were Others who could spit poison. With the way things were playing out tonight, it was probably the latter rather than the former.

I scrubbed a sleeve across my face, but succeeded only in smearing whatever it was. I cursed softly, then thrust upright and scrambled toward the rim of the crater and that brief glimpse of starlight. If I had to fight, then I at least wanted to see my foe.

The ripples of movement didn't immediately resume and, for an all too brief moment, I thought maybe I'd killed them both. It was a thought that swiftly died as those damn waves started up again.

There was nothing I could do. Nothing except keep running. Wraiths weren't stupid; now that they knew I had weapons that could actually hurt them, they'd be a lot more cautious.

But, cautious or not, they were still moving through this muck a whole lot faster than I was. I had one chance, and one chance only—I had to get out and put as much distance between them and me as possible.

The heavy darkness began to slide away from my body. I sucked down big gulps of air, trying to ease the burning in my lungs. It didn't really help. I ran on, my speed increasing as the darkness retreated further, lifting the weight from my shoulders and spine. Then, finally, I was free from its grip and racing over the edge of the crater. I didn't stop. I didn't dare. I needed to gain as much distance as I could . . .

Movement to my right. Instinct had me leaping left. Claws snagged the edge of my coat's sleeve, ripping it from cuff to shoulder but not cutting skin. I twisted away, raised the guns, and fired.

At nothing.

The creature was gone. I had no idea whether speed or magic was involved in that disappearance, and no time to contemplate it. I just kept on running. Stones bounced away from my steps, but this time there were no ghosts to dance in time to the sound.

More movement, this time to my left. I fired again. The

shots ripped across the night but found no target. The stony hillside appeared empty even though the foul presence of the wraiths stained the air itself.

If they were so damn fast—or, indeed, capable of hiding their presence through magic—why weren't they attacking? Had they been ordered not to? Or were they like cats, preferring to play with their prey before closing in for the kill?

If it were the latter, then they were in for a shock, because this little mouse wasn't about to go down without at least taking one of them with me.

The crest of the hill loomed above. Tombs and crosses reached for the stars like broken fingers reaching for help. But there was no safety to be found there, and the tombs themselves were just a reminder of my fate if I wasn't very careful.

Stones clattered to my right; I swung a gun that way but didn't fire. There was nothing there. They were playing with me. Fear pounded through my body, but there was little I could do but ignore it. I'd been in far worse situations than this and survived. I could survive this.

With luck.

I hoped.

The graveyard ghosts gathered near the top of the hill as I drew closer, but their energy was uneasy. Wary. I very much doubted they'd help if I asked for it. There was none of the anger in them that was so evident within the Carleen ghosts, and that probably meant this graveyard—and these ghosts—were pre-war. In which case they'd have no experience with or knowledge of wraiths and no idea just how dangerous they could be.

To my left, one of the creatures appeared out of the night—or, rather, his arm appeared. I ducked under his blow and fired both guns, but in the blink of an eye his limb was gone again. The bullets ricochet off nearby rocks, sending sparks flying into the night.

How in Rhea could I fight—kill—these creatures if I couldn't see them?

I guess I had to be grateful that I could at least hear them. Sometimes. More than likely when they actually wanted me to.

More sound, this time to my left—claws scrabbling across stone. If that noise was any indication, the wraith was closing in quickly. Perhaps it had decided playtime was over.

I couldn't escape them—not in this form. Maybe it was time to try another—

Even as the thought entered my mind, something cannoned into my side and sent me tumbling. I hit the ground with a grunt but kept on rolling, desperate to avoid the attack I could feel coming.

I crunched into a large rock and stopped. The air practically screamed with the force of the creature's approach; I raised the guns once more and ripped off several shots. Then I scrambled upright, only to be sent flying again. This time I hit face-first and skinned my nose and chin as I slid several feet back down the hill.

I had no time to recover. No time to even think. The creature's weight landed in the middle of my back, and for too many seconds I couldn't even breathe, let alone react. Its claws tore at my flesh, splitting the skin along my shoulder and sending bits of flesh splattering across the nearby rocks. It was still playing with me, because those claws could have—should have—severed my spine.

But the blood gushing down my arms and back was warning enough that if I didn't move—didn't get up and get away from this creature—I'd be as dead as any of those who watched from the safety of their tombstones.

And there was only one way I had any hope of escaping— I had to call forth the vampire within me.

So I ignored the creature's crushing weight, ignored the blood and the pain and the gore that gleamed wetly on the ground all around me, and sucked the energy of the night deep into my lungs. It filtered swiftly through every aching inch of me until my whole body vibrated with the weight and power of it. The vampire within rose in a rush—undoubtedly fueled by fear and desperation—and swiftly embraced that darkness, becoming one with it, until it stained my whole being and took over. It ripped away flesh, muscle, and bone until I was nothing more than a cluster of matter. Even my weapons and clothes became part of that energy. In this form, at least, I'd be harder to pin down.

I slipped out from under the wraith and fled up toward the graveyard once again. But I wasn't out of danger yet. I may now be as invisible to the mortal world as any vampire or, indeed, the wraiths themselves, but that didn't mean they wouldn't sense me. Didn't mean they couldn't kill me. The number of vampire bones I'd seen near active rifts over the years was testament to the fact that this particular vampire trick made little difference to a wraith's ability to hunt and kill them.

I finally crested the hill and surged into the cemetery. In this form, I could see the spectral mass that was the gathered ghosts glimmering in the darkness. Their bodies were blurred, barely resembling anything humanoid, which meant I'd been right. These ghosts were very old indeed. Even so, I could taste their fear—of me, not of the things that pursued me. They might not know what wraiths were, but they were familiar with vampires and were now pigeon-holing me as one of them.

They wouldn't help me.

Air began to stir around me again, buffeting my particles and sending a fresh spurt of fear through my body. The wraiths had entered the graveyard—and in this form, I couldn't use my weapons. I didn't even have a vampire's sharp claws to defend myself with. To use my weapons, I'd have to transform both them and my arms back to solidity, and a partial transformation wasn't something I was particularly adept at.

I raced on, heading for Carleen, hoping against hope that the ghosts there would help me. Because if they didn't . . .

I shoved the thought away. I could do this. I *would* do this. The lives of eight children were on the line—or so Nuri believed. I very much doubted that her statement—if I didn't find those children, no one would—had been just an attempt to bring me back into the fold. The desperation and fear in her eyes had been all too real.

Though I heard no sound of approach, claws slashed the trailing tendrils of my energy form. Particles spun away into the night and pain ripped through the rest of me. Panic surged. I really *was* no safer in this form than in the other. In fact, I was probably worse off because I couldn't actually defend myself.

If I was destined to die this night, then by Rhea, I would go down fighting in human form rather than as a vampire.

I called to the darkness and reversed the process, becoming flesh from the head down. As my arms found form, I fired both guns over my shoulder, then to my left and right. A high-pitched scream bit across the night and the rancid, metallic scent of blood washed through the air. I had no idea whether I'd killed one of them, but at least I'd hit one. And if I could do that, I could kill them. Not that I was about to hang around and attempt it.

I raced on through the broken tombstones and shattered remnants of trees, my gaze on Carleen's distant walls even as every other sense was trained on the night around me.

Air rushed past—a wraith, planning Rhea only knows what. I didn't check my speed. Didn't even fire. While my guns weren't yet giving any indication that ammunition was running low, I couldn't imagine this could be too far off. And although I was carrying extra ammo, I didn't have time to reload. The minute I stopped, they would be on me—of that I was sure. The only other weapons I had were the machine rifles—which had already proven useless—and the two glass knives strapped to my wrists. They'd been built as a last resort, a weapon designed for hand-to-hand combat, with a blade that was harder than steel. But there was no way I was about to get into a last-resort situation. Not when it came to wraiths, anyway.

Up ahead, air began to shimmer and spark. A heartbeat later one of the wraiths appeared, blocking my path between two crumbling but ornate tombs. A thick, bloody wound stretched across its gut, and black blood oozed down its torso and legs. But if the wound was hampering it in any way, it wasn't obvious. It flung its arms wide, its claws gleaming and alien, almost icy green. Sparks began to flicker between the razor-sharp tips, then spun off into the night. But they didn't disappear. Instead, they began to cluster together, each tiny spark sending out tendrils to connect to another, and then another, until a rope began to form. A rope that glowed the same alien green as the creature's claws and pulsated with an energy that made my skin crawl.

The wraiths weren't trying to kill me—they were trying to capture me. I had no idea why, and certainly no intention of finding out. I swung left, attempting to outrun the still-forming rope. The wraith appeared in front of me again, the rope longer and beginning to curve toward me.

I switched direction, and the same thing happened. I slid to a halt, raised the guns, and unleashed hell. The wraith's body shook as the bullets tore through its flesh. Blood and gore spattered the ground all around it, but it neither moved nor stopped creating that leash. The two ends of the rope were close to joining now, and I very much suspected I did *not* want that to happen.

One of guns began to blink in warning. I cursed and ran straight at the wraith. Given firing from a distance seemed to have no effect, maybe getting closer would. I had nothing to lose by trying—nothing but my life, and that was already on the line.

The second gun began to blink, but I didn't let up and I didn't stop. The closer I got, the more damage the guns did, but the creature didn't seem to care. Its body and face were a broken, bloodied mass, and still it stood there, resolutely creating its leash. Did these things not feel pain?

The first gun went silent. I cursed again and did the only thing I could—I launched feetfirst at the creature. I hit it so hard that my feet actually went through the mess of its chest, but the sheer force of my momentum knocked it backward and the shimmering around its claws died abruptly as it hit the ground hard. I landed on top of it, caught my balance, and then fired every remaining bullet at its head.

This time, I'd killed it.

But I didn't rejoice. Didn't feel any sense of elation. As the second creature emitted a scream that was both fury and anguish, I tore free the two spare clips from their holders on my pants, reloaded the guns, and ran on.

The twisted, rusting metal fence that surrounded the graveyard came into view. I leapt over it, my gaze on Carleen's broken walls. But the wind that battered my back was warning enough that the other wraith was not only on the move but closing in fast. And I could taste its fury; this one had *no* intention of corralling me, even if that had been their order.

I reached for everything I had left, but my legs refused to go any faster. My body was on fire and my strength seemed to be leaching away as fast as the blood pouring down my arms, back, and face. It was sheer determination keeping me on my feet now, nothing else.

And determination wasn't going to get me much farther. It certainly wasn't going to get me to Carleen. It was simply too far away.

Bear, I wish you could keep your promise to be with me when I die.

But even as that thought crossed my mind, I locked it down. Hard. I might want to die in the arms of my little ones—just as they'd died in mine—but I wasn't about to place either Bear or Cat in the middle of a dangerous situation. There were vampires in this world who could feed off energy—even the ectoplasmic energy of ghosts—and there might well be Others capable of doing the same.

Something smashed into my back and sent me tumbling. I landed faceup, staring at the stars—stars that danced in crazy circles across the wide, dark sky. I could barely even breathe, the pain was so great, but I nevertheless felt the approach of the creature. It was in the air and coming straight at me.

And this time it *wasn't* invisible.

I raised the guns and fired. It wouldn't stop the creature— I knew that—but I didn't have the energy to get up and there was nothing else I could do.

Everything seemed to slip into slow motion. I watched the ripple of air as the bullets cut through it and the creature's gleaming claws gained length and began to drip with sparks. Saw the creature's flesh shudder and jerk in rhythmic harmony with the bullets that tore into its body. Saw the ever-growing gleam of determination and fury in its golden eyes. I might not be able to speak its language, but there were some things that needed no words or explanation. It wanted revenge and it wanted my death, and it didn't care whether it had to die as long as it took me with it.

I can't die. There's still too much I need to do.

But I guess someone else will have to do it.